Acclaim for *The Heart of Redness*

"A major step in the new South African novel—now a polyphony of voices, suddenly freed yet still shadowed by deep and immense riddles."
—*The Village Voice*

"Zakes Mda writes of his troubled homeland with as much affection as outrage, as much love as lamentation. . . . This emotionally rich novel dares to seek redemption . . . devastated lives, Mda finds grace, tenderness . . . the kind of tale . . . their . . . of hardship.
—*The Boston Globe*

"A novel of tremendous scope and deep human feeling, of passion and reconciliation. . . A seamless weave of history, myth, and realist fiction. It is, arguably, the first great novel of the new South Africa—a triumph of imaginative and historical writing."
—*The Seattle Skanner*

"In an unaffected, generous style that blends social and magical realism, oral tradition and written history, Mda spins stories that both read like myth and chronicle ordinary South African life."
—*The Philadelphia Inquirer*

"Jumping handily between past and present, Mda deftly renders the tensions between maintaining an indigenous culture and altering it in the name of progress."
—*Entertainment Weekly*

"Mda tells his country's stories through beautifully realized characters whose search for love and connection take you up close to the black experience, past and present."
—*Booklist*

"A prolific and prominent new voice of South African literature, Mda transforms historical events and invents new ones that express his continued concern, as in these two novels, that the liberators do not become the oppressors . . . A brilliantly profuse novel . . . provocatively offbeat and tragically weird."
—*Los Angeles Times Book Review*

"A nuanced story about belief, memory, and the complex legacies of colonialism and its contemporary heir, global capitalism. [Mda] paints a vivid picture of a new South Africa of uncertain future ... where the past is deeply contested terrain and social equality remains a faraway dream."
—*Mother Jones*

"Mda's fascinating narrative skill reveals the past as a powerful presence in the present: of his characters, and of all of us, as we live."
—Nadine Gordimer

"A work of extraordinary richness, suffused with genuine mythic power: comparable to the recently discovered fiction of Moses Iszegawa and Emmanuel Dongala—and not unworthy of comparison with the masterpieces of Chinua Achebe."
—*Kirkus Reviews* (starred review)

"Rich in the sensuality and exoticism of African life."
—*The Commercial Appeal* (Memphis)

Also by Zakes Mda

The Madonna of Excelsior
She Plays with Darkness
Ways of Dying

The
Heart of
Redness

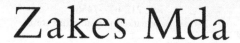

Zakes Mda

Picador
Farrar, Straus and Giroux
New York

THE HEART OF REDNESS. Copyright © 2000 by Zakes Mda. All rights reserved. Printed in the United States of America. For information, address Picador, 175 Fifth Avenue, New York, N.Y. 10010.

www.picadorusa.com

For information on Picador Reading Group Guides, as well as ordering, please contact the Trade Marketing department at St. Martin's Press.
Phone: 1-800-221-7945 extension 763
Fax: 212-677-7456
E-mail: trademarketing@stmartins.com

Library of Congress Cataloging-in-Publication Data

Mda, Zakes.
    The heart of redness / Zakes Mda.
        p. cm.
    ISBN 0-312-42174-5
    1. Triangles (Interpersonal relations)—Fiction. 2. Xhosa (African people)—Fiction. 3. South Africa—Fiction. 4. Villages—Fiction. 5. Casinos—Fiction. I. Title.

PR9369.3.M4 H43 2002
823'.914—dc21   2002025008

First published in the United States by Farrar, Straus and Giroux

First published in South Africa by Oxford University Press

D 28 27 26 25 24 23 22 21 20

DEDICATION

There is a real-life trader in Qolorha, whose name is Rufus Hulley, who took me to places of miracles and untold beauty. He must not be mistaken for John Dalton, the trader of *The Heart of Redness*, who is purely a fictional character. I am grateful to Rufus, and to Jeff Peires, whose research—wonderfully recorded in *The Dead Will Arise* and in a number of academic papers—informed the historical events in my fiction. As for the people of Qolorha, they will forgive me for reinventing their lives.

I wrote this novel in honor of new lives, among which I count my son Zukile, my daughter Zukiswa Zenzile Moroesi, and my daughter's son, Wandile.

THE DESCENDANTS OF THE
HEADLESS ANCESTOR

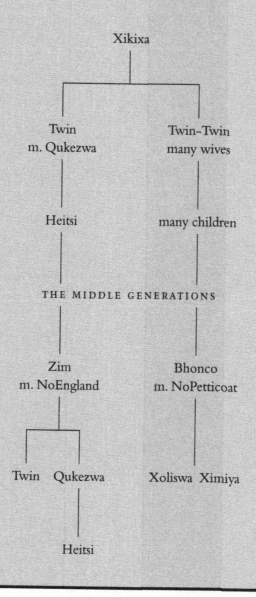

Xikixa

Twin
m. Qukezwa

Twin-Twin
many wives

Heitsi

many children

THE MIDDLE GENERATIONS

Zim
m. NoEngland

Bhonco
m. NoPetticoat

Twin Qukezwa

Xoliswa Ximiya

Heitsi

The Heart of Redness

**I** "Tears are very close to my eyes," says Bhonco, son of Ximiya. "Not for pain . . . no . . . I do not cry because of pain. I cry only because of beautiful things."

And he cries often. Sometimes just a sniffle. Or a single tear down his cheek. As a result he carries a white handkerchief all the time, especially these days when peace has returned to the land and there is enough happiness to go around. It is shared like pinches of snuff. Rivers of salt. They furrow the aged face.

Bhonco is different from the other Unbelievers in his family, for Unbelievers are reputed to be such somber people that they do not believe even in those things that can bring happiness to their lives. They spend most of their time moaning about past injustices and bleeding for the world that would have been had the folly of belief not seized the nation a century and a half ago and spun it around until it was in a woozy stupor that is felt to this day. They also mourn the sufferings of the Middle Generations. That, however, is only whispered.

Bhonco does not believe in grieving. He has long accepted that what has happened has happened. It is cast in cold iron that does not entertain rust. His forebears bore the pain with stoicism. They lived with it until they passed on to the world of the ancestors.

Then came the Middle Generations. In between the forebears and this new world. And the Middle Generations fleeted by like a dream. Often like a nightmare. But now even the sufferings of the Middle Generations have passed. This is a new life, and it must be celebrated. Bhonco, son of Ximiya, celebrates it with tears.

NoPetticoat, his placable wife, is on the verge of losing patience with his tears. Whenever someone does a beautiful thing in the presence of her husband she screams, "Stop! Please stop! Or you'll make Bhonco cry!"

She dotes on him though, poor thing. People say it is nice to see such an aged couple—who would be having grandchildren if their daughter, Xoliswa Ximiya, had not chosen to remain an old maid—so much in love.

It is a wonderful sight to watch the couple walking side by side from a feast. He, tall and wiry with a deep chocolate face grooved with gullies; and she, a stout matron whose comparatively smooth face makes her look younger than her age. Sometimes they are seen staggering a bit, humming the remnants of a song, their muscles obviously savoring the memory of the final dance of a feast.

The custom is that men walk in front and women follow. But Bhonco and NoPetticoat walk side by side. Sometimes holding hands! A constant source of embarrassment to Xoliswa Ximiya: old people have no right to love. And if they happen to be foolish enough to harbor the slightest affection for each other, they must not display it in public.

"Tears are close to my eyes, NoPetticoat," snivels the man of the house, dabbing his eyes with the handkerchief.

"A big man like you shouldn't be bawling like a spoiled baby, Bhonco," says the woman of the house, nevertheless putting her arm around his shoulders.

A beautiful thing has happened. They have just received the news that Xoliswa Ximiya, their beloved and only child, has been promoted at work. She is now the principal of Qolorha-by-Sea Secondary School.

Xoliswa Ximiya is not called just Xoliswa. People use both her name and surname when they talk about her, because she is an important person in the community. A celebrity, so to speak. She is highly learned too, with a B.A. in education from the University of Fort Hare, and a certificate in teaching English as a second language from some college in America.

"They will not accept her," laments NoPetticoat, as if to herself.

"But she is a child of this community," says Bhonco adamantly. "She grew up in front of their eyes. She became educated while others laughed and said I was mad to send a girl to school."

"They will say she is a woman. Remember the teacher who left? He was a man, yet they didn't accept him. They made life very difficult for him. How much more for a woman?"

"They made life difficult for him because he was uncircumcised. He was not a man. How could he teach our children with a dangling foreskin?"

"I tell you, Bhonco, they won't accept her. They will give my baby problems at that school!"

"She is not a baby. She is thirty-six years old. And if they don't accept her it will be the work of the Believers. They are jealous because they don't have a daughter who is as educated," says Bhonco, making it clear that the discussion is terminated.

It had to come back to the war between the Believers and Unbelievers. They are in competition in everything.

The early manifestation of this competition happened a few years ago when the Ximiyas bought a pine dining table with four chairs. The family became the talk of the community, since no one else in the village had a dining table those days. But Zim, of the family of Believers, had to burst the Ximiya bubble by buying exactly the same dining table, but with six chairs. That really irked the son of Ximiya and his supporters.

Since then the war between the two families has become a public one. Their good neighbors await with bated breath the next skulduggery they will do against each other.

The Cult of the Unbelievers began with Twin-Twin, Bhonco Ximiya's ancestor, in the days of Prophetess Nongqawuse almost one hundred and fifty years ago. The revered Twin-Twin had elevated unbelieving to the heights of a religion. The cult died during the Middle Generations, for people then were more concerned with surviving and overcoming their oppression. They did not have the time to fight about the perils of belief and unbelief.

But even before the sufferings of the Middle Generations had passed—when it was obvious to everyone that the end was near—Bhonco, son of Ximiya, resurrected the cult.

He does not care that only his close relatives and himself subscribe to it. Nor does it matter to him that people have long forgotten the conflicts of generations ago. He holds to them dearly, for they have shaped his present, and the present of the nation. His role in life is to teach people not to believe. He tells them that even the Middle Generations wouldn't have suffered if it had not been for the scourge of belief.

Beautiful things are celebrated not only with tears. So Bhonco tells his wife that he will go to Vulindlela Trading Store to buy a tin of corned beef. NoPetticoat laughs and says he must not use the promotion of her baby as an excuse. He needs something salty because he had a lot to drink at the feast yesterday, and now he is nursing a hangover. Whoever heard of sorghum beer giving one a hangover? Bhonco wonders to himself.

"While you are away I'll go to the hotel to see if they have work for me," says NoPetticoat as she adjusts her *qhiya* turban and puts a shawl over her shoulders. But her husband cannot hear her, for he has already walked out of their pink rondavel.

NoPetticoat supplements the income from her old-age pension—or *nkamnkam*, as the people call it—by working as a babysitter at the Blue Flamingo Hotel. Tourists often come to enjoy the serenity of this place, to admire birds and plants, or to go to the Valley of Nongqawuse to see where the miracles happened. They book in at the Blue Flamingo, and leave their children with part-time nannies while they walk or ride all over the valley, or swim in the rough sea.

NoPetticoat is occasionally called by the hotel management when there are babies to look after. However, when many days have passed without anyone calling her, she walks to the hotel to find out if there is any work. She has had to do that since she discovered that the managers call her only as a last resort. Their first choices are the young women whose bodies are still supple enough to make red-blooded male tourists salivate. Almost always when she goes without being called, she finds that indeed there are babies to look after, but a message has been sent to some shameless filly to come for the job. Invariably she fights her way and takes over.

Bhonco drags his gumboots up the hillock to the trading store. His brown overalls are almost threadbare at the elbows and at the knees. He wears a green woolen hat that the people call a skullcap. He does not carry a stick as men normally do.

Under his breath he curses the trader for building his store on the hill. But the breathtaking view from the top compensates for the arduous climb. Down below, on his right, he can see the wild sea smashing gigantic waves against the rocks, creating mountains of snow-white surf. On his left his eyes feast on the green valleys and the patches of villages with beautiful houses painted pink, powder blue, yellow, and white.

Most of the houses are rondavels. But over the years a new architectural style, the hexagon, has developed. On the roofs of these voguish hexagons, corrugated iron appears under the thatch, like a petticoat that is longer than the dress. This is both for aesthetic reasons and to stop the termites. But Bhonco does not believe in this newfangled fashion of building hexagons instead of the tried and tested rondavel.

From where he stands he can see the Gxarha River and the Intlambo-ka-Nongqawuse—Nongqawuse's Valley. He can also see Nongqawuse's Pool and the great lagoon that is often covered by a thick blanket of mist.

Indeed, Qolorha-by-Sea is a place rich in wonders. The rivers do not cease flowing, even when the rest of the country knells a drought. The cattle are round and fat.

Bhonco was born in this village. He grew up in this village. Except for the time he worked in the cities, he has lived in this village all his life. Yet he is always moved to tears by its wistful beauty.

A gale of heat grazes his face. The wind always brings heat from the sea.

Vulindlela Trading Store is a big stone building with a red corrugated-iron roof crowned by an array of television and radio aerials and a satellite dish. In front of the store is a long concrete stoop with a number of wooden yokes and green plows and planters chained together.

Behind the store is the trader's family home, an off-white roughcast modern house with big windows. Between the house and the store, a car and a four-wheel-drive bakkie—both of them Mercedes-Benz recent models—are parked.

Bhonco glances at the television that the trader, John Dalton, has put on a shelf against the wall of the store's verandah. It plays videos of old movies, and children are always crowding here, watching "bioscope," as they call it. Some of these children are herdboys who should be looking after cattle in the veld. No wonder there are so many cases these days of parents being sued because their cattle have grazed in other people's fields.

Bhonco slowly walks into the store, casting a disinterested look at a big blackboard that announces the latest prices for those who want to sell their wool, maize, skins, and hides to the trader, or those who want to grind their corn at his mill. He demands to see his friend the trader. When Missis Dalton says he is away on business, Bhonco insists that he wants to see him all the same. He knows that he is hiding in his office. Dalton has no choice but to skulk out of his tiny office to face the stubborn man.

"What is it now, old man?" he demands.

Dalton is stocky and balding, with hard features and a long rich beard of black and silver-gray streaks. He always wears a khaki safari suit. He looks like a parody of an Afrikaner farmer. But he is neither an Afrikaner nor a farmer. Always been a trader. So was his father before him. And his grandfather was a trader of a different kind. As a missionary he was a merchant of salvation.

Dalton is a white man of English stock. Well, let's put it this way: his skin is white like the skins of those who caused the sufferings of the Middle Generations. But his heart is an umXhosa heart. He speaks better isiXhosa than most of the amaXhosa people in the village. In his youth, against his father's wishes, he went to the initiation school and was circumcised in accordance with the customs of the amaXhosa people. He therefore knows the secret of the mountain. He is a man.

Often he laughs at the sneering snobbishness of his fellow English-speaking South Africans. He says they have a deep-seated fear and resentment of everything African, and are apt to glorify their blood-soaked colonial history. And he should know. His own family history is as blood-soaked as any . . . right from the days of one John Dalton, his great-great-grandfather, who was a soldier and then a magistrate in the days of Prophetess Nongqawuse.

"Don't call me old man. I have a name," Bhonco protests. Although he is old, and to be old is an honor among his people, he has always hated to be called old man since his hair started graying in his late twenties and people mockingly called him Xhego—old man. Now at sixty-plus—or perhaps seventy, he does not know his real age—his hair is snow white.

"It is well, Bhonco son of Ximiya. We are not at war, are we?" Dalton tries to placate the elder.

"I do not fight wars with children. It was your father who was my age-mate. And, ah, the old Dalton looked after me. He was a kind man, your father."

"You didn't come here to talk about my father, did you?"

"I came to ask for *ityala* . . . for credit . . . I need a tin of beef. And some tobacco for my pipe."

Dalton shakes his head, and takes out a big black book from under the counter. After a few pages he finds Bhonco's name.

"You see," he says, "your ityala is already very long. You have taken too many things on credit, and you have not paid yet. You promised that you were going to get your old-age pension soon."

Dalton's wife, who is simply known as Missis by the villagers, thinks it is necessary to rescue her husband. She firmly steps forward and says, "He is not getting any more credit, John."

Bhonco does not take kindly to this interference. He raises his voice. "Let's leave women out of this!"

Fortunately Missis understands no isiXhosa; she is a Free State Afrikaner. Dalton met her when he attended the Cherry Festival in Ficksburg many years ago. She was the Cherry Queen, although it would be hard to believe that now—what with her rotten front teeth and all. The trouble is that she eats too many sweets. Her saving grace is that she hardly ever smiles. She still finds it difficult to understand her husband's cozy relationship with these rustics.

Bhonco adopts a new tactic and becomes very pitiful.

"Ever since Nongqawuse things were never right," he laments. "Until now. They are becoming right a bit now, although not for me. They are becoming right for others. Me . . . no . . . I am still waiting for my nkamnkam.

"This is my seventh year waiting. My wife came here as a child . . . she is many years younger than me. But she now gets nkamnkam. I am very very old, but the government refuses to give me my pension."

Then he goes into a litany of the troubles he has gone through working for this country. He began to work half a century ago at a textile factory in East London, then at a dairy, then at a blanket factory, then . . . He even worked at the docks in Cape Town for more than eight years.

He became permanently crippled—although it is impossible to see any sign of that now—when his sister pushed him down a donga, shouting, "When are you going to mourn for your father?" Since then he has never been able to work again.

Why won't the government give him nkamnkam like all the old men and women of South Africa who are on old-age pensions today? Is it fair that now, even though ravines of maturity run wild on his face, he should still not receive any nkamnkam?

"Maybe it is not fair," says Dalton. "But how are you going to pay me since you get no nkamnkam? Are you going to take your wife's money to pay for your tobacco and luxury items like canned beef?"

"Did you not hear? My daughter is now the principal. I'll pay you."

It is late in the afternoon when Bhonco arrives home. NoPetticoat is busy cooking the evening *umphokoqo*—the maize porridge that is specially eaten with sour milk—on the Primus stove. When the white man has smiled—in other words, when NoPetticoat has been paid at the Blue Flamingo or has received her nkamnkam—she cooks on the Primus stove rather than outside with a three-legged pot.

"I didn't know that the white man has smiled at you," says Bhonco, as he puts the can of corned beef on the table. "Otherwise I wouldn't have humiliated myself begging for ityala from that uppity Dalton."

Before NoPetticoat can admonish him for piling debt on their shoulders, Xoliswa Ximiya walks in. She looks like the "mistress" she is—which is what pupils call unmarried female teachers—in a navy-blue two-piece costume with a white frilly blouse. She has her father's bone structure, and is quite tall and well proportioned—which is good if you want to be a model in Johannesburg, but works against you in a village where men prefer their women plump and juicy. And indeed this is the language they use when they describe them, as if they are talking about a piece of meat. She has a charmingly triste face, and brown-dyed hair that she braids with extensions in Butterworth. But people never stop wondering how she is able to walk among the rocks and gorges of Qolorha-by-Sea in those high heels.

She has just come to see how her parents are doing. She takes it as an obligation to see them occasionally. Her parents—especially her mother—were not happy when she moved out a year ago to stay in a two-room staff house in the schoolyard. At first they insisted that no unmarried daughter of theirs would live alone in her own house. It was unheard of. They had to relent when she concocted something to the effect that as a senior teacher she had to live at school or lose her job. It really frustrates her that her parents insist on treating her like a child.

Bhonco and NoPetticoat are all over Xoliswa Ximiya, congratulating her on her promotion.

"You are going to be the best principal that school has ever had," says her father proudly. "At least you'll be better than that uncircumcised boy the community kicked out."

Such talk makes Xoliswa Ximiya uncomfortable. But she ignores it and announces that although she appreciates the honor of being principal of her alma matter, she would very much like to work for the government.

"But you are working for the government now as a headmistress, are you not?" says Bhonco.

"As a teacher are you not being paid by the government?" echoes NoPetticoat.

"I want to be a civil servant. I want to work for the Ministry of Education in Pretoria, or at the very least in Bisho."

"Bisho! Do you know where Bisho is from here? And Pretoria! Pretoria! No one in our family has ever been there," cries Bhonco. He is choking with anger.

"You want to kill your father?" asks NoPetticoat.

"I know where Bisho is, father," responds the daughter in a cold, sarcastic tone. "It is the capital town of our province. I have been there many times. And Pretoria is the capital city of our country. I have not been to Pretoria, but I have been much farther, father, where none of my family has ever been. I have been to America . . . across the oceans."

"You see, Bhonco, you should never have allowed this child to take that scholarship to America," says NoPetticoat tiredly.

"So now it's my fault, NoPetticoat?"

"If you like towns and cities so much, my child, we have never stopped you from visiting Centani or even Butterworth." NoPetticoat tries to strike a compromise.

"I do not care for towns and cities, mother. Anyway, Centani is just a big village and Butterworth is a small town. Don't you understand? People I have been to school with are earning a lot of money as directors of departments in the civil service. I am sitting here in this village, with all my education, earning peanuts as a schoolteacher. I am going. I must go from this stifling village. I have made applications. As soon as I get a job I am going," says Xoliswa Ximiya with finality.

It is an ungrateful night, and sleep refuses to come to Bhonco. His eyelids are heavy, but sleep just won't come. Oh, why do children ever grow up? How huggable they are when they are little boys and girls, when their parents' word is still gospel, before the poison of the world contaminates their heads. He envies NoPetticoat, who can sleep and snore in the midst of such turbulence.

On nights like this his scars become itchy. He rubs them a bit. He cannot reach them properly, because they cover his back. And the person who usually helps him is fast asleep. Why he has to be burdened with the scars of history, he does not understand. Perhaps that's what prompted him to bring the Cult of the Unbelievers back from the recesses of time.

Yes, Bhonco carries the scars that were inflicted on his great-grandfather, Twin-Twin, by men who flogged him after he had been identified as a wizard by Prophet Mlanjeni, the Man of the River. Every first boy-child in subsequent generations of Twin-Twin's tree is born with the scars. Even those of the Middle Generations, their first males carried the scars.

You can give Twin-Twin any name. You can call him anything. But a wizard he was not. Bhonco is adamant about that. Twin-Twin was a naughty man. Even after he died he became a naughty ancestor. Often he showed himself naked to groups of women gathering wood on the hillside or washing clothes in a stream. He was like that in life too. He loved women. He had a generous heart for *amabhinqa*, the female ones. But Prophet Mlanjeni got it all wrong. Twin-Twin was not a wizard.

The ancestor's name was Xikixa. A patriarch and a patrician of the Great Place of King Sarhili. He was the father of the twins, Twin and Twin-Twin. Twin-Twin was the first of the twins to be born, so according to custom he was the younger. The older twin is the one who is the last to kick the doors of the womb and to breathe the air that has already been breathed by the younger brother.

Twin and Twin-Twin were like one person. Even their voice was one. Mothers who eyed them for their daughters could not tell one from the other. And because they were close to each other, like saliva is to the tongue, they relished playing tricks on the maidens.

The patriarch lived his life with dignity, and brought up his children to fear and respect Qamata, or Mvelingqangi, the great god of all men and women, and to pay homage to those who are in the ground—the ancestors.

The twins were circumcised together with the son of the chief, and therefore became men of standing in their community. They became men of wealth too, for Xikixa did not want them to wait for his death before they could inherit his fields, cattle, and overflowing silos. He divided the bulk of his wealth between them.

Twin-Twin, the first-born twin who was younger than the second-born, loved women, and was the first to marry. And then he married again. And again. Long before Twin could know the warmth of the night. Yet the brothers remained close friends.

Then the news of Mlanjeni reached the homestead of Twin-Twin. And that of Xikixa, which was also the home of Twin. It reached the ears of every homestead in the land.

Mlanjeni, the Man of the River. He was only eighteen. Yet his head was not full of beautiful maidens. It did not throb with stick fights and *umtshotsho* dances. Instead he brooded over the evil that pervaded the world, that lurked even in the house of his own father, Kala. As a result he refused to eat his mother's cooking, for he said it was poisoned. He decided to fast because food enervated him. Women had an enfeebling power on him. So he kept himself celibate.

In order to stay clean he eschewed the company of other human beings, and spent his time immersed to the neck in a pool on the Keiskamma River. There he lived on the eggs of ants and on water grass.

"That son of Kala has something to him," said Xikixa to his twins. "He is a child, but he already talks of big things."

"I have heard his father talking with him about his behavior," said Twin-Twin. "Yet he will not listen."

"Kala is right," said the patriarch. "What does a boy who has not even been to circumcision school know about witchcraft and disease?"

When the time came, Mlanjeni went to the circumcision school. Both Twin and Twin-Twin were among the *amakhankatha*—the men who taught the initiates how to be men. Xikixa was the *ingcibi*—the doctor who cut the foreskin. They saw that Mlanjeni was very thin and weak. They did not think he would survive the rigors of the mountain. But he did, and went on to become the new prophet of the amaXhosa people.

And the amaXhosa people believed in him, for it was clear that he had contact with the spirit world and was charged by the ancestors with the task of saving humankind from itself.

As his teachings unfolded, people knew that indeed he was the next great prophet after Nxele, the man who had revealed the truths of the world thirty years before. And both of them spoke against *ubuthi*, the evil charms that were poisoning the nation, and against witchcraft.

Whereas Nxele had preached about Mdalidephu, the god of the black man; Thixo, the god of the white man; and Thixo's son, Tayi, who was killed by the white people, Mlanjeni worshipped the sun.

Nxele used to talk of the great day that was coming, when the dead would arise and witches would be cast into damnation in the belly of the earth. But his career was stopped short by the British, who locked him up on Robben Island. Before he surrendered he promised that he would come back again. Alas, he drowned trying to escape from the island.

"Can it be that Mlanjeni is the reincarnation of Nxele?" Twin wondered. "After all, the amaXhosa nation is still awaiting the return of Nxele."

As Mlanjeni was praying to the sun, it scorched the earth. There was famine in the land. Cattle were dying. And those that still lived, you could count their ribs. As the Man of the River was waning away from his fasting, men and women of the land were waning away from starvation. And he told them that it was because of ubuthi.

"Leave ubuthi alone," he preached. "As long as there is witchcraft among you, there will be disease. People and animals will die. Cast away ubuthi! You do not need ubuthi to invite good fortune or to protect yourselves! Cast it away, and all come to me to be cleansed!"

"This sickly boy is Nxele himself. Nxele has returned as he promised he would," said Twin.

"No, he is not Nxele," responded Twin-Twin. "Mlanjeni is a prophet in his own right."

This difference of opinion developed into a serious disagreement between the twins, to the extent that they took up sticks to fight each other. Women screamed and called the patriarch. When Xikixa arrived, he was happy. His sons had never disagreed on anything before, let alone fought each other. Now, for the very first time, they were not seeing things with the same eye. A spat over prophets.

"I was becoming worried about you two," he said, taking the sticks away from them. "Now you are becoming human beings."

People came to the homestead of Mlanjeni's father to be cleansed by the wonder child. They came from all over kwaXhosa, even from beyond the borders of the lands that had been conquered by the British. Those who had poisonous roots and evil charms disposed of them and were cleansed. But still, some people held tight to their ubuthi, and lied that they had got rid of it.

Mlanjeni set up two antiwitchcraft poles outside his father's house. Those suspected of witchcraft were required to walk between them. The innocent walked through. Terrible things happened to those who had ubuthi even as they approached the sacred poles.

From early dawn, hundreds of people gathered outside the house. Among them were Xikixa, his wives, his other children from the junior houses, Twin-Twin and his wives and children, and Twin. People had come because word had spread up to the foothills of the Maluti Mountains that Mlanjeni cured the sick, and made the lame to walk, the dumb to speak, and the blind to see.

He was a man of great power. He lit his pipe on the sun, and when he danced drops of sweat from his body caused the rain to fall.

The Man of the River appeared at the door of his hut, and after one word from him people saw the star of the morning coming down from the sky and placing itself on his forehead. Another word from him and the earth shook and the mountains trembled. He disappeared into the hut again. And people began to sing a thunderous song that echoed in the faraway hills. They sang until the sun rose from behind the mountains and moved to the center of the sky.

Mlanjeni emerged again, raised his spear to the heavens, and touched the sun. The sun came down to touch his head, and went through his body until it was bright like the sun itself. People prostrated themselves, shouting, "Mlanjeni! Mlanjeni is our true Lord! The Man of the River is the conqueror of death!"

One by one they began to walk between the poles. The clean were unscathed. The unclean were struck by weakness and fear as they approached the poles. Then they writhed on the spot, unable to move. The people shouted, "Out! Get out, witchcraft!" until the victims staggered through the poles to Mlanjeni, who gave them some twigs that would protect them from further evil and keep them pure.

Twin-Twin's wife from the senior house stood up and slowly walked towards the poles. It was as though she was in a trance. As she moved between the poles she froze. She was paralyzed. Mlanjeni began to dance a frenzied dance around the poles, and the crowd chanted, "She is fixed! She is fixed! She is a witch!"

Twin-Twin rushed to his wife, who was writhing on the ground in agony. He was shouting, "No! No! My wife is not a witch! There must be a mistake!"

A group of zealots grabbed him and dragged him to the donga below Kala's homestead. There they flogged him with whips. They beat him until he was almost unconscious. Then they went back to the Man of the River expecting his praise.

"Twin-Twin is a wizard. That is why he was defending his wife who was clearly identified as a witch by the poles," said Mlanjeni feebly. "But you had no right to beat him up. I have said it before, no person should ever be harmed for being a witch. Witchcraft is not in the nature of men and women. They are not born with it. It is an affliction that I can cure."

Twin-Twin's weals opened up and became wounds. After many months the wounds healed and became scars. But occasionally they itched and reminded him of his flagellation. At the time he did not know that his progeny was destined to carry the burden of the scars.

For a long time he was angry at the injustice of it all. He was not a wizard, and was sure that his wife was not a witch. Yet his own father and twin brother were blaming him for stupidly defending the honor of a woman who had been declared a witch by none other than the great prophet himself. And now both Xikixa and Twin were ostracizing his senior wife.

It did not escape Twin-Twin that this was the second time he had quarreled with his twin brother, and on both occasions the prophet was the cause.

But he continued to defend Mlanjeni. When the British decided to hunt the prophet down—claiming they did not approve of his witch-hunting and witch-curing activities—he was just as furious as the rest of the men of kwaXhosa.

17

Twin-Twin suppressed the bitterness in his heart and went with Twin, his father, and a group of mounted men to meet the white man who called himself the Great White Chief of the Xhosas, Sir Harry Smith. He watched in humiliation as the Great White Chief commanded the elders and even the chiefs to kiss his staff and his boots. And they did. And so did he.

The Great White Chief was running wild all over the lands of the amaXhosa, doing whatever he liked in the name of Queen Victoria of England. He even deposed Sandile, the king of the amaXhosa-ka-Ngqika. This caused all the chiefs, even those who were Sandile's rivals, to rally around the deposed king.

The Great White Chief was relentless in his pursuit of Mlanjeni. He suspected that the prophet was plotting something sinister against the Great Queen and her Empire. He instructed his magistrates to summon him to their offices, where disciplinary measures would be taken. When the prophet refused to hand himself over, the Great White Chief felt personally insulted. One of his most zealous magistrates sent a soldier called John Dalton with a detachment of policemen to Kala's homestead to arrest the Man of the River. But Mlanjeni was nowhere to be found. Queen Victoria's men did not know that he had buried himself under the sacred waters of the Keiskamma River.

The Great White Chief read conspiracy and uprising in this whole sorry affair. He summoned all the kings and chiefs of the amaKhosa people for the usual boot-kissing ritual. He vowed that he would restore law and order throughout British Kaffraria and Xhosaland. But some of the most important kings and chiefs did not attend the ceremony. A further insult to the Empire.

Twin-Twin observed the ceremony from a distance. He reported to the men of his village how the white man who had styled himself the father of the amaXhosa had ranted and raved and threatened to raze the whole amaXhosa nation to the ground.

The people had had enough of the Great White Chief. Mounted men, led by Xikixa, went to the Keiskamma River to consult with the prophet. Mlanjeni ordered that all dun and yellow cattle be slaughtered, for they were an abomination. He doctored the military men for war so that the guns of the British would shoot hot water instead of bullets. The Great War of Mlanjeni had begun.

It was an ugly and tedious war that lasted for three years, during which the Khoikhoi people of the Kat River Valley abandoned their traditional alliance with the British and fought on the side of the amaXhosa. Both Twin and Twin-Twin fought in the war. And so did Xikixa, who was still strong enough to carry a shield and a spear. The Great White Chief was frustrated. He was heard on many occasions talking of his intention to exterminate all amaXhosa.

"Extermination is now the only word and principle that guides us. I loved these people and considered them my children. But now I say exterminate the savage beasts!" he told his field commanders. Some of them were seen marching to war with the word "Extermination!" emblazoned on their hats.

Twin and Twin-Twin fought under General Maqoma in the Amathole Mountains. It was by and large a guerrilla war. They ambushed the British soldiers when they least expected it. The great size of the mountain range made things very difficult for the Imperial forces, and gave the amaXhosa armies many opportunities to destroy the enemy soldiers.

It was at one such ambush that Twin and Twin-Twin—accompanied by a small band of guerrilla fighters—chanced upon a British camp hidden in a gorge. A small group of British soldiers were cutting off the ears of a dead umXhosa soldier.

"What are they doing that for? Are they wizards?" asked Twin-Twin. "Or is it their way of removing *iqungu*?"

Iqungu was the vengeful force generated by war medicines. A soldier who died in war could have his iqungu attack the slayer, bloating and swelling up his body until he died. The amaXhosa believed that the British soldiers had their own iqungu. Therefore, they mutilated the bodies of slain British soldiers to render their iqungu powerless. This was considered savagery of the worst kind by the British, whenever they came across their dead comrades with ripped stomachs on the Amathole slopes.

"It is not for iqungu," explained Twin, who seemed to know more about the ways of the British from listening to fireside gossip. "It is just the witchcraft of the white man. They take those ears to their country. That's what they call souvenirs."

The twins saw that the leader of the soldiers was a man they had met before. John Dalton. He had been one of the soldiers accompanying the Great White Chief during the boot-kissing ceremony. He had been introduced then as an important man in the entourage of soldiers. He spoke isiXhosa, so he was the interpreter. It was the same John Dalton who had been sent with a detachment of policemen to hunt down the Man of the River.

Then, to the horror of the men watching, the soldiers cut off the dead man's head and put it in a pot of boiling water.

"They are cannibals too," hissed Twin-Twin.

The British soldiers sat around and smoked their pipes and laughed at their own jokes. Occasionally one of the soldiers stirred the boiling pot, and the stench of rotten meat floated up to the twins' group. The guerrillas could not stand it any longer. With bloodcurdling screams they sprang from their hiding place and attacked the men of Queen Victoria. One British soldier was killed, two were captured, and the rest escaped.

"It is our father!" screamed Twin. "They were going to eat our father!"

It was indeed the headless body of Xikixa.

"We were not going to eat your father," said John Dalton, prisoner of war, in his perfect isiXhosa. "We are civilized men, we don't eat people."

"Liar!" screamed Twin-Twin. "Why would you cook anything that you are not going to eat?"

"To remove the flesh from the skull," explained Dalton patiently. He did not seem to be afraid. He seemed too sure of himself. "These heads are either going to be souvenirs, or will be used for scientific inquiry."

Souvenirs. Scientific inquiry. It did not make sense. It was nothing but the witchcraft of the white man.

While they were debating the best method of killing their captives, a painful and merciless method that would at least avenge the decapitated patriarch, the British soldiers returned with reinforcements from a nearby camp. Only Twin and Twin-Twin were able to escape. The rest of their party was killed.

It gnawed the souls of the twins that their father met his end in the boiling cauldrons of the British, and they were never able to give him a decent burial in accordance with the rites and rituals of his people. How would he commune with his fellow ancestors without a head? How would a headless ancestor be able to act as an effective emissary of their pleas to Qamata?

In the meantime, the Great White Chief was getting ever more desperate. He was unable to win the war outright. The British firepower was stronger, but the guerrilla tactics of the amaXhosa soldiers were creating havoc. General Maqoma and the Khoikhoi chief, Hans Brander, were giving the Imperial armies a hard time. Mutinies became the order of the day. Queen Victoria's men refused to go to the Amathole Mountains to be slaughtered like cattle by the savage amaXhosa. The Great White Chief was recalled to his country in disgrace, and was replaced by Sir George Cathcart, who proceeded to the eastern frontier to attend to the war with great enthusiasm.

People were disappointed with Mlanjeni's prophecies. None of them were coming true. The Imperial bullets did not turn into water. Instead, amaXhosa men were being killed every day.

But when the amaXhosa were about to give up, the Khoikhoi kept them fighting. At least they had muskets, although they were running out of ammunition. General Maqoma and Chief Brander destroyed more than two hundred farmhouses and captured five thousand cattle from the colonists.

Khoikhoi women sold their bodies to the British soldiers in order to smuggle canisters of gunpowder to their fighting men. Twin and his friends made snide remarks behind these women's backs. They slept with British soldiers, the men remarked. They seemed to forget that it was for the gunpowder that was saving the amaXhosa nation from utter defeat that the women were prostituting themselves.

It was with one of these Khoikhoi women, Quxu, that Twin fell in love. The amaXhosa guerrillas called her Qukezwa. He had seen her leading a group of Khoikhoi women who smuggled gunpowder under their hide skirts, and heard that she was the daughter of an important Khoikhoi chief.

The next time Twin saw Qukezwa it was at the crossroads. She was standing in front of a pile of stones, oblivious of him. She added another stone to the pile, and carefully placed green herbs on top of it. All the while she was chanting softly, "Father of fathers, oh Tsiqwa! You are our father. Let the clouds burst and the streams flow. Please give life to our flocks, and to us. I am weak, oh Tsiqwa, from thirst and hunger! Give me fields of fruit, that your children may be fed. For you are the father of fathers. O Tsiqwa! Let us sing your praises. In return give us your blessings. Father of fathers! You are our Lord, O Tsiqwa!"

She then quietly walked away. She seemed to remember something, and went back to the pile of stones.

"And, O Tsiqwa," she pleaded, "give us strength to win this war! To drive those who have come to desecrate our sacred grounds into the sea!"

Twin was struck with wonder.

"Who is this Tsiqwa you are addressing?" he asked softly. "I do not see anyone."

She was startled. But then composed herself when she saw a smiling umXhosa soldier standing in front of her.

"Tsiqwa is the one who tells his stories in heaven. He created the Khoikhoi and all the world. Even the rocks that lie under water on the riverbed. And all the springs with their snakes that live in them. That is why we never kill the snake of the spring. If we did, the spring would dry out."

Twin was captivated by her wisdom. He did not let on that her words were beyond him, and she felt at ease in his presence. Soon they were chatting like old friends. And in the days that followed he made a point of speaking with her whenever she brought smuggled gunpowder to the caves where the guerrilla fighters were hiding. He was in love. He ignored the mocking laughter of his comrades-in-arms who called her a whore.

From this daughter of joy he learned more about Tsiqwa. Together they sang the song of Heitsi Eibib, the earliest prophet of the Khoikhoi. The song told the story of how Heitsi Eibib brought his people to the Great River. But they could not cross, for the river was overflowing. And the people said to Heitsi Eibib, "Our enemies are upon us, they will surely kill us."

Heitsi Eibib prayed, "O Tsiqwa! Father of fathers. Open yourself that I may pass through, and close yourself afterwards."

As soon as he had uttered these words the Great River opened, and his people crossed. But when the enemies tried to pass through the opening, when they were right in the middle, the Great River closed upon them, and they all perished in its waters.

Whenever they sang this song, Twin wished the same thing could happen to the British.

Sometimes Qukezwa took her beau to the crossroads where there were piles of stones. At different crossroads there were different piles of stones. The lovers added one more stone each time they visited. They also placed green twigs of aromatic herbs such as *buchu* on the stones. She explained, "To place a stone on this grave of Heitsi Eibib is to be one with the source of your soul."

"How can one man have so many graves?" Twin asked.

"Because he was a prophet and a savior," she said. "He was the son of Tsiqwa. He lived and died for all the Khoikhoi, irrespective of clan."

Twin was sad that no one had ever died for the amaXhosa people in the same way that Heitsi Eibib had died for the Khoikhoi.

At night she taught him about the stars. Up in the heavens where Tsiqwa told his stories she showed him the bright stars which she called the Seven Sisters.

"They are the seven daughters of Tsiqwa, the Creator. The Seven Sisters are the star mothers from which all the human race has descended," she explained.

There was no doubt in Twin's mind that he wanted to marry this daughter of the stars. Twin-Twin tried to talk him out of it. He reminded his brother that there were amaXhosa maidens who had never opened their thighs for British soldiers. "What do you see in this *lawukazi?*" he cried.

But Twin was immovable in his resolve to marry Qukezwa.

"At least wait until the war is over," pleaded Twin-Twin. He hoped that time would cure his brother's infatuation.

But Twin would not wait. He married her. And for him she danced the dance of the new rain. And of the new moon.

In the meantime, the war was raging. And Sir George Cathcart would stop at nothing to win it. If he could not defeat the amaXhosa people in the field of battle, he was going to starve them into submission. He ordered his soldiers to go on a rampage and burn amaXhosa fields and kill amaXhosa cattle wherever they came across them, instead of spending their time hunting down guerrillas in the crevices of the Amathole Mountains. When the troops found unarmed women working in the fields, they killed them too.

The great fear of starvation finally defeated General Maqoma's forces, and the amaXhosa surrendered to the British. They turned against Mlanjeni, the Man of the River, because his charms had failed. But other nations continued to believe in him. Messengers from the distant nations of the Basotho, the abaThembu, the amaMpondo and the amaMpondomise visited him, asking for war charms and for the great secret of catching witches.

Six months after the war ended, the great prophet died of tuberculosis.

Although the twins' wealth remained intact—they had hidden most of their herds in the Amathole Mountains—they were disillusioned with prophets. They were devastated by the death of their father, who had ended up as stew in a British pot.

Mlanjeni's war, however, had given Twin a beautiful yellow-colored wife, and Twin-Twin the scars of history.

She starts another hymn. The old ladies pick it up in their tired voices, some of which have become hoarse. They have been singing for the greater part of the night. Her voice remains hauntingly fresh. It is a freshness that cries to be echoed by the green hills, towering cliffs, and deep gullies of a folktale dreamland, instead of being wasted on a dead man in a tattered tent on top of a twenty-story building in Hillbrow, Johannesburg.

She is now singing "Nearer My God to Thee." She is nearer to God. The distance from the havoc, murder, and mayhem in the streets down below attests to that fact.

She is an incongruous mirage. A young woman of hearthly beauty in the midst of shriveled old fogies with shaky voices. She is somebody's *makoti*, or daughter-in-law, judging from the way she is dressed: a respectful doek on her head, a shawl over her shoulders, and a dress that reaches a considerable distance below the knees.

Camagu's eyes cannot leave her alone. Her beauty is not in harmony with this wake. It does not speak of death. It shouts only of life. Of the secret joys that she harbors under her wifely habit.

He wonders who she might be. A relative of the deceased, perhaps? Certainly she is not the widow. Otherwise she would be sitting on a mattress in some dark room, weeping her eyes red, and being fussed over by a bunch of fat females. She is most likely a neighbor. Or a family friend.

Camagu walks out of the tent and joins a group of men who are smoking what smells distinctly like dagga. They are joking about the deceased. From what they say, he must have been a jolly good fellow. But then so are all dead people, especially on the night of their wake. Or on the day of their funeral. The living remember only good things about them.

Camagu wonders who the dead man was. Obviously he was not one of the important people of the slummy flatland: the gangsters and the pimps. Otherwise the wake would have been teeming with fastguns celebrating by firing in the sky. And prostitutes bidding a fond farewell to a business manager by flaunting the wares he'll never exploit again.

He must have been a simple upright citizen, for he is mourned only by the aged and the forgotten. There are no gongs. No dancing girls. No fanfare. No songs of freedom. No fashion parades. Just the grandmothers and grandfathers. The dilapidated orphans of the night. The wanderers whose permanent homes are the tents of the nightly wakes—each night a different vigil. And the young makoti singing the dirge. And Camagu.

Camagu himself is at the wake not because he has any connection with anyone here. He just found himself here.

He was at Giggles, a toneless nightclub on the ground floor, when he decided to take a walk. He is a regular at Giggles because he lives on the fourth floor of this building. He does not need to walk the deadly streets of Hillbrow for a tipple.

Most of Giggles' patrons are disaffected exiles and sundry learned rejects of this new society. He is one of them too, and constantly marvels at the irony of being called an exile in his own country.

It was becoming too hot at Giggles, with the exiles moaning and whingeing, or going on nostalgic reminiscences about what they sacrificed for this country, enduring hardships in Tanzania, Sweden, America, or Yugoslavia.

Others were hurling accusations at him: that he was unpatriotic, that he was deserting his country in its hour of need for imperialistic America.

Perhaps he shouldn't have told them that his suitcase was packed and he was leaving for his second exile tomorrow. He had to tell them, though, because even at this last minute he is trying to sell his old Toyota Corolla. If no one buys it he will have to leave it at some garage, which will sell it for him and cheat him out of a sizable amount.

Giggles was not the place for him tonight.

The band too was not at its best. Screeching saxophones rasped his eardrums. The out-of-tune piano murdered Abdullah Ibrahim with every clunk.

That was why he decided to take a walk. He did not dare go onto the streets. Throughout the night they swarm with restless humanity. Hillbrow never sleeps. Yet he is dead scared of this town. It is four years since he came back from his American exile, but he still has not got used to the fact that every morning a number of dead bodies adorn the streets.

As he stood outside Giggles, planning his next move, a group of old people walked into the building. They were softly singing a hymn. Since the lift is always dead in this building they began to climb the stairs. He decided to follow them. He did not know where they were going. He did not care. He just wanted to get as far away from Giggles as possible.

It was a long climb to the top of the building, where a vigil was in progress in a tattered tent. He was out of breath. The aged ones continued with their song as if climbing Everest meant nothing. He joined the mourners and mourned the dead.

The singing has stopped. A man is declaiming about the wickedness of the city, which has stolen this brother in his prime.

"This brother was gifted," shouts the man. "His hands could create wonders. His fingers were nimble, and could mold enchanted worlds. Yet this city swallowed him, and spewed him out a shriveled corpse. This ungrateful city decided that he could survive only if he created ugly things that distorted life as we knew it. He refused, for he was attached to beautiful things. He waned away as a result, until he was a bag of bones . . ."

The man goes on. The old ones respond with "amens" and "hallelujahs."

But only the image of the makoti lingers in Camagu's mind. He becomes breathless when he thinks of her. He is ashamed that the pangs of his famous lust are attacking him on such a solemn occasion. But quickly he decides it is not lust. Otherwise parts of his body would be running amok. No, he does not think of her in those terms. She is more like a spirit that can comfort him and heal his pain. A mothering spirit. And this alarms him, for he has never thought of any woman like that before. After all, she is a stranger with whom he has not exchanged a single word.

His unquenchable desire for the flesh is well known. A shame he has to live with. Flesh. Any flesh. He cannot hold himself. He has done things with his maid—a frumpy country woman who has come to the city of gold to pick up a few pennies by cleaning up after disenchanted bachelors—that he would be ashamed to tell anyone. Yet he did these things with the humble servant again and again.

There is something about servitude that seems to set the crotches of men of Camagu's ilk on fire. It must have been the same urge that drove the slave master, normally a levelheaded, loving family man with a rosy-cheeked wife and bouncing babies, from his mansion to a night of wild passion with the slave girl in the slave quarters or in the fields. Of course it was wild passion only on his side. To the slave girl, consent was through coercion. It was rape.

In Camagu's case it was not rape, or so he comforted himself when shame confronted him, for the servant encouraged it. She saw it as a chance of making more money from the master.

The makoti starts another hymn. Camagu rushes back to the tent. The dagga smokers are making the place livelier by clapping hands and dancing what looks like the *toyi-toyi*—the freedom dance that the youth used to dance when people were fighting for liberation. Its political fervor has been replaced by a religious one. Camagu joins them. His steps are rather awkward.

He never learned the freedom dance. He was already in exile when it was invented. While it became fashionable at political rallies, he was completing a doctoral degree and working in the communications department of an international development agency in New York. He regrets now that he acquired so much knowledge in the fields of communication and economic development but never learned the freedom dance.

He remembers how in 1994 he took leave from his job and came back to South Africa to vote, after an absence of almost thirty years. He was in his mid-forties, and was a stranger in his own country. He was swept up by the euphoria of the time, and decided that he would not return to New York. He would stay and contribute to the development of his country.

At his first job interview he heard them comment, "Who is he? We didn't see him when we were dancing the freedom dance."

That was when Camagu realized the importance of the dance. He had tried to explain about his skills in the area of development communication, how he had worked for international agencies, how as an international expert he had done consulting work for UNESCO in Paris and for the Food and Agricultural Organization in Rome, and how the International Telecommunications Union had often sought his advice on matters of international broadcasting. The interviewers were impressed. They commended his achievements. He had done his oppressed people proud in foreign lands. And now, the freedom dance? Alas! His steps faltered.

Another interview. They wanted a director of communications in a government department that dealt with land and agricultural matters. This was up his street, and he was confident that he would get the job. They listened patiently and heard about his vast learning and experience. They smiled, gave him coffee with assorted biscuits, and shook his hand. Then they sang the lamentations. "What a pity," a kindly voice whispered. "Unfortunately he is overqualified."

He was being penalized for too much learning.

"Overqualified? I can do the job, can't I?" he asked. "And I find your salary range acceptable. How can I be overqualified?"

"Too much knowledge is a dangerous thing," he thought he heard one of them mutter.

Things would be all right, he told himself. He became an avid reader of the appointments pages in newspapers, and applied for all the jobs for which he was qualified. The broadcasting corporation did not respond, the Department of Health merely acknowledged his application and forever held its peace, the government information service called him for an interview and then forgot his existence. He was gradually losing his enthusiasm for this new democratic society.

The twentieth interview. The big men of the government said to him, "You have been out of the country for many years. What makes you think you can do this job? How familiar are you with South Africa and its problems?"

"How familiar are our rulers, presidents, ministers, and lawmakers—who have either been in prison or in exile for thirty years—with South Africa and its problems?" Camagu asked, not bothering to hide his contempt for the questioner.

He did not get that job.

"You can serve your country in the private sector," the voice of wisdom whispered in his ear. "Why not try the private sector and the parastatals?"

He tried them. He discovered that the corporate world did not want qualified blacks. They preferred the inexperienced ones who were only too happy to be placed in some glass affirmative-action office where they were displayed as paragons of empowerment. No one cared if they ever got to grips with their jobs or not. All the better for the old guard if they did not. That safeguarded the old guard's position. The mentor would always be hovering around as a consultant—for even bigger rewards. The problem with bureaucrats of Camagu's ilk was that they efficiently did the job themselves, depriving consultants of their livelihood.

The beautiful men and women in glass displays did not like the Camagus of this world. They were a threat to their luxury German sedans, housing allowances, and expense accounts.

His joints are not what they used to be. He cannot keep up with the dancers. He decides to stand on the side for a while, making sure that he has an unobstructed view of the beautiful one. He wonders how the old ones manage to be so relentless in their rhythmic movement. And some of them are going to work in the morning. They'll be standing up all day, eking out a meager living as maids, washerwomen, and street vendors. Fortunately he is not going to work. Not tomorrow. Not ever in this country.

Four years have passed, and Camagu is still not employed in what he was trained for. He teaches part-time at a trade school in the central business district of Johannesburg. Well, he was teaching there until yesterday, when he decided to quit.

He had toyed with the idea of taking the advice of an interviewer who once asked him, "With all your education, why don't you start your own consultancy?"

Even as a consultant, he discovered, one needed to dance the free-dom dance in order to get contracts. Or at least to know some prominent dancers. And tipplers at Giggles who were in the booming consultancy trade always complained that the government had more faith in those consultants who had crossed at least one ocean to get to these shores. In any case, one needed money to start a viable consultancy.

The best option for him is to go back to exile.

A woman is declaiming on how the wrath of God will send great flames to incinerate Hillbrow. The vigil responds with "amens" and "hallelujahs."

A man declares that the Lord is always so wonderful. He has blessed this wake with a beautiful young stranger who sings like an angel. Surely the path of the deceased has been cleared by this wonderful voice and he will be welcomed in the house with many mansions. Once more there are "amens" and "hallelujahs."

"Indeed she was sent here by the Lord to accompany her homeboy with her beautiful voice," shouts an old woman. "She is a good child from my village. And she brought us bottles of sea water. She knows that we inland people love to drink the sea because it cures all sorts of diseases. Praise the Lord!"

"Amen!"

"Hallelujah!"

Camagu goes out for a little fresh air and a smoke.

It is dawn.

"Everything now . . . the fruits of liberation . . . are enjoyed only by those from exile or from Robben Island," he overhears a man from the group of dagga smokers complain. "Yet we were the ones who bore the brunt of the bullets. We threw stones and danced the freedom dance."

"Yes, while they were having a good time overseas we were dying here. We were the cannon fodder for those who are eating softly now," adds another one.

Whining and whingeing is the pastime of this new democratic society, thinks Camagu, not recognizing the fact that he was doing exactly the same thing for the greater part of the wake.

"You don't network," Camagu remembers a fellow exile who is now a big man in the government telling him. "You don't lobby."

"Why should I network and lobby when I have the right qualifications and experience?" he asked proudly.

It is pride that has killed Camagu.

The big man from the government laughed. "Do not be stupid," he said. "Come to my office tomorrow. We are going to lobby for you. There is an important post in my department."

"I will not allow anyone to lobby for me to get a job. Are we not all South Africans who should be allowed to serve our country on merit?"

Deadly pride.

Camagu discovered that networking and lobbying were a crucial part of South African life. He was completely inadequate in that regard. All along he had operated under the misguided notion that things happened for you because you deserved them, not because you had the most influential lobbyists.

He had not known that jobs were advertised only as a formality, to meet the requirements of the law. When a job was advertised there was someone already earmarked for it. Not necessarily the best candidate, but someone who had lobbied or had powerful people lobbying on his or her behalf. It helped if the candidate lived vividly in the memory of decision-makers as the best dancer of the freedom dance.

One of Camagu's problems, he discovered, was that he was not a member of the cocktail circuit.

"Join the Aristocrats of the Revolution," advised another big man from the government who had his interests at heart. "I am sure if you try hard enough you can qualify. Of course at first you will belong to the Club of the Sycophants of the Aristocrats of the Revolution. But all in good time, when you have paid your dues, you will be a proper Aristocrat of the Revolution yourself."

Only then did Camagu understand the full implications of life in this new democratic society. He did not qualify for any important position because he was not a member of the Aristocrats of the Revolution, an exclusive club that is composed of the ruling elites, their families, and close friends. Some of them were indeed leaders of the freedom struggle, while others had used their status and wealth to snake their way into the very heart of the organization.

The jobs he had been applying for had all gone to people whose only qualification was that they were sons and daughters of the Aristocrats of the Revolution.

Camagu could easily have benefited from this system if he had played his cards right from the beginning. He knew a lot of people in exile, many of whom were prominent members of the Aristocrats of the Revolution. He had even gone to school with some of them. He had been involved in antiapartheid demonstrations in various capitals of the world with a number of them. It would have been easy to attach himself to them, or even buy a membership card. But he chose to remain independent, and to speak out against what he called patronage. Now that he is unemployed he regrets his indiscretions.

But pride still kills him.

"Why don't you talk with the minister?" asked yet another big man from the government, mentioning a powerful cabinet minister. "I can arrange an appointment for you. If I remember well, you two had a thing going back in the States."

Indeed he had had a few adventures with the honorable minister, many years before anyone ever knew that one day there would be freedom and she would be a member of the cabinet. She was an ordinary poet who composed bad verses and was an aspirant performer of them.

And what breathless adventures! Camagu is quite smug about the fact that he once made the most powerful woman in the country, the woman before whom powerful men tremble, scream for mercy. While he screamed for his mother.

Fatal pride.

Maybe things would come right, he thought. In a year or two, doors would open.

A gravel-voiced man smashes his thoughts with "*Noyana, noyana, phezulu.*" He is slapping his Bible to the rhythm of the bouncy hymn that demands to know whether those congregated here will enter the portals of heaven. The old ones dance around him in a solemn circle. Then the man breaks into a bout of preaching.

"He was in pain before he died, this our brother," he shouts. "It was the pain of the spirit that was being denied the right to soar in its creativity. It was the pain of a suppressed mind. The pain ended up attacking his body. It ravaged his insides. The beauty of death is that it separates us from the pain that racks our bodies."

Camagu's hopes that things would come right were crushed by a strike at the school where he was teaching. The students kidnapped the principal. They demanded that their trade school be transferred from the Department of Labour to the Department of Education. They summoned a cabinet minister, who went cap in hand to negotiate with them.

"We are a liberal and caring government," said the cabinet minister. "The students have genuine grievances. We are now negotiating with them to release the principal."

After many days of negotiations the students released the principal. The minister, a man of the people to the last, was seen on the country's television screens dancing the freedom dance with the triumphant learners.

That incident made up Camagu's mind for him. The minister was doing a jig of victory with people who had committed criminal offenses. In the course of the jubilation the rights of the principal who lost his freedom for a whole week were not considered at all. His children counted for nothing. The message was clear: to get your way with the government you must break the law . . . kidnap somebody . . . burn a building . . . block the roads . . . thrash South Africa!

Yesterday Camagu resigned from the school. His suitcase is packed, and tomorrow he is flying away.

Inside the tent they are praying the final prayers of the wake.

"I'll fly! I'll soar!" shouts Camagu to the indifferent dawn. "Let me soar to the sky like the creations of the dead man!"

The mourners hear him, for now they are streaming out of the tent. The vigil is over. It is time to prepare for the funeral. They laugh and say madness sets in when people begin to talk alone.

They are all going down the mountain. Abseiling the steep rock faces. Camagu misses a step and almost falls when he finds himself next to the makoti.

"Be careful," says the beautiful one.

"You sang those hymns beautifully," says the exile.

"Thank you."

"What is your name?"

"NomaRussia."

"You are not from Hillbrow. You do not look like people from Hillbrow."

"No one is from Hillbrow. Everyone here comes from somewhere else. I am from Qolorha."

"Where is that?"

"Qolorha. Qolorha-by-Sea. Haven't you heard of Nongqawuse?"

Of course, Nongqawuse. He has vague memories of history lessons where he was told about a young girl who deceived the amaXhosa nation into mass suicide. But he never associated her with any real place.

The hearthly one tells him that she came to the city to visit her "homeboy," only to find that he was dead. She is going back to the land of Nongqawuse this very morning. She is saddened by the fact that she won't be able to attend the funeral, for her bus to the Eastern Cape leaves very early in the morning. She is pleased, though, that she was at her homeboy's wake, and was able to sing him a loving farewell.

An old woman drags her away and admonishes her for talking to strangers.

Camagu used to see himself as a pedlar of dreams. That was when he could make things happen. Now he has lost his touch. He needs a pedlar of dreams himself, with a bagful of dreams waiting to be dreamt. A whole storage full of dreams.

While the Unbelievers lament the sufferings of the Middle Generations, Zim celebrates the end of those sufferings. Although both he and Bhonco, son of Ximiya, patriarch of the Unbelievers, are descendants of the headless ancestor, they never see any issue with the same eye.

Zim, the leading light of the Believers, owes his existence and his belief to his great-grandfather, Twin, and Twin's yellow-colored wife, Qukezwa. That is why he named his first-born son Twin, even though he was not a twin, and his yellow-colored daughter Qukezwa.

Zim himself is a yellow-colored stocky man with the high cheek-bones of the Khoikhoi. He has taken more from his great-grandmother's people. So have his children. Their Khoikhoi features were enhanced by their mother. NoEngland, who was from the amaGqunukhwebe, the clan that came into existence from the intermarriages of the ama-Xhosa and the Khoikhoi people even before the days of Nongqawuse.

NoEngland died a year ago, and Zim hasn't stopped mourning her death. Even today as he sits under the gigantic wild fig tree in front of his hexagon, he is wondering how life would have been had the ancestors not decided to call NoEngland so early in her life. And it was indeed early, for she was only forty-four—eighteen years younger than her husband.

The wild fig tree knows all his secrets. It is his confessional. Under it he finds solace, for it is directly linked to the ancestors—all of Twin's progeny who planted it more than a hundred years ago. Now the trunk is as big as his main hut. As soon as it leaves the ground its branches twist and turn in all directions, spreading wide like an umbrella over his whole homestead. Some branches reach as far as the top of the *umsintsi* trees—the coral tree that used to be called kaffirboom during the Middle Generations—and the aloes that surround his yard.

Everyone in Qolorha knows that if you want Zim you will find him under his wild fig tree. He spends most of the day dozing under it, listening to the song of the birds. Neither season nor weather deters him from indulging in this pleasure. He is there in autumn when the tree sheds its leaves, and he is faithful to it even when it remains naked during the winter. When the urge to commune with the tree is strong enough, not even the cold wind from the sea can drive him into the house.

There are four different kinds of ancestors: the ancestors of the sea, the ancestors of the forest, the ancestors of the veld, and the ancestors of the homestead. They are all regular visitors to this tree.

Today the spring weather is particularly beautiful. Green leaves are shyly beginning to appear on the tree. The green pigeons, with their red legs and red beaks, are flying around. Soon they will be feeding on the wild figs that will be ready even before summer. The *amahobohobo* weaverbirds are adding more nests to the city that is already dangling and would be weighing the tree down if it had not gathered so much strength over the generations.

Hundreds of birds inhabit this tree. Perhaps thousands. People think it is foolish of the Believer to be so close to so much meat without killing even a single bird for supper.

Zim is musing about NoEngland, and about the joys of belief. He is rudely awoken by a nest that falls on his head. Sometimes a foolish weaverbird chooses a very weak branch on which to build its nest. As the nest grows bigger it gets heavier. The branch breaks and the nest falls. Whenever that happens Zim becomes very distressed. The bird's labor of many days has been wasted.

He takes the nest and examines the great craftsmanship. It was almost complete. Now the poor bird will have to start its construction from scratch.

He puts the nest on the ground and is about to doze off when Qukezwa arrives and angrily wakes him up. She is shouting, "You see the disgraceful things you do, tata? Now people shout at me at work! Do you want me to lose my job?"

"Why would I want you to lose your job? Dalton gave you that job because he knows you are my daughter," says Zim. "And where do you get your manners . . . talking to your father like that? What did I do?"

But Qukezwa walks into the house in a huff, leaving her father wondering what it is that is eating her. It must be something serious, otherwise she would not have disturbed her father in his musings. She knows how the Believer treasures his moments of meditation. After all, she grew up with the green pigeons and the bright yellow weaver-birds.

She must be angry. In her happy moments she talks with her father in whistles. The Believers talk among themselves in the language of the birds.

"She is only nineteen but she is as feisty as her mother used to be," he mutters to himself.

He wipes his smooth-shaven head and face with a handkerchief. He slowly stands up and drags himself into the house.

It turns out that while Qukezwa was busy scrubbing the wooden floors of Vulindlela Trading Store, where she works as a cleaner, a group of girls came to buy beads, calamine lotion, and other items that young women use to beautify themselves. When they saw her they giggled and pointed fingers at her. She glared back at them, and dared them to say to her face whatever it was they were whispering about her. Even though most of them were older than her, ranging from early to mid-twenties, she was not afraid of them.

One girl stepped forward and shouted, "Your mother was a filthy woman! She must be rotting in hell for what she did to that poor girl!"

"Your friend got what she deserved," responded Qukezwa, rolling the skirt of her dress into her panties, gearing for a fight. "Next time she will leave other people's husbands alone!"

Missis saw what was happening, and shooed them away. The girls ran out of the store giggling.

"And you, Qukezwa," said Missis, "if you bring fights in my store I'll ask Mr. Dalton to fire you."

Everybody knows that Missis has never really liked the bumptious girl.

The great to-do about the "poor girl" who, according to Qukezwa, has learned never to take other people's husbands again, began three years ago when NoEngland bought an old Singer sewing machine from Missis and learned to sew school uniforms. She received an order from Qolorha-by-Sea Secondary School for a number of uniforms, and employed the girl as an assistant to put the dresses together and sew the buttons.

NoEngland and the girl worked together in one of Zim's three hexagons, and became close friends. But the girl had a roving eye which landed on Zim. This interest was quite mutual, for it boosted Zim's ego. Here he was, an undistinguished aging man, the object of desire of a twenty-two-year-old girl of exceptional beauty. His thirst knew no bounds, and he found himself drinking occasionally from the forbidden well, especially on those days when NoEngland went to Butterworth to buy more material.

But the girl became too greedy and selfish. She was not satisfied with the occasional tryst. She wanted Zim for herself alone. So she went to a famous *igqirha*—a diviner—who would give her medicine that would make Zim leave NoEngland and love only her.

"Bring any undergarment of the other woman," said the diviner. "I'll work it, and the man will love only you."

The girl stole NoEngland's petticoat and took it to the igqirha. As soon as he saw it he knew who it belonged to. Instead of "working it" he took it to NoEngland.

"Yes, it is my petticoat," said an astounded NoEngland, "I have been looking for it all this time."

She felt betrayed, and was angry that the girl to whom she had opened her heart was trying to steal her husband. But the diviner told her, "I can deal with this girl for you. Get me an undergarment of hers and I'll work it."

NoEngland contrived to steal a pair of the girl's panties, and gave it to the igqirha. He "worked it" with his medicine.

Since that day the girl has never been able to have another tryst with anyone. Lovers have run away from her because whenever she tries to know a man—in the biblical sense, that is—she sees the moon. Things come in gushes, like water from a stream.

Even now, long after NoEngland's death, the punishment on the hapless girl continues. She has seen a host of diviners, herbalists, and doctors of all sorts. They have tried and failed to help. The famous igqirha has told her, "This can only be reversed by the person who caused it in the first place."

Hence the anger of her friends. It is the anger that many women of the community shared when they first heard of the scandal. Some blamed both women for trying to damage each other just because of a man. *Ukukrexeza*—having lovers outside marriage—is the way of the world, they said.

"What can we do about it?" they asked. "Ukukrexeza has been here since creation. We cannot change the way men and women behave today."

Now everyone has forgotten about it all. Except the girl herself. And her friends who know the sufferings she is enduring, and want to take their anger out on Qukezwa.

Zim tries to talk sense into his daughter's head. "Listen, my child," he says, "you cannot keep on blaming me for things that happened more than two years ago."

She loves her father. And normally they are such great friends. But the taunts of the village girls are becoming too much to bear.

"We are not supposed to talk ill of the dead, but your mother was not so innocent in this matter," continues Zim. "How do you think the igqirha knew that was her petticoat?"

And what would prompt the igqirha to betray a paying customer? Qukezwa now begins to wonder.

"Missis threatened to fire me because of those girls," sobs tata's little girl.

"No, she won't," says Zim adamantly. "I'll talk to Dalton about this."

He knows that he usually gets his way with John Dalton. For some reason, the trader has a soft spot for Zim and his family. He is the one who set his son Twin on the road to the untold fortunes that people who have been to the city of Johannesburg talk about, but that neither Zim nor Qukezwa have seen with their eyes.

Twin liked to do carvings from wood. He made bottlelike figures with turbaned heads, and took them to Dalton, hoping that the wealthy man would buy them. Dalton saw that the boy had a talent which could be developed. Although he was not a carver himself, he explained to Twin how he should carve the arms, hands, legs, and feet, and how he could make the face more realistic by carving detailed ears, eyes, noses, and mouths.

The following week Twin delivered male and female figures, carved exactly as Dalton had shown him. Dalton bought a number of the wooden figures and displayed them on his glass counters. Even today there are hundreds of them in the store, and tourists who come to see where the wonders of Nongqawuse happened buy them.

Zim was proud of his son's talent. He felt that it would work in the Believers' favor in their war against the Unbelievers. He repeated the history of Twin to everyone who cared to listen.

"This child," he said, "worked in Centani selling petrol at a filling station. Then he got very ill with fits. He was also delirious. His ancestor, Twin, visited him in his dreams, and told him to carve people out of wood and he would get well. He carved the beautiful people that you see in Dalton's store, and got well."

But Twin did not live up to his father's expectations. He became a renegade who refused to follow Zim in the battle to preserve the rituals of the Believers. He decided to think like all ordinary people, to follow trends set by others, and to share the same ambition as all the young men of the village: to work in the gold mines of Johannesburg and the Free State.

Zim lost the battle and let him go. He has not seen him since. He has heard that his son has left the mines and is now living in the city, in a building that reaches the sky, where he has accumulated wondrous fortunes from his wood carvings.

Rumor has it that it is because of Xoliswa Ximiya that he has never come back to Qolorha-by-Sea. People have not forgotten that the two were in love many years ago when they were both at primary school. But as time went on, Xoliswa Ximiya outgrew Twin as she became more educated.

He gave up on education in Standard Six. But he never gave up on Xoliswa Ximiya. For many years he hankered after her. That was why he left for Johannesburg, so the gossip goes, to mend his broken heart far away from her. Villagers, however, still hope to this day that the two will eventually marry and bring about peace between the two families.

"Dalton is a good man—although a person is only good when he is asleep . . . or dead," says Zim, blowing out a cloud of smoke and ejecting a jet of spittle onto the floor. "He will not expel you on account of loose tongues. You were just doing your work and those girls came and provoked you. Listen, tomorrow I am getting my nkamnkam. I'll buy you anything you want."

"You do not need to bribe me, tata. I am working for myself now," says Qukezwa proudly.

Indeed, the next day is nkamnkam day. The aged and their hangers-on stream to Vulindlela Trading Store in their finery.

Bhonco and NoPetticoat are among the first to arrive.

He wears his usual brown overalls, gumboots, and skullcap. Loose strands of beads known as *isidanga* hang around his neck. They are completely out of place since they should normally be worn when one is beautifully attired in isiXhosa costume. They make him look like a slob. Over his shoulder hangs a bag made of rock rabbit skin, in which he keeps his long pipe and tobacco. Today NoPetticoat's nkamnkam check is also in this bag.

NoPetticoat is one of the *amahomba*—those who look beautiful and pride themselves in fashion. She is wearing her red-ochred *isikhakha* dress. Her neck is weighted with beadwork of many kinds. There are the square *amatikiti* beads and the multicolored *uphalaza* and *icangci*. Her face is white with calamine lotion, and on her head she wears a big iqhiya turban which is broader than her shoulders. It is decorated with beads which match her *amacici* beaded earrings.

To the amahomba, clothes are an art form. They talk. They say something about the wearer. But to highly civilized people like Xoliswa Ximiya, isiXhosa costume is an embarrassment. She hates to see her mother looking so beautiful, because she thinks that it is high time her parents changed from *ubuqaba*—backwardness and heathenism. They must become *amagqobhoka*—enlightened ones—like her. She has bought her parents dresses and suits in the latest European styles. She might as well have bought them for the moths in the boxes under their bed.

When Zim arrives, heads turn. He is resplendent in his white *ingqawa* blanket which is tied around the waist and is so long that it reaches his ankles. Around his neck he wears various beads such as *idiliza* and isidanga. Around his head he wears *isiqweqwe* headbands made of very colorful beads. He is puffing away at his long pipe with pomp and ceremony.

The aged and their hangers-on are all puffing away, filling the store with clouds of pungent smoke. Women, especially, look graceful with their pipes, which are much longer than men's.

"Tell them to stop smoking, John. We can't even breathe in this smoke," complains Missis in English.

"Those who want to smoke must go outside!" shouts Dalton in his perfect isiXhosa.

"And they must not spit on the floor," moans Missis. "They spit everywhere, these people."

"Don't spit inside the shop. It's not good manners. If you want to smoke and spit, go outside!"

"And lose our place in the queue? Not on your life," says one stubborn graybeard.

"You will smoke when you have received your money then. We are not going to serve anyone who smokes in the shop."

Nkamnkam day is a very busy day at Vulindlela Trading Store. The aged and their hangers-on—daughters-in-law, grandchildren, and sundry relatives—have their checks ready to be cashed by Dalton and Missis. The salespeople are busy behind the counters, for today grannies are buying sweets, biscuits, and corned beef for their favorite grand-children.

Qukezwa drags a big bathtub full of little black notebooks from behind the counter, and puts it on the floor. Each pensioner looks for his or her own book, and gives it to Dalton behind the counter.

Even though the pensioners are illiterate, they know their books very well. And so they should, for in the books their personal ityala is written. Throughout the month they have bought groceries on credit at the store, and Dalton and Missis have diligently recorded their debt in the little black notebooks.

Now Dalton adds up the debt, deducts it from the amount of the check, and gives the balance to the pensioner. For those who have been careless during the month there will be no money. The whole pension check will be swallowed up by their ityala. The next month the vicious cycle of debt will continue.

Bhonco and NoPetticoat are about to reach the bathtub when Zim begins to sing aloud, "*Hayi . . . hayi . . . bo . . .* Even those who don't have a book in the bathtub are here . . ."

People laugh. They know that he is referring to Bhonco. Everyone knows that Bhonco receives no nkamnkam.

Bhonco, son of Ximiya, responds with his own song, "*Hayi . . . hayi . . . bo . . .* Those whose daughters are not secondary-school prin-cipals but sweep the floors of white people should stop talking non-sense . . ."

People laugh again. Qukezwa, who was helping an old lady find her book, glares at Bhonco. And so does Zim.

"Don't you two start your senseless quarrels again. At least not in my store," warns Dalton, who knows from experience that this may lead to a physical fight.

"Don't look at me," protests Bhonco. "That Believer started it. Doesn't he know? It is because his ancestors forced the amaXhosa people to kill their cattle. That is why we are suffering like this. That is why I don't even have nkamnkam."

"Tell the Unbeliever that it is because his ancestors refused to slaughter the cattle even when prophetesses like Nongqawuse, Nonkosi, and Nombanda instructed them to do so. That is why life is so difficult. That is why he has no nkamnkam."

The war of the Believers and Unbelievers!

Afterwards, both Zim and his daughter feel a bit exercised by the tiff at the store. They are in Nongqawuse's Valley. Qukezwa is riding Gxagxa, her father's brown-and-white horse, while Zim walks next to it, holding its reins. They are moving slowly towards Nongqawuse's Pool.

Today the clouds are low, and the mountaintops are wearing them like mourning hats.

"It was all your fault," Qukezwa bursts out. "You embarrassed me, tata. You invited the eyes of the people on me."

They are walking past *usundu* palms among the wild irises that grow in the valley. It is a cool afternoon, and the Namaqualand dove is cooing softly. In Nongqawuse's Pool a variety of eels, springer fish, and river otters are engaged in various antics, showing off to the visitors.

"There used to be aloes around this pool. In the days of Nongqawuse there were aloes," says Zim, talking in whistles.

"Don't change the subject, tata. You heard what I said."

"Even when we were growing up, there were aloes. Also reeds. Reeds used to cover this whole place. Only forty years ago . . . when I was a young man . . . there were reeds. In the days of Nongqawuse the whole ridge was covered with people who came to see the wonders."

He talks passionately about this valley. When he began to walk, he walked in this valley. He looked after cattle in this valley. He was circumcised here. His grandfather's fields were here. His whole life is centered in this valley. He is one with Intlambo-ka-Nongqawuse— Nongqawuse's Valley.

It is clear to Qukezwa that Zim has no intention of discussing his spat with Bhonco. Perhaps she should tell him about her yearning for the city. Now she also talks in whistles. They both sound like birds of the forest.

"You want to go to Butterworth or Centani? You are free to go there anytime you want. No one has ever stopped you."

"I am talking about Johannesburg, tata. I have Standard Eight but I sweep the floors. You heard what old man Bhonco said. Maybe if I go to the city I'll be a clerk and earn better money than the small change that Dalton gives me. I'll be somebody in the city."

This astonishes Zim. Surely it must be the work of the Unbelievers again. His daughter has never been dissatisfied with her lot in the village before. She cannot leave, he tells her, for she is the only one left to carry forward the tradition of belief.

"Your brother left and never came back. He was deceived by the wealth of the city. The ancestors cannot be happy with that sort of thing. I swear in the name of Mlanjeni that they'll beat him up with a thick stick."

"Of Mlanjeni, tata? Even though his prophecies were false?"

"Who teaches you these things? Mlanjeni was a true prophet. All his sayings were true, but everything was spoiled by young men who could not leave women alone. Mlanjeni said so right from the beginning. His medicine and women did not mix. That is why he himself eschewed women all his life."

Then he tells her about Prophetess Nongqawuse.

"Like the Nomyayi bird, she flew to the south," he says. "Nomyayi flew to Gobe to prophesy things that would happen. Nongqawuse used to go with Nomyayi. They were one person."

Zim assures his daughter that if she works hard enough she will end up being a prophetess like Nongqawuse.

At night Qukezwa dreams of Nongqawuse flying with a crow—the Nomyayi bird. She made sure that she slept with her legs stretched out. She will, therefore, be able to run away from her dreams if they become nightmares. One should be able to escape from the witches in one's dreams, or even run away from the dream itself.

But tonight there is no need to run away. She flies with Nomyayi in the land of the prophets.

It was the land of the prophets. Then the gospel people came. Mhlakaza first belonged to the gospel people. But later he was in the company of prophets.

The twins knew all about the gospel people. They knew Mhlakaza, even when he was called Wilhelm Goliath. He carried this strange name because he was a gospel man. He lived in Grahamstown with the white people. Twin and Twin-Twin used to listen to him teach the gospel in the company of a white man called Nathaniel Merriman, the Anglican archdeacon of Grahamstown.

At first he was baptized in the Methodist Church, and married his wife, Sarah, from the clan of the amaMfengu, in that church. But soon enough he deserted his Methodist friends and threw in his lot with the Anglicans. The Methodists, he said, told their hearts in public. He preferred the private confessions of the Anglicans. Also, the Anglicans wore more beautiful robes.

Twin and Twin-Twin did not see any difference between the Methodists and the Anglicans. They were all white people who, according to the teachings of the great Prophet Nxele, had been cast into the sea for murdering Tayi, the son of Thixo. The waves had spewed them on the shores of kwaXhosa. And now they were giving their reluctant hosts sleepless nights.

When Mhlakaza was Wilhelm Goliath, he used to give the people a lot of pleasure. They watched him carry Merriman's baggage, trudging behind the holy man across vast distances. The gospel men walked on foot between country towns and villages, preaching about a man called Christ. For eighteen months they walked all the way from Grahamstown to Graaff-Reinet, and then to Colesberg on the banks of the Orange River. Occasionally when Goliath lagged behind because of the heavy load, Merriman cautioned him against the sin of laziness. When they came to a stream, Goliath washed the holy man's clothes, and while they were drying he preached to whoever was in sight.

The gospel men provided much entertainment everywhere they went. Whenever they came to the twins' village there was great merriment, and people knew that they were going to laugh until their ribs were painful.

Wilhelm Goliath boasted that he was the first umXhosa ever to receive the Anglican Communion. He could recite the Creed, all Ten Commandments in their proper order, and the Lord's Prayer. He spoke the language of the Dutch people too, as if he was one of them.

Sometimes he would break into a fit of preaching. "I urge you, my countrymen . . . change from your evil ways, for they are the ways of the devil. Do away with *ububomvu* or ubuqaba, your heathen practices, your superstitions . . . and become amaGqobhoka . . . civilized ones . . . those who have converted to the path that was laid for us by Christ. Throw away your red ochre blankets! Wear trousers! Throw away your red isikhakha skirts! Wear dresses! For our Lord Christ died for us on the cross, to save us from eternal damnation."

These were utterances that were guaranteed to cause a lot of mirth among his listeners. They found it funny that the way to the white man's heaven was through trousers and dresses. In any case, this Goliath looked hilarious in his ill-fitting black suit that used to belong to Merriman.

The gospel men made sense only when they talked of the resurrection. When Merriman told the people that one day all humankind would rise from the dead, they were joyous. They said they would like to see their grandfathers and all their relatives who had left this world for that of the ancestors.

But still, they continued to find the utterances that came from Goliath's mouth quite ridiculous. Where did he get the nerve to be the spokesman of the god of the white man he knew nothing about?

"This man is from such a distinguished family. His father was King Sarhili's councillor. What is he doing with these people who were cast into the sea?" Twin-Twin asked.

"We had our own prophets who are now with the ancestors," cried Twin. "We had Ntsikana who prophesied the coming of the white man. Then we had Nxele who told us about our own god, Mdalidephu, who was in opposition to Thixo, the god of the white man. Now we have Mlanjeni. We do not need these people with their false prophets and false gods."

This was before Mlanjeni died of tuberculosis.

But Twin shouldn't have mentioned his name, for this inflamed Twin-Twin. He demanded that Twin should withdraw Mlanjeni's name from the list of prophets, because he was not a true prophet.

"Look what happened to us in the war! Where is our father now as we speak?" demanded Twin-Twin.

But Twin was adamant that Mlanjeni was a true prophet in the same league as Ntsikana and Nxele.

Relatives had to be called to separate the twins from a bloody stick duel. The elders of the village had to sit down and negotiate peace between the children of Xikixa. The twins shook hands and swore in the name of their headless father never to fight again.

Once again they became close to each other.

But another evil struck. A marauding disease that attacked cattle in their kraals, in the veld, and even in distant mountain cattle-posts. It crept in during the night, seizing its victims when they least expected it. No one had ever heard of it before, but those who had contact with the white settlements came with the news that it was lungsickness.

Raging lungsickness. Strutting around like a bully. Laughing in the faces of grown men as they wept when they saw their favorite cattle wane away.

White people knew of lungsickness because it came from their country. There were reports that it had killed many cattle across the seas in the land of the whites. It was brought to the land of the amaXhosa nation by Friesland bulls that came in a Dutch ship two years earlier, in 1853. Therefore even the best of the isiXhosa doctors did not know how to cure lungsickness.

The disease was traveling the land of the amaXhosa people and of the amaMfengu like a wild fire. Cattle owners were trying to escape it by driving their herds to mountainous and secluded places. Yet many cattle were lost.

Soon enough the disease attacked the twins' village. Twin-Twin wept as he watched his favorite bull die a horrible and protracted death. First it was constipated. Then it became diarrheic. It gasped for air, its tongue hanging out. When it died he was relieved that at last the pain was over, and he was determined to escape with his remaining herds. Twin did not need persuading. He too had suffered losses. He agreed with Twin-Twin that they should take their families and drive their cattle to new pastures where they could establish new homesteads.

As if lungsickness was not enough, the maize in the fields was attacked by a disease that left it whimpering and blighted. It crept through the roots and killed the plant before the corn could ripen. It certainly was not going to be a year of plenty.

Such a calamity had never been seen in kwaXhosa before. It was the work of malevolent spirits and of ubuthi, of witchcraft. The twins hoped that in a new settlement they would escape all this.

The twins' great trek took many days. It was a slow and painful journey, made even slower by the women and children, and by the pigs and chickens. During the day the trekkers camped so that the cattle could graze and the wives and their daughters could cook food. Those who were tired slept. When night fell they moved on again. They were accompanied and protected by the Seven Sisters, the stars from which the Khoikhoi were descended. The seven daughters of Tsiqwa. He who told his stories in heaven. The Creator.

Qukezwa led the way, for she knew the language of the stars. She rode reinless on Gxagxa, Twin's brown-and-white horse, which seemed to know exactly where to go without being guided by her.

Twin was proud of his wife. She could do things that Twin-Twin's numerous wives could not do. Even though people had constantly laughed at the foreign woman who used to open her thighs for the British soldiers, now her people's stars were leading everyone to fresh pastures. Twin-Twin should be grateful, instead of making snide remarks whenever the couple added a stone and aromatic herbs to the piles of stones they sometimes came across at the crossroads, and then asked someone called Tsiqwa for his guidance and protection.

Every night the twins shook with fear when they saw rivers of fire raging down the mountains. They knew immediately that this was the path to avoid, for it was the path of the disease.

"The stars tell me that we must move until the sea stops us," Qukezwa told them.

After many weeks the twins reached Qolorha. Twin and Qukezwa established their home in the village of Ngcizele. They were so close to the sea that even as they slept at night they could hear the sound of the waves. Here was plenty of grazing land for Twin's cattle.

Twin-Twin and his many wives settled in the small village of KwaFeni a few miles away. Here too were great pastures for his cattle.

Life was beautiful. But it was not completely free of disease. Sometimes the dastardly lungsickness crept in in the deep of the night, seized a prized ox, and drained it of flesh and blood. By this time, experience had taught the twins a few tricks. They separated the sick ox from the rest of the herd until it died. Then they buried the carcass far away from the village.

The twins soon saw Mhlakaza again, for it happened that Qolorha was his ancestral home. He had built his single hut near the Gxarha River, and had called an *imbhizo*—a public meeting—of the people of the Qolorha area, including the villages of KwaFeni and Ngcizele, to discuss the wonders that had happened in his homestead.

Qukezwa knew him at once and whispered to Twin, "Hey, is that not Wilhelm Goliath?"

"Yes," shouted Twin in amazement, "it is the gospel man, Wilhelm Goliath!"

"You dare call me by that name again!" said Mhlakaza angrily. "I am not Wilhelm Goliath. I am Mhlakaza."

Twin did not understand what was wrong, for the man used to call himself Wilhelm Goliath, and would have been angry if he had been addressed as Mhlakaza.

"He is sensitive about being called by that name," a man standing next to them said.

He explained to Twin and Qukezwa that when Merriman stopped walking and was confined to the church in Grahamstown, Mhlakaza's days as a gospel man came to an end. At first the holy man engaged him to teach isiXhosa at a school, and built him a hut in his garden. But he was not a happy man at the holy man's household. Merriman and his wife treated him like a servant, whereas on the road he had been a gospel man in his own right. He felt that Merriman's wife didn't like him. She called him a dreamy sort of fellow. And this convinced him that his enthusiasm for the gospel was not taken seriously by Merriman's family. So he left and came to live next to his sister's homestead near the Gxarha River. He gave up on the god of the white man, and reverted to the true god of his fathers.

"I have called you here, my countrymen, because a wonderful thing has happened!" said Mhlakaza, addressing the small group of men and women who had gathered outside his hut. "Three days ago my niece, Nongqawuse, and my sister-in-law, Nombanda, went to the fields to chase away the birds that like to feed on the sorghum."

"Indeed that is wonderful," said Twin-Twin sarcastically. "His children went to scare the birds in the fields, and he has called the whole nation to tell us about it."

But Mhlakaza ignored the amateur comedian and continued his speech. He called two young girls to stand in front of the people. "This older one is Nongqawuse," he said. "She is fifteen years old. I took her as my own daughter after her parents were murdered by British soldiers during the War of Mlanjeni. This eight-year-old one is Nombanda, my wife's sister. Now, when these children were in the fields, a wonderful thing happened."

"The man has said that already," said Twin. "Get on with the story. Tell us what happened."

"Does he know that we have left our fields and our cattle unattended?" asked Twin-Twin. Others agreed with him.

"Don't be in a hurry for the gravy before the meat is ready," said Mhlakaza, demanding their patience. "Nongqawuse heard a voice calling her name behind the usundu bush."

"Was it not you, Twin-Twin, trying to seduce the poor girl behind the usundu bush? You are well known as a naughty man who loves young blood!" heckled another man, trying to be funny as well. But no one laughed. People were curious to hear more about the voice behind the usundu bush.

Mhlakaza went on, "At first she thought she hadn't heard well, and continued to play with Nombanda and to chase the birds. The voice persisted. She slowly walked to the bush, while Nombanda remained transfixed. At that time mist rose around the bush. The faces of two Strangers appeared in the mist and addressed her."

"What did they say?" people wanted to know. "Who did they say they were?"

"Let the girl tell us herself," demanded Twin-Twin.

"Come, my child, and give us the message of the Strangers," said Mhlakaza.

Nongqawuse shyly stepped forward. She was unkempt and looked like a waif. In the manner of all great prophets she seemed confused and disorientated most of the time.

"Who were the Strangers, my child?" asked Twin.

"I do not know, father," replied Nongqawuse. "They said they were messengers of Naphakade, He-Who-Is-Forever, the descendant of Sifuba-Sibanzi, the Broad-Chested-One."

People were confused. They had not heard of He-Who-Is-Forever, nor of the Broad-Chested-One. Obviously these must be the new names of the god of the amaXhosa people . . . the one who is known by everyone as Qamata or Mvelingqangi . . . the one who was called Mdalidephu by Prophet Nxele.

Nongqawuse continued, "The Strangers said I must tell the nation that all cattle now living must be slaughtered. They have been reared by contaminated hands because there are people who deal in witchcraft. The fields must not be cultivated, but great new grain pits must be dug, new houses must be built, and great strong cattle kraals must be erected. Cut out new milk sacks and weave many doors from *buka* roots. The Strangers say that the whole community of the dead will arise. When the time is ripe they will arise from the dead, and new cattle will fill the kraals. The people must leave their witchcraft, for soon they will be examined by diviners."

Mhlakaza said that at first he had treated the message of the Strangers as a joke. But they had appeared to Nongqawuse again, and ordered her to give the message to her uncle. He had therefore told the chiefs and was given permission to call the imbhizo.

He urged those present not to take the words of the Strangers lightly.

"The rapid spread of lungsickness is proving the Strangers right," he said. "The existing cattle are rotten and unclean. They have been bewitched. They must all be destroyed. You have all been wicked, and therefore everything that belongs to you is bad. Destroy everything.

The new people who will arise from the dead will come with new cattle, horses, goats, sheep, dogs, fowl, and any other animals that the people may want. But the new animals of the new people cannot mix with your polluted ones. So destroy them. Destroy everything. Destroy the corn in your fields and in your granaries. Nongqawuse has told us that when the new people come there will be a new world of contentment and no one will ever lead a troubled life again."

As Camagu drives his Toyota Corolla on the gravel road he concludes that a generous artist painted the village of Qolorha-by-Sea, using splashes of lush color. It is a canvas where blue and green dominate. It is the blue of the skies and the distant hills, of the ocean and the rivers that flow into it. The green is of the meadows and the valleys, the tall grass and the usundu palms.

He is pleased to see that there are some people here who still wear isiXhosa costume. They are few, though. Most of the men and women he passes on the road don't dress any differently from people of the city.

It is sad, he thinks, that when nations of the world wear their costumes with pride, the amaXhosa people despise theirs. They were taught by missionaries that it is a sign of civilization, of *ubugqobhoka*, to despise isikhakha as the clothing of the *amaqaba*—those who have not seen the light and who still smear themselves with red ochre.

Even today the civilized ones condescendingly visit the clothes of the amaqaba, and wear them as curiosities during special cultural occasions. As their everyday attire the civilized ones wear German and Java prints that are embroidered in the West African tradition, but they still boast that they are in African dress. To them, African fashion means West African, and never the clothing of the amaXhosa or some other ethnic group of South Africa.

Camagu parks his car and walks into Vulindlela Trading Store. There is a long line of people who are waiting to be served. He is not sure whether he should go to the counter and make his inquiry or join the queue. He thinks everyone is looking at him with suspicion. To them he looks like the kind of person who thinks he is better than the common village folk, and who will therefore jump the queue. He decides to join it.

It is a long queue and the salesperson behind the counter takes her time. She is passing pleasantries and exchanging snippets of gossip with the customers as she serves them. Camagu amuses himself by watching a teenage boy whose hat has made him very popular with a group of children who are surrounding him. It is a miner's helmet in the black-and-yellow colors of Kaizer Chiefs Football Club. It has many horns that fascinate the kids. He tells them that the horns grew because his grandmother told him folktales during the day. Such stories are supposed to be told only at night.

"Every time she told me a story a horn grew," he tells his captive audience.

Finally Camagu's turn comes and he asks for the owner of the store. He is told that the owner and his wife are not in. They are in the house behind the store. The salesperson asks Qukezwa to take the visitor to the house.

Once they are outside the store Qukezwa smiles at him and impishly says, "I am not married."

Camagu takes a close look at her, his eyes betraying his shock. She is short and plump. She wears a skimpy blue-and-yellow floral dress. Although she is not particularly beautiful, she is quite attractive. Almost half her face is hidden by a black woolen cap which is emblazoned with the P symbol of Pierre Cardin in green and yellow.

"I am available if you want me," she adds.

"What do you mean?"

"You can *lobola* me if you like."

"What is your name?"

"Qukezwa Zim."

They have reached the door of the house. Without another word she runs back to the store laughing. He knocks unsteadily and Missis lets him in.

He sits on the sofa, and looks at a framed picture of a nude African woman carrying a naked baby—a very common poster that he has seen sold by street vendors in every small town through which he has driven.

John Dalton enters the room.

"It is my wife's idea of art," he says, making light of his embarrassment. "I can assure you I am a man of discerning taste."

They both laugh and shake hands.

"What can I do for you?" asks Dalton.

"I am looking for a woman. Her name is NomaRussia. The first person I asked when I entered this village told me that there was someone of that name who used to work at your store."

"NomaRussia?" says Dalton, trying to think very hard. "I don't remember her. Of course that is a common name in these parts. It has historical significance . . . from the days of Nongqawuse. What has she done? Why are you looking for her?"

Camagu concocts some story that she worked for him in Johannesburg, and she inadvertently left with his passport. He dare not tell this white man that he does not know why he is looking for NomaRussia, that he was driving to the airport to catch a plane to America when all of a sudden he took a different direction. He looked at the map and decided to take the ten-hour drive to Qolorha—NomaRussia's name buzzing in his head.

"What is her surname?" asks Dalton. "I know all the families in this region."

Unfortunately Camagu does not know it. Dalton says he is sorry he can't help him. He exclaims, "City people are amazing. This woman worked for you, but you don't know her surname!"

But Dalton is curious about the stranger and wants to find out more about him. They talk about Johannesburg and the political situation, and about America. Dalton is fascinated by an umXhosa man who has spent so many years living in America. He himself has never left South Africa and has spent most of his life in the Eastern Cape. Camagu cannot get over the fact that Dalton speaks much better isiXhosa than he'll ever be able to.

After two hours and many cups of tea, Dalton takes Camagu to his car.

"Is there a place where I can put up for the night?" asks Camagu.

"There is the Blue Flamingo Hotel. It is not a bad place."

"I think I'll stay there for a few days . . . until I can sort out this NomaRussia problem."

As he drives away he sees Qukezwa sweeping the stoop of the store, her yellow thighs glistening in the late afternoon sun.

"What a forward girl!" he says to himself. He is renowned as a man of great venereal appetite. But she is still a child. Young enough to be his daughter if he had bothered to marry and procreate.

It is a beautifully undisciplined dance that the *amagqiyazana*—the young girls who have not yet reached puberty—are performing. They shake their little waists and lift their legs in innocent abandon. Their song rises and falls with the wind. It is the same wind that carries the sonorous sounds of the sea and scatters them in the valleys. The audience claps hands, responding to the rhythms. Everyone finds it charming that some of the girls are consistently out of step.

Camagu is filled with a searing longing for an imagined blissfulness of his youth. He has vague memories of his home village, up in the mountains in the distant inland parts of the country. He remembers the fruit trees and the graves of long-departed relatives. He can see dimly through the mist of decades all the lush plants that grew in his grandfather's garden, including aloes of different types. There are the beautiful houses too: the four-walled tin-roofed ixande, the rondavels, the cattle kraal, the fowl run, the toolshed. Then the government came and moved the people down to the flatlands, giving them only small plots and no compensation.

He was only a toddler when he left with his parents to settle in the township of Orlando East, in the city of Johannesburg. There it was a different life, devoid of the song of the amagqiyazana. And there he grew up until the political upheavals of the 1960s sent him into exile in his late teens. So many things in Qolorha bring back long-forgotten images. He is glad to find himself in the middle of these festivities.

The cacophony of birds, monkeys, and waves had woken him up very early in the morning. To some people this racket from the surrounding woods and from the nearby Indian Ocean may be music, but he would have preferred to enjoy the austere wooden bed of the Blue Flamingo Hotel without further disturbance. His night had not been a restful one because of a recurring dream.

In his dream he was the river, and NomaRussia was its water. Crystal clear. Flowing on him. Sliding smoothly on his body. Until she flowed into the ocean. He ran after her, shouting that she should flow back. Flow back up the river. Upstream. Up his eager body. Climb its lusty mountains, even. When he failed to catch her, he tried to catch the dream itself, to arrest it, so that it could be with him forever. It slipped through his fingers and escaped. He chased it, but it outran him. He woke up, all sweaty and breathless, drifted into slumber, and dreamt the same dream again. Over and over again. For the whole night.

Although he was exhausted from all that running he had to do in the dream, he had jumped out of bed, taken a quick shower, and stepped out of his chalet to face an uncertain day in a strange village.

He had decided to take a walk through the village. Women and children stared at him at every homestead he passed. He was obviously a stranger. All the while he looked very closely at every young woman he met, in case he saw someone who remotely resembled NomaRussia.

He had been called to this gathering by the joyous celebration.

"Are you just going to stand here watching children dance, or are you going to join other men and eat meat and drink beer?"

The furrowed face looks friendly. He cuts a handsome figure in his dark suit and white shirt. His wrinkled necktie has a huge knot. Camagu extends his hand and warmly shakes the old man's.

"I am a tourist from Johannesburg. My name is Camagu, son of Cesane."

"A black tourist!" exclaims the aged one. "We only see white tourists here. Mostly stupid ones who come to Qolorha because a foolish girl once lied that she saw miracles here."

"Ah, Nongqawuse. I learned about her at primary school. We even sang songs about her."

"It is you learned ones who have turned her into a goddess who must be worshipped. Yet she killed the nation of the amaXhosa. Anyway, why do I bother a stranger with the problems of this community? I am Bhonco, son of Ximiya."

This is his homestead, he says. He is the owner of this feast. His daughter has been made principal of the secondary school, so he decided to make a feast to thank those who are in the ground, the ancestors. The stranger from Johannesburg is welcome to share with them the little that has been prepared. He calls a prancing boy to lead the esteemed visitor to the place where he will be served.

The boy leads Camagu towards an umsintsi tree under which some village men are eating meat from a big dish and drinking beer in a tin container that is passed from one man to the next.

Bhonco shouts at the boy, "Hey, *kwedini*! Stupid boy! Why are you taking the visitor to those village bumpkins? Don't you see he's a teacher? Take him to the house where the teachers are!"

The "bumpkins" laugh. An elder among them shouts back at Bhonco that he must not be so high and mighty now that his daughter is the principal of Qolorha-by-Sea Secondary School. He must remember that fortune is like mist. It can disappear anytime.

Camagu joins the elite of Qolorha-by-Sea at table. He discovers that "the little that has been prepared" is a mountain of beef, mutton, chicken, samp, rice, potatoes, tomato, and onion gravy, beetroot, and green salads. And bottles of beer, brandy, and wine. Later he learns that the patriarch spared no expense to celebrate his daughter's elevation. He slaughtered an ox, two sheep, and a number of chickens. Women brewed barrels and barrels of sorghum beer. Xoliswa Ximiya was against the very idea of holding an ostentatious feast in her honor. But the patriarch would not miss the opportunity to show the Believers that it is the Unbelievers who rule the roost in Qolorha-by-Sea.

No one is ever invited to a village feast. When people hear there is a feast at someone's homestead, they go there to enjoy themselves. Others, especially the neighbors and close friends, go beforehand to help with the preparations and to contribute whatever food they can afford. Everyone is welcome at a village feast. Indeed, it is considered sacrilege to stay away from your fellow man's feast.

But none of the Believers have come. The war of the Believers and Unbelievers has gone to that extent. They don't attend each other's feasts. They do attend each other's funerals, though, because death is, as the elders say, the daughter-in-law of all homesteads.

Cynics will say that they attend each other's funerals to make sure that the deceased is really dead. One less person to be irritated about.

But this boycott does not worry Bhonco and NoPetticoat. There are more people at this feast than Zim, the elder of the Believers, would ever be able to muster at a feast of his own. After all, there are more descendants of Twin-Twin's in the Qolorha area than there are of Twin's. This is because Twin-Twin had five wives, who gave birth to many more children than Twin's sole wife was able to do. Another reason is that Twin-Twin was the original Unbeliever. He refused to slaughter his cattle when Nongqawuse gave the orders that the ama-Xhosa should destroy all their herds. He said the prophetess was a liar who had been bought by white people to destroy the black race. Today the village is full of Twin-Twin's progeny, because not many of his children died when famine attacked the land after Nongqawuse's prophecies failed. At the Blue Flamingo Hotel alone, every other charwoman, gardener, waiter, and bartender comes from the loins of those who came from Twin-Twin's loins. Three generations of chefs, trained by Zimbabweans, are from Twin-Twin's line. And everyone is always at pains to stress that Twin's and Twin-Twin's lines are distinct, even though they are joined at the top by the headless ancestor.

The members of Qolorha society who are sitting at the table are discussing precisely these issues, as they stuff themselves with meat and beer. They are laughing about it all. One teacher asks, "How far can you stretch pettiness?" And the rest of the table laughs once more. Camagu notices that Xoliswa Ximiya does not laugh. She merely grins. She seems embarrassed.

The attention turns to the stranger in their midst. After he has introduced himself, Xoliswa Ximiya wants to know, "What puts you in this godforsaken place?"

"Godforsaken? I think it is the most beautiful place on earth," replies Camagu, meaning what he says.

"Perhaps if you are only a tourist. If you were forced to live here forever you'd think twice about it."

"Maybe you are right. I've never lived in a village before."

"It must be something important that has brought you here."

Camagu repeats the concocted story of a young woman called NomaRussia from these parts who worked for him in Johannesburg. He released her from work because he was going to the United States to live there. Only when he was on his way to the airport did he discover that NomaRussia had inadvertently taken his passport with her.

"I am looking for her, and I hope that some of you may know her," he tells them.

NomaRussia is a very common name, one of the teachers explains. The people of this region began giving their valued daughters this name—which means Mother of the Russians—when the Russians killed Sir George Cathcart during the Crimean War in 1854. Cathcart, the teacher further explains, was the much-hated colonial governor who finally defeated the amaXhosa in the War of Mlanjeni, a war that had initially been provoked and launched by Sir Harry Smith, the pompous moron who had styled himself the "Great White Chief of the Xhosas." The colonists called the amaXhosa Xhosas, or even Kosas!

He must be the history teacher of Qolorha-by-Sea Secondary School, judging by the way he coughs out these facts with aplomb, as if he is in the classroom.

"Since then the amaXhosa have been great admirers of the Russians," he adds.

Unfortunately no one seems to know the particular NomaRussia Camagu is looking for. Perhaps if he knew her surname they would be able to help. They cannot fit the description of her that he has given them with any NomaRussia who worked as a maid in Johannesburg.

It is too late for Camagu to amend his story. He must remember next time that NomaRussia did not work for him as a maid. She was merely visiting Johannesburg to attend a funeral. That will narrow the search. Surely not many NomaRussias from Qolorha-by-Sea have visited Johannesburg for a funeral recently. But then how did his passport fall into her hands?

Camagu's eyes are glued on Xoliswa Ximiya. He does not remember seeing anyone quite so beautiful before. Her beauty exceeds that of the hungry women who are referred to as supermodels in fashion magazines. It is the kind of beauty that is cold and distant, though. Not the kind that makes your whole body hot and charges it with electric currents, like NomaRussia's. If only she could bring herself to smile a bit. Her colleagues are now full of boisterous cheer, most of which is obviously induced by the spirits. Yet she remains collected, and throughout maintains her no-nonsense demeanor. Her uncompromising eyes penetrate you when she is addressing you. Deep inside them lurks a sorrow that cannot be remitted.

NoPetticoat enters to find out if the guests need anything. She is introduced to the visitor from Johannesburg. He can see the source of Xoliswa Ximiya's good looks. When he met Bhonco outside, Camagu's eyes could salvage beauty from his aging face. Now here is the mother of the homestead, coming with her own loveliness and grace. She is a sonsy woman, though, not willowy and grave like her daughter.

"You are a family of beautiful people," says Camagu when NoPetticoat has left the room. "Your father, your mother, and you."

She does not thank him for the compliment. Perhaps, thinks Camagu, she has no time for such pettiness as acknowledging compliments or admiring beauty. But then why has she taken the trouble to enhance her own beauty by braiding her hair in such trendy extensions? Her whole mode of dress is elegant. Severe but elegant.

Xoliswa Ximiya is more fascinated by the fact that the stranger was on his way to the United States of America. She informs him that he will be happy in that wonderful country. She herself has lived there, empowering herself with the skill of teaching English as a second language. It is a fairy-tale country, with beautiful people. People like Dolly Parton and Eddie Murphy. It is a vast country that is highly technological. Even though Camagu comes from Johannesburg, he will be fascinated by America. A city like New York is ten times the size of Johannesburg. She remembers when she went to Washington, D.C., and saw the White House, and the Capitol, and the memorial of one historical figure or another. She also remembers when she traveled in a subway in New York. Then she goes on to explain that a subway is a train that moves underground. Very much unlike the Johannesburg–East London train which crudely moves above the ground where every moron can see it.

Before Camagu leaves he must remind her to give him a few pointers on how to survive in America, she adds with a flourish.

America, wonderful America!

Her colleagues are beginning to fidget. Obviously they have been subjected to this harangue before. Camagu is embarrassed on her behalf.

"For how long were you in America?" he asks.

"Six months! I was at a college in Athens, Ohio."

"Athens, like in Greece!" adds a woman who was earlier introduced as Vathiswa. She is sitting next to Xoliswa Ximiya, and is obviously her great fan. She nods vigorously at everything the principal says. Camagu has no heart to tell her that Athens is a college town that is even smaller than the nearby town of Butterworth.

"You must have loved it," says Camagu.

"It is the best country in the world. I hope to go back one day. You are lucky to be going there. I envy you. Are you going for a course—or a conference maybe?"

"No. I am going to work. I can't find a job in South Africa."

She is amazed by his temerity to think that he can just fly to a great country like America and find employment when he can't even find it in South Africa.

"What makes you think you'll find a job in America?"

"Well, I have worked there before. I have a good track record with the organization I worked for."

There is a hint of anger in her eyes.

"You've been in America before?"

"I lived there for thirty years. Practically grew up there. I went there as a teenager."

Now she is really angry. Her colleagues are enjoying this, although they are discreet in their glee, lest they be on the receiving end of her displeasure. Camagu is uncomfortable. He does not know how he can show her that he had no intention of embarrassing her in front of her colleagues. Her subordinates, in fact.

"Why didn't you tell me?"

"You didn't ask me, miss!"

"I am not miss! My name is Xoliswa."

"Ximiya," adds Vathiswa.

She decides that she is now going to ignore Camagu and focus on her other guests, who are arguing aloud about the new developments in the village. Camagu can only catch snippets of the discussion. Apparently a big company that owns hotels throughout southern Africa wants to build a casino on the Gxarha River mouth. They want to introduce water sports in the great lagoon. Tourists will come from all over the world to gamble and to play with their boats and surfboards. At last Qolorha-by-Sea will see progress. But it seems some people in the village are against these developments.

Vathiswa either is out of her depth in this discussion or feels sorry for the stranger who has been left out. She moves closer to him and asks what he studied in America.

"A doctoral degree in communication and economic development," he says, wondering if that will make any sense to her.

"I wish I were you. Maybe you should put me in your suitcase when you fly to America. I want to see all the wonderful things that Xoliswa Ximiya talks about."

Camagu whispers in her ear, "Take everything with a pinch of salt. Her adulation of the place must not mislead you. There is nothing wonderful about America. Unless you think racial prejudice and bully-boy tactics towards other countries are wonderful."

But she is no longer listening. She is giggling. She finds his whispering in her ear rather ticklish. And flirtatious. Perhaps greater things will come out of it.

She tells him about herself. She worked as a nurse in Queenstown. But unfortunately she had a fall.

"A fall?"

"I fell pregnant. At the time they did not allow unmarried nurses to have babies. I then went to model clothes for Mahomedy's in Durban. I was featured in their catalogues."

Now she works as a receptionist at the Blue Flamingo Hotel. Camagu remembers seeing her at the hotel and marveling at her outrageous outfit, which was the height of fashion ten years ago. He wonders why Xoliswa Ximiya does not give her a few tips. After all, what are friends for? Or could it be that the erstwhile catalogue model is all right as she is since she makes Xoliswa Ximiya's flame shine even brighter?

It does not escape Camagu that although Xoliswa Ximiya is ostensibly ignoring him she is furtively listening to his conversation with Vathiswa. When she observes that things may be getting too cozy between them, she makes up her mind that a man who can just fly to America to work there is too important to ignore. He is more of her class than of Vathiswa's, anyway. He is a kindred spirit, because both of them have lived in the land of the free and the brave.

She draws him into the debate about the developers.

"This is a lifetime opportunity for Qolorha to be like some of the holiday resorts in America. To have big stars like Eddie Murphy and Dolly Parton come here for holiday."

"That would be nice," says Camagu without much enthusiasm.

"They go to Cape Town, you know. Cape Town is now becoming a celebrity paradise. Qolorha can be one too if these conservative villagers stop standing in the way of progress. Don't you think so?"

"I don't know the issues. But I am sure you're right."

"Of course I am right. You have seen how backward this place is. We cannot stop civilization just because some sentimental old fools want to preserve birds and trees and an outmoded way of life."

He learns that the leader of those who oppose progress is one Zim, a Believer to the core of his soul. What is sad is that he has now been joined by John Dalton, the white trader. Are whites not the bearers of civilization and progress? Then why is Dalton standing with the unenlightened villagers to oppose such an important development that will bring jobs, streetlights, and other forms of modernization to this village?

Vathiswa has something to say about that. Dalton is only white outside. Inside he is a raw umXhosa who still lives in darkness.

"That is why," she adds, "every weekend he takes white tourists in his four-wheel-drive bakkie to show them Nongqawuse's Pool. Why would civilized people want to honor a foolish girl who killed the ama-Xhosa nation?"

Xoliswa Ximiya freezes at the mere mention of Nongqawuse's name. There is a very strong anti-Nongqawuse sentiment around the table.

"Those people—why can't they let that part of our shame rest in peace?" she asks pleadingly.

Another teacher has a different view of Dalton's motives.

"He is just like all the other selfish white people. Especially those who have built sea cottages along our coastline," he says. "Do you think they care about this community? No. They are here for their own selfish reasons. They have nothing to do with this community. They just come here in summer to have fun in the sea, then leave for East London or other cities where they come from."

"But that's unfair," says another man. "Dalton belongs in this community. He lives here permanently. So have his fathers before him. He was at the same circumcision school as my elder brother. He is the man who has organized the village water-supply project. He has nothing in common with the cottage owners."

Camagu is curious about the cottage owners. The land in the rural villages is not for sale. It is given to the residents by the chief and his land-allocation committees. How do the cottage owners get the land to build here?

This is a sore point with some villagers, he is told. The white people—and some well-to-do blacks from the old Transkei bantustan—bribe Chief Xikixa with a bottle of brandy, and he gives them the land.

"At first it was a bottle of brandy," the history teacher corrects his colleague. "But now the stakes have gone up. Competition for prime land by the sea has intensified. The white folks now bribe the chief with cellphones and satellite dishes. Haven't you heard? The chief has even named one of his daughters NoCellphone. His wife is pregnant. If the baby is a boy he will be named Satellite. A girl will obviously be NoSatellite."

It is illegal to build within a kilometer of the coast. But the cottage owners don't observe that. Most cottages are right on the seashore.

The landscape has changed already. The Unbelievers say it is a good thing, though, because the cottage owners give employment to the local men who wash their cars and to local women who work as maids. None of the men get jobs as gardeners, though, since most cottage owners keep wild gardens planned by landscape artists from East London, and these need no maintenance.

The history teacher says that progress is in the eye of the beholder. He remembers one day when the Minister of Health came to the village to address an imbhizo—a public meeting—about family planning. The minister's emphasis was on the necessity to limit the number of children to three.

An old man asked the minister, "Now, you tell me, my child, how many are you in your family?"

"Eight," said the minister. "But those were the olden days. Things were different then."

"That's not what I am talking about. You say you are eight. What number are you among these eight children?"

"I am the seventh."

"Now tell me, where would you be if your parents had taken the advice you are giving us today?"

The imbhizo never forgot how the old man put the minister in his place.

The table laughs, except for Xoliswa Ximiya, who snarls, "The minister was foolish. Today we don't talk of limiting the number of children. We talk of spacing them properly."

"In any case," says a puny man who has been quiet all along, "that story of the Minister of Health—it did not happen in this village. It's an old joke. I read it somewhere."

The history teacher is offended.

"Cooks read too, do they?" he asks.

"I am not a cook."

"Since when? As far as we all know you cook for white people at the Blue Flamingo Hotel."

"I am a chef, not a cook."

"What's the difference? You cook, so you're a cook."

"You call me a cook again and I'll show you your mother!"

The history teacher is jumping up and down, dancing around the table, shouting, "Cook! Cook! Cook!"

No one knows when the chef got the stick. Like lightning he hits the history teacher on the head. Blood springs out like water from a burst pipe. He falls down. Soon there is a long red stream on the floor. There is commotion. People hold the chef and try to stop him from inflicting further damage on the unconscious history teacher. Xoliswa Ximiya is more concerned with what the visitor from Johannesburg will think of them, behaving like savages in her father's house. She takes Camagu by the hand and leads him outside.

"I am sorry you had to see our worst side," she says.

"It is all right," replies Camagu, trying to make light of the matter. "I have learned a good lesson: never call a chef a cook."

He laughs. She maintains her stern expression.

"Anyway, I must be on my way. But please, can I see you again?"

"Of course."

"Tomorrow?"

"I am free in the afternoon."

In a clearing in front of the pink rondavel, women's upper bodies are vibrating in the umngqungqo dance. Bhonco is joking with the men under the umsintsi tree. He sees Camagu walking away and calls him back.

"Hey, teacher, are you just going to disappear like a fart in the wind, without even saying good-bye?" shouts Bhonco.

"Oh, Tat'uBhonco, I am sorry. I did not see you," says Camagu.

"Did those children expel you so early? The feast is still young."

"I have enjoyed myself, thank you. They entertained me enough."

"With fights? A woman came wailing that the teachers were fighting. I told her to leave us alone to enjoy our beer in peace. The learned ones always fight when they are drunk. What was it all about?"

"I do not know. It started with the discussion about the developers."

"The developers are still going to cause more fights in this village!"

He is passionate about development. His wrath is directed at the Believers who are bent on opposing everything that is meant to improve the lives of the people of Qolorha.

"They want us to remain in our wildness!" says the elder. "To remain red all our lives! To stay in the darkness of redness!"

The Unbelievers are moving forward with the times. That is why they support the casino and the water-sports paradise that the developers want to build. The Unbelievers stand for civilization. To prove this point Bhonco has now turned away from beads and has decided to take out the suits that his daughter bought him many years ago from his trunk under the bed. From now on he will be seen only in suits. He is in the process of persuading his wife also to do away with the red ochre that women smear on their bodies and with which they also dye their isikhakha skirts. When the villagers talk of the redness of unenlightenment they are referring to the red ochre. But then even the isikhakha skirt itself represents backwardness. NoPetticoat must do away with this prided isiXhosa costume. But she is a stubborn woman. Although she is a strong Unbeliever like her husband, she is sold on the traditional fashions of the amaXhosa. But Bhonco is a suit man. He even cried when he saw his beautiful reflection in one of the big windows of Vulindlela Trading Store. In any case, these suits were lovingly bought by his daughter, and it makes her very happy when he wears them.

Camagu wonders why the Believers are so bent on opposing development that seems to be of benefit to everyone in the village.

"It is just madness," shouts Bhonco. "Madness has seeped into their heads. And that John Dalton whose father was my age-mate, that John Dalton is misleading the nation. Now they want to enforce a ban on killing birds. Have you ever heard of such a thing? In the veld and in the forests, boys trap birds and roast them in ant-heap ovens. That is our way. We all grew up that way. Now when boys kill birds, are Dalton and his Believer cronies going to take them to jail? I'll tell you one thing: it is all the fault of Nongqawuse!"

At night Camagu becomes the river again, and NomaRussia flows on him. Yet she remains elusive. So does the dream. It refuses to be arrested. But it keeps on coming back. Until the birds and the waves and the monkeys and the wind tell him it's time to get out of bed. He defies them and sleeps until midday.

After a fulfilling lunch he goes back to Bhonco's homestead. He is met by NoPetticoat, who is talking in whispers. He whispers back that he has come to see Xoliswa Ximiya.

"Xoliswa does not live here," she whispers. "She has her own house at the school."

"Thank you, mama. But why are we whispering?"

She tells him that there is a meeting in progress. The elders of the Unbelievers are sorting out a few problems before they engage in their rituals.

Under the umsintsi tree a motley group of men are sitting and drinking beer. Some are wearing traditional isiXhosa clothes while others are in various western gear ranging from blue denim overalls and gumboots to Bhonco's crinkled suit and tie.

Bhonco sees Camagu and assumes that he is there to visit him. He beckons him to join the elders. Timidly Camagu approaches them, and apologizes for disturbing the old ones in their deliberations.

"Let the young man sit down. He will talk with Bhonco when we have finished upbraiding him," says a grave elder.

Camagu has no choice but to sit down. He cannot tell them now that he has not come to see Bhonco, but his daughter. It will be considered rude and disrespectful if he answers back after receiving such firm instructions to sit down. Even though he has spent so many years in foreign lands, he remembers the culture of his people very well.

Bhonco, son of Ximiya, is being admonished by his peers.

"We do not complain if this son of Ximiya cries for beautiful things," says the grave one. "But he must not betray us by refusing to join us in our grief for the folly of belief that racked our country and is felt even today. He is a carrier of the scars. They will live on his body forever. He has no first son to carry them when he dies, but that is another matter. The ancestors will decide about that. Maybe the scars will be passed to another family of Unbelievers. But that is not what I am talking about now. I am saying that this son of Ximiya must grieve. This descendant of the headless one must lament."

Various elders make their speeches in the same vein. Bhonco is shamefaced. The words of his peers reach deep inside him. His response is one long sharp wail. It is the howl of a mountain dog when the moon is full. Camagu suddenly feels a tinge of sadness.

In a slow rhythm the elders begin to dance. It is a painful dance. One can see the pain on their faces as they lift their limbs and stamp them on the ground. They are all wailing now, and mumbling things like people who talk in tongues. But they are not talking in tongues in the way that Christians do. They are going into a trance that takes them back to the past. To the world of the ancestors. Not the Otherworld where the ancestors live today. Not the world that lives parallel to our world. But to this world when it still belonged to them. When they were still people of flesh and blood like the people who walk the world today.

Like the abaThwa people—those who were disparagingly called the San by the Khoikhoi because to the Khoikhoi everyone who was a wanderer and didn't have cattle was a San—the elders seem to induce death through their dance. When they are dead they visit the world of the ancestors. When the trance is over they rejoin the world of the living. Only the elders do not die to the Otherworld but to the world of the past.

Camagu is not only filled with deep sorrow, he is also filled with fear. He tries to steal away when the elders are dead in their trance. As he tiptoes past the pink rondavel he almost falls on NoPetticoat, who is busy washing a gigantic three-legged cast-iron pot.

"You don't have to steal away like a thief in the night," she says with a smile.

"I am scared. I have never seen anything like this before."

"There is nothing to be afraid of. They are merely inducing sadness in their lives, so that they may have a greater appreciation of happiness."

"I have never heard of this custom before among the amaXhosa."

"It is not there. Even the Unbelievers of the days of Nongqawuse never had it. It was invented by the Unbelievers of today. When the sad times passed and the trials of the Middle Generations were over, it became necessary to create something that would make them appreciate this new happiness of the new age. What better way than to lament the folly of belief of the era of the child-prophetesses and the sufferings of the Middle Generations which were brought about by the same scourge of belief?"

Camagu no longer wants to steal away. He wants to stay and watch the whole ritual. NoPetticoat continues, "The revival of unbelief meant that Unbelievers must learn anew how to celebrate unbelief. Xoliswa's father was one of those who were sent to the hinterland to borrow the dances and trances of the abaThwa that take one to the world of the ancestors."

Under the umsintsi tree the elders present a wonderful spectacle of suffering. They are invoking grief by engaging in a memory ritual. In their trance they fleet back through the Middle Generations, and linger in the years when their forebears were hungry.

Hunger had seeped through the soil of the land of the amaXhosa. It also fouled the ill-gotten lands of the neighboring amaMfengu. Yet that part of kwaXhosa that had been conquered and settled by the children of Queen Victoria—they whose ears reflected the light of the sun—continued to eat.

The sons of the headless one were as diligent as their father used to be before he became stew in a British pot. The patriarch had taught them well about the art of working the soil and looking after animals. When the season was ripe, they cultivated the land. When it was time for hoeing, the women hoed the fields. The maize seemed to be promising. But before the corn was mature the disease attacked. Mercilessly. Once more the plants were left whimpering and blighted.

Lungsickness continued its rampage. It had arrived even at these new pastures. There was no escaping it. It picked and chose at random those cattle it was going to take with it.

At Twin's homestead it displayed the height of arrogance by attacking his prize horse, Gxagxa. No one had heard of lungsickness attacking horses before. But now the beautiful brown-and-white horse was becoming a bag of bones in front of his eyes.

Twin did not sleep. He kept vigil at Gxagxa's stable. Qukezwa brought him sour milk and *umphokoqo* porridge. But he could not eat. As long as Gxagxa could not eat he found it impossible to eat. Qukezwa tried a new strategy and brought him the fermented sorghum soft-porridge known as *ingodi*, and then the fermented maize soft-porridge called *amarhewu*. She knew that these were her husband's favorite drinks, which he found refreshing even after the hardest day's work. But Twin did not touch them. He just sat there and watched Gxagxa go through the stages that he knew so well: constipation, then diarrhea, then weight loss. The poor horse spent days gasping for air, its tongue hanging out. Then it died.

Yet Twin continued his vigil. He was waning away. Qukezwa feared that he was going to follow Gxagxa to the Otherworld. She pleaded. She cajoled. She threatened. Twin continued his vigil over a hide that covered only a pile of bones. Even when the flies and the worms came, he sat motionless and watched them feast.

Qukezwa never really liked Twin-Twin, because he never really liked her. But after praying to the one who told his stories in heaven, she swallowed her pride and went to KwaFeni to appeal for Twin-Twin's assistance. Twin-Twin put his kaross on his shoulder and rode to Ngcizele to see what was ailing his brother.

"It is dead, child of my mother! That horse is dead!" shouted Twin-Twin, greatly exercised by his brother's weakness. Whoever heard of a grown umXhosa man being affected like this by the death of a mere animal. Yes, he himself had felt the pain when his favorite ox died. One or two drops of tears did find their way down his cheeks. But this? Ridiculous! It showed clearly that his brother was a milksop.

For the first time in almost two weeks Twin opened his lips. He uttered something about Heitsi Eibib.

"He was a prophet, the son of Tsiqwa who died for the Khoikhoi people," Qukezwa explained to Twin-Twin.

"What has he got to do with us? This Heitsi Eibib is not one of us for my brother to be delirious about him. It is you, woman, who have put these strange ideas in his head. Now my brother dreams of foreign prophets that have nothing to do with the amaXhosa people. Is it your ubuthi—your witchcraft—that has made him become like this?"

"Would I have called you if I had made him be like this?"

Life seemed to return to Twin's eyes. He smiled and looked at his brother.

"In the same way that Heitsi Eibib saved the Khoikhoi, we need a prophet who will save the amaXhosa," he said.

"We have had our prophets. The prophets of the amaXhosa, not of the Khoikhoi or the abaThwa. We had Ntsikana and we had Nxele. What more do you want?" asked Twin-Twin. He was becoming impatient with this foolish talk.

"Perhaps there is something in this Nongqawuse thing," said Twin. "Perhaps she is the new prophet that will save us."

"She is just a foolish girl," argued Twin-Twin.

"Let us give her a chance, child of my mother. There might be something in her prophecies about the Strangers. She says the Strangers told her that all the animals and crops that we have today are contaminated. And indeed we see them dying every day. Here I have lost Gxagxa. The same Gxagxa who led us to these new pastures. Gxagxa is gone because of the contamination that blankets the land. Even in the new pastures we cannot escape the contamination. Perhaps we shall escape it if we heed Nongqawuse's words and kill all our animals."

"Don't you see, all the words she utters are really Mhlakaza's words? She is Mhlakaza's medium. The same Mhlakaza who was spreading lies, telling us that we must follow the god of the white man. The very white man who killed the son of his own god!"

But Twin was no longer listening. He was humming the song that people sang after Nongqawuse had made her prophecies about the new people who would come from the dead with new animals after all the contaminated ones had been killed.

"Now, I want you to listen very carefully, Twin," said Twin-Twin, trying very hard to muster as much patience as was possible. "I can see you are taking a dangerous path. We have our own god. And he has no son either. Unlike the god of the white man or of your wife's people."

Twin replied defensively, "Unlike the white people, the Khoikhoi did not kill the son of their god."

"It does not matter. What I am saying is, stick to your own god and his true prophets. Leave other people's gods, including those gods' sons, daughters, or any other members of their families."

In the days that followed, Twin seemed to have found peace and calmness at last. He embraced the stories that were beginning to spread that

Mhlakaza had actually visited the land of the dead—the Otherworld where the ancestors lived—and had been caressed by the shadow of King Hintsa. Even though almost twenty years had passed since King Hintsa had been brutally murdered in 1835 by Governor Sir Benjamin D'Urban, the amaXhosa people still remembered him with great love. They had not forgotten how D'Urban had invited the king to a meeting, promising him that he would be safe, only to cut off his ears as souvenirs and ship his head to Britain. There must be something in Nongqawuse's prophecies if Mhlakaza could be caressed by the shadow of the beloved king.

Twin was attracted not only by the good news that new cattle would come with the new people from the Otherworld. Nongqawuse had also pronounced that if the people killed all their cattle and set all their granaries alight, the spirits would rise from the dead and drive all the white people into the sea. Who would not want to see the world as it was before the cursed white conquerors—who were capable of killing even the son of their own god—had been cast by the waves onto the lands of the amaXhosa?

The good news also captured the imagination of King Sarhili, King Hintsa's son. He had not forgotten how he had accompanied his father into D'Urban's camp and had fortunately escaped when his father was held hostage for a ransom of twenty-five thousand cattle and five hundred horses. Since he had heard that his father had been gunned down when he tried to escape, his anger against the British had never diminished. His pained words were recalled every day in many an umXhosa household, "Where is my father? He is dead. He died by the hands of these people. He was killed in his own country. He died without fighting."

These prophecies presented his nation with a great opportunity to avenge itself against the puppies of Queen Victoria.

Although Sarhili was chief of the amaGcaleka clan, he was recognized as the king of all the clans of the amaXhosa. Even those amaXhosa who lived in the lands that were now under British rule paid allegiance to him. When he showed great interest in the prophecies, many amaXhosa people followed him.

There was great excitement at Twin's homestead when the news arrived that King Sarhili would be riding from his Great Place at Hohita to the sea. He was undertaking this journey of a day and part of the night because he wanted to see for himself the wonders that everyone was talking about.

Twin and Qukezwa were at Mhlakaza's homestead early in the morning. On Qukezwa's back was their new yellow-colored baby son, Heitsi, named after the savior of the Khoikhoi. This naming of Xikixa's grandson after his mother's people—instead of his father's, as was the custom—convinced Twin-Twin that his twin brother was now an absolute louse in the seams of his wife's isikhakha skirt. But Twin had already shown on many occasions that when it came to his relationship with Qukezwa he was a man of his own mind.

Although it was in the middle of a very cold winter, people were beginning to gather from all directions. Others had already camped at the banks of the Gxarha River. They had been there for many days listening to Nongqawuse, who was still seeing the Strangers almost every day. Sometimes she would be overwhelmed by the spirit so much that she got sick. Then Mhlakaza would take over and make his pronouncements. But the favorite of the people, and even of the chiefs, was young Nombanda, who talked so sweetly of the beautiful life that awaited those who carried out the instructions of the Strangers.

At midday King Sarhili and his entourage arrived amidst the ululation of women. Neither Twin nor Qukezwa had ever seen him before. He looked impressive in his leopard-skin cape. His long beard was glistening in the winter sun.

The whole place was filled with song and dance. The festive mood permeated the air, the river, and the great ocean. Everyone was filled with love for everyone else. It was wonderful to be there, to be loved so much, and to love others without reservation.

The same voice that had spoken to Nongqawuse spoke to King Sarhili as well. He heard with his own ears the instructions of the Strangers. At a distance on the waves of the sea he saw his own son who had recently died. He was alive and well and living with King Hintsa in the Otherworld. He saw his favorite horse that had also recently died. It was happily frolicking with the very horse his father rode just before he met his fate at the hands of D'Urban's headhunters.

A feast was laid out for the king. He was served a fresh pot of beer by Nongqawuse herself, and was shown a fresh ear of corn. Fresh corn in the middle of winter? This, he was told, came with the new people from the Otherworld.

"I have never tasted such wonderful beer," said King Sarhili as he removed foam from his beard. "It is indeed the beer from the world of the ancestors. A wonderful life awaits my people. But can these wonderful promises of the Strangers not be fulfilled without destroying all the existing cattle?"

"It cannot happen," answered Mhlakaza. "The instructions are firm on that matter. The present animals are contaminated. So are the present crops. The Strangers made it clear that the new ones will not come unless we do as we are told. The new people, our ancestors, will not rise from the dead until we have cleansed the earth by destroying all our cattle and all our crops both in the fields and in the granaries."

"The instructions are clear," said the king. "But my herds are too many. I shall only ask that I be given three months to destroy them all."

In the following weeks the king began to kill his cattle. The first victim was his best bull, which was famous for its beauty in all the land. Poets had recited poems and musicians had composed songs about it. When it fell, people knew that there was no turning back. The cattle had to be killed.

At the same time he sent *imiyolelo*—his formal commands—throughout kwaXhosa that all amaXhosa should obey Mhlakaza's instructions.

Twin and Qukezwa formed part of the regular throngs that went to Mhlakaza's place daily.

"You have been taken up by this foolishness, child of my mother," Twin-Twin warned him, "and you neglect your cattle and fields."

"What is the use of looking after them when they are going to die in any case?" responded Twin. "I am going to destroy them."

Twin-Twin shook his head and went off to look after his animals.

At Mhlakaza's homestead, Twin and Qukezwa joined the multitudes that felt the earth shake and heard bulls bellowing beneath the ground. They were the pedigree bulls waiting to replace those that were to be killed.

All important visitors were introduced to the young prophetesses—Nongqawuse and Nombanda. They were treated to the sight of the girls talking to the spirits. The visitors themselves never heard the spirits, for the spirits could be heard only by the chosen ones. Twin believed that at times he heard them, although he could not say exactly what they were saying.

Nongqawuse's confused look that marked her as a prophet became more pronounced. And in the manner of all great messengers of the spirit world she was unkempt and didn't take any particular care of her looks. She did not even care for the red ochre that girls her age applied on their bodies to beautify themselves. She cared only about the spirits, and every day she led the multitudes to the Gxarha River to show them the wonders from the Otherworld.

A special delegation of chiefs from various parts of kwaXhosa arrived, and Twin, who was gaining more prominence in the homestead of Mhlakaza, was asked to accompany them to the mouth of the Gxarha River where Nongqawuse and Nombanda were already communing with the new people.

As the chiefs approached the river they were overwhelmed by a wonderful fear. There was an explosion and great rocks fell from the cliffs overlooking the river. Soon the whole valley was covered with mist. The air was filled with the bellowing of cattle, the neighing of horses, and the bleating of sheep and goats.

"Cast your eyes in the direction of the sea," Nongqawuse commanded.

And in the sea the chiefs saw hundreds of cattle. Over the horizon a great crowd of people appeared and disappeared again. It did that a number of times. The chiefs pleaded with Nongqawuse to tell the new people to come closer to the shore, so that they might communicate with them.

"The new people will come only when you have killed all your cattle," she told the chiefs. "You cannot talk with them now. Only I can talk with them."

When Twin went back to Ngcizele he spread the news of the wonders he had seen. He even went to KwaFeni to try to persuade his brother to believe in the prophecies.

"That is nonsense," said Twin-Twin. "You people saw what you wanted to see. Of course the sea has its creatures. The sea has whales and dolphins and water buffaloes and sea lions and sea horses. There are even sea people called water-maids. That is what you saw."

"Let me take you there, child of my mother. Then you will see with your own eyes the wonders that I am talking about."

"I have no time to waste, Twin. I have to look after my cattle and till the soil. You have seen how big my homestead has grown, with new children and new wives. Those spirits of yours will not feed my family."

Twin felt sorry for his brother. He went home to slaughter two of his best oxen.

A few days later, Twin decided to go back to KwaFeni to try once more to reason with the stubborn Twin-Twin. He was surprised to see four horses, some still saddled, tethered outside his brother's compound. Was it possible that the very child of his mother's womb could organize a feast without informing him? A feast attended by men of substance too, judging by their fine horses.

Under an umsintsi tree, five men were engaged in serious delibera- tions. Twin-Twin's eyes betrayed his surprise at seeing his brother.

"You are welcome, child of my mother, even though I did not know you would be coming," he said.

"Since when do I need permission to visit my brother's house?" asked Twin.

The men were eyeing him with suspicion. He stared back at them defiantly. He could identify only one of them—Sigidi. He knew him as the senior chief of those amaGcaleka clansmen who lived under the rule of the British in the conquered territory. He was resplendent as usual in his elaborate isiXhosa costume. Twin wondered who the dis- tinguished old man was, with hair as white as the snow on the Ama- thole Mountains. Then there were two younger men in European clothes. The old man himself wore a mixture of European and isiXhosa attire: pants and long-boots, and an animal-skin cape over his shoul- ders. Twin-Twin also looked splendid in his isiXhosa tanned-hide skirt, a zebra-skin cape, and beads of different types. Twin felt small and shabby in his casual donkey blanket—known by that name because of its gray color.

"Twin, this grandfather you are staring at as if he is your age-mate is Nxito, King Sarhili's uncle," said Twin-Twin.

Then he pointed at the men in European clothes. "And this here is Ned, the son of General Maqoma—yes, the man who led us in the War of Mlanjeni. This well-fed one is Mjuza, the son of our great prophet Nxele. Forgive my brother, my father and brothers, he has not been himself since he started believing in false prophets."

Twin was filled with shame for having rudely stared at the aged one. At the same time he was wondering how his brother had come to know such important people.

"I did not mean to be rude, my father and brothers," he said timidly.

"As I was saying," said Nxito, ignoring Twin and his apology, "our god, the great Qamata, knows how to punish those who think they can bully his people."

They were talking about Sir George Cathcart, the victor of the War of Mlanjeni.

Ned was the next to speak. He worked at the Native Hospital as a laborer who was sometimes used as a porter and an orderly, depending on the need. He recounted to the great amusement of all how the white doctor and the superintendent at the hospital were still mourning for the governor even though it was all of two years since he had died at the hands of the Russian soldiers in the Crimean War.

Everyone remembered how the news of Cathcart's death had spread like wildfire, sparking jubilation and impromptu celebrations throughout kwaXhosa. People got to know of the Russians for the first time. Although the British insisted that they were white people like themselves, the amaXhosa knew that it was all a lie. The Russians were a black nation. They were the spirits of amaXhosa soldiers who had died in the various wars against the British colonists. In fact, those particular Russians who killed Cathcart were the amaXhosa soldiers who had been killed by the British during the War of Mlanjeni.

"It is most likely that those Russians were commanded by my own father," mused Twin, who had gathered enough fortitude to join the discussion even though the others seemed determined to pretend that he did not exist.

"How can Xikixa command Russian soldiers when he has no head?" asked Nxito.

Everyone agreed that perhaps that was why the British cut his head off, so that he would not be an effective ancestor.

"It was two years ago when we believed in the Russians, after they had killed Cathcart," said Twin-Twin. "For many months we posted men on the hills to look out for the arrival of the Russian ships. But they never came."

Chief Sigidi laughed and added, "I remember this very Mjuza, son of Nxele, telling everyone that the great prophet had not drowned escaping from Robben Island, but was leading a black army across the seas that would come and crush the British!"

"I was not the only one," said Mjuza defensively. "Many of us believed Mlanjeni had risen from the dead and was the war doctor of the Russian forces. I believed that my father was the leader of the Russians who had returned from the dead until I went to the Gxarha myself and saw that this Nongqawuse is nothing but a fake."

"The Russians may yet arrive," said Twin. "Maybe not as the same Russians who killed Cathcart. Maybe as our ancestors who will rise from the dead after we have killed our cattle. They will emerge from the sea. Nongqawuse says so."

"Nongqawuse is a dreamer. That is precisely why we are gathered here, to see what we can do to save the people from her false prophecies," responded Nxito.

"So it is true what we have heard, Twin-Twin; your brother is a staunch Believer!" said Ned.

"He will change soon enough," Twin-Twin assured his friends.

"Don't talk for me, child of my mother. I have my own mouth. I have seen miracles at the mouth of the Gxarha River with my own eyes. Even your own nephew, Tat'uNxito, King Sarhili himself; I was with him when he saw the miracles. That is why he has issued the formal commands, the imiyolelo, that the amaXhosa nation should obey the instructions of the great prophetess."

Twin-Twin was fuming.

"Who invited you here, eh?" he asked. "This is a meeting of Unbelievers. We are here because we think that King Sarhili is being misled. And you come with your nonsense!"

"Wait, my sons," said Nxito. "Children of a person should not fight on these matters. If we talk about things we'll find solutions."

Although Twin was alone against five Unbelievers he felt very strong. He had only to think of the prophetesses Nongqawuse and Nombanda to feel inspired. He was not afraid of these Unbelievers. He was going to debate with them. He was going to convert them. It was his duty to make them see the light. Some of them might be elders of the nation. Or learned men who worked at white people's hospitals. Or sons of great prophets. But they were lost souls. He would not keep quiet. He would not be intimidated into silence. The future of the amaXhosa nation was at stake here.

"You cannot stop the people from believing in their own salvation!" shouted Twin. "A black race across the sea, newly resurrected from the dead, is surely coming to save us from the white man. Even the armies of The Man Who Named Ten Rivers cannot stand against it! You saw what happened to Cathcart!"

The Man Who Named Ten Rivers was Sir George Grey, the man who had taken over as governor of the Cape Colony after Cathcart's death. He had arrived with great enthusiasm with a mission to civilize the natives. Those amaXhosa who had become amaGqobhoka—the Christian converts, that is—believed in Grey. People like Ned who were on good terms with white people came back with stories of Grey's greatness. He had been a governor in Australia and New Zealand, they said, where his civilizing mission did many wonderful things for the natives of those countries. Of course he had to take their land in return for civilization. Civilization is not cheap. He had written extensively about the native people of those countries, and about their plants. He had even given names to ten of their rivers, and to their mountain ranges. It did not matter that the forebears of those natives had named those rivers and mountains from time immemorial. When Ned told them about the naming of the rivers, a derisive elder had called Grey The Man Who Named Ten Rivers. And that became his name.

"Don't tell me about The Man Who Named Ten Rivers!" said Twin-Twin. "Like all the others he is a thief. Just as he stole the land of the people of countries across the seas, he stole the land of the ama-Xhosa and gave it to the amaMfengu. He stole more of our land to settle more of his people!"

Both Ned and Mjuza were up in Grey's defense. Grey was different from former governors, they said. Grey was a friend of the amaXhosa. Grey was a great reader of the Bible—the big book that talked about the true salvation that would come through the blood of the son of the true god. Grey believed that all men were equal—well, almost equal—as long as they adopted a civilized mode of dress and decent habits. Grey was interested in the health and education of the amaXhosa—that was why he established schools and the Native Hospital. Grey was a great lover of the amaXhosa nation, and was interested in their folk stories, in their animals and in their plants. Instead of being derisively called The Man Who Named Ten Rivers, Grey should be called The Great Benefactor of the Non-European Peoples of the World. Grey was a wonderful man whose only motive for coming to and ruling the land of the amaXhosa was to change the customs of the barbarous natives and introduce them to British civilization. The land that he had grabbed in the process was really a very small price to pay for the wonderful gift of civilization.

"Nonsense," said Twin-Twin, who was losing patience with his fellow Unbelievers. "The only reason your Grey came here is because the white people are full in their country. So they came here to steal our land."

Twin was enjoying this disagreement among the Unbelievers.

"And these are your friends, my brother? These people who believe in the rule of the white man and in his god?" he asked mockingly.

This made Twin-Twin very uncomfortable. His unbelief in the false prophets—beginning with Mlanjeni and now including Nongqawuse and all the others who were emerging and preaching the same cattle-killing message—had forced him to form a strange alliance with people who had deserted their own god for the god of the white man. People like Ned and Mjuza, who were descendants of amaXhosa heroes but were now followers of white ways. Nxito, however, was like him. His unbelief in Nongqawuse was not unbelief in the rites, rituals, and customs of the amaXhosa, and in the god who had been revealed by the likes of Ntsikana and Nxele. Mdalidephu. Qamata. Mvelingqangi. The one who was worshipped by his forefathers from the beginning of time. The one whose messengers were the ancestors.

When Twin left his brother's homestead he was a depressed man. He realized that his brother was too far gone to be saved. He was in cahoots with dangerous people who were servants of the colonial masters.

During the weeks that followed he learned that Mjuza was sometimes seen in the company of John Dalton, the colonial army officer who had fought in the War of Mlanjeni. Dalton was often sent by the magistrates of The Man Who Named Ten Rivers to discipline those amaXhosa chiefs who did not toe the colonial line. When Dalton's name was mentioned, Twin always saw his father's head being tossed into a boiling pot. How could Twin-Twin associate with Mjuza, who was a lackey of the people who had rendered Xikixa headless? Was this the end of the road for their twinhood?

It was like that in many families. Believing brothers fought against unbelieving brothers. Unbelieving spouses turned against believing spouses. Unbelieving fathers kicked believing sons out of their homesteads. Unbelieving sons plotted the demise of believing fathers. Unbelieving fathers attempted to kill believing sons. Siblings stared at each other with eyes full of blood. Many amaXhosa killed their cattle in order to facilitate the resurrection. Many others killed them unwillingly under the threat of their believing relatives.

The amaXhosa people called the Believers amaThamba—those whose hearts were soft and compassionate. The clever ones, whose heads caught fast. The generous ones. The Unbelievers were called amaGogotya—the hard ones. The unbending ones. The selfish and greedy men who wanted to hoard their cattle and thereby rob the entire amaXhosa nation of the sweet fruits of the resurrection.

Whenever Twin's spirit was beginning to flag, he went to the place of miracles with Qukezwa. And there they ate and danced until midnight. They drank sorghum beer. And early in the morning hours they saw cattle in the bushes and in the sea. Some of the people could even see their old friends and relatives who had long been dead. One morning Twin himself saw the risen heroes emerge from the sea. Some were on foot, others were on horseback, passing in a glorious but silent parade, then sinking again among the waves.

The following day Twin and Qukezwa went home and slaughtered more of their cattle with greater vigor. At the same time they proceeded to enlarge their kraals in anticipation of the new cattle, and to renovate their houses so that the new people—the resurrected relatives—could be welcomed in newly thatched huts.

Throughout kwaXhosa Believers were killing hundreds of cattle every day. People were not allowed to eat meat of cattle that had been killed the day before. Every day new cattle were slaughtered and the previous day's meat was thrown away. Soon the stench of rotting meat filled the villages. The stomachs of the Believers were running from eating too much meat. And again the stench filled the villages.

Twin and his wife went on to dig out the corn from their underground granaries and threw it into the river.

Some Believers sold their corn and cattle to the unbelieving amaMfengu and to the markets of Kingwilliamstown and East London at a fraction of the market price.

Twin-Twin was disturbed by all these activities. At an imbhizo at the chief's place, when arguments were hotting up between Believers and Unbelievers, he shouted, "I say to you, Believers, bring that foolish girl Nongqawuse to me so that I may sleep her. I will give it to her so hard that she will stop spreading lies! She is telling all these lies, dreaming all these dreams, seeing all these imaginary visions, because she is starved of men!"

It was too late for Twin and his fellow Believers to close their ears to avoid being contaminated by such blasphemy.

Camagu tells Xoliswa Ximiya about the memory ritual of the Unbelievers. The graceful pain that captivated him. She is surprised that such a highly educated man who has lived in America for three decades is fascinated by such rubbish.

"It is embarrassing, really," she says. "I do not know why they do not want to forget our shameful past."

"I thought it was beautiful."

"Don't patronize my people."

"Really. You don't have to be a Romantic poet to know that sadness is essential in our lives."

Xoliswa Ximiya makes it clear that she would rather talk about other things. She tells him about her wish to leave Qolorha-by-Sea, to be away from the uncivilized bush and the hicks who want to preserve an outdated culture. Her friends have important posts in the government. She would like to join the civil service too. She has made many applications but all she gets in the post are letters of regret. Perhaps she should follow his example and fly to the good ol' U.S. of A.

Apart from her obsession with America, Camagu finds her quite attractive. The sadness in her eyes gives him a strong urge to hold her very tightly and protect her from the harsh world. But he knows that if he dared succumb to the temptation, she would not hesitate to put him in his place.

After a glass of orange squash, and a promise that he will see her tomorrow, he takes leave of her. He wants to see more of the seashore before it gets dark.

He is walking in Nongqawuse's Valley when a whirlwind approaches and almost blows him off his feet as it passes by. Then it turns back and stops right in front of him. It is Qukezwa riding bareback and reinless on Gxagxa. She giggles.

"Hello, stranger," she says, as she dismounts and lets Gxagxa graze on his own. She takes out a panga from the sheath she is wearing and starts waving it about. He moves back in fear. She enjoys this and laughs.

"You are scared? Don't worry, I won't chop your head off—at least not yet."

She starts chopping away at some bushes.

"Who are you?" he asks.

"Qukezwa Zim."

"Oh, you are the girl at the shop. The girl who told me—"

"Told you what?"

"Come on, you know that we met at the store where you work. You actually propositioned me, naughty girl!"

"I have never seen you before."

"Okay, I'll take your word for it. But I know that we met."

She continues to chop the bush.

Maybe this girl will know NomaRussia. Camagu decides there is no harm in asking her.

"I am looking for someone."

"NomaRussia? I heard."

"But you said you have never seen me before."

"This NomaRussia—you really love her, don't you? Coming all the way from Johannesburg to look for her! Do you really know her? Did she tell you about herself? Did you taste her womanhood and then decide you were going to follow her to the end of the earth?"

"Don't be outrageous!"

"Did you meet her at some drinking place where your drunken eyes saw a goddess in her?"

"I did not meet her at a drinking place!"

"Oh, I forgot, she was working for you and left with your passport."

"Who told you that?"

"Do you think I am a baby? Do you think everyone is a baby in this village?"

"Of course not!"

"NomaRussia never worked for you. She doesn't work for anyone."

"Do you know her then? Please tell me where I can find her."

"No. I don't know her. Never heard of her."

"Please. It is very important that I find NomaRussia."

"What if she is a married woman? What if she has someone?"

He remembers that she was dressed like a newly married woman— a makoti. He had not thought of this when he drove all the way from

Johannesburg. Now he fears that the villagers will not take kindly to the fact that he is busy inquiring after someone's wife.

"Is she married then?" he asks, dreading the answer.

"What if she suffers from an incurable disease?"

"Don't toy with me, girl!"

"What if she is the daughter-in-law of a vicious ogre who will not hesitate to castrate the first man who gives her a second look?"

"I am sure you know her. Please—I beg you . . ."

"No, I don't know her. I don't want to know her. So leave me alone about NomaRussia!"

She chops the bush even more aggressively.

"Do you know what I call what you are doing?" he asks sneeringly.

"Chopping down a stupid plant, what else?"

"Vandalism. Why are you destroying these beautiful plants that have such nice purple flowers?"

"Nice purple flowers? They are blue as far as I am concerned."

"Because they are blue as far as you are concerned they deserve to die?"

"Nice plants, eh? Nice for you, maybe. But not nice for indigenous plants. This is the inkberry. It comes from across the Kei River. It kills other plants. These flowers that you like so much will eventually become berries. Each berry is a prospective plant that will kill the plants of my forefathers. And this plant is poisonous to animals too, although its berries are not. Birds eat the berries without any harm, and spread these terrible plants with their droppings."

Suddenly she emits a sharp whistle, which brings Gxagxa galloping to her. She mounts the horse and rides away—brandishing her panga.

Camagu shouts after her, "Thanks for the lesson!"

Then under his breath: "Bloody bitch."

At night he becomes the river and NomaRussia its cool, crystal-clear water. He wakes up in a cold sweat when the panga-wielding girl of Nongqawuse's Valley defiles his dream by intruding into it. She is squeezing the purple juice of the inkberries into the river, turning its water into purple slime.

He cannot sleep again after that.

 Since the rebuke of the elders, Bhonco, son of Ximiya, has changed. He now laments the sufferings of the Middle Generations. He still cries for beautiful things. But he does not believe in not grieving anymore. We cannot say he believes in grieving, for as an Unbeliever he does not believe.

It is as it should be.

At this public meeting he is gearing for a fight. If Chief Xikixa is so weak that he cannot put his foot down and take a sensible position on this matter of development, he will show the Believers that there are still men in the village of Qolorha-by-Sea. The chief is the kind of person who is swayed by each speaker's argument, and at the end of the imbhizo he does not know what side to take.

Those who like to make snide remarks are often heard saying of the chief, "How do you expect him to have a head for good reasoning or for anything else for that matter? He is named after a headless ancestor."

But it is difficult for many people to know which side to take. Even Camagu, with all his learning, cannot make up his mind. Every day of the two weeks he has been at this village he has spent time with

Xoliswa Ximiya. Sometimes just an hour or two after school, or almost half a day during weekends. It is understandable, then, that at this imbhizo he is more sympathetic to the position of the Unbelievers.

Xoliswa Ximiya stands unyieldingly next to him. If only his mates at Giggles could see him now, in the company of this model-type in all her clinical elegance!

He has tried to observe the patterns of believing and unbelieving at this village, to try to make sense of them. And they remain beyond his comprehension. He has talked with Bhonco at length. Unfortunately he has not had any opportunity to talk with Zim. Camagu concludes that these people select positions in such a way that they are never found to be on the same side on any issue. Even at the *inkundla*, where they are both councillors and counsellors at Chief Xikixa's court, they are always at loggerheads.

"The Unbelievers stand for progress," asserts Bhonco, to the assenting murmurs of his followers. He exudes graveness and anger as he punches the air with his fist. The whiff of friendliness that Camagu once observed on his furrowed face has flown with the reproof of the elders. "We want to get rid of this bush which is a sign of our uncivilized state. We want developers to come and build the gambling city that will bring money to this community. That will bring modernity to our lives, and will rid us of our redness."

Xoliswa Ximiya is proud of her father's position. If only he had asked NoPetticoat to press his suit. But even a wrinkled suit is better than no suit at all. Far better than beads and traditional isiXhosa costume, even though a rock-rabbit-skin bag hangs over the elder's off-white shirt and twisted tie.

Zim stands up, looking regal in his traditional finery. He is smiling.

"This son of Ximiya talks of progress. Yet he wants to destroy the bush that has been here since the days of our forefathers. What kind of progress is that?" he asks. He is very deliberate in his manner and in his speech.

"What does the bush do for you?" shouts Bhonco. He has lost patience with the stupidity of the Believers. "The new developments will bring tourists. The new developments will create employment for us all. The new developments will bring people from all over the world. From America!"

His last point, thinks Camagu, comes from the elder's daughter.

"Yes. Those people!" scoffs Zim. "Those so-called tourists! They come here to steal our lizards and our birds."

"Who wants lizards, anyway?" asks Bhonco contemptuously. "Do you eat lizards, Zim? Why do you complain about lizards and birds? Does a grown man like you eat birds like a young shepherd? Like a herdboy in the veld?"

"They come to steal our aloes and our cycads and our usundu palms and our *ikhamanga* wild banana trees," insists Zim.

Bhonco is exasperated. He has never heard such foolishness oozing from every pore of a man who is supposed to be an elder of the village. Will progress and civilization stall because of such madness? Yes, people have been caught smuggling cycads and reptiles out of Qolorha, which is the height of foolishness. Why arrest a man for taking wild things that belong to no one in particular? And they are ugly too, these lizards. And these plants are of no use at all to the people. They are good neither as wood nor as food. And when there is progress, who would need wood from the forest anyway?

"People will be using fire from electricity," says Bhonco proudly, "like my daughter does in her house in the schoolyard where, as you know, she is the principal."

Xoliswa Ximiya has recently bought two hot plates, since the school joined the Blue Flamingo Hotel and Vulindlela Trading Store as the only places in the village that have electricity drawn from Butterworth. Well, the only places if you exclude the holiday cottages, most of which are connected to electricity lines or have their own generators.

But she is not pleased when her father mentions her great achievement. That is why she did not want to come to this imbhizo in the first place. She knew that in the course of the quarrel between the feuding families, things would get personal. She heard what happened at the store during nkamnkam day when her name was thrown into the fray by her own father. Camagu prevailed on her to come, so she now finds herself being pierced by a hundred pairs of eyes while her utilization of electricity is bandied about so shamelessly. Camagu gives her a reassuring smile.

"When there is progress," adds Bhonco, "there'll even be streetlights."

"Why should we fight about this?" asks Zim. "We are all descendants of the headless one."

Trust Zim to use that trick. Whenever he gets stuck in a debate he resorts to sentimental appeals to their common ancestry. Yet he will continue to hold desperately to a bad argument, as if his very life depends on it.

It is as it should be, for as a Believer it would be sacrilege to be in harmony with any position taken by the Unbelievers. Camagu suspects that even if a miracle were to happen, and Bhonco were to change his position and denounce the developers, Zim would suddenly do an about-face and support the developers.

"When it suits you we are all descendants of the headless one," sneers Bhonco. "But when you laugh at my misfortunes, such as my not getting nkamnkam from the government even though I am an aged one, you forget that we are both of the headless one. Or when you want to destroy the people by standing in the way of progress. You are a wily one, Zim. You are just waiting to stab me in the back in the same way that your fathers stabbed my fathers. In the same way that your fathers led this nation to destruction by following the teachings of Nongqawuse."

Zim resorts to ridiculing Bhonco. He laughs mockingly. His followers join the mirth. No one knows what they are laughing at. Bhonco is livid.

"This man who believes in progress—"

But even before Zim can complete his words Bhonco points his stick at him with indignation. "I do not believe in progress," he shouts in a pained voice. "I am an Unbeliever. None of us Unbelievers believe! We stand for progress!"

"Okay, he stands for progress," says Zim graciously. "Yet he hasn't progressed from the old-style rondavel to the modern hexagon. Some of us have hexagons aplenty in our compounds. He has a single pink rondavel. What kind of progress is that?"

o o o

It is a cowardly thing to laugh at a man for his possessions or lack of them, mumble the people as they go their different directions. It is clear that Zim has run out of reasoning. If Chief Xikixa and his development committees had any balls at all, they would certainly follow Bhonco's way. They would make a ruling once and for all that the development work should begin.

"Chiefs cannot just issue orders," the history teacher from the secondary school says, trying to calm Bhonco as he walks with him towards his homestead. "That is what democracy is all about. Citizens must first debate these matters. There must be consensus before a decision is taken."

"Such are the ills of democracy!" remarks Bhonco.

"But it was like that even in the days of our forefathers," says the teacher. "Chiefs never made decisions unilaterally. That is why they had councillors who would go out to get the views of the people first. That is why they held imbhizos which all the men were obliged to attend. Things were spoiled during the Middle Generations when the white man imposed a new system on us, and created his own petty chiefs who became little despots on behalf of their masters."

"Get away from me, small boy! Who invited you to walk with me?" shouts Bhonco. "Who are you to teach me how things were done in the days of our forefathers?"

The impertinent teacher withdraws. He sees Xoliswa Ximiya and Camagu walking away together, and rushes to join them. It is clear that the headmistress too finds his presence irritating. But Camagu welcomes him and wants to find out where he stands in this great debate.

"I do not know," says the teacher.

"You do not know?" asks Xoliswa Ximiya with disgust. "A whole secondary school history teacher is ignorant of developmental issues! What did your parents send you to school for?"

"These are difficult issues, Miss Ximiya," says the teacher apologetically. "Sometimes I find myself tilting more to the position of the Believers. I think it is important to conserve nature . . . our forests . . . our rivers . . ."

"What about jobs? What about the tourists?"

"We can still get tourists. Different types of tourists. Those who want to commune with nature. Those who want to admire our plants, which they regard as exotic. Those who want to photograph our birds."

"Those who want to see the natives in their primitive state, you mean," says Xoliswa Ximiya disdainfully. "The only people who will get jobs from that kind of a tourist are the con artists, NoManage and NoVangeli."

Camagu learns that NoManage and NoVangeli are two formidable women who earn their living from what John Dalton calls cultural tourism. Their work is to display *amasiko*—the customs and cultural practices of the amaXhosa—to the white people who are brought to their hut in Dalton's four-wheel-drive bakkie, after he has taken them on various trails to Nongqawuse's Valley, the great lagoon, the ship-wrecks, rivers, and gorges, and the ancient middens and cairns. Often when these tourists come, NoManage pretends she is a traditional healer, what the tourists call a witch doctor, and performs magic rites of her own concoction. At this time NoVangeli and the tourists hide some items, and NoManage uses her supernatural powers to discover where they are hidden. Then the tourists watch the two women polish the floor with cow dung. After this the tourists try their hand at grinding mielies or sorghum on a grinding stone or crushing maize into samp with a granite or wooden pestle. All these shenanigans are performed by these women in their full isiXhosa traditional costume of the amahomba, which is cumbersome to work in. Such costume is meant to be worn only on special occasions when people want to look smart and beautiful, not when they are toiling and sweating. And the tourists pay good money for all this foolery!

Xoliswa Ximiya is not happy that her people are made to act like buffoons for these white tourists. She is miffed that the trails glorify primitive practices. Her people are like monkeys in a zoo, observed with amusement by white foreigners with John Dalton's assistance. But, worst of all, she will never forgive Dalton for taking them to Nongqawuse's Pool, where they drop coins for good luck. She hates Nongqawuse. The mere mention of her name makes her cringe in embarrassment. That episode of the story of her people is a shame and a disgrace.

"What is strange about people like Dalton," muses Xoliswa Ximiya as if to herself, "is that his white forebears in the days of Nongqawuse were grouped with the amaGogotya—the Unbelievers—as people who would be swept into the sea on the day of the rising of the dead. But here is John Dalton today standing with the amaThamba—the Believers—in fighting against progress."

Camagu excuses himself. He has a few letters to write in his hotel room. He gives her a peck on the cheek, and promises to see her tomorrow.

Wagging tongues follow him as he makes his way to the Blue Flamingo. Here is someone who has come to save Xoliswa Ximiya from spinsterhood, the people at beer parties gossip. But others think that he is suspect. Why is he not married at such an old age? The wiser ones say that he has not had the time to marry. He has been at school all these years. Haven't they heard that his head is rotten with education? He is so learned that he has reached the highest possible class in the world. Vathiswa has even spread it that he is a doctor, although not the kind that cures illnesses. There are other kinds of doctors, she has assured them, who have earned that title by reaching the destination beyond which all knowledge ends.

It is clear that the community has been worried that their head-mistress might die an old maid. It is well known that men are intimi-dated by educated women. And by "educated women" they mean those who have gone to high schools and universities to imbibe west-ern education, rather than those who have received traditional isiXhosa education at home and during various rites of passage. Men are more at home with the kind of woman they can trample under their feet. Even educated men prefer uneducated women. Perhaps this stranger from Johannesburg is a different breed of educated man. He is not intimi-dated by the dispassionate beauty. Otherwise why would he have been seen with her every day for the last two weeks? People have eyes. They can see. They have ears. They can hear.

In the morning he lies in bed for a while, planning his future. It dawns on him that he really has no future to plan—not in this village. His money will not last forever at this hotel. His mission to find Noma-Russia has failed. Anyway, if he found her what would he do with her? It was a foolish quest. He must prepare to leave. He must work his way back to Johannesburg. Back to the disrupted journey to the airport. Back to Xoliswa Ximiya's U.S. of A. With this thought he sinks into utter depression.

A knock interrupts his thoughts. He opens the door for the house-maid. He goes to the bathroom to take a shower while the woman makes up his bed. All of a sudden she gives a chilling scream that brings him scuttling out of the bathroom.

"What the hell?" he demands.

Even before she can answer he sees a brown snake uncoiling itself slowly on his blankets. The woman darts out shouting for help. In no time a battalion of gardeners, handymen, and even a petrol-pump attendant rush in armed with spades and sundry weapons.

"Wait!" screams Camagu. "No one will touch that snake."

"He says we must not kill the snake!" shouts the petrol-pump attendant.

"Why? Is he crazy like those Believers who want to protect lizards?" asks a gardener.

"No," says Camagu. "This is not just any snake. This is Majola."

It begins to register on the men.

"You are of the amaMpondomise clan then?"

"Yes. I am of the amaMpondomise. This snake is my totem."

Camagu is beside himself with excitement. He has never been visited by Majola, the brown mole snake that is the totem of his clan. He has heard in stories how the snake visits every newborn child; how it sometimes pays a visit to chosen members of the clan to give them good fortune. He is the chosen one today.

The men understand. They are of the amaGcaleka clan and do not have snakes as totems. As far as they are concerned, snakes are enemies that must be killed. But they know about the amaMpondomise of the Majola clan. They know also that in their upbringing they were taught to respect other people's customs so that their own customs could be respected as well. As they walk away, they talk of Camagu in great awe.

They did not expect a man with such great education, a man who has lived in the lands of the white people for thirty years, to have such respect for the customs of his people. He is indeed a man worthy of their respect.

Camagu cannot contain his joy as he walks on the sandbank of the great lagoon singing to himself. He has left the snake lying on his bed. It will go on its way when it feels like it. He breaks into a jog, but stops when he runs out of breath. Age has indeed caught up with him. There was a time when he could run for hours. And that was not so long ago.

"Hello, stranger!"

He is startled. He looks around, but cannot see anyone. She whistles at him, and he sees her head bobbing in the water. It is that confounded girl again! The one who sullies crystal-clear water with poisonous juices, turning it into purple slime.

"Is it not possible to be anywhere without you sneaking around?"

She walks out of the water. She struts about in panties and a bra, as if she were a fat model in a top-of-the-range bikini. She reaches for a dress that was left on a rock to dry. Although it is still wet she puts it on, and joins him on the sandbank. He tries very hard to pretend that he does not see the buxom curves that are accentuated by the wet dress that desperately clings on her body and has become see-through.

"Sneaking around? I should think you are the one who is sneaking around. This is my lagoon. I live here. You live in Johannesburg. And if I were you I would go back there and stop bothering innocent people."

They glare at each other for a while. Then she breaks out laughing. He self-consciously inspects himself, in case his fly is open.

"I shall not let you spoil my day," Camagu says, walking away. "Today I was visited by my snake. I thought it was going to be my lucky day."

"So soon?" she asks.

He stops and looks at her.

"So soon?" he repeats, wondering what on earth she means.

"I didn't think you would see through your thin girlfriend so early in your affair. I agree with you: Xoliswa Ximiya is a snake."

"I am talking about my totem snake, foolish girl!"

He walks away in disgust. She follows him. He walks faster still. She keeps up the pace. It frustrates him that he cannot get rid of her.

"Honestly, she is a snake. Don't you see her beauty? It is not normal. When a woman is that beautiful my people say she has been licked by a snake. I know her very well. She was my teacher at Qolorha-by-Sea Secondary School. She has no patience with those who lack beauty."

By this time Camagu is running. But the girl is keeping a steady pace behind him, all the while yapping about the beauty of Xoliswa Ximiya. In class, the irritating girl continues, Miss Ximiya used to begin her lessons by reading from a newspaper cutting the story of a Taiwanese woman called Hu Pao-yin. She killed her mother-in-law and stabbed her mother with a knife because they were not pretty enough to deserve to live. Hu Pao-yin declared, "I am the most beautiful woman in the world and the existence of other women is unnecessary."

Exactly Xoliswa Ximiya's sentiments.

She read this story to her class before every lesson. At the end of the story she would remark breathlessly, "Isn't it romantic?"

Camagu cannot run forever. He sits down on a rock, completely out of breath. Qukezwa stands in front of him, arms akimbo, and says, "She read the story of Hu Pao-yin over and over again, until the newspaper cutting went yellow with age. She wished she could have the courage to do what the Taiwanese woman did. In the long run we couldn't stand it. We stole the newspaper cutting and destroyed it. She was never the same after that."

"Never the same?"

"The way you see her now. A frozen statue."

"You are a nuisance, you know that? You even slander your former teacher. What kind of a child are you?"

"Child? Is that all you see in me? Child? I am nineteen, you know. I am going to be twenty in two months' time. Many of my age-mates are married with children."

"To me you are a child."

"It's because you are an old man. Old. Finished and klaar. A bag of old bones. A limp that cannot be saved even by Viagra. I don't know what you're doing chasing young children like NomaRussia!"

Ouch!

Camagu decides he cannot compete with this girl's acerbic tongue. Get her on your side, he tells himself. She can be a deadly enemy. Get her on your side. She may even lead you to NomaRussia. It is obvious that she knows her.

"Listen, I don't want to exchange insults with you," he says. "What did I ever do to you? I don't want to be your enemy. Let's be friends, okay?"

"Don't pretend to be nice to me. I can't help you. I do not know the NomaRussia you are looking for."

The witch!

"Did I tell you that I passed Standard Eight? I may not be an 'Excuse Me' from Fort Hare like your thin girlfriend, but at least I can read and write."

"Well, congratulations!" He spits the words out, making sure that she does not miss the sarcasm in his voice.

But she is no longer paying any attention to him. She is clapping hands for a group of five women who are walking rhythmically on the sandbank, singing and ululating. Each woman has a bundle of mussels and an *ulugxa*, a piece of metal that they use to harvest *imbhaza* and *imbhatyisa*—as mussels and oysters are called—from the rocks when the waves have uncovered them. Some of the women are wearing gumboots while others walk barefoot. Two of them, NoGiant and Mam-Cirha, are also holding plastic bags that are full of oysters. They stop to talk with Qukezwa.

"Yo! This child of Zim! You have not gone to work today?" asks NoGiant.

"This child of Zim has wonders! That Dalton lets her do what she likes," adds MamCirha.

"Hey, Qukezwa! Why don't you ask your friend to buy our harvest?"

"There is plenty of imbhaza here to last him for many meals."

"And imbhatyisa too. Men love imbhatyisa!"

They all giggle knowingly.

Camagu is curious. He inspects the bundles of mussels. He is not one for seafood, and was not aware that the amaXhosa of the wild coast eat the slimy creatures from the sea. Qukezwa explains that they sell the best of their harvest to the Blue Flamingo Hotel, or to individual tourists. Male tourists like to buy imbhatyisa and eat them raw on the spot. Those imbhaza and imbhatyisa that have not been bought, the women take home to their families. They fry them with onions and use them as a relish to eat with maize porridge or samp. Although this is very tasty and healthy food, children are not allowed to eat oysters because they are an aphrodisiac. They make men frisky. That is why they are called imbhatyisa—that which makes one horny.

NoGiant and MamCirha try to persuade Camagu to buy some of the oysters, seeing that now he has the attention not only of the head-mistress but of Qukezwa as well. One giggles and whispers to the others, "A man needs all the strength he can get."

They burst out laughing. Camagu appreciates the joke, although he is a bit embarrassed by it. He laughs with them.

NoGiant says, "Seriously, though, you don't have to eat imbhatyisa raw. When you have fried it, it is such wonderful meat! Once you taste it you will never leave it again."

But Camagu tells her that he is staying at the hotel, where all his cooking is done for him. If he bought their harvest he would have nowhere to cook it. The women bid them good-bye, and continue their boisterous and songful walk to the village.

"You could have asked your thin girlfriend to cook it for you," says Qukezwa.

"Don't you start with me again," pleads Camagu.

"I doubt if she can even cook. What with her long red nails . . . like the talons of a vulture after ripping open a carcass."

"I didn't know you were Zim's daughter. I would like to meet your father," says Camagu, trying to change the subject.

"What for?"

"I would like to know why he is against progress."

Qukezwa laughs for a long time. Then she says, "Your thin girl-friend has been feeding you lies. That's the only thing she knows how to cook."

"I was at the imbhizo. I heard him opposing the building of the gambling complex that will create jobs and bring money into the village."

"Are you aware that if your gambling complex happens here I will have to pay to swim in this lagoon?"

"Why would you pay to swim in the sea?"

"Vathiswa says they made you a doctor in the land of the white man after you finished all the knowledge in the world. But you are so dumb. White man's education has made you stupid. This whole sea will belong to tourists and their boats and their water sports. Those women will no longer harvest the sea for their own food and to sell at the Blue Flamingo. Water sports will take over our sea!"

"There will be compensation for that. The villagers will get jobs at the casino."

"To do what? What do villagers know about working in casinos? What education do they have to do that kind of work? I heard one foolish Unbeliever say men will get jobs working in the garden. How many men? And what do they know about keeping those kinds of gardens? What do women know about using machines that clean? Well, maybe three or four women from the village may be taught to use them. Three or four women will get jobs. As for the rest of the workers, the owners of the gambling city will come with their own people who are experienced in that kind of work."

Camagu is taken aback both by her fervor and her reasoning. She is right. The gambling city may not be the boon the Unbelievers think it will be. It occurs to him that even during its construction, few men from the village, if any, will get jobs. Construction companies come with their own workers who have the necessary experience. Of course, a small number of jobs is better than no jobs at all. But if they are at the expense of the freedom to enjoy the sea and its bountiful harvests and the woods and the birds and the monkeys . . . then those few jobs are not really worth it. There is a lot of sense in what Qukezwa is saying. He is grudgingly developing some admiration for this scatterbrained girl with a Standard Eight education who works as a cleaner at Vulindlela Trading Store.

She walks away.

He follows her unquestioningly. She does not even look back to ask why he is following her. They waddle on the sand, past the holiday cottages and below the part of the village that faces the sea. They walk silently among tall grasses that are used for thatching houses. Then they get to the rocks that are covered with mosses of various colors. Camagu is fascinated by the yellows, the browns, the greens, and the reds that have turned the rocks into works of abstract art. Down below he can see a hut of rough thatch and twigs. It looks like the nest of a lazy bird. Outside, naked *abakhwetha* initiates are sitting in the sun, nursing their newly circumcised penises. The white ochre that covers their bodies makes them look like ghosts. One shouts at Camagu, asking for tobacco. But he walks on, following the relentless girl.

After about thirty minutes they reach Intlambo-ka-Nongqawuse—Nongqawuse's Valley. They are greeted by the sight of partridges and guinea fowls running among the cerise bellflowers, and among the orchids, cycads, and usundu palms.

When they reach Nongqawuse's Pool, Qukezwa speaks for the first time, asking him to throw some coins into the pool. He finds a few two-cent pieces in his pocket and throws them into the pool.

"That is not how things are done," she says softly. "You cannot throw brown money into the sacred pool. You need to throw silver so that your road will shine with good fortune. Your thin girlfriend should have advised you that when you came to Qolorha for the first time you ought to have come here to throw money into the sea, for that is where the ancestors are—the people that Nongqawuse spoke about."

"She is not my girlfriend, and she is not thin!"

"And she does not believe in the ancestors! Just like all of you whose heads have been damaged by white man's education."

"I believe in the ancestors, dammit! Where do you get off telling me I don't believe in the ancestors?" he shouts, throwing two shiny five-rand coins into the pool.

A white wild fig tree stands out among the green bushes. Camagu is lost in the antics of the birds that are eating the figs. Qukezwa pulls him by the shirtsleeve to the bank of the Gxarha River where it spews its water into the Indian Ocean. A flock of Egyptian geese takes off from the river. Camagu's eyes follow the brown, white, and black patterns until they disappear in the distance, far away, where the sea breathlessly meets the sky.

"Those birds used to come here only in summer," says Qukezwa. "But now they stay here all year round."

"You know a lot about birds and plants."

"I live with them."

Mist rises on the sea.

They are now walking among the broad-leafed wild strelitzia.

"These look like banana plants. I didn't know bananas grew in the Eastern Cape."

"It's not really a banana tree. It is called ikhamanga. White people call it wild banana. But it bears only the banana flower, never the fruit. Birds enjoy its nectar and its seeds."

The mist thickens.

Qukezwa has a distant look in her eyes.

"We stood here with the multitudes," she says, her voice full of nostalgia. "Visions appeared in the water. Nongqawuse herself stood here. Across the river the valley was full of ikhamanga. There were reeds too. They are no longer there. Only ikhamanga remains. And a few aloes. Aloes used to cover the whole area. Mist often covers this whole ridge right up to the lagoon where we come from. It was like that too in the days of Nongqawuse. We stood here and saw the wonders. The whole ridge was covered with people who came to see the wonders. Many things have changed. The reeds are gone. What remains now is that bush over there where Nongqawuse and Nombanda first met the Strangers. The bush. Ityholo-lika-Nongqawuse."

Camagu is seized by a bout of madness. He fights hard against the urge to hold this girl, tightly, and kiss her all over. It is different from the urge he once had: to hold and protect Xoliswa Ximiya. This woman does not need protecting. He does. He is breathing heavily as if he has just climbed a mountain, and his palms are sweating. Every part of his body has become a stranger to him. He convinces himself that this is temporary insanity: he is merely mesmerized by the romance of the place and the girl's passion for the prophets.

Yet his heart is pumping faster than ever!

He must run away from this siren. Away from her burning contours. After only two strides he trips over a pile of stones and falls. She helps him up, and her touch exacerbates the madness. Wonderful heat is consuming his whole body. Like the fires of hell.

She adds a stone to the pile.

"It is a cairn," she explains. "The amaXhosa call it *isivivane*. People from my Khoikhoi side said these were the graves of their prophet, Heitsi Eibib, the son of Tsiqwa. They were found at many crossroads. If you want the protection of the ancestors for a safe journey, you add a stone to the pile. Come on. Add a stone. Then you'll have a safe journey to America."

Camagu gingerly puts a stone on the cairn.

Qukezwa added another stone and sang a song in praise of Heitsi Eibib. Twin added a few twigs of aromatic buchu herbs. He gave another twig to Heitsi, who was wrapped in a blanket on his mother's back. She bent down so the child could put the twig on the stones. Then they continued on their way. Even though the crossroads was near their destination, they had made it a habit never to pass Heitsi Eibib's graves without performing the ritual.

The multitudes had already gathered at Mhlakaza's homestead. They wanted to see more miracles. They were demanding the presence of their forefathers from the spirit world. But Nongqawuse told them that the people who came from the sea were invisible. Those pilgrims who were favored by her were sent back to their homes to fetch a head of cattle each before they could be introduced to the new people.

Since Twin and Qukezwa no longer had cattle to look after, having killed all of them, they spent almost all their time at Mhlakaza's. They went to their homestead at Ngcizele only once a week to sweep the floors of their huts and the ground outside, so that when the day of the rising of the dead came, the headless Xikixa and the other ancestors before him would be welcomed to a clean homestead.

Twin and Qukezwa had become part of the prophets' hangers-on who were fed from the big pots of meat and samp that were steaming

all day long. The daily feasting, the spirit of brotherhood and sister-
hood that permeated the very air that they were breathing, the singing
and dancing, the hope for the future, all made the multitudes forget
about the troubles of the outside world and the lungsickness that tor-
tured the Unbelievers. Many of those who gathered daily at the banks
of the Gxarha River were like Twin and Qukezwa. They no longer had
any cattle to worry about. Lungsickness was a distant nightmare.

Sometimes the new people came riding on the waves. As usual only
Nongqawuse and Mhlakaza could see them. Or only those who had been
given permission by the prophets were able to see shadows of the new
people. Or at best silhouette images at the place where the sea met the sky.

In most cases, even the prophets themselves could not see the new
people with their eyes, for they manifested themselves in the form of
imilozi, the whistles that are the language of the spirits. Nongqawuse
and Nombanda spoke with the new people in whistles. Then they
translated their messages into the language of humans.

The fact that only Nongqawuse, Nombanda, and Mhlakaza could
see or speak to the new people enhanced the prestige of the prophets.
Many of those who were tempted not to believe were converted by
this fact.

"The new people say that as long as there are some among you
who refuse to kill their cattle, the dead will not arise," announced
Nongqawuse. "The new cattle that are free of disease will not come. As
long as the amaGogotya—the Unbelievers—continue to unbelieve, the
prophecies shall not be fulfilled."

This caused a lot of anger among the people. A beautiful life
awaited the amaXhosa nation. Yet there were traitors, the amaGogotya,
who wanted to spoil everything for everyone. They were the enemies
of the nation. Something had to be done. While Nongqawuse was
leading Qukezwa and a group of visitors to the valley to listen to the
lowing sounds of the new cattle in the aardvark holes and in the bush
where the Strangers had first appeared, Twin gathered the men behind
Mhlakaza's solitary hut. The only topic on the agenda was the course of
action that had to be taken against the Unbelievers.

"What choice do we have? Kill the amaGogotya! Destroy their
crops! Kill their cattle! Burn their houses!" the men shouted.

❋ ❋ ❋

Twin's heart began to bleed for Twin-Twin. He had not spoken with his brother for three weeks, since the last time they had exchanged insults. Twin-Twin had walked all the way to Ngcizele to persuade his brother one more time to stop the foolishness of killing his cattle, and to stop believing in the dreams of a sex-starved girl. To his astonishment he found that Twin had already killed all his cattle. His homestead was buzzing with flies, and the stench of rotten meat assailed one a mile away.

"It is your wife," Twin-Twin had screeched. "It is this terrible foreigner who made you do this stupid thing."

"She is not a foreigner. She is the original owner of this land," said Twin proudly.

"She is not an umXhosa woman. She is a prostitute."

"You call my wife that again and you will regret that you were ever born."

"Everyone knows that she opened her thighs for the British soldiers."

"For your freedom. You ungrateful little man. Now go and never darken my homestead with your evil presence. I never want to see you again."

That was the last time Twin had seen his brother. He had heard many stories about him. That he was riding around with Mjuza and Ned, in the company of no less a murderer than John Dalton. That they were denouncing the prophets and coercing people into defying the instructions of the Strangers.

"Can we trust Twin?" asked one man. "His twin brother is one of the staunchest Unbelievers. Will he not reveal our plans to him?"

Twin was angry at such impertinence. He stood up and addressed the man directly, pointing at him threateningly.

"Who are you, if I may ask? You only joined the Believers yesterday, long after my wife and I had been coming to the banks of the Gxarha River to commune with the new people through our humble prophets. I have on occasion even seen the new people with my own eyes. And you have the temerity to express doubts about me. Now let me assure those who may be stupid enough to listen to you. I am just as angry with the Unbelievers as everyone here. In fact, I am angrier! My twin brother is not just a passive Unbeliever. He is riding around with John Dalton, causing havoc to the Believers in the countryside. And do you know who John Dalton is? He is the man who beheaded my father. He and his comrades cooked the head of my father in a cauldron. It is the return of this headless ancestor that I am waiting for here at this spot where the Gxarha River spews its sacred waters into the sea. Do you, foolish man, still doubt me?"

The men apologized profusely, and reprimanded their colleague for speaking out of turn. They said that indeed Twin had a lot to lose if the resurrection failed due to the selfishness of the Unbelievers. The man shook Twin's hand. He had not meant any harm, he said. He suggested Twin's name as the leader of the secret force that would destroy the cattle and crops of the Unbelievers. And so Twin became a leader by acclamation.

He was determined to show everyone that he meant business, by leading a raid against his own brother. And although he normally shared everything with Qukezwa, he kept this plot a secret. But people talk. Soon she got to know of the plan and confronted him.

"This is terrible, Father of Heitsi! The ancestors will not like this," she warned.

"How can they not like it? I am doing this for them. So that they should be able to come back and join us. They won't rise from the dead if we don't kill all the cattle living. The white people will not be swept into the sea, but will continue to rule us."

"But he is your brother, from the same womb, at the same time."

"When did you become his defender? You know how he hates you."

"You are only doing this to impress the men. I heard how at first they doubted you. You are not doing it for the dead. You are doing it for the living."

For the first time Twin decided to go against the wishes of his wife. The life of the nation was at stake. His family would not be the first one to be at war over this matter. It was happening throughout the land. Not just between siblings. Even between husbands and wives. The women of the amaXhosa were the main cultivators of the land. Many of them refused to go to the fields even when their husbands were the staunchest of Unbelievers. Women became the strongest supporters of the prophets. Many of them left their husbands and went to live with their parents. Women were the leaders of the cattle-killing movement. Twin was therefore surprised that Qukezwa, she who had taught him how to talk directly with the one who told his stories in heaven, should seem to be getting cold feet at this dire hour.

Twin-Twin was not making things any better for himself. It was clear to everyone that he had immersed himself deeply in the shameless company of headhunters such as John Dalton. His unbelieving had started as a matter of common sense. At first he had no truck with those who were Unbelievers on the basis of their being followers of the god of the white man—those who called themselves amaGqobhoka or Christians. He continued to be faithful to the god of his fathers. But lately he was being seen more often with the likes of Mjuza and Ned, men who were benefiting from the new opportunities offered by the rule of the white man. Believers or amaThamba like Twin, on the other hand, belonged to the ranks of the common people, whose only salvation from the yoke of conquest lay in the fulfillment of the prophecies.

There were two groups of amaGogotya: those who built their homesteads deep inland in case there was truth in the prophecies that Unbelievers would be swept into the sea together with the white people, and those who defiantly established their homes by the sea, openly challenging the validity of the prophecies. Twin-Twin was becoming so fervent in his unbelief that it was rumored he was considering moving his vast homestead from KwaFeni to Ngcizele, to be close to the sea. Twin never got to know whether there was any truth in that, because it was at the time when he was no longer speaking to his brother. But the rumor strengthened his resolve to burn down Twin-Twin's homestead before he could become his neighbor.

The Unbelievers had powerful chiefs such as Sigidi and Nxito on their side. They worked closely with the government to root out the cattle-killing movement. This was against the wishes of Sarhili, the king of all amaXhosa, who had issued orders that the prophets must be obeyed.

John Dalton was having the best of times. He was the most enthusiastic of government agents, working directly under the magistrates who had been placed by The Man Who Named Ten Rivers and his predecessors at the courts of all the senior chiefs of the amaXhosa. He rode in the countryside routing out those who were thought to be Believers. This sent most of the movement underground, and made Twin and his followers even more determined to wage a guerrilla war against the Unbelievers and their colonial masters.

Twin led his men to destroy the Unbelievers' fields in the dead of the night. He started with his own brother's fields. He opened Twin-Twin's kraals and drove his cattle onto his fields and gardens to trample the crops. Then his men stabbed some of the prize bulls with spears. When Twin-Twin's family woke up the next morning, they were consumed by an explosive rage. The Unbelievers had great difficulty in stopping Twin-Twin from riding to Mhlakaza's homestead to show the traitors that he was not made of clay. It was at that very moment that the news arrived that Twin-Twin's senior wife, the one who had once been identified as a witch by Prophet Mlanjeni many years before, had run away to join the Believers on the banks of the Gxarha River.

He was devastated.

The hand of the Believers was strengthened by five more prophets who emerged in those lands of the amaXhosa that were under British rule. All of them claimed they were messengers of the ancestors that would rise from the sea to bring freedom to the people. Their message was the same as that of the great prophets of the Gxarha River—Nongqawuse and Nombanda. People had to kill their cattle and refrain from cultivating the land. One of the prophets, the wife of Councillor Bhulu, prophesied that on top of Ntaba kaNdoda Mountain there would be endless supplies of wild animal skins of all types and beautiful ornaments for wearing. These would be provided by the new people only if the amaXhosa gave up their witchcraft and killed all their cattle.

Another prophet, the daughter-in-law of Phetsheni, ordered the people to buy new axes to build kraals for the new cattle that would come with the new people. Like the rest of the prophets, she told the people, "Do not associate with white people! Do not join those who murdered the son of their own god! Or the god of the amaXhosa will punish you!"

While those chiefs who supported the cattle-killing movement did so secretly lest they incurred the wrath of the colonial magistrates, Chief Maqoma openly admitted to supporting it. Since he was the general who had gained great respect during the War of Mlanjeni, his support further strengthened the resolve of the Believers. Maqoma ordered that all those who lived in his chiefdom should actively participate in the activities of the cattle-killing movement. Those who disobeyed the orders were threatened with banishment.

But chiefs who were Believers continued to cultivate their land. Their territories became targets of Twin's marauding destroyers.

Not long after destroying Twin-Twin's crops, Twin led a party of armed men to his brother's homestead again. They went first to his kraals, their spears ready for a massacre. But the kraals were empty, except for three milk cows. Twin-Twin had sent his remaining cattle with his sons to hide in the Amathole Mountains.

The armed men turned their wrath on the huts and set them alight. Crackling sounds filled the air, and a black cloud billowed above the homestead. A large swath was splashed with an orange glow as the flames raced to the sky, only to be swallowed by the black cloud. Shadows of screaming women and children ran helter-skelter. Some were trying to save their valued belongings from the burning houses. Twin-Twin was urging them to leave everything and save their lives. He was running from hut to hut, making sure that all his children were safe, when he came face-to-face with his brother, leading the men who were now singing triumphantly and dancing around the burning homestead.

"You . . . child of my mother . . . you did this to me?" he croaked in a voice stifled by horror.

But Twin did not answer. Instead he beckoned his men to move on. There were more homesteads to burn.

o o o

Twin-Twin and his wives and children found themselves exiled in the mountains. There were many other families who had also lost everything. They were huddled under the cliffs, where old Nxito's councillors ministered to them. Chief Nxito himself was in exile at a secret place, having been driven away from his chiefdom at Qolorha near the Gxarha River by the activities of the Believers.

Most of the refugees in the mountains were the Unbelievers who believed—it was in the days when Unbelievers believed—in Qamata, the god of the amaXhosa. The one who was called Mdalidephu or Mvelingqangi by various prophets of old. Those Unbelievers who believed in Thixo, the god of the white man, were rumored to have been given succor on the grounds of the magistrates' courts, and some as far afield as the Native Hospital in Kingwilliamstown. They were supplied with blankets and food.

This was the most humiliating time for Twin-Twin. Here he was, a man of means and standing, reduced to a beggar. He was sitting around a fire with other wretched people, where they would spend the night under the stars.

It was clear to him that some Unbelievers were beginning to waver. He listened in distress to idle gossip about Unbelievers who were converting into Believers and were throwing their spades and plows into the river. He heard of women who attempted to cultivate their fields but were fixed to the ground, unable to move. Some women were carried into the sea by strong winds when they tried to sow. And a man who went to cut the bush in order to fence his compound was swept up by a whirlwind, which left him suspended in the air.

Although these stories were told in great laughter, Twin-Twin found them very distressing.

His scars began to itch. They transported him to his flagellation by Prophet Mlanjeni's men years before. The itching was so severe that he had to roll himself on the rough ground and scratch himself against a boulder.

Bhonco's scars are playing up again. Whenever he is upset by the Believers the scars itch. And when that happens he is blinded even to the beautiful things that make him weep. He is blinded by anger. He needs NoPetticoat by his side. She has a way of soothing him, and scratching the scars gently, almost caressing them, until he is lulled to sleep. And in his sleep he joins his forefathers wandering on the mountain, digging out roots to feed their children and lamenting the folly of belief.

When he wakes up he is fresh again, and eager to enjoy life. He is ready to cry for beautiful things. And these include the fresh breeze that comes from the sea. He takes a walk with the view of bathing his lungs in the air.

"Tat'uBhonco!"

It is Camagu. The elder is glad to see him. He has heard things about this man and his daughter. But he pretends he knows nothing. He will pretend he knows nothing until an official delegation from the young man's family—for to him he is a young man—comes and asks for the girl's hand. And from what the gossips have told him it may be soon.

"I have not seen you for a long time," says the elder. "Since the day of that imbhizo that I do not even want to think about. Has this village been taking care of you well?"

"Very well, my father. So well that I think I want to stay here and build a new life among the people of Qolorha."

Bhonco smiles. Then he remembers that as an Unbeliever he is not supposed to smile. He is supposed to be angry about the folly of belief that started before the Middle Generations, and about the sufferings of the Middle Generations. And that must be reflected in his face. Oh, the burdens that have been placed on his kindly disposition by his Cult of the Unbelievers!

He replaces the smile with a frown.

"So, you want to stay here now? Have you told the chief about this? If you are going to be one of his subjects you need to put the matter before him," advises Bhonco.

"At the moment I am just toying with the idea," says Camagu.

Are the gossips true then, that things have developed to such a serious extent between this learned man and his daughter? Why else would he want to give up the comforts of the city of Johannesburg, and of the wonderland that is America? He begins to pity those misguided souls who laughed at his daughter's spinsterhood. See who will have the last laugh! And with a man who has seen the world joining his family, a man who knows what development is all about, the Believers do not stand a chance. This may yet be a thing to weep about.

In his head he can already hear the bridesmaids singing *umbhororho* songs in preparation for the wedding that future generations will talk about. He cannot wait to tell NoPetticoat the wonderful news.

"You will excuse me, son," he says. "I must rush home. I forgot something."

As he rushes home he remembers that lately his daughter has been talking of going to live in the city to work for the government. She has been showing her unhappiness with her lot in the village, even though as principal of Qolorha-by-Sea Secondary School she is the second most important person in the village after the chief. And the chief is a headless twit whose only function in society is to eat bribes. What if this Camagu is the passport to the city that his daughter has been looking for? Then he will never see his daughter again. He will lose all the prestige he is currently enjoying due to his daughter's position. Perhaps he shouldn't be too enthusiastic about this wedding after all.

Camagu climbs the hill to Vulindlela Trading Store. From the top he is moved by the view below: the waves that smash against the rocks with musical violence, the Gxarha River that flows into the Indian Ocean with misty grace, the sacred ikhamanga bushes, and the pining Nong-qawuse's Valley. He left his car at the hotel and walked on foot precisely because he wanted to enjoy this view. He thinks of Qukezwa. He hopes to have a glimpse of her. That is why he is going to Vulindlela Trading Store. To have a glimpse of Qukezwa, even if it's a fleeting one.

He has not seen her since he was attacked by a fit of madness a week ago. He has returned to the lagoon and to Nongqawuse's Valley over and over again, hoping she would be there, but she has been nowhere to be found.

Unfortunately the store is not busy today. He had hoped that it would be possible to lose himself among the customers while his eyes furtively searched for Qukezwa. But all the eyes of the salespeople are on him. It is obvious that wagging tongues have been doing the rounds. John Dalton comes out of his small office to greet him.

"I hear that things are happening between you and Bhonco's daughter," the trader says with a naughty glint in his eyes. "Maybe now you'll decide to stay with us for a while . . . especially because you haven't found your passport yet."

"How do you know that?"

"Well, this is a village. People talk. They say you haven't been able to locate NomaRussia, but at least you have found love."

"If I decide to stay for a while it won't be because of Xoliswa Ximiya. My soul has been captured by this valley."

"So you will stay then?"

"Just for a while. Until I sort my thoughts out. I need to earn a living, though. I have a few ideas in my mind."

"That is wonderful. You could be very useful in our self-help projects."

"Hey, I don't want to be part of the war between the Believers and Unbelievers."

"Why should you? Most people here don't care about those petty quarrels. They want to see development happening. They want clean water. They want health delivery services. They see Bhonco and Zim and their small bands of followers as clowns who are holding desperately to the quarrels of the past. But the whole thing frustrates development."

"Some people may say you are the one who is frustrating development since you have joined the Believers in opposing the casino and holiday resort."

"I have not joined the Believers. On this issue of the gambling city they happen to be on the same side as me. The gambling city will destroy this place."

Camagu agrees. He says that at first he did not understand the reasons for the opposition to what the Unbelievers call progress. But now it is clear to him that the gambling city will not benefit the village. He does not mention that he received this piece of wisdom from Qukezwa.

"Instead of creating jobs," adds Camagu, "it will take all the little money that there is in the village. I have been to casinos in other parts of the country and in Lesotho. During the day you find all sorts of ordinary poor people, mostly women, gambling their money away, hoping to hit that elusive jackpot. That is what we'll find here. While husbands toil in the mines of Johannesburg, their wives will be gambling their sweat away."

"You are so right. The men themselves will gamble their fortunes away when they are on leave. But let's think about you. If you're staying here for a while you need to get proper accommodation. You can't stay at the hotel indefinitely . . . unless, of course, you are a millionaire."

Dalton tells him about a sea cottage that is owned by a doctor who lives in Butterworth. She rents it out to inland people who want to hold parties or wedding receptions at the sea. This happens mostly in December during the holiday season. Most of the year the cottage is unoccupied. Dalton thinks that the doctor will be happy to have someone looking after it. He undertakes to talk with her about letting Camagu stay there as a caretaker.

They decide to go and see Zim at his homestead to tell him the good news. As they climb into Dalton's four-wheel-drive bakkie, Camagu sees Qukezwa cleaning a number of big pots on the lawn near the store. He waves at her. She does not wave back.

When they get to Zim's homestead, Zim is reclining under his tree, in the company of his amahobohobo weaverbirds. He is talking to the birds in whistles.

"It is the language of the spirits," he explains to his visitors after greeting them. "It is the language that the prophets used when they talked with the new people."

He says he is happy to see Camagu, although he does not understand what he is doing here. Everyone knows that he has been bought by the Unbelievers with the thighs of Bhonco's daughter. People have even seen him at the memory rituals of the Unbelievers.

"They say you are a total Unbeliever," adds Zim. "You have been brought here by them to reinforce their stand in destroying our forests and our birds and our lizards."

"There is no truth in that," says Camagu, trying to hide his annoyance.

"Then what were you doing at Bhonco's place, where they arrogantly go back to the world of the ancestors to bother them with their petty problems? Where they take glory in the pain of yesterday instead of savoring the pleasures of today?"

"They glory in pain to enjoy the pleasures of today better."

"See?" says the elder excitedly. "He even knows their things. He is defending them. He is one of them."

John Dalton comes to Camagu's defense. "Do not fight with the stranger, Tat'uZim," he says. "He is on our side."

"Since when? Is he not Bhonco's son-in-law?"

"I am not anyone's son-in-law," says Camagu, beginning to lose his patience. "And I am not an Unbeliever. I am not a Believer either. I don't want to be dragged into your quarrels. My ancestors were not even here among yours when the beginning of your bad blood happened. I come from a different part of the country."

"Yes," adds Dalton, "let us leave believing and unbelieving out of this. We have come to talk about development."

"Well, you cannot claim that your ancestors were not here too, Dalton," says Zim, ejecting a black jet of nicotine-filled spittle. It lands on the ground in front of the visitors.

"I wish you wouldn't do that, Tat'uZim," says Dalton.

Spitting is one thing he is not prepared to tolerate among his people. They spit anywhere, anytime, especially when they are puffing on their long pipes.

"You forget that this is my homestead, Dalton. This is not Vulindlela."

The birds are making too much noise. They are overly excited today. It means that soon the weather will change. They are talking of rain. And since the men have to shout to hear one another, Zim suggests that they go into one of his hexagons. Camagu is relieved, for they have been standing all this time, while the elder addressed them from his reclining position.

The room is sparsely furnished. They sit at the pine table and talk about their strategies in opposing the casino and holiday resort. Camagu learns that a project of this magnitude cannot be built without cutting down the forest of indigenous trees, without disturbing the bird life, and without polluting the rivers, the sea, and its great lagoon.

"But what alternative do we offer?" asks Camagu. "If we oppose development projects that people believe will give them jobs, we must be able to offer an alternative. I heard that day at the imbhizo that they think you are taking this stand for John's benefit. They say as things stand now, only his store and the Blue Flamingo Hotel benefit from tourists. And of course John's lackeys—NoVangeli and NoManage."

"Surely you don't believe that," protests Dalton.

"The important thing is that they do. We need to work out a plan of how the community can benefit from these things that we want to preserve. We need—"

His heart skips a beat as he catches a glimpse of Qukezwa passing at the door. She is whistling to the birds, and they whistle back excitedly.

"Come, Qukezwa," says her father. "Let me introduce you to the visitor from Johannesburg."

She walks into the hexagon. She looks quite haggard in her blue-and-yellow floral dress and her black Pierre Cardin woolen cap. She greets the guests respectfully.

"This is my daughter . . . the only child I have. Her brother, Twin, was swallowed by the big city."

"I have met her a few times before," says Camagu as he shakes her hand.

"I do not remember meeting you," she says abruptly, and then walks out.

"Prepare something for the visitors," Zim calls after her.

A few moments later she returns with steaming plates of samp cooked with beans and relished with boiled oysters and mussels.

Fixing her eyes on Camagu, she announces, "This relish is im-bhatyisa."

"I always come here when I want to eat the food of the ama-Xhosa," says Dalton, digging into the samp with a spoon. The sauce splashes all over his beard.

"It is delicious," says Camagu.

"Some people like to fry imbhatyisa with onion," explains Zim. "But I like them boiled. The secret lies in boiling them without salt, for they have their own salt from the sea."

The next day Camagu is at the great lagoon. He comes here every day, even though he has now lost all hope of meeting Qukezwa again. He simply cannot understand her. Yesterday, for instance. Why did she pretend not to know him? And she was not just doing that for the benefit of her father and Dalton. She has done this before. Once when they met at Intlambo-ka-Nongqawuse. She vowed that they had never met before. Yet she was the one who first planted the seed in his mind when she propositioned him the very first time they saw each other. Out of the blue.

He is not used to being approached by women in such a manner. It is obvious that she usually does this sort of thing. Who knows how many traveling salesmen who come to Vulindlela Trading Store she has approached this way? How many tourists? She might be a reservoir for all sorts of diseases. He must completely forget about her, and resume his friendship with Xoliswa Ximiya. And his search for NomaRussia.

But Qukezwa will not allow him to forget about her. She approaches from the opposite direction, stamping her feet so hard that they dig deep footprints on the sandbank. She is holding an ulugxa, the piece of iron that is used to harvest oysters, mussels, and even abalone. She smiles at him and says, "How did you like the imbhatyisa yesterday?"

He is absolutely fed up with her. He grabs her arm and demands, "Why did you pretend you didn't know me?"

"How did you like the imbhatyisa?" she insists.

"It was good. Now answer my question."

"Didn't it do something to your body?"

"Like what? Don't be crazy."

But she is doing something to his body. He turns away so that she should not see his shameful state. She giggles and wants to know what is wrong.

"Nothing," he says. "Did you come to harvest the sea?"

"Yes. But it cannot be done today," she explains, "when the tide is like this. See? The water has turned from blue to black. The sand has become blue. Water covers the rocks. Those who try to harvest imbhatyisa or imbhaza will not get them today. When the sea is like this you can expect a terrible storm."

"So what are we doing here if there's going to be a storm?"

"I don't know what you are doing here. I love the sea. The sea loves me."

She had always been scared of the sea, she tells him. Until her mother's death three years ago. Her mother, NoEngland, always warned her never to go to the sea alone or with other children. Whenever she wanted to visit the sea, she had to ask her mother, who would then request an adult to accompany her. The chaperone was given strict instructions not to allow her even to put her feet in the water. As a result she never learned how to swim. She used to envy girls her age who could go out to swim or harvest imbhaza, imbhatyisa, and amangquba—which is the abalone or perlemoen—from the rocks of the ocean.

Once, when she was a student at Qolorha-by-Sea Secondary School, she nearly drowned. She went to the sea with a friend without her mother's permission. She took off her school uniform and tried to swim in her panties. She became stuck between two rocks, and couldn't move an inch. Waves came, buried her, receded, only to come back again. She thought she was going to die. Her friend ran to the village to call for help.

That night NoEngland gave her a thorough hiding.

Since her mother's death she has learned how to swim, and has become quite an expert at harvesting the sea. Now she swims with a vengeance and is not scared of the most vicious storms.

"As for you," she says sadistically, "when the storm comes it will sweep you away. You didn't cleanse yourself when you first came here.

You must drink water from the sea when you are a stranger, so that the sea can get used to you. Then it will love you. Even your skin will be smoother, and you'll look a bit more beautiful. You need it."

She walks away. She does not even say good-bye. She just walks away. He looks at her with pitiful eyes. How he longs to lose his breath in hers. But then, after that had been done, what would they talk about?

John Dalton was telling Chief Nxito's councillors that all Sir George Grey wanted was to spread British civilization. His magnanimous wish was to convert the amaXhosa from their barbarous ways. It was for their own good that they should discard their customs and follow the ways of the English. There was no saving grace in the culture and religion of the natives. The cattle-killing movement proved this beyond all doubt. It was a great setback to his civilizing mission.

"But he is taking more and more of the land of the amaXhosa," complained Twin-Twin.

"What is land compared to civilization?" asked Dalton impatiently. "Land is a small price to pay for a gift that will last you a lifetime . . . that will be enjoyed by your future generations. The gift of British civilization!"

"The Man Who Named Ten Rivers' civilizing mission is taking food from the mouths of our children," insisted Twin-Twin. He had shown on many occasions that he was not in awe of this British officer who had beheaded his father. And he had not forgotten that incident either. As far as he was concerned it was for his own convenience that they were on the same side today. One day the opportunity to avenge his father's head would present itself.

Dalton shook his head pityingly. He had never really trusted this man. He was not happy when Ned and Mjuza suggested that he should be saved from his mountain refuge and set up in a new homestead in Qolorha, near Chief Nxito's deserted Great Place, where he would receive protection from the marauding bands of Believers. Dalton had to go along with the idea because it was important to show the natives—especially those who were heathens like Twin-Twin—that people who were on the side of the British Empire would receive full protection. But this man had shown with his needling questions and comments that he was not really on the side of Her Imperial Majesty.

"Your savage practices are taking food from your children's mouths, not Sir George," said Dalton. "Sir George did not kill your cattle or burn your crops. Your own people did."

People murmured among themselves that there were rumors among some Unbelievers that in fact The Man Who Named Ten Rivers was responsible for the cattle-killing movement, so as to break the might of the amaXhosa and subjugate even those lands across the Kei River that the British had failed to conquer. Some were even saying that one of the Strangers Nongqawuse saw behind the bush was in fact The Man Who Named Ten Rivers in person. But John Dalton did not hear these rumors. He was going on about Sir George's magnanimity of spirit, his intelligence, his charm, and his unconditional love for the native peoples of the world, which he had already demonstrated to the natives of a country called New Zealand across the seas.

Dalton was preparing his listeners for the forthcoming visit of The Man Who Named Ten Rivers, who was riding throughout kwaXhosa, calling on chiefs and on the colonial magistrates attached to those chiefs. He was expected to visit Nxito the following day. The sad thing was that this visit was not going to happen at Nxito's chiefdom, in Qolorha near the Gxarha River. The aged chief was still keeping his distance from the Believers, who had taken over that whole area and were acting as if they themselves were the chiefs.

"But the governor does not want any ceremony," warned Dalton. "He wants this visit to be as quiet as possible. He just wants to talk to the chiefs about the affairs of the nation, and to discuss with you the benefits of accepting British rule without question or rebellion."

Even though John Dalton had told them that The Man Who Named Ten Rivers wanted no ceremony, his hosts did lot expect him to arrive as quietly as he did, accompanied only by a small entourage which included Dalton and John Gawler, the young magistrate in Chief Mhala's district.

Twin-Twin remembered the boot-licking rituals of Sir Harry Smith, the erstwhile Great White Chief, and the pompous ceremonies of Sir George Cathcart, whose demise at the hands of the Russians was celebrated by the amaXhosa. He remembered the Great White Chief riding arrogantly all over the place, making a show of his power as a representative of the British Empire, and even whipping some of the revered elders of the amaXhosa.

The Man Who Named Ten Rivers was different. He did not even want a public meeting. He just wanted to talk privately with the chief and his most trusted councillors. Twin-Twin felt honored that he was one of those councillors. As usual, John Dalton was the interpreter.

"I am visiting all the chiefs in Xhosaland with the same message of peace," he said in measured tones. "You want peace, we want peace, all decent human beings want peace. It is possible for us to live together in harmony."

He went on to say that he had come to see Nxito because, as King Sarhili's uncle, and as a respected elder who was almost eighty years old and who was also an Unbeliever, the chief could have great influence on his fellow chiefs. He could even persuade his nephew to stop supporting the cattle-killing movement and to acquiesce to the good intentions of the British government, who wanted only to bring civilization and progress to the amaXhosa people. The British government was coming with a new administrative system, devised by the governor himself. He made it clear that the chiefs had no option but to accept it. He had already visited a number of them privately, each in his own district, where he outlined the grand plans he had drawn up. The chiefs were all happy with them. But the cattle-killing movement was a serious distraction to the new system. It was crucial that it be stopped.

"What can Nxito really do, since he himself is in exile far away from his chiefdom at the Gxarha River?" asked Twin-Twin.

"The chief must go back to his chiefdom," said Gawler. "Otherwise the Believers will think they have the upper hand."

"It is dangerous for the chief," pleaded Twin-Twin.

"And why is it not dangerous for you?" asked Dalton. "We have recently established your homestead at Qolorha near the Gxarha River. We have given you adequate protection there. We can do the same for the old man."

But it turned out that Nxito's situation was complicated. His son, Pama, a staunch Believer, had taken over his chiefdom. Nxito's was a house divided. It was the same with many families. Even a great Believer like Chief Maqoma, the revered general of the War of Mlanjeni, was opposed by his sons, Ned and Kona, who were not only staunch Unbelievers but Christians as well. Ned even worked at the Native Hospital. Then there was the rift between Twin and Twin-Twin. And there was Mjuza, whose father was the great Prophet Nxele. Yet Mjuza was an Unbeliever. Families were being split apart.

The Man Who Named Ten Rivers did not really care how they dealt with Nxito's problem. He could not be expected to solve every petty problem for them. The important thing was that Nxito was Sarhili's uncle. He had a duty to warn his nephew of the dangers of his ways.

"I have written to Kreli and warned him that the continued cattle-killing will cause starvation and disorder," said The Man Who Named Ten Rivers. Kreli was the name the colonists used for Sarhili. "I am going to hold him fully responsible for anything that happens as a result, and I will punish him severely. I am a good friend of Kreli and his people. It is my desire to continue so. But if he forces me to take a contrary course, he shall find me a better enemy than I have been a friend."

The governor then broke into a smile, and told them how he loved the amaXhosa people and that he didn't want to see them destroying themselves. He had established health programs for them, which were an unqualified success. There was, for instance, a Dr. Fitzgerald who had come with him from New Zealand. He was an ophthalmic surgeon, and he performed cataract operations that gave him fame throughout kwaXhosa as a man of miracles who could make blind people see. Fitzgerald was treating more than fifty people a day. But what amazed The Man Who Named Ten Rivers was that even those amaXhosa who benefited from Fitzgerald's medicine continued to go to their own traditional doctors as well.

"It is because Fitzgerald heals only the ailing body," explained Twin-Twin. "But our amaXhosa doctors are also spiritual healers. They are like priests in your churches of amaGqobhoka. They don't only end there. They heal the head and the mind."

"That is precisely what we must change," said the governor. "We must get rid of all these superstitions. That is what civilization will do for you. That is another matter I have been discussing with the chiefs. You see, I plan to open a school in Cape Town for the sons of chiefs, where they will grow up in the bosom of British civilization. They will learn to appreciate the might of the British Empire and will acquire new modes of behavior. They will give up their barbaric culture and heathen habits, and when they take over in their chiefdoms they will be good chiefs. I want all the chiefs to undertake to send their sons to this school."

"The chiefs that you have already met . . . what do they say?" asked Nxito.

"For some reason they are reluctant. They don't understand. They think they will be giving up their children. It is for elders like you who have a better understanding of these things to convince them otherwise."

The Man Who Named Ten Rivers said he was heartened by the manner in which he was received by the chiefs throughout the territories he visited. It showed that his pacification and civilizing missions were succeeding. As soon as he reached Cape Town in a few weeks' time he would write to the colonial secretary of state in England to brief him fully that the Xhosa people were not at all hostile to the colonial administration.

"A few weeks' time?" asked Gawler. "Does this mean His Excellency hasn't completed his rounds on the frontier?"

"I still have a few chiefs to see before I go back to Cape Town," replied the governor.

"I fear for His Excellency's health," said Gawler. "This trip has been quite rigorous."

The Man Who Named Ten Rivers was irritated. He felt that the young upstart was undermining his manliness and his vast experience as an English explorer who had pioneered some of the most dangerous places in the new world, who had walked uncharted territories in Australia and New Zealand, and who had given names to ten rivers. Gawler apologized and assured His Excellency that he had not meant to be disrespectful.

Perhaps the governor should have heeded the magistrate's friendly warning. Before his rounds on the wild frontier were over, he suffered a nervous breakdown and had to be sent back to Cape Town hallucinating and blubbering.

While Twin-Twin was discussing civilization with The Man Who Named Ten Rivers, Twin was dreaming of Heitsi Eibib. He used the dreams to transform himself into the new Heitsi Eibib of the ama-Xhosa people, the one who would lead them across the Great River, in the same way that the true Heitsi Eibib of old had led the Khoikhoi people. The same way that he had instructed the water to part, and when it obeyed he led his people to safety. But when the enemy tried to cross between the parted water . . . when the enemy was in the middle . . . the water closed in again, and the enemy drowned. Only in Twin's dreams, the enemy that was swallowed by the Great River was led by The Man Who Named Ten Rivers, accompanied by none other than the famous headhunter, John Dalton.

Whenever Twin awoke from such dreams, his fervor for the girl-prophets multiplied tenfold.

He was distressed about the rift between himself and Twin-Twin. He blamed it all on his twin brother's stubbornness. And on his father's headlessness. Because the British had cut his head off, Xikixa was not being an effective ancestor. A good ancestor is one who can be an emissary between the people of the world and the great Qamata. A good ancestor comes between his feuding descendants whenever they sacrifice a beast to him, and brings peace among them. Without a head Xikixa was unable to bring cohesion to his progeny. That was why they were fighting among themselves, and were destined to do so until his headless state was remedied.

Only the resurrection of the dead could restore the elder's dignity. And the dignity of all the amaXhosa people, dead or alive. It would bring about a regeneration of the earth. The new redeemer that the girl-prophets talked about, son of Sifuba-Sibanzi the Broad-Chested One, would lead this re-enactment of the original creation. The long-departed relatives of the amaXhosa people would come back from the world of the ancestors and would once more walk the earth of the living. The white colonists would disappear. So would the lungsickness that they had brought from across the oceans.

The greatest joy of the Believers was that Prophet Nxele—who had drowned trying to escape from Robben Island some thirty years before—would come back and lead the people to victory over the colonists, in the same way that he had led the Russian army that had vanquished Cathcart in the Crimean War. It did not matter that Mjuza, Nxele's son and heir, had rejected the prophecies of Nongqawuse. Mjuza was a lost cause who had been deceived by his colonial masters.

These were the happiest times for Twin and Qukezwu. They had few cares in the world. They wandered on their uncultivated fields or on the sands of the sea, daydreaming of the wonderful life that awaited them. They sang the praises of Mhlakaza, Nongqawuse, and Nombanda. Their hearts overflowed with love and goodwill. So did the hearts of all Believers.

And they looked beautiful too. Ever since Nongqawuse had ordered her followers to adorn themselves in their finery in celebration of the imminent arrival of the ancestors, Qukezwa would not be seen without her makeup of red and yellow ochre. Even old women who had long given up the practice of decorating themselves were seen covered in ochre and resplendent in ornaments. They knew that as soon as the ancestors arrived from the Otherworld, their youth would be restored.

Finally the date of the resurrection was set by the prophets. The full moon of June 1856. The Believers waited with anticipation. But the day came and went like any other day. No miracles and wonders were seen at the Gxarha. Nor anywhere else in the lands of the amaGcaleka and throughout kwaXhosa. This was the First Disappointment.

Some Believers began to unbelieve, and King Sarhili was roused to anger. He called an imbhizo at his Great Place, where all the important men of the amaGcaleka clan were invited.

"How can we trust these prophets when they fail to keep their word?" he asked. "Why are they keeping the new people from rising? Until the prophets keep their word I shall command that the slaughter of the cattle should stop."

"Mhlakaza must be forced to show us the new people!" cried the men. "He must prove to us that his word is true!"

When the prophet of Gxarha was finally hurled before them, he explained that the ancestors had failed to arise because on that day they had gone on a visit to an inaccessible corner of the Otherworld. He had been unable to get hold of them. Why, they had even been beyond the reach of greater prophets like Nongqawuse and Nombanda.

"But since then we have spoken with them," he assured the elders. "The rising of the dead will still happen. The next full moon will be the moon of wonders and dangers. On that great day two suns will rise in the sky. They will be red like the color of blood. In the middle of the sky, over Ntaba kaNdoda, our sacred mountain, they will collide, and the whole world will be in darkness. A great storm will arise, and only those huts that are newly thatched in preparation for the arrival of our ancestors will survive it. Out of the earth, at the mouths of all our great rivers, the dead will arise with their new cattle. Our forefathers will finally come wearing white blankets and shiny brass rings. And be warned, all you Unbelievers: the English and their collaborators, all those traitors who wear trousers, will be swallowed by the sea, which will take them back to the place of creation whence they came . . . to be re-created into better people."

The next full moon was in mid-August. Twin and Qukezwa did not sleep that night. They joined the revelers at the banks of the Gxarha River, and filled the valleys of Qolorha with song and laughter. The hills echoed the joyous sounds, and sent shivers down the spines of the colonists.

While all the carousing was going on, Heitsi slept on a grass mat behind Mhlakaza's hut. He was not alone. There were other toddlers and babies of the Believers. They were looked after by those girls who were too young to participate in the revelry. Heitsi was getting used to this. Of late he was spending a lot of time with strangers while Qukezwa attended to matters of belief.

Soon the night was a memory. Everyone was tired. But no one slept. They wanted to see with their eyes the wonders and dangers.

Qukezwa sat on the bank of the Gxarha River, rocking Heitsi on her lap and singing a lullaby that she had learned from her Khoikhoi people. Her eyes were looking fixedly at the horizon, waiting for the two red suns to burst out of the pink-and-purple skies. Her husband sat behind her, and joined in the call-and-response parts of the lullaby. His eyes were red and his breath reeked like a pigsty. When he belched, one could actually see waves of deadly fumes assailing the crisp air of dawn. His head was pounding with a hangover and lack of sleep. Yet he was going to soldier on for the rest of the day. If he slept, who would welcome Xikixa and the rest of the distinguished ancestors?

The sun that rose was not red. Perhaps it would change color on the first steps of its journey across the sky. Perhaps a second one would rise. The Believers watched in breathless anticipation. The solitary sun walked across the sky as if it was just another day. It took its time, as it always did when it was watched. No other sun came. No great collision happened. No darkness. Instead the day was brighter than usual. The people had waited in vain. The ancestors did not venture out of the mouths of the rivers.

This was the Second Disappointment.

Once more there was anger directed at the sacred persons of the prophets. While the staunch Believers held tightly to their belief, the weak let disillusionment get the better of them. King Sarhili summoned Mhlakaza, who denied that he was the source of the prophecies. He put all the blame on Nongqawuse.

"She is the one who talks with the new people," he said. "I am merely her mouth."

King Sarhili retreated to Manyube, a conservation area and nature reserve where people were not allowed to chop trees or hunt animals and birds. He had often told his people, "One day these wonderful things of nature will get finished. Preserve them for future generations." There he was able to think things over in a peaceful environment. He decided to issue a decree that chiefs should ban all further cattle-killing activities in their chiefdoms.

But a few days later the Believers were encouraged by new reports that the new people had been seen taking a stroll in the countryside near the mouths of the great rivers. This proved that the prophecies had not failed completely. Perhaps something had gone wrong somewhere. Soon the truth was discovered. The fault lay with the people who had sold their cattle off instead of slaughtering them. And those who slaughtered them without going through the ritual of preserving their *imiphefumlo*, their souls.

This explanation of the Second Disappointment was good enough for Sarhili. He issued new orders that the cattle-killing should continue. This time he pushed it relentlessly. He was like a man possessed. He rode once more from his Great Place at Hohita to Qolorha, where he conferred with the prophets.

Qukezwa and Twin were among the multitudes that accompanied the king to the river. He rode further than the mouth of the Gxarha River, all the way to the mouth of the Kei River. And there he saw his father, the great King Hintsa, who had been beheaded by the British twenty-one years before. He was among a host of new people who appeared in boats at the mouth of the river. They told the king that they had come to liberate the black nations, and that this message must be passed throughout the world. In the meantime the cattle-killing movement must be strengthened.

Sarhili was very excited. He announced to the multitudes, "I have seen my father! I have seen Hintsa face-to-face."

That night, as provisions were being cooked for the king and his entourage for the long ride back to his Great Place, he decided to take a walk. When he came back he announced that he had seen his father again.

"I met my father among the wild mielies," he said. "He gave me the spear that was buried with him. I have it now."

His words sparked a new wave of cattle-killing. And a new fervor in Twin and Qukezwa. Sacred fires were burning in their chests, jetting out of their mouths in the form of sermons that rendered the words of the prophets to the multitudes.

King Sarhili took the message of the new people seriously. As soon as he returned to his Great Place he sent emissaries to other black leaders in the region, to exhort them to kill their cattle. King Moshoeshoe of the Basotho people sent his own messengers to Qolorha to find out what all this cattle-killing meant. But none of the other kings heeded the prophecies.

At the same time, Mhlakaza was extending a hand of reconciliation to the white settlers. He was asking them to kill their cattle and destroy their crops as well, for the sake of their own redemption. He invited them to come to the Gxarha River to see for themselves and hear the good news of the resurrection.

"It is not enough for you to read the big black book," he warned them. "You must throw away your witchcraft. The people that have come have not come to make war but to bring about a better state of things for all."

But the colonists were too stubborn to accept his invitation. What the Believers had suspected all along, that the whites were beyond redemption, was confirmed. What else would one expect from people who were a product of a different creation from that of the amaXhosa, people who were so unscrupulous that they killed the son of their own god?

While Twin was trying to come to grips with issues of faith, Twin-Twin was grappling with his conscience. It seemed to him that his unbelief was sinking him deeper into collaboration with the conquerors of his people. Although he was strong enough to resist conversion, some of his fellow Unbelievers were becoming Christians. And when they did, they sang praises of the queen of the conquerors, asking some god to save her. That worried him a lot. He did not want the queen to be saved. He wanted nothing more than to see the complete disappearance of the colonists from kwaXhosa. But the way of Nongqawuse was not the way.

Chief Nxito seemed to depend increasingly on Twin-Twin's counsel, especially because Twin-Twin was now stationed at Qolorha under the protection of the British government, and was able to see what was happening in the old man's chiefdom. Whenever the chief had to meet representatives of The Man Who Named Ten Rivers—even if it was merely John Dalton—Twin-Twin was required to be there.

He was there when Dalton and Gawler arrived with new instructions from The Man Who Named Ten Rivers. The chiefs would henceforth receive a monthly salary in colonial money. They were no longer allowed to impose fines on those who were found guilty at the chiefs' courts. Councillors like Twin-Twin who assisted the chiefs in exchange for a share of those fines would now also be paid by the government. This would make them loyal to the government instead of to the chiefs. The work of the chiefs was now made lighter because they would no longer be allowed to judge legal cases on their own. At every case there would be a British magistrate, who would do most of the work. This was because the governor valued the chiefs so much that he did not want them to be burdened with such mundane matters as presiding over cases.

Nxito and his councillors seemed pleased with the new arrangement. Colonial money was reputed to be very powerful in the purchase of goods that could be bought only in the trading stores that were emerging throughout kwaXhosa. Many people bought such goods with grain. But those who had colonial money, the very money adorned with the image of Her Britannic Majesty, were men of status in the league of Ned and Mjuza.

But Twin-Twin, ever ready to bring others down to earth, asked, "Now, if we are going to have this white man judging our cases, whose law is he going to apply?"

"The law we apply every day," answered Nxito. "Our law."

"The white man does not know our law," said Twin-Twin vehemently. "He does not respect our law. He will apply the law of the English people. This is a way of introducing his laws among our people. As for the colonial money, The Man Who Named Ten Rivers is buying our chiefs. When they are paid by him, they will owe their loyalty to him, and not to the amaXhosa people, and not to our laws and customs and traditions!"

Twin-Twin was right on both counts. The intention of The Man Who Named Ten Rivers was to break the power of the chiefs. After he had recovered from his nervous breakdown he called his senior officers and briefed them about his tour of the frontier and the new judicial system he was introducing to the natives.

"It will gradually undermine and destroy Xhosa laws and customs," he said. "European laws will, by imperceptible degrees, take the place of their own barbarous customs, and any Xhosa chief of importance will be daily brought into contact with a talented and honorable European gentleman, who will hourly interest himself in the advance and improvement of the entire tribe, and must in process of time gain an influence over the native races."

The applause was deafening. Here at last was a governor who knew how to deal with the native people without incurring the great expense of war. At the ball that evening he was the toast of the genteel society of Cape Town. Admirers surrounded him, eager to learn more about the situation on the frontier.

He told them about the great cattle-killing movement. The whole thing was a conspiracy of Kreli and Moshesh, the king of the Basotho people, he explained, using the colonial names for Sarhili and Moshoeshoe. The latter was bent on uniting black resistance against white domination in the whole of southern Africa. That is why he had sent an emissary to Kreli. The Basotho king had grown too ambitious ever since he defeated the British under Governor Cathcart at the Battle of Berea a few years back.

"Mhlakaza is merely an instrument in the hands of Kreli and Moshesh, working on the superstition and ignorance of the common people," said the governor.

"What would these chiefs gain from the cattle-killing?" an officer wanted to know.

"Simple, my dear friend. The mind of the native can be very devious," said the governor sagaciously.

Everybody agreed that indeed the native had the slyness of the devil himself.

"This whole cattle-killing movement is not just superstitious delusion. It is a plot by the two chiefs . . . a cold-blooded political scheme to involve the government in war, and to bring a host of desperate enemies upon us."

It was clear to the governor that his admirers were not bright enough to understand the intricacies of this political intrigue. Their faces were blank.

"Kreli and Moshesh want to drive the pacified Xhosas into a war they do not want against the English. Hunger will make them desperate and they will fight. They will steal cattle from the white people and the Thembus to provide their fighting men with food. Now they are killing their own cattle so that they will have none to guard, and more men will be available to fight. Those are the true reasons for the cattle-killing."

Then he entertained the listeners with his stories of Australia, where he had succeeded in imposing English law in the place of the bloodthirsty aboriginal law. He had made it a point that aboriginal people were not allowed to congregate together and practice their old uncivilized habits. Instead they were scattered all over the settler country, where they could be equipped with education and skills that were necessary for their survival in the modern world.

"That's what I plan to do with the Xhosa people as well," he explained, giving a conspiratorial wink.

Whereas previous governors like Sir Harry Smith had talked of exterminating the natives, his was a humane policy that aimed at civilizing them, and bringing them up to the supreme levels of the English.

In Australia the policy of extermination had borne fruit, but in the Cape Colony it had already failed even when its advocate, Sir Harry, had tried actively to implement it.

"The natives of the Cape Colony and British Kaffraria must be grateful that my philosophy is an enlightened one," the governor said. "They must seize the opportunity, and they must be disciplined. We have taken a few lessons from our success in Australia."

In New Zealand he had had similar success. He told the genteel folks amid sighs of admiration how he had disciplined a Maori chief called Te Rauparaha. He had been getting too big for his boots and was surely going to give the settlers some problems in the future, so Grey had accused him of plotting to kill white settlers and rape their women. The chief was arrested, and was released only after his people agreed to hand over three million acres of prime land for white settlement. This added more land to the millions of acres that Sir George had gained by various means from the Maori, including court-martialing and executing their uncooperative leaders and transporting some of them to Australia.

As for Te Rauparaha, although there had been a great uproar that he had been falsely accused, it was well worth his sacrifice. His people received the greatest gift of all: education and British civilization. The governor built schools and hospitals for them. He could do the same too for the natives of the Cape Colony and British Kaffraria if they walked the road of civilization and did not fill their heads with idle thoughts of killing settlers and raping white women.

"But I am afraid that is exactly what those cattle-killers of the frontier plan to do . . . kill settlers and rape white women," said the governor. "And I will deal with them in the same manner that I dealt with Te Rauparaha."

The sufferings of the Middle Generations are only whispered. It is because of the insistence: *Forget the past. Don't only forgive it. Forget it as well. The past did not happen. You only dreamt it. It is a figment of your rich collective imagination. It did not happen. Banish your memory. It is a sin to have a memory. There is virtue in amnesia. The past. It did not happen. It did not happen. It did not happen.*

John Dalton's friends think that memory is being used to torment them for the sins of their fathers. Sins committed in good faith.

Next week two of them are leaving, one for Australia and the other for New Zealand. One owns a cottage at Qolorha-by-Sea and the other lives in Port Elizabeth. Today they and a few other cottage owners gather in the garden of the emigrant, braaing meat on an open charcoal stand and drinking beer.

Dalton is one of the guests.

"What will happen to this nice cottage?" he asks.

"I am selling it," says the emigrant. "My house in East London too. And my ostrich farm in the Karoo. I am leaving everything in the hands of my estate agents."

Perhaps Camagu will be interested in this cottage, thinks Dalton. He seems so happy in Qolorha, and is involving himself in the life of the community. He has even established a business with some village women.

It all started with the oysters and mussels that he ate at Zim's. He was sold on the taste. When he moved to the sea cottage he is currently taking care of on behalf of the Butterworth doctor, he made it a habit to buy fresh oysters and mussels from the women. Two women in particular, NoGiant and MamCirha, became regulars at his cottage. Every other day they brought him oysters and mussels kept in a bucket of sea water to prevent them from going bad. They told him that sea-harvest can last for many days in a bucket of sea water. Since then he has not had any need to buy meat.

Later on, Camagu wanted to learn to harvest the sea himself. But the women would not teach him. He was good as a customer and not as a competitor. One morning he found Qukezwa harvesting the sea. She was in a good mood and offered to teach him the art of catching mussels and oysters, or imbhaza and imbhatyisa. She told him that the best time to catch this valued seafood was in the morning between seven and nine.

"When the moon is red," she explained, "or is dying, with only a small piece remaining, then we know that the next morning will be good for harvesting the sea."

She taught him how to walk into the sea, sometimes with the water rising up to his chest, how to use his hands to feel the rocks at the bottom, and how to use an ulugxa to dislodge imbhaza and imbhatyisa from the rocks. She also taught him how to get amangquba and *amaqonga*, the varieties of abalone that look like big snails. He learned fast, for there was no guarantee that Qukezwa's good mood would still be there the next morning.

NoGiant and MamCirha were not happy that he was no longer buying their seafood now that he could harvest his own. In fact, he could not eat all his harvest, and this gave him a good idea. He had no means of earning a living in this village. Soon his money was going to run out. His Toyota was sitting idle since he hardly went anywhere in it. He made up his mind to catch oysters and mussels, keep them in sea water as he was taught by the women, take them in his car, and sell them to hotels in East London and the surrounding smaller towns. He was not going to compete with the women. Instead he would form a cooperative society with them.

Indeed, the business was established, with NoGiant and MamCirha leading a committee of very enthusiastic women. It is not as lucrative as they might wish. It is struggling on. But Camagu, for the first time after many years, is a very fulfilled man.

Although he has not said it in so many words, he regards Qolorha as his home now, and it is reasonable for Dalton to suspect he will not be thinking of going to America or even back to Johannesburg in the near future. He often says this is the most beautiful place in the world. Even if he leaves, there is no harm in investing in property, especially such a prime one. Dalton will certainly bring the matter to his attention.

"This is one of the things we'll miss," says the second emigrant to the first. "I don't think where we're going we'll get such beautiful land for a bottle of brandy."

Everyone laughs. Except Dalton.

"You are the only one who will remain in this mess, John," says a cottage owner who sees himself as a prospective emigrant down the line. "Everyone is leaving."

"Not everyone," says Dalton, not bothering to hide his irritation. "The Afrikaners are not leaving."

"Do you fancy yourself an Afrikaner, just because you married one?"

"I am staying here," says Dalton. "I am not joining your chicken run. This is my land. I belong here. It is the land of my forefathers."

"That is self-delusion, John," warns the first emigrant.

Dalton is now getting angry. Against his better judgment he raises his voice and says, "The Afrikaner is more reliable than you chaps. He belongs to the soil. He is of Africa. Even if he is not happy about the present situation he will not go anywhere. He cannot go any-where."

Everyone is taken aback by his outburst. No one understands why he takes their ribbing so seriously. So personally. They all look at him in astonishment.

"He can go to Orania," says another prospective emigrant, trying to recapture the jolly mood.

"That is the problem. You call the Afrikaner racist when he wants a homeland for his own people. You laugh at his pie-in-the-sky Orania homeland as a joke—which it is—but you are not aware that you yourselves have a homeland mentality. Your homelands are in Australia and New Zealand. That is why you emigrate in droves to those countries where you can spend a blissful life without blacks . . . with people of your culture and your language . . . just like the Orania Afrikaners. Whenever there is any problem in this country you threaten to leave. You are only here for what you can get out of this country. You think you can hold us all to ransom."

"Us? You are not a native, John. You may think you are, but you are not," says the second emigrant, jokingly using the "native" tag of a bygone era.

"At least in Australia they killed almost all their natives," titters the first emigrant.

But the other cottage owners are not prepared to take Dalton's accusations lying down. How dare he call them racists when they are well-known liberals who fought against apartheid? Dalton himself knows very well how they used to demonstrate against the injustices of the system even in their early university days, how they were activists in liberal student organizations, how they always voted for the sole progressive party of the day. How dare he compare them to people with a laager mentality? Does he mean they must stay and watch while the country is being sucked into a whirlpool of crime, violence, affirmative action, and corruption? Is he blaming them for thinking of the future of their children?

"Yes, you prided yourselves as liberals," admits Dalton. "But now you can't face the reality of a black-dominated government. It is clear that while you were shouting against the injustices of the system, secretly you thanked God for the National Party which introduced and preserved that very system for forty-six years."

He is walking away as he utters these words. His friends remain wondering whatever went wrong with a man who used to be so upstanding.

The first emigrant says sadly, "It's very much unlike him. He must be under a lot of stress."

"Stress my foot!" exclaims the second emigrant. "The man has mastered the art of licking the backsides of the blacks. He has even joined the ruling party."

John Dalton gets into his four-wheel-drive bakkie and drives away. He has had it with these clowns and their attitude. They can all leave for all he cares. Yes, let them go. He does not need them. He has his community of Qolorha-by-Sea. And his wife's people.

Somebody is flagging down the bakkie. It is Bhonco, son of Ximiya.

"Where does that road lead to, son of my dead friend?" he asks.

"To my store, of course. Where does yours lead to?"

"To the Blue Flamingo Hotel," says the elder.

"Jump in."

The old man struggles to climb into the back of the bakkie. Even though Dalton is alone in the front seat, customs do not die easily. Dalton can see a hint of anger on the elder's face. But he dismisses it as the natural anger of the Unbelievers.

On the road that branches off to the Blue Flamingo Dalton stops, and Bhonco jumps down. He stumbles a bit. Dalton is about to drive away when Bhonco shouts that he has left his stick and knobkerrie where he was sitting on the bakkie. He reaches for his weapons.

"Hawu! What now with the weapons?" asks Dalton.

"Because I am going to fight!" answers the angry elder.

"Oh, no! Not the war of the Believers and Unbelievers again. Will you people ever stop your silly wars of the past?"

"It is not the Believers I am going to fight, although after what you and they have done to stop the development of Qolorha, I would be happy to give all of you one or two bumps on your stupid heads."

Bhonco explains that he is going to fight the white tourists at the Blue Flamingo Hotel. They insulted his wife. NoPetticoat came home from babysitting fuming that white people from England—a middle-aged couple and their three teenage children—made a monkey of her. They had what Dalton understood to be a camcorder, and took photographs of her. They all posed with her. She did not mind that. Tourists do that all the time. But that was not enough for these characters from the queen's own country. They asked her to talk into the machine in her language. And say what? Anything. Any old thing as long as it is in the clicky language. She uttered some words which meant absolutely nothing. Then they asked her to sing. She sang a few notes into the machine, even though by this time she was feeling foolish. Fellow workers were looking at her, laughing. Then the tourists asked her to dance. Her dignity was hurt, but she had to do it since she didn't want the hotel manager to accuse her of being rude to his guests.

"Can you believe it, son of Dalton . . . making my wife look foolish like that?" asks Bhonco. "Do you think they would do that kind of thing to their own mothers?"

Although Dalton does not really understand what the fuss is about, he tries to calm the elder. It would not be a nice thing for the future of Qolorha if he went to fight tourists at the hotel. Is he not one of the people who want to attract more tourists to the region by building a gambling resort? How will tourists come when they hear that villagers go to hotels to attack them for no apparent reason?

"For no apparent reason?" bristles Bhonco. "Would you be happy if they did that to your wife?"

"Tat'uBhonco, your wife works at that hotel. In the evenings she sings *izitibiri* for the tourists. Why is she offended now?"

Dalton is referring to the concerts that are held in the bar of the Blue Flamingo. Saturdays are seafood nights at the hotel. Huge bedecked billiard tables heave with raw oysters and grilled prawns, langoustines, abalone, mussels, and line fish. These are served with garlic butter and chili sauce, and fried rice. When the tourists have stuffed themselves, they relax with wine and beer. The women who work as cleaners, babysitters, waitresses, and chefs' assistants form themselves into a choir and sing izitibiri, the songs that are popular at school concerts and are also known as "sounds." The workers clown around, entertaining tourists, who donate money in a plate that is passed around. At the end of the concert the workers share the proceeds of their weekly ventures into the world of showbiz.

"That is different!" protests Bhonco. "That is a concert where everyone sings and dances. It is not an attempt to ridicule my wife."

To placate the elder, Dalton invites him over to his store. He promises him that they will sit down and explore other ways of solving the matter. After expressing his doubts about Dalton's ability to solve anything, especially now that he is in cahoots with the enemies of progress, Bhonco jumps back into the back of the van. Dalton drives on to Vulindlela Trading Store.

He regrets this indiscretion as soon as they arrive at the store. Zim and Camagu are sitting on the wooden yokes bundled together on the verandah, waiting for him. A noisy group of herdboys is watching an ancient black-and-white movie on the television screen against the wall. Camagu wonders how they are able to follow the dialogue, which is all in English. And they laugh at the right places too. They egg the hero on and condemn the villain. They follow and understand every detail of the story. Then he remembers that he should not be surprised. As an urchin in the townships of Johannesburg, he used to be a regular in the dingy movie houses. He and his friends followed the exploits of Roy Rogers and Tex Ritter in all their intricacies, although none of them knew any English.

Zim's face turns sour as soon as he sees Bhonco. Camagu smiles, stands up, and extends his hand to the elder. Bhonco ignores it.

"So it is true what they say," says Bhonco sadly. "You have now joined the Believers."

"It is not true, Tat'uBhonco. I do not belong to the Believers, in the same way that I do not belong to the Unbelievers. I am just a person. My ancestors were not here when these quarrels began with Prophetess Nongqawuse."

"You see, he is a Believer!" exclaims Bhonco triumphantly. "He even calls her a prophetess. She was no prophetess. She was a fake. She was used by white people to colonize us."

"I want you to understand this, both of you," says Camagu firmly. "To me you are both respected elders. I do not care about your being Believers or Unbelievers. I respect you both in the same way. Please don't drag me into your quarrels. Neither of you must expect me not to be friends with the other."

Bhonco looks at Dalton, and whispers to him in exasperation, "And they say this is the boy who wants to marry my daughter. He can't even stand like a man in support of the side of his future in-laws.

He comes with all this learning from America. Yet he does not see the value of having more tourists come here."

"Don't you realize, Tat'uBhonco," says Dalton patiently, "that the tourists who come to spend their money here . . . they come precisely because the place is unspoiled?"

"Spend money on whom?" asks Bhonco. "On you, of course, because they buy food from your shop. You take them around in your van to see the places of our shame. You stand to benefit the most if things stay the way they are. And so do your friends who own the hotel."

"We employ people from the village."

"Exactly. Now these developments you are trying to stop will employ even more people. Everyone will benefit."

Zim is looking up in the sky, humming a song, as if none of these matters concern him.

Then softly, as if to himself, he says, "I hear that some people depend on their daughters to build houses for them. Where were they when men were working for themselves?"

"If you are talking about me, why don't you address me directly? What are you afraid of?" asks Bhonco. "Or are you jealous that my daughter can afford to build her father a house because she is the principal of a secondary school instead of cleaning after white people?"

Those, like Camagu, who do not follow village gossip closely learn for the first time that Xoliswa Ximiya has built her father a second house—a four-walled tin-roofed ixande—saving him from the ridicule of having only one pink rondavel at his compound. The Unbelievers see this as a wonderful gesture from a daughter who has obviously been brought up well. The Believers, on the other hand, think it is a shame that a man who should have worked for himself to fill his compound with many rondavels, hexagons, and at least one ixande has to depend on a girl to build him a house. The fact that the man is an Unbeliever, and Unbelievers are expected to be well off since they did not kill their cattle during the days of Nongqawuse, makes his relative penury even more remarkable. He must have led a careless life. Or his fathers before him were merciless in their feasting on Twin-Twin's wealth during the

Middle Generations. They devoured cattle that had escaped the cattle-killing frenzy without thinking of future generations.

But there are those who look at him with compassion and mutter that the poor man's cattle got finished when he educated his daughter right up to university level. This education swallowed even the money he had accumulated in his younger days when he worked in East London and Cape Town. And now the government is not even giving him any old-age pension, any nkamnkam.

"I think it is a wonderful thing that your daughter has built you a house, Tat'uBhonco," says Dalton. "Don't you think so, Camagu?"

"I agree," rejoins Camagu. "You are truly blessed to have a daughter like Xoliswa Ximiya."

Zim pierces them with his wounded eyes.

"Didn't I hear of some man who was bought with the thighs of someone's daughter?" he asks in a contemptuous voice.

"Are you insulting my daughter, Zim?" fumes Bhonco. "Are you insulting the principal of this village? Is it my fault that no decent man will look at your floor-scrubbing daughter?"

Dalton steps between the elders, and tells them that if they want to start their nonsense again they should do it elsewhere. Camagu suggests that now that they are all together it would be better to try to close the chasm that exists between Bhonco and Zim through dialogue. For the sake of the village it is better if the elders lead their followers into working together rather than pulling in different directions. He offers to mediate.

"You cannot be a mediator," says Zim. "We all know about you and Bhonco's daughter. We have heard already that you are going to be his son-in-law."

"How can you say that when Dalton and I have eaten in your house, and have made it clear where we stand on these issues?" rebuts Camagu.

"Aha!" shouts Bhonco. "So I was right. You have chosen your side already. I defended you when the villagers were accusing you of taking the side of redness. When we heard of your decision to stay in this village we were happy. We said among ourselves, now here was an educated man who would see our point of view . . . who would support the introduction of civilization to our lives. You disappointed many people when you joined the side of this child of Dalton and his Believers."

Dalton makes a feeble attempt to explain that he is not a Believer. But Bhonco, son of Ximiya, has not finished with him yet.

"You shut up! I am talking to this boy from Johannesburg who I doubt is even circumcised! As for you, Dalton, you can thank God that your father is no longer alive to see this shame. He was a man of progress, your father. He would be ashamed to see you dragging this village into darkness. He used to tell us every day that we were savages who needed some enlightenment. Now that enlightenment is coming to the village you fight against it!"

By this time a number of people who have come to the shop are surrounding the men. They heckle their agreement or disagreement with the speaker. It is clear that the majority of those assembled are on the side of civilization, as represented by the gambling resort and water-sports paradise. Dalton skulks away into the shop. Camagu thinks that this may be the opportunity to thrash out these differences. But it seems that each side wants to play to the gallery. Zim, for instance, is prancing about, mouthing invective against those hecklers who agree with Bhonco's point of view.

"I do not see how you people can agree with these Unbelievers," he says. "These are the very people who consort with white business-men from Johannesburg who want to destroy our trees," he says.

He has played into Bhonco's hands. It is as if the elder was waiting for just that kind of stupid statement.

"It is clear that the Believers are mad," he says. "It is foolish to talk of conserving indigenous trees. After all, we can always plant civilized trees. Trees that come from across the seas. Trees that have no thorns like some of the ugly ones you want to protect. Trees like the wattle and the bluegum that grow in the forest of Nogqoloza. You know that Nogqoloza is a beautiful forest because the trees there were planted in straight lines many years ago. Although we do not like white people for causing the sufferings of the Middle Generations, we must at least thank them for planting the forest of Nogqoloza."

Most people agree that the Believers have gone overboard in their madness. Dalton, for instance, has been urging the chief to stop the boys from taking the eggs of birds from their nests. Whoever heard of such nonsense? Don't all boys grow up doing that? From time immemorial? And this business of banning boys from hunting wild animals with their dogs, where does it come from? And what gives Dalton the right to change the ancient practices of the people? How dare he try to influence Chief Xikixa on such matters? And of course the headless chief is capable of bending to the slightest breeze, although in this case he has not been stupid enough to accede to Dalton's exhortations.

"You have heard with your own ears, my people," says Zim, seizing the opportunity to score a point. "This son of Ximiya says the very white people who took our land are wonderful people just because they planted bluegum trees at Nogqoloza. That is why he now wants us to consort with whites who plan to turn our village into a business from which we won't benefit. He is a tool of white people, just like his forefathers who became tools of The Man Who Named Ten Rivers."

"What is Zim talking about?" cries Bhonco. "Is he not the one who is working with the white man Dalton to drag our village deeper into redness?"

"Dalton is not really white," says Zim in the trader's defense. "It is just an aberration of his skin. He is more of an umXhosa than most of us. He was circumcised like all amaXhosa men. He speaks isiXhosa better than most of you here."

The impromptu meeting degenerates into a free-for-all din. Everyone thinks he or she has something wise to share with the rest. And everyone wants to dispense this wisdom at the same time. All of a sudden Dalton and Missis rush out. Missis screams so sharply that everyone suddenly keeps quiet.

"This is not a beer hall," she shrieks. "You can't hold your meeting here!"

As he walks away, Camagu catches a glimpse of Qukezwa standing at the door with some of Dalton's workers watching the show outside. He has not seen her since the morning she taught him how to harvest the sea, almost four months ago. He has passed Zim's house, and has pretended to visit Dalton at his store, all the while hoping to catch a glimpse of her. He has taken lonely walks in Nongqawuse's Valley, and has visited sacred cairns. He has looked longingly at the great lagoon, which on a clear day he can see from his seaside cottage. But Qukezwa has been nowhere to be seen. Perhaps all for the better, he convinced himself. All for the better. She is not the type of woman he should be associating with.

He has been too wary to ask anyone about her whereabouts, lest people question his interest in Zim's daughter. He has continued his steady friendship with Xoliswa Ximiya, fueling further rumors in the village about the imminence of their marriage. And bringing further anxieties on Bhonco and NoPetticoat that they are going to lose their daughter to Johannesburg or America. Yet at the same time they are looking forward to a glorious wedding that will enhance their status in society and bring prestige to the rest of the Unbelievers. There is hope yet. The man has started a business with some village women. He may not take her away after all.

And now here is Qukezwa standing at the door, laughing at Missis shooing the rowdy villagers away.

Camagu remembers that in fact he and Zim had come to discuss the botanical garden that Dalton wanted to establish. He goes back to the store. As he enters he looks at Qukezwa and smiles. She smiles back. She actually smiles back at him!

His mind is no longer on the botanical garden. It is wandering somewhere in the clouds. Dalton is telling him how the brilliant idea came to him one lovely day. He was at the river with the water project committee that included Bhonco and Zim, inspecting the water pump that had been constructed with money that he had raised from his business friends and from the government. The pipes were laid to draw the water up to the village. Next to the concrete embankment near the pump, Bhonco showed the committee a small piece of land surrounded by wild irises, orchids, and usundu palms. On it grew protea flowers, which was strange since they are found nowhere else in the Eastern Cape. He told his colleagues that it was his land that had been left for him by his father. Dalton suggested that they develop the land into a botanical garden where they would cultivate rare indigenous plants, especially those that were endangered.

The next time Dalton went to inspect the water pump he found that Bhonco had planted maize on that piece of land. Apparently the elder thought that Dalton had an ulterior motive concerning his land.

"What's the use?" asked Dalton, laughing loudly. "Monkeys will eat those mielies!"

But it was no laughing matter when he also discovered that a rare fig tree that he had pointed out to the committee of the water project had also been chopped down.

"It is this son of Ximiya," Zim had said at the time. "He came in the middle of the night and chopped the tree so that no one else could enjoy it."

But Bhonco denied that he had had anything to do with the destruction of the tree.

Dalton is obviously having a good time recounting these stories. And many others about the problems the war of the Believers and Unbelievers has caused him. He goes on about his plans to develop the village, what a wonderful team he and Camagu will make, and how their "Let the Wild Coast Stay Wild" campaign will succeed if only they play their cards right. But Camagu can only hear his droning voice, as if from a distance.

He excuses himself. He must get away from these surroundings that are haunted by Qukezwa's aura. He must fight the demons that take hold of him at the mere thought of her smile. He must try to be in control. This wild woman cannot possibly be of any good to him.

That evening he visits Xoliswa Ximiya. She is glad to see him. After a glass of orange squash and Tennis biscuits, he suggests that they enjoy a walk in the full moon.

Distant fires speckle the silvery night with golden orange. Shadows of lovers assume monstrous shapes. Unseen eyes follow Camagu and Xoliswa Ximiya as they are drawn slowly by the song of the silvery girls who are dancing on the village playground.

Tomorrow more stories shall be told, seasoned as usual with inventive spices by whoever is telling the story at the time.

Xoliswa Ximiya comments that it is shameful that the girls are frolicking about topless, wearing only traditional skirts. Camagu responds that he does not see anything to be ashamed of. The girls are from a culture that is not ashamed of breasts.

"That brings me to this thing about Majola," says Xoliswa Ximiya. "I've been wanting to talk to you about it for months."

"My totem snake, you mean. What about it?"

"Don't you think you are reinforcing barbarism in this village?"

"Then I am a barbarian, because I believe in Majola, in the same way that my parents before me believed in him."

"You are an educated man, Camagu, all the way from America. How do you expect simple peasants to give up their superstitions and join the modern world when they see educated people like you clinging to them?"

"I am not from America. I am an African from the amaMpondomise clan. My totem is the brown mole snake, Majola. I believe in him, not for you, not for your fellow villagers, but for myself. And by the way, I have noticed that I have gained more respect from these people you call peasants since they saw that I respect my customs."

"You have messed up everything. I thought we were going to have a beautiful walk in the moonlight," says Xoliswa Ximiya, walking away from him. "You will call me when you have come back to your senses."

He calls after her, but she walks on. He decides it is not worth pursuing her. He should rather go home to his cottage by the sea. He does not understand why his joy at being visited by Majola so long ago should cause him so much trouble on such a silvery night. And why Xoliswa Ximiya should feel so strongly about it.

It is like this Nongqawuse thing. Everyone seems to be ashamed of her. There is a lot of denial in this village about Nongqawuse. She is an embarrassment. Some say she never existed and that the story is a lie concocted by white people to defame blacks. Others say she existed but not in this village. She must have lived somewhere else, in Umtata or even in Cape Town. Another group says that even if she did live in these parts, she was a liar and a disgrace. They don't want to hear or know anything about her.

It is only the family of Believers and their few followers who take Nongqawuse seriously and are proud of her heritage. That is why there is such anger against Zim among the amaGqobhoka—the enlightened ones like Xoliswa Ximiya—that he is bringing back the shame of the past. And against Dalton, who takes tourists to Nongqawuse's Pool in his four-wheel-drive bakkie.

When these white tourists throw money into the pool, the Unbelievers lament, "What a waste! Why don't they give that money to us?" To the Believers, however, it is proof of the power of Nongqawuse. White people are trying to appease her for all their sins.

"They say when an owl of the night hoots at daytime, then we must brace ourselves for misfortune," observes a silvery voice.

He is startled out of his reverie. A silvery beast stands right in front of him. She is sitting on top of it, all silvery in her smug smile. As usual, she rides on Gxagxa bareback and reinless. Over her shoulder she is carrying an *umrhubhe*, the isiXhosa musical instrument that is made of a wooden bow and a single string. Women play the instrument by stroking and sometimes plucking the string, using their mouths as an acoustic box.

"What do you mean?" he demands.

"I saw old Bhonco getting the better of you. You men are useless," she declares, with a naughty twinkle in her silvery eyes.

"Where did you come from?"

"It is a night not to be wasted. Come, let me give you a ride."

He panics.

"Like that? Without a saddle? Without reins? Where will I hold?"

"Don't be scared. Climb up. Gxagxa is strong. He can carry two people."

She helps him up. He sits behind her, and holds tightly around her waist as Gxagxa gallops away. He must try to forget his circumstances. He must try to ignore the havoc that is being caused to his body. He must talk about something.

"Why do white people drop money into Nongqawuse's Pool?" he asks breathlessly. "Surely they don't believe in her like you do."

"Have you heard of Gqoloma?"

"No. What is Gqoloma?"

"It is a snake that lives in Nongqawuse's Pool. It lives under the water. When Gqoloma goes out of the pool it causes a great storm. When it pays a visit . . . moving from the pool at the Gxarha River to another pool at the Qolorha River . . . it causes havoc in its wake, like a tornado. It destroys houses. It uproots trees."

He is not sure if she has answered his question.

Gxagxa gallops on, climbing hills and descending hillocks. He gallops on the rough silvery rocks that dot the coastline above the silvery ocean. She bursts into a song and plays her umrhubhe musical instrument. She whistles and sings all at the same time. Many voices come from her mouth. Deep sounds that echo like the night. Sounds that have the heaviness of a steamy summer night. Flaming sounds that crackle like a veld fire. Light sounds that float like flakes of snow on top of the Amathole Mountains. Hollow sounds like laughing mountains. Coming out all at once. As if a whole choir lives in her mouth. Camagu has never heard such singing before. He once read of the amaXhosa mountain women who were good at split-tone singing. He also heard that the only other people in the world who could do this were Tibetan monks. He did not expect that this girl could be the guardian of a dying tradition.

For some time he is spellbound. Then he realizes that his pants are wet.

It is not from sweat.

Perhaps if he takes his mind off his dire situation, and sends it to dwell on Xoliswa Ximiya's icy beauty, there might be some respite. She is so beautiful. Xoliswa Ximiya. So staid and reliable.

Qukezwa is not burdened with beauty. She is therefore able to be free-spirited.

Twin and Qukezwa sat all day long on the banks of the Gxarha River near the estuary. They watched the sun as it walked across the sky, while the amorous shenanigans of the waters of the river with the tides of the sea filled the couple's idle lives with monotonous moans. They sat like that every day, hoping the sun would turn red, and other suns would emerge from behind the mountains or from the horizon and run amok across the sky and collide and explode and their embers rain on the earth and burn the hardened souls of the Unbelievers. But every day the sun rose as it had risen in the days of their forefathers.

Sometimes Heitsi would be with them, chasing locusts and fashioning inept flutes from grasses and reeds. He was growing up to be a handful, this Heitsi. At first he had enjoyed being with his parents all the time. But now he preferred to spend most of the day sprinkling sand on the heads of the Believers' toddlers. If these were normal times, he would be chasing calves and lambs in the fields.

It was the middle of October. Blossoms scented the air.

Twin and Qukezwa sat and watched the sky. And watched the horizon. And watched the sand. He sat behind her, his arms covering her tightly. She sat ensconced between his sinewy thighs. She played the umrhubhe, the musical instrument that sounded like the lonely voice of mountain spirits. She sang of the void that the demise of Gxagxa, Twin's brown-and-white horse, had left in their lives. She cursed the lungsickness that had taken him away. She spat at those who had brought it into the land. When she closed her eyes she saw herself riding Gxagxa on the sands of the beach, completely naked. Gxagxa began in a canter. And then gathered speed in a fiendish gallop, raising clouds of dust. Again Twin's thighs were around her. He was sitting behind her, while Heitsi was wrapped in her thighs at the front. Gxagxa continued his wicked gallop until they all disappeared in the clouds. Through the voice of the umrhubhe she saw the new people riding on the waves, racing back according to the prophecies, and led by none other than Gxagxa and the headless patriarch.

The song of the umrhubhe creates a world of dreams.

Twin and Qukezwa sat and watched the sky. Their eyes were now inured to the sharp rays. From a distance they could hear a cry that was carried by the wind from the village. The cry floated above the tidal moans. Above the song of the umrhubhe. She stopped playing and listened carefully.

"It sounds like a war cry," said Qukezwa.

"It does sound like the village crier. But it cannot be war," Twin assured her. "There cannot be a war at a sacred time like this."

He was wrong. It was a war cry. It came from the homestead of Pama, Nxito's believing son who now acted as chief of Qolorha in his exiled father's place. Men were beginning to gather from all corners of the village. When Twin's ears had confirmed that it was indeed a war cry he ran up from the river to Pama's Great Place and joined the men who had already gathered.

"All men must take up arms!" shouted Pama, addressing the meeting. "We are being invaded. The Man Who Named Ten Rivers has done what he has been threatening to do all along. You all know about the letters he has been writing to our king, Sarhili, making what we thought were empty threats. The threats were not so empty after all. A ship full of his soldiers has been seen entering the mouth of the Kei River!"

The mouth of the Kei was only a few miles from the Gxarha mouth. In no time, armed amaXhosa soldiers were at the banks of the river, watching the ship HMS *Geyser* sail slowly up one of the channels. More amaXhosa soldiers were arriving from other villages and chief-doms.

Twin started a war song, and all the men joined in a fearsome unison.

The earth shook. And HMS *Geyser* stood still. The people in the ship lowered a boat to the river. But it overturned, and the men in it nearly drowned. One of the men refused to get back into the boat. He swam to the shore and ran away like a scared rabbit, to the guffaws of the amaXhosa soldiers. They did not chase him, though. They wanted him to reach East London safely, so that he could warn his masters that it was not the wisest of things to trifle with the amaXhosa people.

There were cheers among the villagers when HMS *Geyser* shame-facedly sailed back without attacking.

Twin started another song. The men joined in triumphal unison. Piercing ululation filled the air. Twin could hear a distinct howl. He knew at once that Qukezwa was among the ululants. She had never mastered the art of producing the sharp undulating wails that every umXhosa woman produced so well. He turned and looked among the women who were singing in the rear. Indeed there she was, with Heitsi at her back, singing in the peculiar manner of the Khoikhoi, now and then making her vain attempts at ululating.

"Why did you come?" asked Twin impatiently. "You are supposed to be looking after Heitsi at Mhlakaza's, and not running around the war front."

"We had to come, Father of Heitsi," said Qukezwa sweetly. "We cannot let you fight a war alone."

"I am not fighting a war alone! I am with the other soldiers."

"Women must do their bit as well. That is why I rallied them from the village to come and ululate their men to victory."

"Oh, Qukezwa," pleaded Twin, "you shouldn't have come. Men don't understand our relationship. They will say I am under the isikhakha skirts of my wife."

The victory over The Man Who Named Ten Rivers' ship started a new frenzy of cattle-killing. It was a sure sign that the new people were powerful, and were about to show themselves according to the prophecies of Nongqawuse. The faith of those people who were beginning to waver was reinforced. A number of Unbelievers became Believers. Even those Believers who had long finished destroying their cattle, and were beginning to get hungry, gained more courage. Although Twin and Qukezwa had long finished destroying their cattle, they could not be counted among those who were hungry or lacked courage. They spent almost all their time at Mhlakaza's, where they had all their meals. Some believing families who still had cattle and grain were taking them to Mhlakaza's for the daily feasts.

This new frenzy was discouraging to Chief Nxito and his counsellors. They accused The Man Who Named Ten Rivers of bad faith.

"He pretends to be talking with us in order to resolve these matters peacefully," said the aging chief, "yet he secretly sends his ship to attack our people. Now look what has happened! His ship was defeated and now the people are killing more of their cattle."

"I have always warned that you cannot trust any of these people," said Twin-Twin. "Their word is like a rock that has been made slippery by the urine of rock-rabbits. You cannot cling to it."

Twin-Twin was so angry at the treachery of The Man Who Named Ten Rivers that his scars of history were itching. He had to scratch them constantly. They reminded him that prophets could not be relied upon to make sound judgments. He therefore became more steadfast in his unbelief. But some Unbelievers became Believers when they heard about the defeated ship.

Major John Gawler, the no-nonsense magistrate, heard about the rumblings of the people he considered allies, and sent John Dalton to talk to them.

"Sir George Grey had no intentions of attacking the amaXhosa," explained Dalton. "He merely wanted to scare the Believers with HMS *Geyser*. The ship was on its regular route from Natal to the Cape Colony. Sir George decided that it should make a call at the Kei mouth to demonstrate the British naval power."

No one believed Dalton.

When he had left, Twin-Twin said, "They would make excuses for their spectacular defeat at the hands of the Believers, wouldn't they?"

What worried Twin-Twin most was that as a result of this so-called demonstration of the queen's sea power the Believers were becoming even more arrogant. They were once again going around attacking Unbelievers. And The Man Who Named Ten Rivers was refusing to give the victims of these attacks any assistance. When his representatives in the region, people like Gawler and other magistrates, sent urgent messages that the Unbelievers should be assisted, he responded that the British government could not send parties throughout what he called Kaffirland to defend each person who might be attacked.

"In any case," he added, "if we were to do that, we would be playing right into the hands of Kreli and Moshesh, who are plotting a war against the colony. That would give these diabolical chiefs an excuse to attack."

The only thing that could be done was to ask the unbelieving chiefs to give refuge to the seeing Unbelievers and to ensure that they were not harmed. There was nothing else that could be done, unless the problems spread to the lands that were set apart for white occupation.

This attitude reinforced Twin-Twin's view that The Man Who Named Ten Rivers had planned the whole cattle-killing movement. And that he had cleverly invented these prophecies and used Nongqawuse, Mhlakaza, and Nombanda to propagate them among the amaXhosa people. He wanted the amaXhosa to destroy themselves with their own hands, saving the colonial government from dirtying its hands with endless wars. This view was gaining currency among those Unbelievers who were not Christians.

"The Strangers that Nongqawuse saw," explained Twin-Twin, "were The Man Who Named Ten Rivers himself, maybe with Gawler and Dalton."

Those Unbelievers who were Christians, such as Ned and Mjuza, did not agree with this view. They echoed The Man Who Named Ten Rivers' view that Nongqawuse's visions were nothing more than a plot by Sarhili and his friend, Moshoeshoe of the Basotho nation, to starve the amaXhosa into rebellion against the British Empire.

❂ ❂ ❂

The Believers couldn't be bothered with these debates. They had debates of their own. A new prophetess had arisen at the banks of the Mpongo River. She was Nonkosi; the eleven-year-old daughter of a well-known traditional doctor called Kulwana.

Nonkosi's visions began early in January. She saw Strangers who were similar to those seen by the great prophetesses of the Gxarha River. They first emerged to her when she was playing near a pool in the Mpongo River. They showed her a great number of cattle in the water and the new people that would rise if the amaXhosa destroyed all their cattle. They told her of various peoples who were going to be destroyed for not believing, and these included the Basotho, the amaMfengu, and of course the English, who would run to King-williamstown and be destroyed there.

The strange thing about the daughter of Kulwana was that she did not look confused and unkempt in the manner of great prophets. She was not waifish and malnourished. She was zestful and liked to spend the whole day playing children's games instead of sitting with the gray-beards teaching them about the happy times that were coming with the new people from the world of the ancestors. But when she was called to order, her message was clear and resounding. It came out of her little mouth in musical peals. It made grown men cry with joy.

Although Nonkosi's message was similar to Nongqawuse's, she gained a new following. Among the young Believers it became fashion-able to identify oneself as Nonkosi's follower rather than Nongqawuse's. Whereas Nongqawuse urged her followers to wear ornaments and makeup, Nonkosi's teachings were that ornaments should be disposed of. She further gave instructions that fires for cooking or for any other purpose should be made only of sneezewood, instead of the more pop-ular mimosa.

Kulwana became his daughter's staunchest supporter. He told her followers that he too had heard the cattle lowing and bellowing from the pool.

It seemed that there was competition between the two prophets. In reality the competition was between their followers. The prophets spoke with one voice and did not see each other as rivals. All they wanted was to save the amaXhosa nation.

Twin and Qukezwa were curious about the new prophet. They undertook a two-day journey to visit her at the Mpongo River banks. It was an arduous trip, for Heitsi slowed them down considerably. But they did not regret it one bit. They were energized by Nonkosi, and were filled with new hope. She led them, together with hundreds of other followers, to a pond near the river, and there they saw newly circumcised abakhwetha initiates dancing on the surface of the water. They joined in the song and danced, albeit on solid ground. They saw the horns of cattle emerging from the water, then sinking again, and heard the lowing of cows and the bellowing of bulls. In the evenings they participated in the *ukurhuda* rituals where the wonderful prophetess administered sacred enemas and emetics to her followers. They vomited and their stomachs ran all night long.

Like all of Nonkosi's followers, Twin and Qukezwa shaved off their eyebrows in order to distinguish themselves from Unbelievers.

Although two denominations of Believers had emerged, Twin and Qukezwa decided that they would follow both prophets. When they returned to the Gxarha they introduced the fashion of shaving off the eyebrows. The Believers there happily adopted it, even though it was Nonkosi's invention.

Using the herbs they had brought with them from the Mpongo River, Qukezwa and Twin frequently indulged themselves with revelries of vomiting and purging.

The problems of redness!

Camagu is facing the irritation of Xoliswa Ximiya. And this threatens to put a damper on his housewarming party. She does not seem to care at all that she is a guest in his house. Guests, like hosts, are generally expected to be gracious. That is why the other guests—the elite of Qolorha-by-Sea such as John Dalton, the teachers of the various schools in the area, and Vathiswa, the receptionist at the Blue Flamingo

Hotel—are fidgeting on their seats. Some of them may agree with Xoliswa Ximiya's point of view, but they do not think that it is right to attack a man at his own housewarming party. And Camagu seems determined to stand his ground.

"I say it is an insult to the people of Qolorha-by-Sea," Xoliswa Ximiya screeches. "My people are trying to move away from redness, but you are doing your damnedest to drag them back."

"To you, Xoliswa, the isikhakha skirt represents backwardness," says Camagu defensively. "But to other people it represents a beautiful artistic cultural heritage."

Camagu is the only one in the village who calls Xoliswa Ximiya just by her first name—besides her parents, of course. This is one of the things that have fueled rumors that something is cooking between them. This, and the fact that they argue all the time. And then there are the visits to her house in the schoolyard, which sometimes take place in the evening. Others believe that he has slept there on occasion, although no one can vouch to have seen him with their own eyes.

"Even in magazines people wear isikhakha," says Vathiswa. Although she is known as Xoliswa Ximiya's lackey, she feels that this time, in the presence of all these honorable guests, she must contribute her little piece of wisdom as honestly as she can. But Xoliswa Ximiya's glaring eyes silently reprimand her for her treachery.

"It is true," says Vathiswa, asserting her independence. "Even on television I saw some cabinet ministers wearing isikhakha at the opening of parliament."

"It does not matter if the president's wife herself wore isikhakha," says Xoliswa Ximiya dismissively. "It is part of our history of redness. It is a backward movement. All this nonsense about bringing back African traditions! We are civilized people. We have no time for beads and long pipes!"

The curse of redness!

It all started with the people of Johannesburg. When they heard that Camagu had not gone to America after all, but was hiding on the wild coast of the Eastern Cape, they sent messages that he should buy them traditional isiXhosa costumes. These were becoming very popular among the glitterati and sundry celebrities of the city of gold since the advent of the African Renaissance movement spearheaded by the president of the country.

Camagu saw this as an opportunity for his cooperative society to expand its activities to the production of traditional isiXhosa costumes and accessories such as beaded pipes and shoulder bags, to be marketed in Johannesburg. His partners, NoGiant and MamCirha, were keen on the idea. After all, harvesting the sea for imbhaza and imbhatyisa did not earn them that much. They even invited NoManage and No-Vangeli to join the cooperative, but these cohorts of Dalton's were too busy milking gullible tourists with their displays and performances of isiXhosa culture.

When these activities reached the ears of Xoliswa Ximiya, she was not amused. Her lack of amusement has continued to this day, and is now showing itself at her host's housewarming party.

Vathiswa looks quite rueful for contradicting her mentor. After her intervention, the other guests feel free to stand with Xoliswa Ximiya and become vocal about the matter. Those whose views fall in line with Camagu's wisely keep quiet. John Dalton knows how to tread carefully at times like these. He keeps his opinion to himself.

"What can we say about a man who believes in a snake?" Xoliswa Ximiya sneers.

"It is precisely because I was visited by Majola that my fortunes have changed for the better. The house . . . the business . . ."

Camagu does not wait for Xoliswa Ximiya's rejoinder. He excuses himself and goes outside to join the villagers who are sitting on the verandah eating meat and drinking beer. He would have liked them—especially elders like Bhonco—to sit at the table inside the house with the rest of high society. But they refused. They said the custom was that they enjoyed their feasts under the trees while the "teachers" sat in the house. The best compromise that Camagu could reach was that they should at least sit on the verandah.

"Hey, teacher," cries NoPetticoat. "I hear now you are sewing skirts."

"You can laugh as much as you like, Mam'uNoPetticoat, but you will swallow your laughter as soon as you see those women who have joined the cooperative society getting rich," says Camagu.

"Those women, teacher," teases Bhonco, son of Ximiya, "do their husbands who work in the mines of Johannesburg know that they are running around with you here?"

"Very soon those women will be earning more than their husbands in the mines," Camagu boasts.

"In that case you can count me in," says NoPetticoat. "I am tired of cleaning the bottoms of the children of white people at the Blue Flamingo."

Everyone can see that beer has already run into NoPetticoat's head. Not only is she unsteady, but she has become quite vociferous.

"You, NoPetticoat? What a laugh!" says Bhonco.

"You don't think I can do it, Bhonco?" challenges NoPetticoat. "You don't think I can work with beads?"

"What would Xoliswa say?" asks Bhonco.

Everyone agrees that Xoliswa Ximiya would not like that at all. Bhonco and NoPetticoat would not want to make Xoliswa Ximiya unhappy.

"Especially now that she has built you that lovely ixande house," adds Camagu, making sure that the sting of his remark is felt. He has learned that here at Qolorha-by-Sea a man who does not hit back becomes the playing ground of other men . . . and women.

People mumble that it is unbecoming for this Camagu, son of Cesane, to direct such snide remarks at his prospective father-in-law. Some ask how Bhonco can be his prospective father-in-law when the man has not even asked for his daughter's hand in marriage.

"How do you know he has not asked?" asks a woman. "You do not know the things that happen in other people's homesteads."

"We would know. We would know," says a man. "A daughter's hand in marriage is never asked in secret. It becomes a public occasion."

They all shut up when NoPetticoat glares at them disapprovingly. It is fortunate that Camagu does not hear what they are talking about from his position near the door.

"You see, son of Cesane," says Bhonco in a hurt voice, "not all of us are rich like you. Not all of us can afford to buy sea cottages like this one that we are warming today."

Camagu apologizes and says he did not mean to sting the elders with words. He did not buy this sea cottage because he is rich. When Dalton told him that it was for sale when the owner emigrated to Australia, he tried very hard to raise money to buy it. He went to banks from Butterworth to East London, but they all refused to give him a bond, for they said he was unemployed. He pleaded with John Dalton to stand surety for him, but he refused. "Such things spoil friendship," he said.

It was only after he sold his car that he had the money to put down as a deposit, and only after he showed the bank the accounts of the cooperative society that they agreed to give him a mortgage. They decided that he was self-employed rather than unemployed.

"This son of Cesane," says NoPetticoat, laughing mockingly, "they say he has learning that surpasses even that of our daughter. He has come after many years across the seas. But what is he doing loitering in the village? Of what use are his long letters? At least our daughter has done something for her parents. Is he able to do anything for his parents when he runs around catching imbhaza and imbhatyisa with women, and sewing skirts and beads?"

Camagu ignores the old woman. But others will not let the matter rest. Some praise his cottage in hope that he will take out more beer. Indeed, they say, here he will live like a white man. He even has taps of water inside the house, in the kitchen and the bathroom. His toilet is inside the house, unlike the pit latrines at their homesteads.

"Don't even mention water," says Bhonco. "He has all this water in every room while our communal water taps have been closed! Now our wives have to go to wells far away, or to the rivers."

"We should be asking you why the taps are closed, son of Ximiya," says another old man. "You are on the water committee, are you not?"

"Ask Dalton, not me," says Bhonco defensively. "He and his Believers closed the water. Or ask this son of Cesane."

"No. Not me," says Camagu. "I am not on the water committee. No one ever elected me there."

"No one ever elected you in any of these quarrels between the Believers and Unbelievers. Yet you have chosen a side," says Bhonco.

"Hey, John, come out here," Camagu calls into the house. "I am not going to be a martyr for your sins."

John Dalton walks out. He seems relieved to be rescued from the harangue of the intellectuals in the house. But his face soon changes when he realizes that he is in for interrogation out here. The people want to know why the water taps have been closed.

"You know very well why they are closed, my mothers and fathers," says Dalton. "For many months now you have not paid for the water. You know that those water pumps have to be maintained, and it takes money to maintain them. It takes money to buy diesel too."

"But some of us have been paying regularly ever since the communal taps were constructed," pleads a woman.

"It is true, some of you have been paying," admits Dalton. "But most of you have not been paying. The taps shall remain closed until all of you have paid."

"It is unfair. We suffer for the sins of those who have not paid."

"We open the water just for you, even those who have not paid will get it. It is up to you to see to it that your neighbors pay so that everyone can get water."

"What about you and Camagu? You have water."

"Because we have paid and ours are not communal taps. Those who can afford to have taps that go straight to their homesteads and have paid for them continue to get water."

"It is a plot of the Believers!" shouts Bhonco. "I want everyone to know that I disagreed with this closing of the taps at the committee meetings. I disagreed completely. But I was outvoted by the Believers!"

"It is like this election thing," says NoPetticoat. "We thought things were going to be better. But look who they put in to run our affairs: people we don't know. People from Butterworth who know nothing about our life here."

This is a sore point for the villagers. When local elections came a few years back, people thought that at last they were going to run their own affairs. But the ruling party had different ideas. It imposed its own people nominated by party bosses from some regional headquarters far away from Qolorha. And the villagers did not know these candidates.

As a result many people refused to vote, even though they were supporters of the party. The same thing happened at the last general election, and it will happen again at the next local election unless people learn to fight for their rights.

"It is the same at the provincial and national level too. Leadership is imposed from above," says Dalton. "But I do not see what that has to do with the water taps. The water committee was not imposed on anyone. It was elected by the villagers."

"Don't even talk, Dalton," says Bhonco. "You have messed up our lives. You and your Believers. Now we can't even cut our own trees."

"That is unfair," says Camagu. "You all know it is not John's law. It is the law of the land. And it is for your benefit."

"What benefit?" Bhonco fumes. "Our forefathers lived to be graybeards without imposing such stupid laws on themselves."

"Perhaps you need to learn more about your forefathers," says Dalton. "King Sarhili himself was a very strong conservationist. He created Manyube, a conservation area where people were not allowed to hunt or chop trees. He wanted to preserve these things for future generations."

"Don't tell us about Sarhili," cries Bhonco. "He was a foolish king. A king of darkness. That is why he instructed his people to follow Nongqawuse!"

The argument is broken by the arrival of Zim. Everyone bursts out laughing. Zim looks very strange. It is as if he does not belong to this world. He has shaved off his eyebrows. And he has cocooned himself inside a red blanket, without any of the beautiful ornaments for which he is known far and wide. There is not even a single strand of beads. His feet are bare. No shoes. No anklets.

"I greet you, children of the amaGcaleka clan, even though you welcome me with the rudeness of your laughter," says Zim, sitting down among his peers.

"What have you done to yourself, Tat'uZim?" asks Camagu. "You were not like this yesterday when I saw you."

"It is the new look of the Believers, in accordance with the teachings of Nonkosi, the prophetess of the Mpongo Valley," explains Zim.

"What happened to Nongqawuse now?" asks NoPetticoat laughing.

"Oh, she is still there all right. But she is not the only prophet, you know. We Believers have a number of prophets. Nonkosi taught her followers to shave their eyebrows so as to distinguish themselves from the Unbelievers."

Zim is clearly taking the war to new heights. He says it came to him through the birds that he had neglected some practices of the Believers of old. Maybe that's why his son left and never came back. From now on he is going to shave his eyebrows.

His discovery of Nonkosi, the eleven-year-old prophetess of the Mpongo Valley, has injected new life into his belief. He has now adopted a new set of rituals that combine the best from the two denominations. For instance, he takes regular enemas and emetics to cleanse himself, as he comes into contact with Unbelievers like Bhonco on a regular basis. This ukurhuda ritual is a basic tenet of the teachings of the daughter of Kulwana.

All the while Bhonco is shaking his head pityingly.

"A person who does not get any pension from the government can shake his head until it flies off his neck," says Zim, not looking at Bhonco.

"How foolish can people be!" rejoins Bhonco.

"How foolish can people be!" echoes NoPetticoat.

"If Unbelievers have their rituals, there is no reason why we cannot have our own too," says Zim. "If they can induce sadness in their lives, there is no reason why we should not purify our bodies and our souls by purging and vomiting."

"Our rituals don't leave a stink!" shouts Bhonco.

"Your rituals are not even your own," Zim shouts back. "You stole them from the abaThwa!"

"The abaThwa people don't dance around to invoke grief! Grief is our thing, and no one else's."

"The abaThwa dance around to induce a trance that takes them to the land of the ancestors. You stole that from them!"

"We didn't steal it! They gave it to us!"

"Thieves! Thieves!"

"You call me that again, Zim, and see if Nongqawuse and Nonkosi will protect your head from the damage that my stick will cause on it."

"You and whose army, Bhonco?"

"Stop!" cries Camagu. "You are the elders of the village. You are here to bless my new house, not to desecrate it with your bad blood!"

"How can your house be blessed when you have run out of beer?" asks NoPetticoat, standing up and shaking her upper body in the *tyityimba* dance. Everyone cheers and claps hands and sings for her.

It is true that Camagu underestimated the number of people who would come to his housewarming party. He had thought that only those he had invited would come. He had forgotten that in the village a feast belongs to everyone. But he has only himself to blame, because MamCirha and NoGiant, his business partners who brewed the beer for him, did warn him that the malted sorghum he bought was too little to satisfy the thirsty throats of the guests. Camagu thought they were referring to the guests he had invited, and not to the whole village. So he dismissed their concerns. Now everyone is complaining that he is tightfisted and stingy like all learned people.

He goes into the house and comes out with a bottle of brandy. It is only for the elders, he tells them, and not for everyone. He pours some brandy in the bottle cap, in the manner that brandy is normally served, and gives it to the shriveled old woman nearest him. She swallows it in one gulp and grimaces with burning pleasure. He does the same for every older guest, each one swallowing and grimacing. This continues for several rounds, until the brandy in the bottle is finished.

"You gave him five capfuls of brandy," complains Zim, wagging his finger at Bhonco. "Why do you only give me four?"

"I was not counting," says Camagu. "I just passed the bottle cap around."

"It is the greed of the Believers!" shouts Bhonco. "He got five like everyone else!"

Another battle is about to erupt, but Camagu and Dalton put a lid on it. Dalton makes the mistake of saying that their ancestors must be ashamed of them for the way they behave. Both elders give him a stern look.

"Leave our ancestors out of this," says Zim. "What do you know of them?"

"He knows them all right," says another elder. "His forebears cooked them in their cauldrons."

"Yes," rejoins Bhonco. "This Dalton here . . . he is a descendant of headhunters. Yet no one holds that against him."

"It is not true! It is not true!" shouts Dalton, flushed with shame.

On this matter Camagu is on the side of the elders. He says it is true. In one of his travels abroad he went to the Natural History Museum—part of the British Museum—in London to see the reconstructed skeletons of dinosaurs. He chanced upon some scientists from his university in the United States who had been given access to examine some items that were not on display. He was shocked to discover that there were five dried-out heads of the so-called Bushmen stored in boxes in some back room of the museum.

He has never understood this barbaric habit of the British of shrinking heads of the vanquished people and displaying them in these impressive buildings where ladies and gentlemen go to gloat and celebrate their superior civilization.

"Maybe that is where the head of our great-great-grandfather ended up," says Zim.

"Yes, the head of the great Xikixa must be in that building," agrees Bhonco.

There is sudden silence. Everyone is taking in what has just happened. Some stare in disbelief. Believers and Unbelievers have just agreed on something!

"The heads of our ancestors are all over Europe . . . trophies collected in military action and in executions," continues Camagu. "Not only heads. In Paris the private parts of a Khoikhoi woman called Saartjie Baartman are kept in a bottle!"

Bhonco bursts out laughing.

"The Khoikhoi are Zim's people," he says, still laughing. "He descends from a Khoikhoi woman called Quxu. They changed her name to Qukezwa so that people would think she was an umXhosa. Zim himself married a woman of the amaGqunukhwebe. And we all know who the amaGqunukhwebe are."

"The way I see it, it is no laughing matter," says Camagu.

"It is a laughing matter from where I am sitting," says Bhonco. "I have an unobstructed view of Zim's face. I wonder what he plans to do about the femaleness of his great-grandmother that is kept in a bottle in the land of the white man."

Zim stands up, casts an evil eye on both Camagu and Bhonco, and walks away from the feast.

"Please, Tat'uZim, come back! Do not leave like this!" Camagu shouts after the old man. But he walks on, and does not look back for one moment.

"You see now?" says Dalton to Camagu. "That's what you get when you dig out the past that is best forgotten."

"It is not the past," says Camagu emphatically. "It is the present. Those trophies are still there . . . today . . . as we speak."

"Let him go! Who needs him here?" shouts NoPetticoat drunkenly.

"You cannot say that about my guests," says Camagu sternly. "This is not your feast. You wouldn't like it if somebody did this at your feast."

"This child of Cesane, now he is boasting about his feast," says Bhonco, standing up and uxoriously holding NoPetticoat's hand. "Why doesn't someone tell him that it is not the first time we have seen a feast? He can stay with his feast for all we care."

He helps NoPetticoat up, and leads her away. All the while she is singing an umtshotsho song, and shaking her upper body in the style of the tyityimba dance. Bhonco joins in the song as they stagger away together.

Although the elite stays until late at night, dancing to compact discs that have been brought by Vathiswa, Camagu has lost interest in his own housewarming party. Right up to the end, Xoliswa Ximiya does not stop nagging him about his encouragement of redness in the village. Even when he accompanies her to her house, the harangue continues. Normally he cannot drink enough of her chilled beauty. But at this moment he wishes she would just disappear.

Qukezwa is the best antidote to Xoliswa Ximiya.

Qukezwa. He has not seen her since the silvery night, months ago. He thought he had freed himself from her inebriating power, until she started invading his dreams, as NomaRussia used to do. Orgastic dreams. Dreams in slow motion. Dreams that sweep the NomaRussia water from the river. The riverbed lies naked. Dreams in slow motion. Very messy dreams.

The following day he goes to Zim's compound under the pretext of making peace with the elder. But Zim is not under his tree. He has gone to the dongas to purge himself of the contamination he got from mixing with Unbelievers yesterday, Qukezwa tells him.

"You are lucky he is not here," she adds. "He does not even want to hear your name mentioned."

"I came to make peace with him, even though I do not know what I have done," says Camagu.

"You do not know? After spreading lies throughout the village that my grandmother's femaleness lives in a bottle in the land of the white man?"

"I never said such things!"

"Is my father lying then? Is he lying when he says he became the laughingstock of your feast after you made such ludicrous claims about our relative?"

"Saartjie Baartman is not your relative. She was a Khoikhoi woman, but you don't know if she was your relative! I was merely stating a fact about what white people did to her. What happened to her was not your fault either. I do not know why you should bear that shame."

Qukezwa is not convinced. "All the Khoikhoi are one person," she says. "You cannot say the private parts of that woman have nothing to do with me."

Camagu begs her to come down to the lagoon so that they can talk about this.

She glares at him. She is angry, not only because of the femaleness that lives in a bottle. Of late he has been featuring in her dreams. And she tells him so. She does not like that. He has no business imposing himself on her dreams, performing unsavory acts. Everyone in the village knows he belongs to Xoliswa Ximiya. He must do those dirty things in the headmistress's dreams.

"I should be angry with you too, because you feature in my dreams," says Camagu. "It is not for anyone in this village to decide to whom I belong!"

"If I feature in your dreams it is your own fault. Just don't mess up my dreams."

"Please," pleads Camagu, "let's talk about this. Let's go down to the sea."

Mutual dreams. Messy dreams.

She offers him food: fried *amaqongwe*, or cockles, with maize porridge. Then she says he should go and wait for her at the lagoon.

On the way he meets members of his cooperative society coming up with the day's harvest. NoGiant and MamCirha tease him that it is too late in the day if he thinks he can catch any mussels and oysters.

"You must learn to wake up early, teacher," says MamCirha.

"He needs a wife, don't you think?" asks NoGiant. "I tell him every day that a man of his age needs a good woman who will look after him."

"Well, he cannot say we did not advise him," says MamCirha, to the laughter of the other women. "He can't say there are no eligible young women in this village. There is Xoliswa Ximiya for instance."

"What is happening to their thing? Is it getting cold?"

"Men are afraid of Xoliswa Ximiya. There is Vathiswa. Vathiswa is a good woman, even though she had a fall."

He just smiles and waves them away. They have a way of discussing him as if he is just a piece of meat, these business partners. That is how they communicate with him: by completely ignoring him and addressing each other about him, and supplying the answers on his behalf.

He has grown to love them, though. And they love him too. To the extent that their husbands were beginning to get jealous. Until they saw the money their wives were bringing home.

Black economic empowerment is a buzzword at places like Giggles in Johannesburg, where the habitués are always on the lookout for crumbs that fall from the tables of the Aristocrats of the Revolution.

But the black empowerment boom is merely enriching the chosen few—the elite clique of black businessmen who have become overnight multimillionaires. Or trade union leaders who use the workers as stepping-stones to untold riches for themselves. And politicians who effectively use their struggle credentials for self-enrichment. They all have their snouts buried deep in the trough, lapping noisily in the name of the poor, trying to outdo one another in piggishness.

Disillusioned with the corruption and nepotism of the city, Camagu had come to Qolorha in search of a dream. And here people are now doing things for themselves, without any handouts from the government.

But why is there still a void in his life?

Finally Qukezwa comes riding Gxagxa. After a long wait. Yet she is unhurried.

"You kept me waiting," complains Camagu.

She does not dismount.

"Why do you want to see me?" she asks.

"It is polite to apologize when you have kept someone waiting."

"I didn't ask you to wait. It was your choice. And it is not for you to teach me manners. Go and teach that girlfriend of yours to stop being a bat."

"Girlfriend? A bat?"

"Are you going to pretend that Xoliswa Ximiya is not your girlfriend? In that case you are the only one in the village who doesn't know that you two are lovers. Yes, she is a bat, because she does not know whether she is a bird or a mouse."

He does not know how to answer that.

"If you don't know why you wanted to see me I'll be on my way," she says.

"Please give me a ride on Gxagxa . . . like the other night," he pleads.

She laughs, and says, "Only if we ride naked. Do you think you can do that, learned man? Strip naked? Gxagxa loves to be ridden naked."

She does not wait for his answer but gallops away. Camagu just stands there, openmouthed and looking foolish.

Qukezwa does not get far before a group of about six girls emerges from the bushes and howls at her. She stops and faces them defiantly.

"So this is what you are up to, Qukezwa! Sneaking around with other women's men?" cries one of the girls.

"Does Xoliswa Ximiya know that you sleep with her man?" asks another.

"You have taken after your mother! What she did to our friend is terrible!" yells yet another girl.

"She must be burning in hell for what she did to the poor girl!"

"And all because of your father!"

"Our friend is getting worse now! Are you going to be happy when she dies?"

"You are all a family of whores and perverts!"

"Your friend is the whore in this whole matter," Qukezwa finally shouts back, and gives Gxagxa two slaps at the back. The horse neighs and charges at the girls. They run in different directions, screeching. One falls down and Gxagxa gives her a kick in the stomach before he gallops away. The girls utter various invectives pertaining to NoEngland's sojourn in the house of Lucifer as they rush to assist their fallen comrade.

Camagu wonders what this is all about.

He is eating the evening meal when there is a sharp knock on the door. It is Vathiswa, and she says she has come to fetch her compact discs that people were dancing to at the housewarming party. Camagu invites her to join him at table. There are more oysters and mussels fried with onion in the pan. At first Vathiswa is hesitant. People in this village talk, she says. They will tell Xoliswa Ximiya that now she is eating her supper in Camagu's house.

"Xoliswa Ximiya is my friend," she adds. "I wouldn't like her to think I have designs on her man."

"Her man? Xoliswa does not own me!" says Camagu. "Why is everybody on my case about this Xoliswa Ximiya?"

He tells her about the girls who attacked Qukezwa just because they saw her standing with him.

"It was not really about you," says Vathiswa. She tells him about the girl who had a tryst with Zim, and the activities of NoEngland and her igqirha that left the poor girl gushing to this day.

"If you can keep a secret, I can tell you that Qukezwa is pregnant," says Vathiswa.

This comes as a shock to Camagu. He does not believe it, and he says so.

"It is true. But she cannot name the man. She says it just happened on its own. The grandmothers who examined her confirmed that she has not known a man before."

"She didn't say anything about this when I met her today."

"Why would she want to tell yon about that?"

Camagu laughs mockingly and says, "Her virginity was broken by horse-riding, and she conceived from that?"

"The grandmothers say she is still a virgin," says Vathiswa seriously.

Camagu cannot understand why he is filled with anger and bitterness. He remembers the silvery night when she sang him to an orgasm. He recalls the dreams.

He looks at Vathiswa munching away nonchalantly at rice, oysters, and mussels. It occurs to him that this is the longest he has ever been celibate. Has his famous lust deserted him at last? This is the land of starvation. He has learned to use his fingers. But only in the mornings that follow the nights that are not populated by messy dreams.

He remembers MamCirha and NoGiant talking of the troubles the young women of the village go through. In their oblique communication with him, MamCirha said that in the early days of her marriage, when her husband was away in the mines and the desire of the flesh attacked her, she would lie on her stomach for two hours while the urge slowly burnt itself away. She had not yet learned to use her fingers to create her own worlds of passion.

**8** Everybody is talking about the concert. It is the highlight of every year. For the past two weeks the students of Qolorha-by-Sea Secondary School have been practicing izitibiri, the lively songs that are also known as sounds. Sounds are very popular with school and church choirs, and are a staple at concerts.

The main aim of the concert is to raise funds for the secondary school. But it also serves to celebrate the end of the school year. It brings together people from all corners of Qolorha and the neighboring villages.

Those villagers who like the limelight are also preparing themselves for a few minutes of fame. They will "buy" themselves the right to go onto the stage and render a song, a dance, or any clownish thing that they think will make the audience laugh. Indeed, most money at concerts is raised when members of the audience go to the chairperson's table and pay some money, "buying" that they or some other member of the audience should perform some act or other. The money that is made at the door is only a tiny fraction of the fortunes that are raised when enthusiastic citizens "buy" one another.

The workers from the Blue Flamingo Hotel are practicing hard too. For a change they will be singing for the whole village, instead of just a few tourists in the hotel bar on Saturday evenings. They will not be buying themselves to perform, but have been specially invited by Xoliswa Ximiya to support the school choir.

NoPetticoat is the natural leader of izitibiri. Her fellow choristers give most of the solos to her. To Bhonco's chagrin, she has been spending all her evenings for the past week or so practicing at the hotel. Bhonco has had to cook his own supper. But he suffers in silence for the sake of his daughter's school. And for the prestige of having a wife who is a chorister by invitation rather than by being bought to sing. The concert is so highly regarded that receptionists like Vathiswa participate in the choir, even though they are too important to sing for tourists on Saturday evenings.

While Bhonco is languishing for his wife, Zim is pining for the Russians. In the same way that he resuscitated the practice of shaving his eyebrows and cleansing his soul with enemas and emetics, he has revived another age-old practice: that of standing on the hill and watching the sea for the approach of Russian ships.

The Russians were supposed to come during the days of Nongqawuse, led by the departed amaXhosa generals and kings. Believers of old stood on the hill waiting for them. The Russians did not come. It was one of the prophecies that were not fulfilled because of the selfish Unbelievers who refused to slaughter their cattle.

When Zim is not dozing under his gigantic tree, listening to the rolling songs of the spotted-backed amahobohobo weaverbirds, he spends hours on the hill, gazing longingly at the place where the sea meets the sky. He knows the Russians will not come. But he waits for them still, in memory of those who waited in vain.

In the days of Nongqawuse the Russians were black and were the reincarnation of amaXhosa warriors. Zim knows very well that today's Russians are white people. After all, sons and daughters of the land who have spent decades in exile, some living in the houses of the very same Russians, have said as much. But the spirit of the ancestors continues to direct their sympathies. That is why they fought the English. That is why all those who benefited from the sufferings of the Middle Generations hated them. That is why they armed and trained those sons and daughters of the nation to bring to an end the sufferings of the Middle Generations.

It is with a sense of pride that he stands on the hill. That he pines. That he waits for the Russians even though he knows they will not come. They have already come in a guise that no Believer expected. They came in the bodies of those who fought to free the Middle Generations. It is an honor to pine on behalf of those who waited in vain.

Camagu pines too. He has convinced himself that it is for NomaRussia, the woman he followed to Qolorha. However, for some strange reason he has taken to walking past Zim's homestead several times a day. Even when his destination is Vulindlela Trading Store, he takes the longer route that detours past Zim's homestead. And when he gets to the store his eyes seem to dart around, looking for something he never finds. He exchanges a few words with Dalton about this or that development, and then tells him that he is rushing to the women of the cooperative society. Again he takes a circuitous route that passes Zim's homestead. Sometimes he is brave enough to enter, and finds the old man dozing under his tree. He makes some small talk while his eyes search for something that they never seem to find.

The old man reprimands him for the hundredth time for making wild claims that the private parts of a Khoikhoi ancestor live in a bottle in the land of the white man. Camagu apologizes for the hundredth time for making this statement at a public feast, but insists that it is true. He says the old man's anger is directed at the wrong person. He should be angry with those who did dirty things to Saartjie Baartman instead of venting his wrath on him. He is only the messenger.

On occasion he sees the old man in the distance, walking up the hill. Or standing on top of the hill looking intently at the horizon. Camagu walks to the homestead pretending he does not know that the old man is not there. He knocks on every door. But no one is there. He knocks again and again. He stands out there for some time, praying for a miracle, then he slowly walks away.

Yet he pines for NomaRussia.

There are many others who pine at Qolorha-by-Sea. Rumor has it that the principal of Qolorha-by-Sea Secondary School herself is pining. But instead of waning away and languishing in her heartache, as people who pine are wont to do, she lashes out at everyone in anger. They say her problems began when she discovered that the man she intended to marry had impregnated a nondescript girl who used to be her student. The man himself is said to be pining for this former student who has been dispatched by her father to a distant village to live with relatives until the baby is born.

It is uncanny how the people of Qolorha-by-Sea know things about their fellow citizens that the unhappy compatriots do not know about themselves.

Perhaps the concert will bring some relief to languishing souls.

While pining is doing the rounds in the village, John Dalton is preoccupied with water affairs. It is weeks now since his water committee closed all the communal taps. The villagers are refusing to pay. When the chief calls a public meeting, an imbhizo, to discuss the matter, the few who come say, "You, son of Dalton, you got money from your business friends and from the government to start this water project. Why don't you ask those people who gave you the money to maintain these taps? How do they think they will be maintained if they do not come to maintain them?"

Dalton runs to Camagu with his woes.

"We must coopt you into the water committee," he says. "Maybe you will come up with new ideas on how to make these people pay for the water."

"That will be impossible," says Camagu. "My hands are full already with the cooperative society."

The cooperative society is not doing badly. Business would be booming if the banks were interested in assisting small-business people. The women sell their sea-harvest to hotels and restaurants in East London. They now want to expand their market to inland cities like Queenstown, Kingwilliamstown, and Grahamstown. They have signed a contract with a hotel chain for large supplies of mussels, oysters, and cockles. But now they need money to harvest on a larger scale. Most important, they need to buy a cold storage vehicle that will deliver the food. At the moment they use cooler bags filled with ice. For transport they depend on lifts from Dalton, the four-wheel-drive van from the Blue Flamingo, or buses and taxis.

They have tried to get loans from banks, but to no avail. The banks want security. They do not look at the potential of the business and the profits that will come from the contract with the hotel chain. Camagu fears that they will end up losing this big order, since the hotel chain will opt for a supplier who is able to deliver.

It was the same in Johannesburg too. The banks frustrated him after he had taken the advice to open his own consultancy. He got a two-million-rand contract to do a feasibility study for a new satellite television network. The television company was prepared to advance him 30 percent of the money provided he secured a guarantee from the bank. But the banks refused to give him a guarantee. He did not want a single cent from them, yet they failed to assist him. They did not want to take the risk, even on the basis of his qualifications, which clearly showed he could do the job. He lost that contract. The banks lost a lucrative account and destroyed one more entrepreneur.

History is repeating itself. His cooperative society is on the verge of success. But the South African banks are determined that it should not succeed. So much for black empowerment!

Hopefully the beadwork and isiXhosa costumes they are sending to Johannesburg every month will make enough money to put down on a secondhand vehicle, even if it does not have cold storage.

"But you can spare a few minutes a day to attend to the problems of water," insists Dalton.

"No, I cannot," says Camagu. "You went about this whole thing the wrong way, John. The water project is failing because it was imposed on the people. No one bothered to find out their needs."

"That is nonsense," says Dalton. "Everyone needs clean water."

"So we think...in our infinite wisdom. Perhaps the first step would have been to discuss the matter with the villagers, to find out what their priorities are. They should be part of the whole process. They should be active participants in the conception of the project, in raising funds for it, in constructing it. Then it becomes their project. Then they will look after it."

Camagu is of the view that, as things stand now, the villagers see this as Dalton's project. He thought he was doing them a favor when he single-handedly raised funds for it and invited government experts to help in its construction. It was only later that the community was involved. Dalton hand-picked a committee of people he thought were enlightened enough to look after the project. The villagers were given a ready-made water scheme. It is falling apart because they don't feel they are part of it.

"That is the danger of doing things for the people instead of doing things with the people," adds Camagu. "It is happening throughout this country. The government talks of delivery and of upliftment. Now people expect things to be delivered to them without any effort on their part. They expect somebody to come from Pretoria and uplift them. The notions of delivery and upliftment have turned our people into passive recipients of programs conceived by so-called experts who know nothing about the lives of rural communities. People are denied the right to shape their own destiny. Things are done for them. The world owes them a living. A dependency mentality is reinforced in their minds."

"Are you trying to say I don't know what I am doing?" asks Dalton. "You come all the way from America with theories and formulas, and you want to apply them in my village. I have lived here all my life. So have my fathers before me. I cannot be called an expert from outside the community. I am one with these people."

"That is the main problem with you, John. You know that you are 'right' and you want to impose those 'correct' ideas on the populace from above. I am suggesting that you try involving the people in decision-making rather than making decisions for them."

John Dalton has a wounded look. Camagu assures him that he is not belittling his efforts to develop his village. He is merely being critical of the method.

But Dalton walks away without saying another word.

Camagu decides to go and while away time at the concert. People are beginning to gather at Qolorha-by-Sea Secondary School. The village is already filled with the peals of bells, alerting people that the concert is about to start. On his way to the school, Camagu passes Bhonco's homestead. Under the tree in front of the pink rondavel the activities of the elders of the Unbelievers are going on. Camagu wonders if they will not be going to the concert even though NoPetticoat is one of the star attractions.

The Unbelievers are engaged in their memory ritual. When the pangs of unbelief gnaw them, they are undeterred even by important community activities like school concerts. Bhonco, son of Ximiya, would have loved to bask in his wife's glorious voice at the concert. But when the elders of the Unbelievers came early in the morning and demanded the invocation of unhappiness, he had to give the concert up. Of course there may still be time to catch up with it if the Unbelievers return from the time of the ancestors early enough. The concert normally goes on for the whole day.

The Unbelievers like to explore various strategies in pursuit of happiness. Whereas Believers have a tendency of wanting to stay ignorant of the things that could make them unhappy, the Unbelievers like to induce sadness in order to attain happiness.

They are now dancing the painful dance that will send them into a deep trance in which they will commune with some of the saddest moments of their past.

Mjuza and Ned, the notorious amaGqobhoka, were talking their Christian nonsense again. They were telling Twin-Twin and old Nxito that it was wrong to seek happiness in this world. Happiness could be achieved only after death.

"That is a mad idea if ever I heard one," argued Twin-Twin. "How would you attain happiness after death if you failed to attain it when you were still living? Even the ancestors would kick you out of their ranks if you came to them as a failure like that."

"As for me," said Nxito, "I do not think happiness is obtainable. I have been living in this world for many years. I have seen men and women search for it. But when they think they have got hold of it, it escapes. They have to begin searching once again. It is an illusion. That is why our people are now dying of starvation. All in pursuit of happiness."

"Don't tell us about those," responded Ned. "They are stupid heathens."

"For me," said Twin-Twin, "the pursuit of happiness is fulfillment enough."

"Happiness can only be achieved after death, when we join the Lord and sit at his right-hand side," insisted Mjuza.

"At his right-hand side? Why at his right-hand side?" asked Twin-Twin.

"Well, that's where people sit when they join the Lord," said Mjuza sheepishly. "That's where Jesus sits."

There was silence for some time, while the men pondered this heavy matter. They puffed rhythmically on their long pipes, blowing out rings of smoke that hung like halos over their heads.

"Perhaps followers of the religion of the white man like Mjuza and Ned have a point," Nxito said finally. "It is better to forget about happiness. Look what its pursuit has done to my people. They thought it would finally be achieved when the new people came."

"The followers of the god of the white man are lost, Old One," appealed Twin-Twin. "I know that many of our people are beginning to resort to this white god. It is because prophets who purport to speak for our god have let us down. But if we commune with the ancestors, and do all that is right by slaughtering for them, they will give us happiness. Of course they will never come back as the amaThamba, the Believers, have been deceiving the people. Only we shall go to join them when Qamata so decides."

Mjuza and Ned decided it was futile to try to convert these people. They were set in their ways. It did not matter, though. They remained friends still. Unbelievers, whether they were Christians or heathens, could be relied upon as allies of The Man Who Named Ten Rivers. Or so Mjuza and Ned thought.

"Anyway," said Mjuza, "it is clear that we shall not see the question of happiness with the same eye. Let us talk about what you called us here for."

"We summoned you here because messages from the Gxarha River are becoming more frantic," Nxito explained. "Hardly a day passes without a messenger coming to say that Nongqawuse and Nombanda are demanding my return to my chiefdom. What should I do? What do

Gawler and Dalton, the representatives of The Man Who Named Ten Rivers, want me to do in this case?"

"I wonder why Nongqawuse is so keen that you return to Qolorha, when it is her Believers who drove you away in the first place," said Ned.

No one seemed to have an answer. Could it be that the prophetesses feared the wrath of the ancestors should the aged Nxito die in exile, far away from the graves of his fathers?

"Perhaps they are afraid that when Nxito's ancestors arise from the dead they will not be happy to see that their son has been exiled," said Mjuza sarcastically.

"What does the elder think?" asked Ned. "Perhaps things will depend on what Chief Nxito himself wants to do. We'll take your message to the magistrate. I am sure he will want to know what your own view is."

"I am sure the old man is longing for his home," added Mjuza.

"I think that if the old man returns on the orders of these young girls then he'll be giving them more power," said Twin-Twin. "People will believe in them even more."

While Twin-Twin was grappling with the grave issues of happiness and the demands of girl-prophets, Twin and Qukezwa were sitting on top of a hill watching for the approach of Russian ships. They no longer sat on the banks of the river or on the beach, but now preferred the hill since it gave them a good vantage position. From here they would wait until the new people came riding on the waves, or until the long-promised Russian fleet sailed to the shores of Qolorha to destroy The Man Who Named Ten Rivers and his white settlers.

Heitsi was digging out roots a short distance away. The days of glorious feasting were over. The euphoria that soaked the land after the defeat of HMS *Geyser* had long since bubbled itself out, and people were faced with the stark reality of starvation. Twin and Qukezwa were now dependent on wild roots. Even these were hard to find, since starving hordes of Believers had long invaded the veld and the hills to dig them out. Old people, children, the weak, and the infirm were fainting from hunger. At least one person, the son of a believing diviner, was known to have died from the famine.

Yet Twin and Qukezwa's belief was not weakening. They refused to cultivate their fields. Like everyone else, they were hungry. To ease the pain of hunger they tightened leather belts around their stomachs. On days when they could not find any roots, they survived on the bark of mimosa trees. They even had to eat shellfish, which was not regarded as food at all by the amaXhosa. Yet the hope that the prophecies would ultimately be fulfilled burned even brighter in their hearts.

They replenished their belief by going down to Mhlakaza's hut at the Gxarha River. Often they found Believers there whose belief was gradually fading, pestering the prophets and demanding that they be saved from a looming death.

"Go and adorn yourselves!" Nongqawuse told them. "There is no time for weeping! There is time only to celebrate the coming of the new people!"

Once more the people were invigorated. They dressed up in their red ochre costumes and beaded ornaments. Tottering old women were resplendent in new isikhakha skirts and in brass jewelry, hoping that with the rising of the dead they would have their youth restored to them. Twin and Qukezwa were torn between the austere teachings of Nonkosi, which demanded that Believers should eschew all forms of beautification, and Nongqawuse's instructions. On some days they followed Nonkosi and on others Nongqawuse.

But hunger was no respecter of beauty. It attacked even the best dressed of people. The Believers appealed to the believing chiefs to be rescued from its pangs. The chiefs in turn appealed to King Sarhili. After all, he had taken the responsibility of the cattle-killing upon himself. Even Chief Maqoma, the general who had brilliantly led the amaXhosa forces against the British in the War of Mlanjeni, was sending persistent messages to Sarhili. Maqoma was a leading Believer, and had now taken over from his brother as the chief of the amaNgqika clan. He had led his clan into a frenzy of cattle-killing, and into famine. King Sarhili in turn appealed to Mhlakaza and his teenage prophetesses. He tried to force them to come up with a new date for the fulfillment of the prophecies.

"There is nothing I can do," said Mhlakaza. "Nongqawuse and Nombanda have spoken. They say that the dead will not arise as long as Chief Nxito remains in exile. The chief must first return to his chiefdom near the Gxarha. Only then will the new day be known."

Twin-Twin was adamant that old Nxito should not go back to his native place on the instructions of the girls. He was angry because, in spite of the protection that had been guaranteed by the British magistrate and his crony, Dalton, Believers had entered his homestead and had stolen grain from his silos and milk from his two cows. There was also talk that they were looking for his cattle, which were hidden in cattle-posts in the Amathole Mountains under the care of his many sons. Twin-Twin suspected the hand of his twin brother in all this. But he couldn't have been more wrong. Twin was interested only in the rising of the dead. He had no wish to steal anyone's food. He was fulfilled in his hunger. All he wanted to do was to sit in a dazed state with his Qukezwa and Heitsi, and await the Russian ships and the coming of the forebears riding on the waves.

Twin-Twin was now rekindling his old lust for the prophetesses, particularly for Nongqawuse. He was spreading the news throughout Qolorha that copulation was the only medicine that would drive out the wild prophecies from her head. But of course this remained only talk. He would never dare get near Mhlakaza's homestead to seduce or rape the prophetess, even with his phalanx of bodyguards.

Pressure was mounting on Chief Nxito, and finally in November 1856 he yielded and rode back to Qolorha in the company of Twin-Twin and a number of his unbelieving followers. His son, Pama, handed back the chieftainship to him without any argument. After all, it was the wish of the prophetesses that the old man should rule.

The first thing he did, on the very first day of his arrival, was to go to Mhlakaza's homestead. He wanted to talk with Nongqawuse personally. But she seemed disorientated and confused, in the manner of all great prophets. It was left to Mhlakaza and Nombanda to speak for her.

"Nongqawuse says that the new people—" began Mhlakaza.

"The new people?" asked Nxito.

"The ancestors who will rise from the dead," explained Nombanda.

"Nongqawuse says that the new people no longer wish to speak through a commoner like myself," Mhlakaza continued. "They want to speak through you, Chief Nxito. That is why the prophetesses insisted that you come back to your chiefdom. The new people have chosen you, a senior chief of kwaXhosa, to be their spokesman."

"How is that possible?" asked Nxito.

"Nongqawuse says the new people—"

"Nongqawuse says? But she did not say anything," shouted Twin-Twin. "We didn't hear her say anything. She just sits there staring at nothing and you keep on lying that Nongqawuse says, Nongqawuse says . . ."

Nxito's entourage mumbled its agreement, while the Believers expressed their indignation at such blasphemy. Some said it was a pity that Twin was no longer interested in the affairs of the state. He no longer attended imbhizos but sat all day long on the hill. If he were here he would have taught his stubborn brother a thing or two about respecting those who had been chosen by the ancestors to be their messengers.

"Nongqawuse says soon the new people will present themselves to Chief Nxito," continued Mhlakaza, ignoring Twin-Twin's comment. "And when that happens he must call an imbhizo of all commoners and chiefs of kwaXhosa. The multitudes must gather to await the return of the ancestors."

Chief Nxito and his entourage laughed all the way back to his Great Place. What did Mhlakaza take them for? Did he think they were fools?

But the Believers read the return of the old chief and his meeting with the prophets in their own way. Soon word spread that Chief Nxito had been converted from his unbelief. This gave more hope to the Believers that the prophecies would soon be fulfilled. Some even said that the rising of the dead would take place at the next full moon. Once more euphoria swept the land. And the rivers thundered their laughter.

❂   ❂   ❂

The weather is swollen, and the rivers continue to thunder their laughter. The elders of the Unbelievers have fallen on the ground in a trance. Izitibiri sounds that have leaked through the cracks of the Qolorha-by-Sea Secondary School hall are filtering through the heavy air and seem to lull the elders into a deeper trance.

Eventually, Bhonco, son of Ximiya, is the first to open his eyes. Perhaps it is NoPetticoat's voice flavoring the izitibiri that hauls him from the pain of the ancestors' world to the world of joyous school concerts. Hazy figures of little men take shape before him. He looks around. The fellow elders are still in a trance. But to his shock they are all surrounded by a group of abaThwa, the small people who were called Bushmen by the colonists of old.

"Wake your friends up," says the leader of the abaThwa, mixing isiXhosa with his own language which is composed of clicks. "Wake them up!"

"Hey, what is the matter?" Bhonco asks.

"We demand the return of our dance!" says the leader.

"Woe unto the amaGcaleka who have given birth to me!" cries Bhonco.

He tries very hard to wake up the other elders. Slowly they return. Their bodies are drenched with the sadness of the past. They are emerging from the trance ready to face the world and to battle with the Believers. They are taken aback when they hear that the abaThwa are demanding the return of their dance. This is a setback that none of them is prepared for. How will they survive without the dance?

They ask the abaThwa to sit under another tree while they confer.

"Didn't these people give us this dance? How can they demand it back?" asks one elder.

"It is now our dance," asserts another. "They gave it to us."

"But now they want it back," says Bhonco. "I do not think there is anything else that we can do."

"We shall not give them the dance. What can they do?"

"Yes, what can they do? Will they beat us up?"

The elders would be laughing at this ridiculous notion if the elders were other people. Who can imagine little men like the abaThwa beating up giants like Bhonco? But Unbelievers are not prone to laughter.

Or if they laugh at all, it must be in secret. No one must ever know about it. That is why the elders once reprimanded Bhonco when they thought he was becoming too loose with his expression of joy.

"Of course they will not beat us up," says Bhonco. "But we do not want to upset people who have such a powerful dance . . . a dance that can send one to the world of the ancestors and back again. We do not know what other powerful medicine they have that they can use against us should we anger them. We must tread lightly when we deal with these people. If they say they want their dance back, we must give it to them."

"But how are we going to survive without the dance? How are we going to induce sadness in our lives without visiting the sad times of our forefathers?"

"And how do we visit the sad times of our forefathers without the dance?"

"We must negotiate. We must beg them to lend us the dance again," says Bhonco.

"These selfish abaTbwa!" shouts another elder. "I shall not be surprised if they have been put up to this by the Believers. That Zim! He is related to these people, is he not? He must have put them up to this!"

"It is possible that the Believers have had some influence on the abaThwa," says Bhonco. "But Zim is not related to the abaThwa. He is related to the Khoikhoi. They are different people, although if you don't know their language you may think it sounds the same. They look different too."

"You cannot teach us about the abaThwa and the Khoikhoi," says the first elder dismissively. "We have lived with them since the days of our forefathers, although we did not call the Khoikhoi by that name. We called them amaLawu or amaQheya."

Bhonco sighs appreciatively at the elder's use of these derogatory isiXhosa names for the Khoikhoi and people of mixed race. It is the next best thing to laughter.

After a long debate, during which the abaThwa become impatient under their tree, the elders of the Unbelievers agree that the abaThwa must be given their dance back.

"We must be nice to them so that we can borrow it again when we need it," says an elder.

"We are like a sparrow that is wearing the feathers of an eagle," says Bhonco. "We must invent our own dance. At first it will not have the power of the dance of the abaThwa. But it will gain strength the more we perform it. Perhaps one day it will take us to the world of the ancestors just as efficiently as the dance of the abaThwa."

Bhonco is fuming as he makes his way to the concert. Today he will have a showdown of all showdowns with that Believer, Zim. If he wants to fight dirty by sending the abaThwa to take back one of the valued rituals of the Unbelievers, he too, the son of Ximiya, has a few tricks up the sleeves of his wrinkled suit.

After paying his admission fee, Bhonco saunters into the school hall. The hall is full, but a young member of the audience stands up and gives Bhonco his seat. The elder throws his eyes around the hall. They fall on Zim, who is sitting in a self-satisfied manner next to Camagu. The eyes of the elders meet. Bhonco sneers. Zim smiles. Camagu is engrossed in the sounds of the school choir.

Across the aisle John Dalton sits next to Xoliswa Ximiya. He is not with Camagu because things have been a bit icy between them since Camagu's indiscretion of criticizing his efforts to develop his village. Things are a bit icy between Camagu and Xoliswa Ximiya too. Not only because of their divergent views on civilization and barbarism. The little matter of Qukezwa finally reached Xoliswa Ximiya's ears, and she did not hesitate to confront Camagu about it.

It was during one of his visits to her home. Even before he could take a seat, she asked, "Is it true what I hear about you and that child?"

"Child? What child?"

"Don't play dumb with me. I am talking about Qukezwa."

"That child, as you call her, is not dismissive of beautiful things. Where you see darkness, witchcraft, heathens, and barbarians, she sees song and dance and laughter and beauty."

"So it is true! You are a dirty old man! I have lost all respect for you!"

"What is true? And why am I a dirty old man all of a sudden?"

"You made her pregnant. Everyone in the village says so."

"That's the problem with you. You listen to village gossip. No one made that woman pregnant."

"Woman? She is no woman. She was my student here only yesterday. And of course she made herself pregnant, did she?"

"The grandmothers confirmed after a thorough examination that she is still a virgin. I never had anything to do with her."

"You believe in that mumbo jumbo? You are a disgrace to all educated people!"

People talked of Xoliswa Ximiya's fury spreading like a veld fire. It was affecting everybody: her colleagues, her parents, and her students. She was right to be angry, too, they said. This Camagu was proving to be a scoundrel. He must be the one who messed up Zim's daughter, even though the grandmothers have certified her a virgin. Otherwise how did the seed get into her? Who planted it? In what manner?

People's thirst for knowledge must be quenched.

The history teacher is the chairman of the concert. He rings the bell and the choir stops singing. He stands up, obviously enjoying the power that he wields.

"Silence please, the chair is speaking!" he shouts. "Here we have Miss Vathiswa from the Blue Flamingo Hotel. She is buying with her twenty cents that the school choir must take a rest for the duration of three songs, and must be replaced by the choir from the Blue Flamingo Hotel!"

People applaud as the school choir walks from the stage. The Blue Flamingo choir takes the stage, and NoPetticoat's voice rings in a new izitibiri song. Vathiswa herself joins the choir and dances around clownishly. But even before they have gone halfway through the song the bell rings again. The choir stops.

"For twenty-five cents this young man here . . . he is a student at Qolorha-by-Sea Secondary School . . . he says that he will not allow anyone to treat his school choir like that," says the chairman. "The Blue Flamingo choir should go home to sleep, and the school choir should come back to the stage."

The school choir has sung only one song before Vathiswa buys it off the stage again. The buying battle between Vathiswa and a group of students, now also joined by some parents, continues until the price is five rand. Vathiswa throws in the towel, and the choir from the secondary school dominates the stage. It sings three songs in a row, which reverberate around the walls of the hall, overwhelming everyone with joy. The very joy that is reflected on the faces of the students as they sing and dance.

The fourth song is not izitibiri but a formal classical piece that is conducted by Xoliswa Ximiya herself. Halfway through the song the bell rings.

"We have this man here who won't tell us his name," says the chairman. "He says that he is not stopping the song. After all, it is such a beautiful song by one of our greatest composers, Michael Mosoeu Moerane. He merely wants to comment on the beautiful smiles on the children's faces as they sing with their lovely voices that sound like drops of rain. But he is not happy that the conductor herself does not have a happy smile. The conductor looks sad. He is therefore buying with his three rand that that man who is sitting in the audience, Camagu, son of Cesane, should come to the stage and tickle the conductor, Miss Xoliswa Ximiya, as she conducts this song. We have never seen Miss Xoliswa Ximiya laugh, the buyer says."

Xoliswa Ximiya gives both the buyer and the chairman a very stern look. Camagu is embarrassed, but laughs in the spirit of the game. He goes to the chairman's table. The bell rings again.

"Camagu is buying with his three rand fifty that he will not tickle Miss Xoliswa Ximiya because the buyer has neglected to mention which part of Miss Ximiya's body he should tickle," the chairman announces.

People laugh. Some students shout, "On the hips! On the waist!" while others yell, "On the sole of her feet! Tickling is more effective there!"

But the chairman rings the bell and says, "No use shouting! Only money talks at the concert! Come to the table and buy if you want to say anything."

Xoliswa Ximiya casts a deadly look at the buyer, and then at Camagu, as she walks to the chairman's table. The bell rings.

"Miss Ximiya says with her five rand that there shall be no tickling, and that is final," announces the chairman. He looks around for the buyer, hoping that he will pay more money to have his way, and for the first time the people of Qolorha-by-Sea will see their headmistress reeling with laughter. But the buyer is not brave enough to contradict Xoliswa Ximiya.

The choir continues with Moerane's song until it comes to an end. Then they lunge into an energetic izitibiri song and dance. The bell rings.

"Things are becoming hotter and hotter," says the chair man, "Here we have Qukezwa, daughter of Zim . . . "

Camagu's eyes nearly pop out of their sockets at the mention of the name. There is Qukezwa, looking as cocky as ever, leaving the chairman's table and going to sit next to the buyer who bought that Xoliswa Ximiya should be tickled. This tickling business must be her idea. He wonders from which hole she has emerged after all these weeks.

"She is buying with her five rand that every woman in the audience whose name is NomaRussia should come to the stage and parade as if in a beauty contest," says the chairman, "and Camagu should be the judge of which NomaRussia is the most beautiful."

This has gone beyond a joke, thinks Camagu. He came to the concert to enjoy himself, not to be the center of so much ridicule. But the NomaRussias of Qolorha-by-Sea do not see this as ridicule. It is fun, and a moment of fame for many of them. They stream to the stage, in every shape, size, and age, about fifteen of them in all. They clown around and parade on the stage, to the great amusement and cheers of the audience.

Camagu walks to the chairman's table, intently looking at the NomaRussias, hoping against hope that his own NomaRussia is among them. But she is not. He buys with ten rand that he will not be the judge, and the NomaRussias must get off the stage so that the choirs can continue. He adds that the next choir to take the stage should be the hotel choir. The amount is too big for anyone to argue with.

The bell rings.

"Here is a group of girls. They say they are not stopping the choir. It must remain on the stage. For two rand they only want Qukezwa to come to the stage and explain the pain of their friend which Qukezwa seems to enjoy," says the chairman. Then he adds, "I must admit I do not understand what it is exactly that the young ladies are buying. But Qukezwa must come to the stage and explain the pain."

Qukezwa walks to the stage. She smiles condescendingly at the girls who have bought her. It is not the first time she has had a confrontation with them. Nor will it be the last. They are the same girls who attacked her at work many moons ago. The very girls who insulted her in the presence of Camagu at the lagoon.

"The girls want me to explain the pain of their friend," says Qukezwa defiantly. "Well, the explanation is a very simple one. Their friend caused the pain on herself."

She is about to walk down the stage when the chairman stops her with his bell.

"Another person has bought you, Qukezwa," laughs the chairman. "You see, you started the whole thing by buying the NomaRussias. Now people are buying you. For twenty rand John Dalton is buying you to sing in your split-tone manner. He says he has heard your beautiful voice as you went about working in his store. But today you need to share it with the rest of the audience."

One thing Qukezwa is not ashamed of is her singing. She opens her mouth and sings in many voices. There is utter silence in the hall. Camagu remembers the silvery night when she sang him to an orgasm on top of Gxagxa.

Qukezwa sings in such beautiful colors. Soft colors like the ochre of yellow gullies. Reassuring colors of the earth. Red. Hot colors like blazing fire. Deep blue. Deep green. Colors of the valleys and the ocean. Cool colors like the rain of summer sliding down a pair of naked bodies.

She sings in soft pastel colors, this Qukezwa. In crude and glaring colors. And in bright glossy colors. In subdued colors of the newly turned fields. All at the same time. Once more wetness imposes itself on a hapless Camagu.

The song ends. She surveys the audience. Utter silence ensues. It follows her as she walks down the stage and out of the door. Panic grips Camagu. She will disappear again. And if she does he will never be able to find her. He will not let her disappear from his life again. He jumps out of his seat, calling her name. The scandalized eyes of the audience follow him as he bolts out of the door.

"Please, Qukezwa, wait for me," he pleads. "We must talk."

"We have nothing to talk about," says Qukezwa, walking on, almost running.

"We have a lot to talk about! Please don't run away from me!"

She breaks into a run. He cannot keep up.

"I love you, Qukezwa! I love you!" he shouts breathlessly.

"You know nothing about love, learned man!" she shouts back. "Go back to school and learn more about it!"

She is gone. He stands there mortified. Why on earth did he utter such damnable words: *I love you?* What came over him?

He cannot go to the concert now. He has disgraced himself. He walks slowly to his cottage at the sea. The wind bombards his eardrums with sounds that have escaped through the cracks of the school hall.

Things remain happening in the school hall. After Camagu bolts out there is stunned silence for a while. Then Bhonco, son of Ximiya, angrily stands up and walks towards Zim.

"This is all your work, is it not?" he fumes. "You put your daughter up to this! You used your medicine to make that poor man run after her!"

"Why would I do that? I don't need that demented man in my homestead!"

"You would do it to spite me, wouldn't you? To make a laughing-stock of the house of Ximiya! Yes, to spite us! In the same way that you influenced the abaThwa to take their dance away!"

While the younger members of the audience find this commotion exciting, the older ones are shocked. Xoliswa Ximiya is clearly ashamed of her father's outburst. So is NoPetticoat, who stands frozen on the stage, in the midst of her fellow choristers.

The chairman is ringing the bell and shouting, "This is a concert, gentlemen. Money talks. If you have anything to say to anybody, you

come to the table and buy. You don't just exchange words among yourselves like that!"

"Just tell this Bhonco to leave me alone," says Zim. "I have nothing
to do with what has happened here. I have nothing to do with the
abaThwa taking their dance either, although it serves him right!"

"Money talks! Not just your mouth! Not just empty words! It is
money that talks at a concert!" shouts the chairman.

At last there is calm. The concert resumes. The choir from the Blue
Flamingo Hotel sings another izitibiri song.

The bell rings. The music stops.

"Tat'uZim is buying, ladies and gentlemen," announces the chairman. "He says this choir from the hotel washes his heart. Its music is
like the music of the angels. But there is something missing somewhere
there. Ululation! Such beautiful music must be accompanied by ululation. With his ten rand he buys NoPetticoat to ululate from now right
up to the end of the concert."

This would have been great fun if it had not come from Zim. But
now no one takes kindly to it. NoPetticoat has no choice but to ululate.
At first she enjoys ululating and prancing about. But by the third song
she is exhausted. Bhonco goes to the table and buys with eleven rand
that his wife should stop ululating. But Zim buys with twelve rand that
NoPetticoat should ululate for the rest of the concert. Bhonco has run
out of money, but Xoliswa Ximiya gives him some more. She is furious
that her mother has been turned into a "bioscope."

It seems that Zim has come prepared. His rock-rabbit-skin bag is
full of money. He keeps on buying NoPetticoat back on the stage
whenever Bhonco buys her off the stage. The stakes have now risen to
one hundred rand. The Ximiya family has run out of money and
cannot buy anymore. People are exclaiming that the vindictive Zim is
finishing all his nkamnkam or old-age-pension money on a concert.

NoPetticoat ululates. Choirs come and go. NoPetticoat ululates for
all of them. By the end of the concert her voice is gone. It became
hoarse and then disappeared. The villagers are angry that Zim has
spoiled the concert, but there is nothing they can do about it. It is only
money that talks at a concert.

This does not sit well with Bhonco, son of Ximiya. He challenges Zim to a stick fight. "Let's see if money will buy you out of a duel," he says. "You have made a fool of my family and you must pay for it. *Uzidla ngemali*—money has made you too proud!"

But Dalton, ever the water that extinguishes wildfires, talks them out of the fight. The law has no mercy on people who engage in such foolish activities. They may find themselves in jail, he warns them.

The following days Bhonco plans a different type of vengeance. He tells the gathering of the elders of the Unbelievers, "Since this Believer loves ululation so much, I am going to engage a group of *abayiyizeli*, the ululants, to ululate for him."

Abayiyizeli are women who take their ululation seriously. They look forward to those occasions when they are needed to ululate. When Bhonco engages them, they take to their task with gusto. They ululate outside Zim's homestead during those serious moments when he is resting under his giant wild fig tree, in the company of his ama-hobohobo weaverbirds. They know that he loves to have a siesta after midday meals. They choose that very moment to pierce his eardrums with the sharpest possible ululation. At first he ignores them. He thinks they will ultimately get tired of it. But they never do. Instead they mobilize more ululants to work in shifts at all hours.

Soon things develop to the extent that the abayiyizeli ululate every time they see Zim. They follow him through the village ululating. Even young girls who were not part of the original group of ululants ululate when they see him. Female passersby stop whatever they are doing to ululate whenever he approaches.

Zim does not know what to do about this. He goes to Chief Xi-kixa, but the chief is powerless. When the ululants are summoned before him, they claim that they are innocent people who enjoy ululat-ing along village pathways. And this is not against the law in the new and democratic South Africa.

Finally Zim gets his revenge. He sends *ing'ang'ane* birds, the hadedah ibis, to laugh at Bhonco. They are drab gray, stubby-legged birds with metallic green or purple wings. Three or four birds follow him wherever he goes, emitting their rude laughter. They sit on the roof of his ixande house, and continue laughing.

There is a feeling that things are getting out of hand. There is talk in the village that the war of the Believers and Unbelievers has advanced beyond human prowess. It is rumored that Bhonco is about to enlist the assistance of the *uthekwane*, the brown hammerhead bird. With its lightning it will destroy Zim's fields, or perhaps his homestead. But some people laugh the whole matter off. They say it is an empty threat. Bhonco does not know how to talk with birds. Only Zim can talk with birds. Yet others feel that it is a shame that these elders have now stooped to the level of sending such innocent creatures as birds to battle on their behalf.

While these battles are going on, Camagu is hiding in his sea cottage. He is ashamed to show his face in public. Days pass. He cannot even venture to Vulindlela Trading Store. He hears about the quarrel that is threatening to swallow the whole community from NoGiant and MamCirha when they come to work. They tell him of the ululation that happened at the concert, and its consequences. They beg him to go and talk with the elders, to convince them to stop destroying each other this way. The women think that the elders will listen to him. But Camagu does not think so. He believes that after his behavior at the concert he has lost their respect.

One day he gets a surprise visit from John Dalton. He says they need to bury their differences because there are greater things at stake. The developers are coming to hold a public meeting with the villagers, to explain their plans to turn Qolorha-by-Sea into a tourist paradise. Dalton will not be able to attend this imbhizo because he is going to Ficksburg in the Free State on an urgent family matter. He has come to ask Camagu to attend the meeting because it is important that some-one should be there who will be able to articulate the view of those villagers who are opposed to the tourist paradise as envisaged by the developers.

"It is good that you want us to bury our differences," says Camagu. "I never had any differences with you in the first place. I merely expressed a different point of view about the water project . . . after you had solicited my opinion."

"Okay, maybe it was childish of me to take it personally," admits Dalton, "but let's talk about this imbhizo. Will you be able to attend?"

"Who will listen to me after what I did at the concert?"

Dalton laughs.

"I don't know what came over you," he says. "But this meeting is important. The whole future of the village depends on it. We cannot let your personal problems—"

"Okay, okay, I will go."

The developers, two bald white men and a young black man, come early on a Saturday morning and insist that the meeting be held at the lagoon so that they can demonstrate their grand plans for the village. The young black man is introduced as Lefa Leballo, the new chief executive officer of the black empowerment company that is going to develop the village into a tourist heaven. He looks very handsome in his navy-blue suit, blue shirt, and colorful tie. The two elderly white men—both in black suits—are Mr. Smith and Mr. Jones. They were chief executive and chairman of the company before they sold the majority shares to black empowerment consortia. Now they act as consultants for the company.

Most of the villagers have gathered. When Camagu arrives they titter and point fingers him. He walks defiantly to the front, and to his consternation he finds himself standing next to the teachers of Qolorha-by-Sea Secondary School. Xoliswa Ximiya just looks forward and pretends that he does not exist. The history teacher who was the chairman at the concert smiles at him. He smiles back.

His eyes search for Bhonco, the most vocal supporter of the holiday resort project. There he is, surrounded by his supporters. The hadedah ibises have given him some respite and are no longer mocking him with their laughter. The abayiyizeli, the ululants, have also taken a break from slashing Zim's eardrums with their razor-sharp ululation, and have assumed the role of ordinary citizens. Zim sits with his daughter and a few supporters. Both elders look tired and drained.

After the chief has introduced the visitors, Lefa Leballo makes a brief speech. He tells the villagers how lucky they are to be living in a new and democratic South Africa where the key word is transparency. In the bad old days such projects would be done without consulting them at all. So, in the same spirit in which the government has respected them by consulting them, they must also show respect to these important visitors, by not voicing the objections that he heard some of the villagers were having about a project of such national importance. He then gives the floor to Mr. Smith.

Mr. Smith talks of the wonders that will happen at Qolorha-by-Sea. There will be boats and waterskiing and jetskiing. People from across the seas will ride the waves in a sport called surfing. This place will be particularly good for that because the sea is rough most of the time. Surfing will be a challenge. There will be merry-go-rounds for the children, and rides that go up to the sky. Rides that twist and turn while the riders scream in ecstatic fright.

"Right here," says Mr. Smith, "we shall see the biggest and most daring rides of all roller coasters in the world . . . over the rough sea. This will be the place for roller coaster enthusiasts who spend their lives traveling the world in search of the biggest and most daring rides."

Bhonco and his supporters applaud. Except for people like Xoliswa Ximiya, none of them have seen a roller coaster before. But it does not matter. If it is something that brings civilization, then it is good for Qolorha.

"That is not all, my dear friends," says Mr. Smith excitedly. "We are going to have cable cars too. Cable cars shall move across the water from one end of the lagoon to the other."

"These are wonderful things," says Bhonco. "But I am suspicious of this matter of riding the waves. The new people that were prophesied by the false prophet, Nongqawuse, were supposed to come riding on the waves too."

Lefa Leballo explains that this has nothing to do with old superstitions. This riding of the waves is a sport that civilized people do in advanced countries and even here in South Africa, in cities like Durban and Cape Town. But the waves here are more suited to the sport than the waves of other big cities in South Africa. The waves here are big and wild.

Lefa Leballo then interprets Bhonco's concerns to the consultants. They find this rather funny and laugh for a long time. The villagers join in the laughter too.

But Camagu is not impressed.

"You talk of all these rides and all these wonderful things," he says, "but for whose benefit are they? What will these villagers who are sitting here get from all these things? Will their children ride on those merry-go-rounds and roller coasters? On those cable cars and boats? Of course not! They will not have any money to pay for these things. These things will be enjoyed only by rich people who will come here and pollute our rivers and our ocean."

"Who are you to talk for the people of Qolorha?" asks Bhonco. "You talk of our rivers and our ocean. Since when do you belong here? Or do you think just because you run after daughters of Believers, that gives you the right to think you belong here?"

"Hey you, Bhonco! If you know what is good for you, you will leave my child out of this!" shouts Zim. "She did not invite that stupid man to follow her. Today this son of Cesane is talking a lot of sense. This son of Cesane is right. They will destroy our trees and the plants of our forefathers for nothing. We, the people of Qolorha, will not gain anything from this."

"You will get jobs," says Lefa Leballo desperately. Then he looks at Camagu pleadingly. "Please don't talk these people against a project of such national importance."

"It is of national importance only to your company and shareholders, not to these people!" yells Camagu. "Jobs? Bah! They will lose more than they will gain from jobs. I tell you, people of Qolorha, these visitors arc interested only in profits for their company. This sea will no longer belong to you. You will have to pay to use it."

"He has been put up to this by that white man, Dalton," says Bhonco. "He is Dalton's stooge. Dalton is hiding himself and has sent this man here because he has a black face. Dalton wants us to remain in the darkness of our fathers so that he can grab our land as his fathers did before him."

"You are a liar, Bhonco!" cries Zim. "You lie even in the middle of the night. This young man is talking common sense from his own brain. It has nothing to do with Dalton."

"You have nothing to offer these people," says Mr. Jones to Camagu. "If you fight against these wonderful developments, what do you have to offer in their place?"

"The promotion of the kind of tourism that will benefit the people, that will not destroy indigenous forests, that will not bring hordes of people who will pollute the rivers and drive away the birds."

"That is just a dream," shouts Lefa Leballo. "There is no such tourism."

"We can work it out, people of Qolorha," appeals Camagu. "We can sit down and plan it. There are many people out there who enjoy communing with unspoiled nature."

"We are going ahead with our plans," says Lefa Leballo adamantly. "How will you stop us? The government has already approved this project. I belong to the ruling party. Many important people in the ruling party are directors of this company. The chairman himself was a cabinet minister until he was deployed to the corporate world. We'll see to it that you don't foil our efforts."

"Well, how will you stop progress and development?" asks Mr. Smith, chuckling triumphantly.

"Yes! How will he stop civilization?" asks Xoliswa Ximiya.

For a while Camagu does not know how to answer this. Then in an inspired moment he suddenly shouts, "How will I stop you? I will tell you how I will stop you! I will have this village declared a national heritage site. Then no one will touch it. The wonders of Nongqawuse that led to the cattle-killing movement of the amaXhosa happened here. On that basis, this can be declared a national heritage site!"

"That damned Nongqawuse again!" spits Bhonco.

"That Nongqawuse of yours is already burning in the fires of hell," says Xoliswa Ximiya.

"This son of Cesane is brilliant!" cries Zim. "I knew that Nongqawuse would one day save this village!"

It is clear that the majority of the people have been swayed by Camagu's intervention. Bhonco bursts out in desperation, "This son of

Cesane, I ask you, my people, is he circumcised? Are we going to listen to uncircumcised boys here?"

"How do you know he is not circumcised?" asks Zim.

"Why should that matter?" says Camagu. "Facts are facts, whether they come from somebody who is circumcised or not."

"Yes, it does matter," says Zim. "That is why this Unbeliever brings it up. He has been defeated by facts and reason. That is why he now talks about circumcision. Of course, if this son of Cesane is uncircumcised we shall not deal with him, though he has been useful in our cause."

At first Camagu is stubborn. He says he does not see why the worth of a man should be judged on whether he has a foreskin or not.

"You said you respected our customs," says Bhonco. "So you respect them only when it suits you? Clearly you are uncircumcised!"

"I challenge you, Tat'uBhonco, to come and inspect me here in public to see if I have a foreskin," says Camagu confidently. He knows that no one will dare take up that challenge. And if at any time they did, they would not find any foreskin. He was circumcised, albeit in the most unrespectable manner, at the hospital.

Zim's supporters applaud.

Mr. Jones adopts a more conciliatory stance. In measured tones he tries to convince them how beautiful the place will be, with all the amenities of the city. There will be a shopping mall, tennis courts, and an Olympic-size swimming pool.

He is struck by a new idea, which by the look on his face is quite brilliant. "We can even build new blocks of town houses as holiday time-share units," he says.

"Time-share units? We didn't talk about time-share units," says Mr. Smith. "We talked about a hotel and a casino."

"Well, plans can always change, can't they?" says Mr. Jones.

"If the plans change at all, I rather fancy a retirement village for millionaires," says Mr. Smith. "This place is ideal for that. We can call it Willowbrook Grove."

"Grove?" exclaims Mr. Jones. "How can we call it a grove when we're going to cut down all these trees to make way for the rides?"

"We'll plant other trees imported from England. We'll uproot a lot of these native shrubs and wild bushes and plant a beautiful English garden."

The developers seem to have forgotten about the rest of the people as they argue about the profitability of creating a beautiful English countryside versus that of constructing a crime-free time-share paradise. Even Lefa Leballo is left out as they bandy about the most appropriate names: names that end in Close, Dell, and Downs. At first the villagers are amused. But soon they get bored and drift away to their homes, leaving the developers lost in their argument.

Late in the evening Camagu is eating his supper of fried eggs, oysters, and steamed bread. He is quite happy with himself. He feels that he has redeemed himself in the eyes of the villagers. He hears the neighing of a horse outside. He ignores it. The neighing continues irritating. He reluctantly walks to the door and opens it. There is Qukezwa sitting on top of Gxagxa.

She giggles.

"I love what you did today," she says.

"And you came all the way just to tell me that?"

"Come here. Don't be afraid. I won't eat you."

He hesitates, then slowly goes to her.

"You can touch Gxagxa if you like," she says, grabbing his hand and brushing the horse with it.

"Please," he blurts out. "I want a ride. I want to repeat the ride of that night."

"But there is no moon tonight," she says softly.

"It does not matter," he cries with urgency. "I want that ride now. I want to feel what I felt. Maybe I'll understand how that conception happened."

Qukezwa lets him climb behind her, and Gxagxa gallops away. She sings in many voices. But Camagu cannot feel a thing. The silvery night cannot be recaptured. Gxagxa picks up speed. Qukezwa strips and throws all her clothes away. He follows her lead.

"We'll pick them up on our way back," she cries.

They both ride bareback, reinless and naked.

When they get to Intlambo-ka-Nongqawuse—Nongqawuse's Valley—they run naked on the lush grass, chasing each other. Then he follows her lead once more and jumps into the pool. He can't swim. She swims like a fish. She begins to teach him, showing him a few strokes. When they jump out of the pool his whole body is itchy and has a fine rash. He screams.

"Don't be such a baby," she says as she rubs it with some leaves. "It is only the *thithiboya* caterpillar that has walked on you. Or poison ivy. So far no one has died from either."

John Dalton was becoming impatient. He dared not show it, though. John Gawler, on the other hand, sat calmly and appeared intensely interested in Sir George Grey's ramblings. He had not become a magistrate at the tender age of twenty-six by displaying impatience at stories told by colonial governors. He had a long life full of brilliant service and lucrative promotions ahead of him. If the older Dalton wanted to interrupt the governor of the Cape Colony, it was his own problem. The older Dalton had nothing to lose. His career in the service of Her Majesty's Government was almost over in any case. He was already talking of opening a trading store somewhere in British Kaffraria.

"Sir, perhaps we should get back to the matter at hand," said John Dalton.

"The matter at hand? Is that not what we are talking about?" asked Sir George.

"The disaster in British Kaffraria," said Dalton. "When he heard that you would be in Grahamstown, John Maclean, your chief commissioner of British Kaffraria, sent us with the message that things are getting worse. The natives are dying in their hundreds from starvation."

"Their customs are to blame," scoffed Sir George. Then he addressed the younger man. "You will be happy, Gawler, to hear that I have commissioned an exhaustive research of native laws and customs in support of my system of magisterial rule in the eastern Cape. When you know their customs, you will be a much more effective magistrate over the natives."

"That will be very useful, sir," assented Gawler.

"In the meantime they are dying, Sir George," Dalton appealed. "In spite of everything, the cattle-killing continues. What should we do? The prophets of Gxarha have the people firmly in their power."

"You know, in Australia and New Zealand I did the same thing," boasted Sir George. "I built an important collection of the languages, customs, and religions of the natives. It is important to record these because they are destined to disappear along with the savages who hold them, don't you think, Gawler?"

"It is so, Sir George."

"The advance of Christian civilization will sweep away ancient races. Antique laws and customs will molder into oblivion," proclaimed the governor.

"It is already happening, Sir George. We, your magistrates, are advancing your policies to the letter," said Gawler, feigning enthusiasm.

"The strongholds of murder and superstition shall be cleansed," said Sir George spiritedly, "as the gospel is preached among ignorant and savage men. The ruder languages shall disappear, and the tongue of England alone shall be heard all around. So you see, my friends, this cattle-killing nonsense augurs the dawn of a new era."

"In the meantime, what do we do about this current emergency?" asked Dalton. "What do we tell the chief commissioner?"

"Who is this man?" Sir George asked, looking at Gawler and pointing at Dalton disdainfully.

"John Dalton, sir," answered Gawler.

"I know that, but who is he?"

"He is a military veteran of the frontier wars. He is very useful in translating and interpreting the native tongues."

"I interpreted for you on your last tour of the frontier, Sir George," said Dalton helpfully.

"Then teach him that being given the privilege of an audience with me is quite different from addressing mobs of natives. He must stop interrupting me."

"Yes, sir," said Gawler.

"My apologies, sir," said Dalton, who then sulked for the rest of that day.

"As for the prophets of Gxarha, why don't you just arrest them?"

"The chief commissioner fears an uprising," said Gawler.

"An uprising of people who have been rendered powerless by starvation? An uprising of dying people?"

When the two officers got back home they laid down their plans for the arrest of the prophets. But they were advised by the unbelieving elders to wait until the problems between Chief Nxito and some of his subjects had been sorted out. It seemed that an armed confrontation between the Believers and Unbelievers of Qolorha was imminent. If the prophets were arrested at that time, it would exacerbate the situation.

After Chief Nxito's return to his chiefdom, rumors were flying around that he had converted and joined the Believers. He, on the other hand, was eager to prove to all his subjects that his supposed conversion was a figment of the Believers' imagination.

He also wanted to find a way of demonstrating once and for all that the prophecies were false. He demanded that Mhlakaza should display to the chiefs of kwaXhosa those new people he was claiming had already risen from the dead. The prophets of Gxarha played for time, but Nxito was persistent.

Finally Mhlakaza announced that the new people had agreed to show themselves to Chief Nxito. The wizened chief was suspicious. He sent Twin-Twin to reconnoiter the appointed meeting place and make sure that there was no chicanery. Unfortunately, Mhlakaza's spies discovered Twin-Twin hiding in the donga near the sacred place where the new people were expected to appear just for Nxito's benefit.

"Nxito has insulted the new people!" screamed Mhlakaza. "He has placed an Unbeliever on their path! How do you expect them to come when their path is obstructed by the evil shadow of an Unbeliever like

Twin-Twin? The new people have left in anger for the mouth of the Great Fish River. Nxito must bear all the blame!"

The Believers were fuming. Once more the Unbelievers were responsible for the delay of the rising of the dead. Some questioned Twin-Twin's intentions. Hadn't he publicly expressed his desire for the sacred body of Prophetess Nongqawuse? Was he not trying to kill two birds with one stone: putting obstacles in the path of the new people while at the same time waylaying the prophetess on her daily route to commune with the new people at the banks of the Gxarha River?

"You never know with these amaGogotya, these Unbelievers." That was all Mhlakaza could say. "In any event, the new people have spoken. Nongqawuse says they say they have decided not to rise, because of the appeals that are being made to them by the ancestors of the Unbelievers. The ancestors of the Unbelievers are worried that their descendants will be doomed for disregarding the prophecies. In their infinite compassion the new people still hope that the Unbelievers will change their minds and kill their cattle."

But King Sarhili was no longer prepared to let Mhlakaza off so easily. He demanded that he should set a definite date for the coming of the new people. The messengers the king had been sending to the Gxarha were coming back with the bad news that no wonders were seen over there. Only those people who wanted to see miracles saw miracles. They were saying that as far as they were concerned the whole story of the new people and new cattle was a deceit.

Small cracks of doubt were opening in the armor of some Believers.

Twin and Qukezwa did not share these doubts. They were among the hungry and the weak who walked the whole day from Qolorha to Butterworth, where more than six thousand believing amaXhosa had already gathered, waiting for the dawn of the new day of miracles and wonders that had been announced by Mhlakaza.

The mood was joyous in Butterworth. At last the resurrection was going to happen. There was very little food but plenty of singing and dancing. Everyone was waiting for the next full moon, which was to fall on 10 January 1857. The moon was going to be blood-red and the dead would arise.

Twin was rather unhappy that none of the prophets could be seen in the joyous crowd. Mhlakaza was not there. Neither were Nongqawuse and Nombanda. Even Nonkosi, the eleven-year-old daughter of Kulwana, who had emerged as a new prophetess at the Mpongo River, was nowhere to be seen. Perhaps her absence could be explained, the people whispered. The new date had not emanated from her denomination.

"Are you beginning to doubt the prophets?" asked Qukezwa.

"No, I do not doubt the prophets," Twin assured her. "But it would have been nice if they were here to welcome the new people personally."

"The new people are not coming to Butterworth, Father of Heitsi," Qukezwa reminded him. "We are merely here to celebrate their arrival at the Gxarha. The prophets insisted that only King Sarhili and his trusted councillors should be on hand to witness their approach to the shores of kwaXhosa, riding on the waves."

"I know, I know. Those were the instructions of the new people themselves."

"So you see, all the prophets must be at the Gxarha mouth to welcome the new people."

Qukezwa and Twin did not know that problems had arisen at the Gxarha mouth. King Sarhili and a group of councillors had ridden down there on the third day of January, only to find that Mhlakaza and Nongqawuse had vanished. They had left a message that the new people had angrily returned to the Otherworld because of the despicable behavior of the unbelieving chiefs. The king and his people should wait for the full moon of February instead.

The king was sad and humiliated. For the first time, he faced criticism from angry crowds. When he tried to address them they heckled him, and the imbhizo ended in chaos. A broken man, he decided to ride back to his Great Place at Hohita. On the way he tried to kill himself with his father's spear. His councillors stopped him. They were forced to keep a close eye on him and hide all the knives, spears, and other weapons from him.

✪ ✪ ✪

Yet Twin and thousands of the staunch Believers remained in Butter-worth. Early in February, hope was rekindled. Even the dejected Sarhili gained some courage. There were rumors that the prophecies had already been fulfilled in the land of Moshoeshoe. At the next full moon they would surely be fulfilled in the land of Sarhili. The king rode back to Butterworth to be with the celebrating masses.

The masses were hungry, but they lived on faith.

The prophecies had spoken that during the resurrection the sun would rise late in the morning. It would be red like blood. It would not venture far, but would return to its starting point only to set again. The earth would then be covered in absolute darkness. There would be a raging storm accompanied by thunder and lightning, during which the dead would arise.

"I am staying!" declared King Sarhili, addressing the multitudes. "I am staying with you here to see my father, Hintsa, and his cattle rise again!"

The people cheered and ululated.

The king asked local traders to sell his people candles so that they might have some light during the great darkness. John Dalton was seen going up and down selling candles to the Believers. He had crateloads of candles and was supplying even other traders whose stores had run out. Whereas the traders expected the Believers to come to their stores to buy this essential commodity, Dalton took his candles right there to the multitudes. He worked up a sweat peddling the candles the entire day. That was the beginning of his trading empire.

The more practical Believers did not spend their time singing and dancing like Twin and Qukezwa and the multitudes that gathered in Butterworth. They prepared for the new people by sewing new milk sacks, renovating their houses and making new doors for them, and rebuilding their kraals. Even those widows who had remarried left their current husbands and returned to their old homesteads to await the res-urrection of their first loves.

On 16 February 1857, the long-awaited day dawned. The sun rose. It was not the color of blood. It looked like any other sun. It did not rise late either. The Believers watched it in disbelief as it moved across the sky. There was no darkness. No thunder. No lightning. The dead did not arise.

The Unbelievers went about their usual work. But for the Believers it was the day of the Great Disappointment.

Perhaps on the following day things would be different, sighed the Believers. But nothing happened. And the next day. And the next. Until all hope faded away.

Twin and Qukezwa slowly made their way back to Qolorha. Their hunger belts were fastened even tighter. They lived on grass and ants. They were angry. But not with the prophets. The Great Disappointment was the fault of Nxito and his spies, who had insulted the new people. It was the fault of all Unbelievers, who had refused to slaughter their cattle and continued to cultivate their lands.

But King Sarhili had finally lost all hope. He took the blame upon himself for issuing the imiyolelo, the orders that people should obey the prophets of Gxarha. He told John Dalton, "I have been deceived. I must explain this whole matter to The Man Who Named Ten Rivers personally. Please send a message to him that my people and I do not want any war."

"I will see what I can do," said Dalton, "although at the moment I am busy setting up my trading store. I have retired from full-time service in Her Majesty's Government."

Twin and Qukezwa went back to Mhlakaza's homestead to replenish their faith. There was Mhlakaza preaching to a small group of desperate Believers who were hoping to hear words of encouragement. Nongqawuse and Nombanda were standing next to him. As usual Nongqawuse looked confused and disorientated, and Nombanda had a distant look in her eyes.

"Nongqawuse says the new people say they do not want to be troubled with the importunity of the amaXhosa, and will make their appearance when they think fit."

"There is no hope," whispered Qukezwa. "The prophets are forsaking us."

"There is some hope," replied Twin. "Mhlakaza says they say they will still make their appearance. In spite of what the Unbelievers have done to them, they have not deserted us completely."

"Blame the amaGogotya, the Unbelievers!" declaimed Mhlakaza. "They have refused to kill their cattle. The new people were ready to rise. The great Naphakade, He-Who-Is-Forever, was ready to lead them to our shores, driving more than six thousand cattle. But the ancestors of the Unbelievers still want to save their descendants from eternal damnation. They hope that the stubborn Unbelievers will change their minds and kill their cattle. Only then will the dead arise. It is for you, beautiful amaThamba, you the Believers, to see to it that these prophecies are fulfilled. It is for you to see to it that all cattle in the land are killed."

There was general fury against the Unbelievers. Believers invaded Unbelievers' kraals and cattle-posts. They also stole grain from their granaries. And chickens from their fowl-runs. Even dogs were not spared. Back in Hohita, at his Great Place, King Sarhili made things worse when he declared, "I cannot starve. There are still cattle in the land, and they are mine. I will take them as I require them."

Twin-Twin vowed that he was going to protect whatever cattle he had left with his life. His grain was threatening to run out. He had not been able to cultivate the land since he had been placed under protection in Qolorha. He feared that the Believers would burn his fields.

He was going to nurse his grain until the next harvest. Hopefully the Believers had learned their lesson and would start cultivating the land instead of destroying the crops of those who wanted to feed their families.

He did not give a hoot for the plight of the Believers. He felt no pity even when he heard stories that his twin brother, his brother's yellow-colored wife, and their yellow-colored son were surviving on the bark of the mimosa tree.

His praise name was not He Who Wakes Up With Yesterday's Anger for nothing.

The mimosa tree, or the *umga*, as the amaXhosa call it, is plentiful and grows easily. It is the only tree a person can chop without the chief's permission. For all other trees, even foreign ones, one is supposed to get permission before one can chop them down.

It is for the crime of chopping down a tree that Qukezwa appears before the court, the inkundla, of Chief Xikixa. Camagu is among the people who have come to listen to the case. He wonders what came over Qukezwa to make her chop down trees, when she has always presented herself as their protector. Part of her objection to the planned holiday paradise is that the natural beauty of Qolorha-by-Sea will be destroyed. But here she is, standing before the graybeards of the village, being charged with the serious crime of vandalizing trees. What is worse, she was not even in need of firewood. She just chopped them down and left them there.

Yet she stands defiant. Like her father, she has taken to shaving her head, although she has not gone to the extent of shaving off her eyebrows. The red blanket that she wears over her shoulders reaches down to her ankles. But it cannot hide the protruding stomach. She looks forlorn in her defiance.

An elder sums up the charges against Qukezwa, daughter of Zim. Yesterday she was seen cutting down a number of fully grown trees in Nongqawuse's Valley. She continued with impunity even when women from Xikixa's Great Place shouted at her to stop. She displayed her bad upbringing by daring anyone to physically stop her.

Bhonco stands up to object.

"This is highly irregular," he complains. "Where have you seen a child this age being charged or sued for anything? According to our customs and tradition, when a minor has committed an offense it is his or her father or legal guardian who is charged."

"I am twenty years old," says Qukezwa.

"You are a minor still. Even if you were thirty or fifty you would still be a minor as long as you are not married," explains Chief Xikixa.

"That is the old law," cries Qukezwa, "the law that weighed heavily on our shoulders during the sufferings of the Middle Generations. In the new South Africa where there is no discrimination, it does not work."

"Now she wants to teach us about the law," mutters the chief.

"She may be right on the question of minority when a woman is not married. But still she is under twenty-one," says a councillor of the chief. "The law is clear that she is a minor."

"They vote at eighteen nowadays," says another elder helpfully.

"Perhaps she thinks that just because she is with child she can stand for herself," moans Bhonco, ignoring all the niceties of what the law says or does not say. "Or does she think her illicit liaison with this son of Cesane who has brought nothing but trouble to this village qualifies as a marriage?"

"I have nothing to do with this case. I do not know why this elder drags my name into it," protests Camagu, looking at the chief for protection.

"Why is Zim hiding behind his daughter's skirts? Why doesn't he stand up like a man and take the rap?" asks Bhonco.

Zim gracefully stands up and gives a mocking chuckle in Bhonco's direction.

"How can I be hiding myself when I am here in person?" Zim wonders. "Was it me who said you must charge my daughter instead of me? I know the laws, customs, and traditions of our people as well as any man. You people, you cowards, decided to charge my daughter instead of me! Is that my fault?"

"Do you hear what you are saying, Zim?" asks the councillor. "Are you insulting this inkundla by calling us all, including the chief, cowards?"

"That is your own interpretation," says Zim, sitting down.

"Perhaps I should explain how this girl got to be charged," says Chief Xikixa. "When we sent a messenger to Zim's homestead he found this girl. She insisted that she was the one who should be charged. She and not her father cut the trees, she said. And she boasted that she was going to cut them again and again. It seems that my messenger got angry and decided to teach her a lesson by charging her instead of her father. In the course of it all, he forgot about our judicial customs and traditions. The fact of the matter is that Zim is the one who must answer for his daughter's actions."

"I do not mean to be rude to you, my elders," says Qukezwa, displaying a humble demeanor that some might see as uncharacteristic. "I cut the trees, and I shall cut them again."

"This stubborn girl must sit down or get away from here. Since when do girls attend an inkundla? Since when do they address their elders with such disrespect? Is it the seed of this son of Cesane that is jumping about in her womb that makes her talk like this?" demands Bhonco.

The men laugh. Another one shouts, "It is the modernity that you Unbelievers are fighting to introduce here at Qolorha!"

But Camagu will not let the elder get away with libeling him like this. He shouts from where he is sitting, "Hey, Tat'uBhonco! Do you have cattle to pay for my name that you are dragging in mud? I shall sue you dry!"

"This girl must get away from here," insists Bhonco, ignoring Camagu.

"She cannot go away, because she is a witness in this case," says the councillor. "Although we are charging Zim, she is the one who cut the trees. She must explain why she did it."

"She has already admitted that she cut the trees. All we need to do is to fine her father," argues Bhonco.

The inkundla agrees that there is no need to waste time on this matter. The girl has admitted that she committed the crime. The graybeards cannot sit here all day long when there are other matters to deal with. There is, for instance, this question of the developers who are said to be bringing civilization to Qolorha. Today they must thrash it out. Camagu must explain exactly what he meant when he said the place could be turned into a national heritage site, and how that would benefit the people of Qolorha.

"The chief must mete out an appropriate fine so that we may move on," an elder suggests.

"Don't be in a hurry," says Zim. "You cannot talk of meting out a fine when you have not heard from our side."

"What is there to hear from your side?" asks Bhonco.

"This girl has cut down the inkberry before, yet no one complained about that."

"The inkberry is poison. It is well known that it destroys everything before it!"

"So do the trees that I cut down," says Qukezwa. "They are foreign trees! They are not the trees of our forefathers!"

"Are you going to cut down trees just because they are foreign trees?" asks Bhonco indignantly. "Are you going to go out to the forest of Nogqoloza and destroy all the trees there just because they were imported from the land of the white man in the days of our fathers?"

"The trees in Nogqoloza don't harm anybody, as long as they stay there," explains Qukezwa patiently. "They are bluegum trees. The trees that I destroyed are as harmful as the inkberry. They are the lantana and wattle trees. They come from other countries . . . from Central America, from Australia . . . to suffocate our trees. They are dangerous trees that need to be destroyed."

"The law says only the umga, the mimosa, can be cut without permission," insists Bhonco, son of Ximiya. "The law does not mention any other tree."

"Then the law must be changed," says Qukezwa, explaining once more. "Just like the umga, the seed of the wattle tree is helped by fire. The seed can lie there for ten years, but when fire comes it grows. And it uses all the water. Nothing can grow under the wattle tree. It is an enemy since we do not have enough water in this country. If the umga can be cut without permission because it spreads like wildfire, so should the wattle . . . and the lantana for that matter. So should the inkberry, which I have always cut without being hurled before the elders."

Most of the elders nod their agreement. Some express it in grunts and mumbles. One mutters his wonder at the source of Qukezwa's wisdom when she is but a slip of a girl. Shouldn't she be focusing her interest on red ochre and other matters of good grooming and beauty?

"The law is the law," insists Bhonco. "It cannot be changed for the sake of this impetuous girl. The law says only the mimosa can be cut without permission. We must not apply the law selectively. Remember that only a month ago two white tourists who were staying at the Blue Flamingo were arrested by the police, no less, for smuggling cycads from our village. Remember that last week we punished boys right here at this inkundla for killing the red-winged starling, the *isomi* bird."

There can be no comparison here, the elders say all at once. The isomi is a holy bird. It is blessed. No one is allowed to kill it.

The chief's councillor is obviously moved. He stands up and

declaims, "Shall we now be required to teach revered elders like Bhonco about our taboos? It is a sin to kill isomi. Yes, boys love its delicious meat that tastes like chicken. But from the time we were young we were taught never to kill isomi. We ate these birds only when they died on their own. We watched them living together in huge colonies in the forest or flying in big flocks of thousands. We only desired them from a distance. We rejoiced when they fought among themselves, often to death, for we knew that only then were we allowed to eat them. These are sacred birds. If an isomi flies into your house your family will be blessed. Isomi is a living Christ on earth. If you kill isomi you will be followed by misfortune in every direction you go. When we punish boys for killing red-winged starlings, we are teaching them about life. We are saving them from future misfortune."

"I say the same rules that apply to the mimosa must apply to the wattle tree and to the lantana," shouts Zim out of turn.

"Perhaps we should look at the intentions of Qukezwa before we pass judgment in this case," suggests Camagu.

They look at him as if he is something a naughty puppy has just dragged into the house from the garbage heap. No one thought he would have the audacity to contribute his say in this matter. After all, everyone now knows that he was fed a powerful potion by the Believers, which turned him against a well-mannered and educated woman of the Unbelievers, only to run like a puppy after this tree-cutting siren. Now she is even carrying his child. Of course the village is divided on the matter of the child, as the grandmothers long since proclaimed that she has not known a man—in the biblical sense, that is. And no one can question their expertise in these matters.

Wouldn't it have been wise if he, as an interested party, had kept his mouth shut? But then every man of the village participates in the inkundla court cases. No one ever recuses himself, even when he is related to the disputing parties.

Bhonco stands up to respond and put this spineless foreigner in his place. But all the attention of the men is drawn to a cloud of smoke that is billowing in the distance. Herdboys suddenly appear with buckets of water, running towards the blaze that is rising to the sky.

"*Umzi uyatsha!* A homestead is burning!" they shout.

The inkundla breaks up and the men rush to assist in extinguishing the fire. Camagu takes advantage of the confusion to talk with Qukezwa.

"Why can't you just let things be?" he asks.

"So you agree with them?"

"No, I don't. But the baby . . . it can't be good for the baby if you put it under all this stress."

She smiles, and looks at her stomach.

"Don't worry, they won't pursue the matter," she assures him.

"Oh yes they will, Bhonco will see to that."

"Go and help them put out the fire."

"First promise you won't chop down any more trees."

"We'll talk, okay?"

She walks away. He follows her with his eyes for a while, then rushes to the billowing smoke. He is shocked beyond words to find that a number of homesteads are on fire, and one of them belongs to his business partner, NoGiant.

That, in fact, is where the fire started, a tottering old woman informs him.

The wind is making things worse. It had been a cool and quiet day when they were at the inkundla, but all of a sudden there is a raging wind that is spreading the fire and frustrating the efforts of the people who are trying to put it out.

"What happened, *makhulu*?" asks Camagu.

"Go ask NoGiant," says the old lady angrily. "It is her carelessness that has left me homeless. And this unpredictable weather of Qolorha! It is because there is a lot of witchcraft here. It is the land of Nongqawuse."

The battle against the fire is eventually lost. A number of houses have been burnt to the ground.

The fire is a setback to the cooperative society. NoGiant has lost everything, including the sewing machine and a pile of material and beads that belonged to the cooperative.

Camagu regrets ever asking the women to work from home rather than in the room he had allocated for that purpose at his sea cottage. He thought they were being more productive at home. At his cottage

MamCirha and NoGiant spent a lot of their time gossiping. Or talking about their cesarean operations. They compared the scars, paying particular attention to their sizes and their shapes. They exclaimed that the scars never really bothered them, even when the weather was bad. "I often hear people say that when the weather is cloudy or cold the scars itch. I would be lying if I said mine did the same," NoGiant would say. "Mine too. It never itches at all. I always forget that it is even there," MamCirha would respond.

At their homes they are on their own. Their husbands toil in the mines of Johannesburg and the Free State, and the children are either at school or in the veld looking after cattle. There is no one to gossip with, so productivity increases.

The following day Camagu decides to go to Ngcizele to see NoGiant, who is receiving temporary shelter under MamCirha's roof.

"I will come with you," says Qukezwa. "I will show you where she lives."

"I know where she lives," replies Camagu. He really does not want her to come with him. He is still uncomfortable when people see them together and point fingers and giggle. "Remember I went there a few months ago when MamCirha had her misfortune?"

Misfortune seems to dog the women of Camagu's cooperative. MamCirha had fallen asleep while breast-feeding her baby, the one who had caused the famous cesarean scar. Her huge breasts had suffocated it and it died. Camagu had gone to her house to pass his condolences, and then later to attend the funeral. He went again with Dalton to talk members of her family into some form of reconciliation when they were accusing her of murdering her own baby so that she would be free to gallivant around making money at the cooperative society. She valued money more than her child, they said.

"I still want to come," insists Qukezwa. "They must get used to seeing us together, and talk until their tongues are twisted. Unless you want to chicken out."

He does not understand how she is able to read his thoughts so accurately, and to put his fears into words.

Early in the morning they walk to Ngcizele, a village that lies across deep gorges.

NoGiant is still very shaken. After insisting that she wants to talk to Camagu alone, without Qukezwa, she tells him how the fire started. Her husband, who was on a brief holiday from the mines, demanded his conjugal rights. She assured him that she was prepared to give him as much conjugal rights as his body was capable of taking, provided he took a bath first.

That made him furious.

"You think that just because you now make all this money running around with educated people I am no longer good enough for you?" he yelled.

He was pouring paraffin all over the rondavel while ranting and raving about her unreasonable demand that he should wash his body. Since when have conditions ever been set before he could enjoy the pleasures of marriage? Where was the bath when he paid his father's cattle for her? What gives her, a mere woman, the right to pass judgment on the state of his cleanliness or lack thereof?

He set the house ablaze.

"Where is he now?" asks Camagu.

"The police got him. They are charging him with arson."

On their way back home, Camagu briefs Qukezwa on the cause of the fire. He tells her he is disturbed that the success of the cooperative society is causing its members so many problems with their families.

"You should not worry yourself about that," says Qukezwa. "Men are insecure when women make more money. It makes women more independent. Men will just have to get used to it."

She leads him down to the sea; this, she says, is the shortest route between Qolorha and Ngcizele. But what she wants him to see is a shipwreck, the *Jacaranda*. She tells him that it got lost at sea many years before she was born, and crashed against the rocks of the wild coast. All the white people from the boat were saved. But they spoke no English, nor any other language known to the people of Ngcizele. Her father believed it was a Russian ship, which was more than a century late. It was during the sufferings of the Middle Generations, when people were looking to be saved.

She clambers up the skeleton of the ship, and perches herself on what remains of the railings of the deck. He is scared that they will break and she will have a rude fall. But she is in too reckless a mood to care. A gust of wind almost blows her over. She lets go of her red blanket. It splashes into the water and starts sailing away on the waves. She screeches in laughter as she remains in her flimsy dress. It is clinging to her body for dear life. Her body is full. Her stomach is fuller.

He stands at the keel and appeals to her to come down before she hurts herself. She dares him to come up.

A bird laughs: *wak-wak kiririri!* They laugh with it, competing to see who will produce the closest imitation. Their eyes search for it. But they can't find it.

"That is uthekwane, the hammerkop," says Qukezwa.

"No, that is *uxomoyi,* the giant kingfisher," says Camagu.

"Man of the city, what makes you think you can argue with me about birds?"

The bird hovers over them, and perches on the mast. It is a long-beaked bird with fine white spots on black. The breast is brown on white. It certainly has no hammerhead, for it is the giant kingfisher.

"How did you know? It does sound like uthekwane!"

"I have the best of teachers: you."

She loves to hear this. She laughs so much that the kingfisher flies away yelping its own laughter.

"You are cleverer than you look, man of the city. Come here and kiss me. Don't be such a coward."

He gathers courage. He might as well be reckless. He makes his way up the skeleton of the ship and joins her on the railings. He kisses her. Just a shy peck. She takes his hand and places it on her belly. Blood pumps fast and hot in his body.

"What do you feel?" she asks.

"It's kicking like there is no tomorrow."

"It's laughing! I can hear it laugh!"

"It's the uxomoyi bird, silly."

❍ ❍ ❍

Late in the afternoon Camagu goes to Vulindlela Trading Store. This time his eyes do not wander around looking for something that will ease his pining. He pines no more. He just needs somebody who will help him contain his unseemly effervescence. Dalton will serve that purpose. Dalton's feet are firmly planted on the ground. Although there are still some traces of tension in their relationship, things are returning to normal between them. He joins Dalton in his office, where he is relaxing with a magazine. Missis is busy with some paperwork.

Camagu bubbles about his discovery of the *Jacaranda*. But he does not mention his shipboard romance. Dalton tells him the *Jacaranda* was a Greek cargo ship, which foundered in September 1971. The sailors were drunk, partying all the time. They had not been paid for six months, so they wrecked the ship.

"What were you doing at that remote place?" Dalton asks.

"Just exploring," Camagu lies. "Just learning more about this lovely country."

"Just exploring, eh? With that daughter of Zim?" Dalton chuckles naughtily.

Missis gives Camagu a disapproving look. He is by now used to her sneering attitude and does not pay any attention to it. He does not answer Dalton's question either.

"I don't know what he sees in that crude girl," comments Missis, as if to herself.

Still Camagu does not answer. He just smiles politely.

"She is a rotten apple, that one. I am glad she no longer works here. I would have fired her long ago if it were not for John, who seems to be compassionate to the worst of these people," continues Missis. "Take Xoliswa Ximiya, for instance. Now that's a lady. Very educated. Polished. I don't know why your friend dumped her, John."

"Don't believe everything you hear from village gossips," says Camagu.

"You didn't dump her then?" asks Missis incredulously.

"Hey, let's not pry into the man's affairs, dear," says Dalton.

"There was no reason to dump her in the first place. There was never anything between us."

He omits to add that Xoliswa Ximiya, like the village gossips, doesn't seem to think so. She has been sending daily messages that she wants to see him. Cold and distant notes through schoolboys. Summoning him to her presence. One day, a messenger even arrives in the person of Vathiswa. He has been ignoring all these royal commands. And has been avoiding any path that passes near Qolorha-by-Sea Secondary School or Bhonco's homestead. The messages are becoming more frantic by the day. They no longer sound like orders. They sound like entreaties. If she were not such a refined lady, she would have long since gone to his cottage to rout him out of his snakehole. But she is too proud for that. The last thing she wants is a showdown with that unschooled girl who, according to gossip, now openly frequents the cottage.

"She is a lady, that Miss Ximiya," observes Missis as she serves them coffee and biscuits that were brought in by a maid. "Not like the red girl. I hear now that one is even cutting down trees."

"That reminds me," says Dalton. "How did the case go?"

"It hasn't ended," says Camagu curtly.

"She's a crazy, that one! Fancy cutting down trees!" Dalton laughs.

"I too thought so, John. I thought she was mad. Until I heard her side of the story. She has a point, John."

Dalton and Missis look at him closely, as if to make sure whether he too hasn't lost it.

"You are aligned with destructive forces, Camagu," says Dalton. "I hear that your women of the cooperative killed a swarttobie bird, the black oystercatcher. They said it was competing with them for mussels."

"That was wrong," admits Camagu. "I warned them against it. I told them that the African black oystercatcher is an endangered bird and they must never kill it again. It is just ignorance, John. I think we all need some education on these matters. All of us. Even you, John. Then we will understand why Qukezwa chopped down those trees."

Camagu suggests that instead of having his verandah television play old movies that have no relevance to the people of Qolorha-by-Sea, he should consider playing videos on developmental issues. Documentaries that will encourage community dialogue. It is important that people should start talking about things that affect their lives. The problem, of course, is where to find such videos.

Camagu is not aware that while he is busy drinking coffee with the Daltons, things are happening at Zim's homestead. Hecklers and ululants have gathered once more, and are creating such a din that even the amahobohobo weaverbirds are reeling about and flying against one another.

Bhonco has resumed his offensive! To the abayiyizeli, the women whose greatest joy in life is to ululate, he has added the hecklers. They are young men whose greatest pleasure is to heckle at the slightest provocation. They have perfected heckling to the extent that they can heckle even when no one is talking. They have only to look at a person, imagine his speech in their heads, then heckle him. Bhonco has promised them beer brewed by the expert hand of NoPetticoat at the end of each day of heckling.

At this very moment, Qukezwa is giving birth in one of the rondavels. She is surrounded by the grandmothers who are village midwives. She is heaving and screaming. Ululants are ululating outside. Hecklers are heckling. Zim sits at the door of the rondavel, his head buried in his hands.

The gathering of the hecklers and ululants sees his pain and increases the volume.

"Try again, my child," says a grandmother. "Push!"

"The head is already appearing," says another grandmother.

She pushes once more. She hears the yelping laughter that Camagu insisted was not the baby's but the giant kingfisher's. The bloody thing crashes its way out. It immediately starts screaming. It is as though it wants to compete with the ululation outside, and the heckling.

"It is a boy," says a grandmother.

"A boy," says Qukezwa, forgetting the pain. "His name is Heitsi."

"Heitsi!" shout the grandmothers in unison. "What kind of a name is that?"

 It is ages since rivers of salt have run down the gullies of Bhonco's face. Beautiful things have become estranged from his life since Camagu, son of Cesane, imprecated himself upon this village and became the bane of the Unbeliever's family. And then the abaThwa came and took their dance, wrenching away the cord that connected him to essential pain. How will the Cult of the Unbelievers survive without the dance? The Unbelievers cannot afford to be marooned in this world, without occasionally traversing misty mountains and plains to the pains of the past.

And then there is Zim and his despicable Believers. Zim whose medicine has turned influential people like Dalton and the detestable Camagu to his side. Zim whose daughter has cast a spell on the spineless Camagu, wresting him away from the esteemed daughter of the Unbelievers. The very daughter who lives and is prepared to die for civilization. Zim who will soon be driven crazy by ululations and heckles, until he plunges down a cliff. Zim. Zim. Zim. It is a name that buzzes in his vengeful head.

And then there are the hadedah ibises that have now taken to loitering outside his pink rondavel, sharing corn with the hens and their broods. Although the ibises are bigger and uglier birds, the hens are no longer bothered by them. Three or four of the accursed birds still follow him whenever he ventures out of the homestead. They hover above him clumsily, emitting their raucous laughter.

Beautiful things are hard to come by.

It is in the midst of the elder's brooding on this dearth that Xoliswa Ximiya visits the homestead. He can sense that she is despondent, even though she wears a brave face. She tells her parents that she is earnestly looking for a job in the government.

"We thought you had forgotten about that," says Bhonco.

"I thought I had forgotten about it too. I was resigned to staying here and building my school. But this place is not for me. There can be no growth for me here."

"This place is for you. This is your village. You were born here. Your forefathers walked this land. If anyone must go, it is that Camagu!" shouts Bhonco.

"It has nothing to do with Camagu!" Xoliswa Ximiya shouts back.

"She wanted to go to the city long before Camagu came here," agrees NoPetticoat.

"But she was no longer talking of it, NoPetticoat. She was no longer talking of it until that Camagu cast his evil shadow on our village."

"Maybe she is right, Bhonco," pleaded NoPetticoat. "Maybe we should allow her to go. Many young women from our village have gone to work in the cities. And they are not half as educated as Xoliswa."

"You cannot allow me to go, mother. When I want to go, I will go. I am not a child anymore. I was not asking for your permission. I was informing you. When the school closes next week I am going to Pretoria to make personal applications. Many of my former schoolmates are high up in the ruling party. They will lobby for me. I must go because it works out much better when one is there. It is high time I went to live in more civilized places."

"Do you hear what she is saying, NoPetticoat? And this is what you support?"

"She is a big girl, Bhonco. Let her go."

Bhonco, son of Ximiya, storms out screaming, "The Believers have won again! They are taking my child away from the place where her umbilical cord is buried . . . where she has made her name as the principal of the secondary school."

"You have upset your father," says NoPetticoat calmly.

"I can see that."

"This Camagu, did you really love him?"

"It has nothing to do with Camagu, mother."

"He is not worth it, you know?"

"He is not my business. My only concern is that he is taking this village back to the last century, and many people now seem to agree with him."

"Maybe we have judged him too harshly," says NoPetticoat deliberately. "Maybe there are indeed many different paths to progress."

"How can you say that, mother?"

"The clothes that they make at the cooperative . . . they are so beautiful. The isikhakha skirts. The beaded ornaments. The handbags."

"They are the clothes of the amaqaba, mother—of the red people who have not yet seen the light of civilization."

"Oh, how I miss the beautiful isiXhosa clothes of the amahomba!"

Xoliswa Ximiya stares at her mother in disbelief. NoPetticoat has that distant look that speaks of a deep longing for what used to be. The silence is broken by Bhonco's screams outside. Both women rush out.

The bees that have built their hive on the eaves of his four-walled tin-roofed ixande house are attacking him. The women shriek and open the door of the rondavel for him. He rushes in and they shut the door. He has numerous stings on his skin. His whole face is swelling fast and his eyes can no longer see. His scars are itching. He sits on the chair and moans, "How can the ancestors do this to me?"

"It is the bees, father, not the ancestors," says Xoliswa Ximiya. "We'll just have to take you to the clinic."

Education has made this girl mad, thinks Bhonco. Has she forgotten that, according to the tradition of the amaXhosa, bees are the messengers of the ancestors? When one has been stung, one has to appease the ancestors by slaughtering an ox or a goat and by brewing a lot of sorghum beer.

"It must be that scoundrel Zim," moans Bhonco. "He must have talked our common ancestor into sending me these bees. And the headless old man complied! Don't they know? Bees are not for playing games of vengeance!"

But at this moment Zim's thoughts are drifting a distance away from schemes of vengeance. They are with NoEngland, who resides in the Otherworld. He has been thinking of NoEngland for some days now. He misses her. He thinks that things would have been different if she were here. If she had not hurried to the world of the ancestors, leaving her husband and children in a world that has been so defiled by lack of belief. NoEngland has been in his mind all the time lately, to the extent that he has not touched his food. He just lies under his giant tree. He does not even hear the ululants and the hecklers. They are becoming discouraged because they are not making a dent in his indifference. They don't know that nothing can penetrate his mind now, for it is occupied by NoEngland.

He does not even notice when Camagu comes and greets him. Camagu does not know what to do. He thinks that perhaps the old man is asleep. Yet his eyes are wide awake. And there is a smile on his face. He greets again. And again.

"I have come to see Qukezwa and the baby, old one," Camagu says aloud, so that his voice can rise above the cacophony of ululations, heckles, and amahobohobo weaverbirds. The women who are fussing over Qukezwa and Heitsi in the rondavel hear him and appear at the door.

Ah, at last some people who might help. It is a week now since the new Heitsi was born to ululations and heckles. A week of searing loneliness for Camagu. He has been languishing alone in his cottage, pining for Qukezwa, and reflecting on what this place has done to him. It has rendered him unrecognizable to himself. He used to be a man-about-town. A regular at Giggles. But he hasn't had a tipple since he came to Qolorha-by-Sea. He has also found himself losing interest in cigarettes. Even his famous lust has deserted him. Since coming here he has only known a woman—in the biblical sense, that is—in his messy dreams.

His old self would have taken advantage of the raw talent that he encounters every day in this village. Lots of talent. Vathiswa. Even the waitresses and charwomen at the Blue Flamingo. It is all because of the effect that Qukezwa has had on him. The effect that has even cleansed NomaRussia out of his life, out of his recurrent dreams.

He pined and pined in his cottage, until he gathered enough strength to walk to Zim's homestead with the intention of pleading to be allowed a glimpse of the woman and her child.

"You cannot see Qukezwa and the baby," screeches a woman at the door.

"Did she say so? Did she say she doesn't want to see me?" asks Camagu.

"Don't you see this reed? It means that no man is allowed into this house."

She is pointing at a reed that is jutting out from the roof just above the door.

"He grew up in the land of the white man. He does not know that a reed like this means there is a newborn baby in the house and no man is allowed," observes another woman sympathetically.

"But he is the father of the child," says another one. "Fathers are not barred from the reed."

"Who says he is the father? The grandmothers said Qukezwa was a virgin."

More women come out of the house and join the debate, completely ignoring Camagu, who just stands there looking foolish.

"Even if he is the father," asserts a toothless wizened hag, "he is not married to this daughter of Zim. When the custom says a father is allowed into the reed it means a father who is married to the mother of the baby."

"Yes," adds another one, "it does not mean those men who have just ejected their seed illicitly."

"It does not mean the eaters of stolen fruit," shout others.

But some disagree. A father is a father, they say. It is cruel not to let a father see his baby. A custom is a custom, says the opposing view. Men must learn not to urinate all over the place without taking responsibility for their actions by marrying the women they have urinated upon.

"But who says this son of Cesane is the one who has spoiled this daughter of Zim?" a voice of sanity pipes up above all the din. But Camagu cannot hear it. He is drifting away from Zim's homestead. Wandering aimlessly at first. To be as far away as possible from the jabbering women. Away to the sea. Aimfully. To his haunts with Qukezwa. To the ship at Ngcizele where he last saw her. To the *Jacaranda*.

He sits on the railing where Qukezwa sat. The uxomoyi kingfisher sits on the mast and mocks him again. He laughs back at it. It did not expect this response. It flies away. He turns to the waves and conducts them as if they are a choir. They sing even louder and crash against the reefs with greater violence, creating snow-white surf. The children of Ngcizele shriek as they clamber down the rocks to the sea to swim and to draw the medicinal sea water that their parents use for drinking and douching. They wonder at the strange man who is playing on the skeleton of the ship. He beckons to them and they paddle away laughing. He creates his own Qukezwa, holds her very tightly, and dances around vigorously. The children watch in wonderment and laugh. They mimic him and dance around the ship.

In the meantime the Qukezwa of flesh and blood is sulking at the women who are fussing over her. She heard how Camagu came to see her and was not allowed to enter the rondavel. They could at least have called her out to talk to him, she moans. If she never sees him again, she and her baby will never forgive them. Heitsi bears witness to this by bawling for the entire world to hear. He bawls all the time. The women say it is because the sacred rituals of his father's clan have not been performed for him, since his father is not known.

Heitsi bawled for the entire world to hear. Qukezwa sang a lullaby, hoping he would sleep. She was beginning to despair. Twin walked in front of her, humming a song about the coming salvation. He did not waver in his belief. Other Believers were disappointed in him, though. They were complaining that they had elected him by acclamation to be the leader of the secret forces that would destroy the houses, crops, and cattle of the Unbelievers. But he seemed to have lost all interest in the raids. He just wanted to sit on the hill with Qukezwa, and await salvation that would come from the Russian ships. Somehow his belief had made him lethargic.

The staunch Believers continued their raids without him. But they were collecting less and less booty. The Unbelievers had hidden their cattle in those chiefdoms that had strong unbelieving chiefs. Twin-Twin, for instance, hid all his herds in the Amathole Mountains where his numerous sons looked after them. They had established permanent cattle-posts with protected villages deep in the gorges that were hard to reach.

In the other villages, though, the raids continued unabated. Hordes of hungry Believers burnt down the Unbelievers' homesteads after looting them. The Unbelievers appealed to Gawler and his master, The Man Who Named Ten Rivers, for protection. Although Gawler pro-tected Twin-Twin personally, for the man was considered useful by the colonial government, the rest of the Unbelievers were without protec-tion. All The Man Who Named Ten Rivers would say was that the Unbelievers should hold their ground. But he would not send his mili-tary force to defend them. He made it clear that the military would be sent only if the hordes strayed into white settlements and farms.

The raids were not on Twin's mind as he led Qukezwa down the hill. Even the bawling Heitsi did not get on his nerves. He was thinking only of one thing: salvation.

"Father of Heitsi, the child is hungry," said Qukezwa feebly.

But Twin did not respond. He marched on, humming his hymn. Qukezwa rushed past him and stood in front of him. She threw the child into his arms.

"What now, Qu?" he asked.

"He is your child too, Father of Heitsi! And he is hungry!"

"We'll get something to eat at Mhlakaza's. If you are tired of carry-ing the baby, I don't mind helping you. In any case, Heitsi is old enough to walk on his own. You spoil him when you carry him on your back at this age."

"He can't walk, Father of Heitsi. He is hungry. And we won't get anything at Mhlakaza's. We didn't get anything there last time. Mhlakaza himself was hungry. So were the prophetesses."

As they approached Mhlakaza's homestead they were welcomed by the wailing of women. The sound was subdued yet searing. Twin knew at once that there was a death in this house. He handed Heitsi back to Qukezwa and ran to Mhlakaza's house. There were more women inside, kneeling around Mhlakaza's skeletal corpse. Another casualty of starvation. Nombanda and her brother Nqula were there as well. They were not wailing. They just sat there and stared into nothingness. As usual they were unkempt. But Nongqawuse was nowhere to be seen. It was whispered that she had taken refuge with one of the believing chiefs.

"He was a great man!" declared Twin. He would have cried, but his eyes no longer had tears. He just knelt down next to the dried-out corpse and whimpered softly. He lamented the demise of the robust gospel man and the effervescent guardian of the prophetesses, who was now reduced to a bundle of bones.

"The dogs of the government are here!" screamed a woman outside.

It was Mjuza. He was accompanied by a group of fourteen men on horseback. They were all in police uniform. Mjuza was now a member of Major Gawler's police force.

"We have come to arrest Mhlakaza and the girls," announced Mjuza.

"You will have to go to the world of the ancestors to arrest him," said Twin triumphantly.

"What? Is he dead?" asked a disappointed Mjuza.

"How else do you join the ancestors?" asked Twin.

"We are too late," said Mjuza, addressing his men. "He has escaped justice. But we'll take the girls with us."

"That is sacrilege!" shouted Twin. "You cannot touch the prophetesses."

"Try to stop us," mocked Mjuza, getting down from his horse and walking into the rondavel. Two policemen followed him. The Believers watched helplessly as they walked out of the house dragging Nombanda and Nqula with them.

"Where is Nongqawuse?" barked Mjuza.

Nobody answered.

"I will find her, if it's the last thing I do."

"If it is Mhlakaza and Nongqawuse that you want, why are you arresting Nombanda? And what has her brother Nqula done?" demanded Twin.

"Nombanda was Mhlakaza's prophetess as well," said Mjuza. "She spoke as much as Nongqawuse, and was often preferred to her. And the boy Nqula, he was Mhlakaza's messenger. He was the one who was often sent to the chiefs."

Twin shouted after the policemen as they rode away with the boy and girl, "You will pay for this, Mjuza! The ancestors will punish you! Your own father, our great Prophet Nxele, will twist your neck for consorting with the conquerors of his people, they who have murdered the son of their own god!"

Mjuza only laughed at his empty words.

People remained asking themselves what had happened to Mjuza. He was the son of Nxele, the prophet who prophesied the resurrection of the dead in 1818! He who was known far and wide as a great anticolonial militant! He who was a war hero, who burnt down a mission station in Butterworth in 1851 and was shot in the stomach by a colonial bullet! He who had announced at the beginning of the cattle-killing movement that his father was coming back at the head of the Russian army to liberate the amaXhosa people! Here he was today, a servant of his colonial masters, a hero of the Unbelievers! Indeed burning embers gave birth to ashes!

Meanwhile, Twin-Twin was happy to hear that the power of the prophets of Gxarha had finally been broken. He rejoiced even more when he heard later that Nongqawuse herself was finally routed out of her hiding place and arrested. And so was Nonkosi, the prophetess of the Mpongo River. They were all in the custody of Major John Gawler.

Perhaps now the madness will come to an end in the land and families will come together, thought Twin-Twin. But after all the pain inflicted on him by the scourge of belief, he would not forgive Twin. He would not forgive his own senior wife either. She who was once identified by Mlanjeni as a witch. She on whose behalf he had suffered the humiliation of flagellation. She who had defected to the Believers. His scars itched terribly at the thought of the treacherous woman.

The saddest thing about NoPetticoat's defection to Camagu's cooperative society is that no one scratches and soothes Bhonco's scars when they itch in anger. Although the once-happy couple live in the same house, they don't talk anymore. And Bhonco, son of Ximiya, is determined that he will not talk to her until she returns to her senses.

She, on the other hand, is determined never to come to any senses other than those that she has at the moment. These are the senses that made her long for her beautiful isiXhosa costumes of the amahomba after seeing the work done by MamCirha and NoGiant at the cooperative society; that made her defy her husband and daughter by joining the cooperative; and that have turned her into a traitor in the eyes of the members of her family, especially now that she sees the issues of development in the village with the same eye as the Believers.

To Bhonco this is the ultimate betrayal. The furrows on his face have become deeper and sadder. Once more the Believers have won a battle. Only a battle, not the war. The war is going to be a protracted one. The Unbelievers will win in the end, because civilization is on their side. Is it not written that victory shall be achieved over the forces of darkness? Light always overcomes darkness and banishes it away.

This thought brings joy to his heart. But instead of crying—it is his habit to cry for beautiful things—he bursts out laughing. He just melts into laughter. He has finally found it taxing to be grave and angry all the time. He walks all over the village laughing. The hadedah ibises retreat, unable to compete with his laughter. He is disgraced among his fellow Unbelievers. The story is relayed from one mouth to another. "Did you hear the latest? Bhonco laughed!"

The turncoat NoPetticoat is blamed for his debilitated behavior.

Bhonco laughs all the way to Vulindlela Trading Store. Here he finds Camagu pleading with Dalton to go with him to Zim's to ask for Qukezwa's hand in marriage. They suddenly stop their conversation. They are alarmed to see the elder laughing.

"I greet you, destroyers of my people!" says Bhonco cheerfully.

"Is something wrong, Tat'uBhonco?" inquires Dalton, looking at him closely.

"Should there be anything wrong, besides the mess you have all dragged us into?"

Camagu and Dalton observe that the laughter is only in his voice. His eyes are sadder than ever.

"Give me ityala, you son of my dead friend, and stop asking me stupid questions," says Bhonco, waving his hands dismissively.

He demands that Dalton give him credit for corned beef and pipe tobacco. He must write it in his black book, because his daughter, the school principal, will pay. His name, he says, is Bhonco, son of Ximiya. He does not depend on his wife's nkamnkam or old-age pension. He has educated his daughter precisely so that she could look after him in his old age. As far as he is concerned—and he indicates that he is saying this for the benefit of Camagu—his wife can eat all her money with the Believers who have bewitched her into their camp.

"Your wife joined the cooperative because she wanted to," says Camagu, as Dalton puts the goods the elder wants on the counter in front of him. "No one enticed her there. It is for her own good and the good of her family. Soon she will be making more money than the nkamnkam she gets from the government."

Bhonco bursts out laughing, takes his canned beef and tobacco, and walks out of the store. The two men shake their heads pityingly.

"Is the world coming to an end?" asks Dalton.

"There is nothing cheerful about that laughter," observes Camagu. "It is the laughter of sadness."

"You know, what you want me to do . . . my wife will be very angry with me," says Dalton, reverting to what they were discussing before the laughing elder walked in. "She does not understand what you see in Zim's daughter."

"Your wife will never understand. I know that even my friends in Johannesburg would never understand. Sleeping with her, yes. But marrying her! They would certify me mad."

"This is highly irregular, Camagu," says Dalton. "I am not your relative. Normally three of your relatives would go to ask for the woman's hand."

"I don't have a relative here, John. So you qualify."

Zim is sitting under his big tree with four of his male and female relatives when Dalton and Camagu arrive. The ululants and hecklers are not here today. No one knows why Bhonco has recalled them. He has been doing inexplicable things ever since he started this business of laughing.

After greeting the elders, Dalton says, "So you got the message that we would be coming to talk about the *intombi*—the young woman?"

"Are you the visitors we are expecting?" asks Zim incredulously.

"It is us, Tat'uZim," says Dalton.

The relatives inspect them from head to toe. All the while they are puffing on their long pipes and ejecting jets of spittle onto the ground. It is a habit that Dalton hates, but he ignores it. He is a beggar here and he cannot dictate how people should behave. Two chairs are brought for them. The relatives are sitting on the ground. They look disappointed.

"We are listening," says Zim.

"We have come to ask for the intombi," says Dalton.

"Has the young man already spoken with our intombi?" asks one of the relatives.

"Please allow us to confer first," pleads Dalton.

The relatives look at one another in amazement.

"Confer? This is a simple question. But we'll allow you to confer," says Zim.

Dalton and Camagu walk out of the relatives' earshot.

"Have you asked Qukezwa to marry you," asks Dalton, "and has she agreed? That is what the relatives want to know."

"I have not. I could not," admits Camagu. "They would not let me see her."

"You have sent us here to make fools of ourselves. They will ask Qukezwa. What if she says no? Women don't like to be taken for granted, you know?"

"Okay, let me just say I asked her and she agreed!"

"You are lying!"

"You are my messenger. You don't know what went on between us. Just tell them what I say."

They go back to join Zim and his relatives. Dalton tells them that the *umfana*—the young man in question—has indeed spoken with the intombi.

"If that be the case, it is well," says one relative. "Go and fetch the young man. We'll decide on a new day to meet. We'll have our intombi at hand."

"He is here already," says Dalton, pointing at Camagu. "He is the suitor."

Again the relatives are taken aback. They look at Zim angrily.

"Did you know about this?" asks an uncle.

"I did not even know who the visitors were going to be," Zim defends himself.

"This is highly irregular," says the uncle. "The suitor has come personally on the very first day. He is supposed to come on our demand. He is not supposed to negotiate his own marriage."

"I have no relatives here to do that for me, my fathers and mothers. It is for that reason I came myself with this son of Dalton."

"He is not an umfana," observes an old woman. "He is too old for our daughter."

"Age has never mattered to our people," says an old man. "If it does not matter to the intombi, why should it matter to us?"

"Has he ever been married?" inquires the uncle.

"I have never been married before, my fathers and mothers."

"Then he is an umfana, whatever his age," says another old woman.

"Does he know the situation of our daughter?" Another uncle directs this question to Dalton. "We must not talk here as if we have a daughter who can wear white on her wedding day."

"He knows it very well," says Dalton.

"Maybe he is even responsible for it," adds a younger relative.

"No, it cannot be," says Zim emphatically. "The grandmothers have said she has never known a man."

"I do not care," says Camagu desperately. "I am willing to take responsibility. I can even claim paternity if need be. All I want is to marry your daughter."

"Go back home," says the uncle. "You will come back again. You know what to bring."

The days that follow are very hectic for Camagu. He sends people out to nearby villages to purchase three head of cattle that must be driven to Zim's homestead on the second visit. These are not yet for the lobola. The first one is payment for the very act of asking for marriage, the second one is for the face of the woman, and the third one is for the room where the newlyweds will sleep, known as *ikoyi*.

In the meantime, Camagu is asked by the chief to address the elders on the alternative plans for the development of the village, since he is one of the instigators of the rejection of the gambling complex that the consortium from Johannesburg wanted to build. He holds a series of meetings where he outlines his plans. At every meeting the Unbelievers are very vocal in advocating the holiday paradise that will bring civilization to the village, and he has to defend his plans vigorously. He even has to appear before the regional and provincial executives of the ruling party, who are not happy that there are obstacles to the injection of such wonderful investment into the village economy. At every meeting his plans become more thought out.

At these meetings with political big shots, he never forgets to remind them that all the black empowerment groups in Johannesburg and other big cities empower only the chosen few. They do not create employment for the people. Instead, whenever these big companies are taken over by these groups, there follows what is euphemistically called rightsizing in order to maximize profits. Thousands of workers are retrenched. These black empowerment groups do not empower workers by creating jobs for them. Instead, workers lose jobs.

It is the same with the company that wants to turn Qolorha into a holiday haven. Only a chosen few will benefit: the party and trade union bosses who are directors. They live in their mansions in Johannesburg and have nothing to do with the village. The villagers will actually lose more than they will gain from the few jobs that will be created. Very little of the money that is made here will circulate in the village. As for the dream—no, the nightmare—of town houses and the "English" retirement village for millionaires, the less said about it the better.

"The less said about it the better because you have no alternative plan!" cries Bhonco, son of Ximiya. Laughter has deserted him once more. He has told his fellow Unbelievers that it was temporary insanity planted in him by the Believers.

"I do have a better suggestion," says Camagu.

The villagers must come together, and using the natural material that is found in the village, the very material that they use to build and thatch their houses, they must build a backpackers' hostel in Qolorha. There are many tourists who like to visit unspoiled places for the sole purpose of admiring the beauty of nature and watching birds without killing them. Such tourists would enjoy the hospitality of the ama-Gcaleka clan in self-catering rondavels or in the hostel with a kitchen and a dining room. Authentic food of the amaXhosa such as *umngqusho,* the maize samp that is cooked with beans, would be prepared for the guests. So would various types of shellfish such as amaqonga, imbhaza, amangquba, and imbhatyisa, which are plentiful in the rough sea. Many people would come for the seafood, especially if it is cooked in the unique manner of the people of Qolorha. Here he has in mind Qukezwa's cooking that converted him to seafood when he first visited Zim's homestead.

"The gambling city is going to bring electricity to the village," says Bhonco.

"Electricity must come to the village . . . but not because of the gambling city," Camagu responds. "The government must bring electricity here because the village needs it. It is the policy of the government now to electrify even the most remote villages."

Then all of a sudden he gets excited and shouts, "Come to think of it, we can even create our own electricity! From the sun! There is plenty of sunshine here! We can harness the sun to light our hostel and our houses! We can even cook and warm our water with the sun!"

People shake their heads in wonderment. Even Camagu's supporters think he is crazy. He tries to explain to them the wonders of solar energy. These are not just dreams, he tells them. Such things are already happening in other places.

Bhonco and his Unbelievers are getting worried that more people are being swayed by the picture that Camagu has painted.

"The man is obviously a crook," shouts Bhonco. "He says now we must build a hotel. For whom are we building this hotel? For him. He wants to use us to make himself rich in the same way he has used some of the foolish women of this village."

"Those foolish women, Tat'uBhonco, are making good money that you will not see even in your dreams," replies Camagu. "And they make this money from their own business. I do not own the cooperative society. Its members own it. The same will happen if the villagers come together to build this holiday place that will give travelers the opportunity to experience life in an African home. The villagers who come together to build the place will own the place. They will not be working for anyone but themselves. It will not be big and wonderful like the gambling city with roller coasters and cable cars. But it will be ours. The Chinese have a saying that it is better to be the head of a chicken than to be the backside of an elephant."

"What have the Chinese got to do with this?" asks Bhonco derisively. "It is in the nature of Believers to put their faith in all these strange foreign people from across the seas. First it was the Russians. Now it is the Chinese!"

Those who understand what Camagu meant by the Chinese adage laugh.

"After we have built the place, how will the tourists know about it?" asks a young woman.

"We'll advertise the place throughout the South African backpackers' network. But we'll also target different types of tourists. There are those who will come, for instance, because of the historical significance of the place. Remember this is a place of miracles! This is where Nongqawuse made her prophecies!"

"That damned Nongqawuse again!" fumes Bhonco, walking out of the meeting.

Camagu is pleased with himself. There is no doubt that most of the villagers support his idea.

❁ ❁ ❁

Zim has heard about his performance, and congratulates him as they sit under the giant wild fig tree with John Dalton, waiting for Zim's relatives to continue haggling over Qukezwa. Zim does not attend the meetings anymore. He seems to have lost interest in anything that has to do with the village. When Camagu asks him about his lack of interest he says, "You will complete that work. My thoughts are no longer here. They are with NoEngland. Even now she has given me respite only in order to complete this matter of Qukezwa's marriage."

"You talk in riddles, old man," says Dalton. "What are you trying to tell us?"

But before the elder can respond, some of his relatives arrive. And soon thereafter a boy comes driving the three head of cattle with which Camagu will be asking for Qukezwa's hand in marriage. Women welcome the cattle with ululation.

"Now that the cattle have arrived, we can proceed," says an uncle.

"But the brandy . . . where is the brandy?" asks another relative.

Dalton rushes to his four-wheel-drive bakkie parked near the gate and comes back with a case of brandy.

"We know the customs, my elders," he says. "This occasion cannot be complete without the brandy that has been brought by the suitor."

"Let the girl be called," says the uncle.

Qukezwa stands in front of Zim, his relatives, and the suitor's delegation that comprises only the suitor himself and John Dalton. Camagu has not seen her since she gave birth to Heitsi. She does not look at him. She is looking to the ground. She is expected to be shy on an occasion like this. Camagu laughs inside. Qukezwa looks so strange when she is shy.

"Do you know these people?" asks the uncle.

She casts a furtive glance at Camagu. He is dying inside. And praying that she will give the correct answer. He has not asked her before. He prays that she does not think that he takes her for granted. There was no way he could meet her to ask her to marry him. And there was no way he could wait for such an opportunity to present itself. He wants her to be with him. As soon as now!

Camagu sighs with relief when Qukezwa says, "Yes, I know them." If she had said she did not know them, that would have been the end of the story. It would have meant she was turning Camagu down.

"From where do you know them?" inquires an aunt.

"Here in the village of Qolorha," responds Qukezwa.

"To prove that you really know them, what is their clan name?" asks the uncle.

"They are from the amaMpondomise people. They are of the Majola clan. They are the people whose totem is the snake," says Qukezwa with confidence.

Camagu smiles to himself.

"You have heard her. She agrees," says the uncle with satisfaction.

"We have heard her," responds Dalton.

"You can go, my child," commands the uncle.

She gives Camagu a naughty wink before she turns away and walks to her rondavel that still has a reed jutting out.

"My work is finished now," says Dalton.

"No, it is not finished," says the aunt. "We have not talked about the lobola."

"Twelve head of cattle," says Zim.

"Tat'uZim! That's rather steep," pleads Dalton. "Unless of course each head of cattle is worth three hundred rand."

"Twelve cattle, and that is not negotiable," insists Zim. "Qukezwa is a child of the spirits. Each head of cattle is worth a thousand rand."

"Let's take it before they change their minds," Camagu whispers to Dalton.

"They can't change their minds. It is the custom to negotiate . . . to try to bring them down," Dalton whispers back. Then to the relatives he says, "We have decided to agree with your terms."

"It is agreed," they say in unison.

"After three days the girl's uncle and some other relative will take her to our new son-in-law's house," says Zim. "According to custom we should be taking her to Camagu's parents' home, not to his house. But this is not a regular marriage. We are giving our daughter to a man whose parents and whose home we don't even know."

"Indeed it is an irregular marriage," agrees the uncle. "When we take this girl to your house, son of Cesane, you know that a goat known as *tsiki* must be slaughtered. Then our daughter has to be given a new name by the eldest daughter of her new family. But in your case, who is going to give our daughter a name?"

"Yes," adds an aunt, "and who will give the bride the leg of a goat?"

"We'll improvise," says Camagu. "MamCirha and NoGiant will do all the things that are supposed to be done by my female relatives. They are like my relatives now."

"Look after our daughter well," warns Zim.

The women bring food from the house. There is plenty of mutton, samp, potatoes, and spinach. The meat is served in a big dish and the men use their own knives to cut it. The other food is served on individual enamel plates. There is no sorghum beer, though. Instead they serve the brandy brought by Dalton.

"I had hoped our daughter-in-law would cook us her usual specialty of abalone, mussels, and oysters fried with onion and served with samp," says Dalton as he munches away.

"This child of Dalton!" exclaims the uncle. "Where do you come from? Don't you know that our custom demands that on occasions like this, proper meat should be served and not your snakes from the sea?"

They all laugh and say that young people like to change tradition. They roar even more when one of them makes the observation that both their new son-in-law and Dalton are not so young, but are middle-aged, and should in fact be preserving customs instead of trying to change them.

"Don't allow our daughter to cut any more trees," an aunt advises Camagu, "otherwise you will run around in court all your life."

"By the way, what happened to her case?" asks the uncle.

"It just fizzled out. No one talks of it anymore," says Zim proudly. "That Unbeliever Bhonco tried very hard to resuscitate it. But the elders of the village have more important things to deal with."

The talk turns to that evil Bhonco and his Cult of the Unbelievers. The gathering mocks the folly of unbelief. They ridicule their rituals and praise the abaThwa for taking back their dance. They curse Bhonco's forebears for refusing to kill their cattle, thus destroying the amaXhosa nation. The Unbeliever's foolish forebears must take the responsibility for the failure of the prophecies.

"I for one think that on this matter of Nongqawuse, Bhonco has a point," says Dalton quite unwisely. "It is your forebears who were foolish for killing their cattle."

They look at him as if he has uttered the worst of blasphemies. Camagu suspects that the brandy has run to his head. No sober man, no sane man, can risk saying anything nice about Bhonco in the midst of such hard-core Believers. He is fortunate that they are in such a good mood after the successful negotiations that went completely in their favor. Otherwise they would be eating him alive. Instead of making a meal of him, they are dumbfounded.

"Has this child of Dalton been bought by the Unbelievers? Didn't you tell me that he is on the side of the Believers, Zim?" asks the uncle.

"He is a fickle man," says Zim.

Dalton doesn't seem to notice the stir he has caused. He just goes on gulping his brandy and talking in a very careless manner.

"No, I am not fickle. And I am not on the side of the Believers. Neither is Camagu. We just happen to agree with you, or you with us, on this matter of development, of preserving the indigenous trees, plants, animals, and birds. That is all. We are not Nongqawuse's people."

"Well, John, this is not the time and the place to argue about such things," Camagu pleads.

"The truth must be told, Camagu," says Dalton. "Otherwise they will be expecting you to participate in their quarrels and their rituals."

"This child of Dalton says our forebears were foolish," says Zim sadly. "Is that why his forebears cooked them?"

"Will you ever forget about that?" appeals Dalton. "You people are just like Bhonco. Whenever we don't see eye to eye on the smallest of things, you bring up this cooking business!"

"Foolish?" ponders the uncle. "Our belief is foolish? This child of Dalton has been bought by the Unbelievers."

"No, he did not mean it that way, my fathers," says Camagu. "There is nothing foolish about belief."

"Nothing foolish about belief!" exclaims Dalton incredulously.

"Dead people and cattle rising from the sea! And you say there is nothing foolish about that?"

"If your Christ can walk on the sea and turn water into wine, so can Nongqawuse's cattle rise from the sea," declares Zim. "And they did rise. People saw them, didn't they? Even kings like Sarhili saw them. There were witnesses to these miracles, in the same way that your Christ had witnesses to his. Of course, the cattle rose only to prove the truth of the prophecies. They rose only to be seen among the waves, then went back to the world of the ancestors. They would not have gone back if the Unbelievers had not continued to unbelieve."

"The old man is putting it well," says Camagu. "Believers are sincere in their belief. In this whole matter of Nongqawuse I see the sincerity of belief, John. It is the same sincerity of belief that has been seen throughout history and continues to be seen today where those who believe actually see miracles. The same sincerity of belief that causes thousands to commit mass suicide by drinking poison in Jonestown, Guyana, because the world is coming to an end . . . or that leads men, women, and children to die willingly in flames with their prophet, David Koresh, in Waco, Texas."

"I do not know if you can compare our prophets with prophets who come from white people's books," says the uncle.

"What I am saying is that it is wrong to dismiss those who believed in Nongqawuse as foolish," says Camagu. "Her prophecies arose out of the spiritual and material anguish of the amaXhosa nation."

Dalton feels betrayed. It is fine to humor these people sometimes, to go along with their foibles before putting them on the correct path. But this Camagu seems to believe what he is saying. He is not merely ingratiating himself with his in-laws. He speaks with conviction. The Believers, on the other hand, hear his words. But they don't mean anything to them. Educated people, they say, like to mystify the most straightforward of things. To cloud them with meaningless words.

"You know very well, Camagu, that Nongqawuse was a little girl who craved attention," Dalton says. "She had vaguely heard of the teachings of Nxele about the resurrection . . . and the Christian version of it, as her uncle had been a Christian at some stage. She therefore decided to concoct her own theology . . . which gathered momentum as she gained more prestige as a great prophetess. These were the delusions of a young girl!"

This Dalton does not give up. His tongue becomes more careless as the bottles get emptier and as the sun creeps towards its resting place.

"Miracles are miracles, John. She was a young girl, yes, and young girls are prone to seeing visions," says Camagu.

"If somebody I know who is a principal at the secondary school were here, she would tell you that the statement you have just made is highly sexist," laughs Dalton.

"It is true, you know? Who's always seeing visions of the Virgin Mary? Young girls. Our Lady of Fátima . . . our lady of this and that . . . all places where young virgins saw visions of the Virgin!"

The following day Camagu is shamefaced. He sits on the stoop while the rays of the morning sun warm his naked torso. He regrets that he argued with Dalton at Zim's place. They made fools of themselves in the presence of his in-laws. They must have sounded arrogant and vain, arguing about people's beliefs as if they were the fountains of all wisdom. Blabbering in loud voices while the elders watched in undisguised disgust. No wonder they have no respect for so-called educated people. It was all Dalton's fault. He was drunk. Camagu himself did not touch the brandy at all, although he got louder with those who did. Dalton was gulping it like water. By the time they left he was staggering and singing boisterously.

He is thinking of how he will redeem himself to his in-laws when Dalton arrives in his four-wheel-drive bakkie. The trader is in a jolly mood. He greets Camagu and carries on about the great success of their mission yesterday. He stops when he sees that Camagu is sullen.

"What is wrong, man? What have they done to you now?"

"You embarrassed me yesterday."

"Is that how you thank me for getting you a bride?"

"You got too drunk. What will those people think of us?"

"Those people are my people, man. I know them. They know me. I grew up with them. I am one of them. I do not know why you should be concerned how I behave when I am with them. Anyway, I came to talk about the plans you outlined at the meeting the other day."

"Ja. What about them?"

Dalton says he has thought long and hard about them. He feels that they are good. But they can still be improved. Instead of building a backpackers' hostel with self-catering chalets for nature-loving tourists, they should construct a cultural village owned and operated by the villagers. He already has two formidable women in NoManage and NoVangeli who are experienced in entertaining tourists by displaying cultural performances and practices of the amaXhosa. This is a proven kind of business. Tourists like visiting such cultural villages to see how the people live. The village will have proper isiXhosa huts rather than the newfangled hexagons that are found all over Qolorha. Women will wear traditional isiXhosa costumes as their forebears used to wear. They will grind millet and polish the floors with cow dung. They will draw patterns on the walls with ochre of different colors. There will be displays of clay pots and other earthenware items. Tourists will flock to watch young maidens dance and young men engage in stick fights. They will see the abakhwetha initiates whose bodies are covered in white ochre. They will learn how the amaXhosa of the wild coast live.

"The abakhwetha initiates? Right there in the middle of the cultural village? What will the initiates be doing in the village?" wonders Camagu.

"These will be actors, man, not the real abakhwetha."

"Then we won't be showing the tourists the true picture of how the amaXhosa live. In the real-life situation you don't find abakhwetha hanging around the village, women in their best amahomba costumes grinding millet and decorating walls, while maidens are dancing, and right there in front of the house young men are fighting with sticks. It's too contrived."

"That's the purpose of a cultural village: to show various aspects of the people's culture in one place."

"That's dishonest. It is just a museum that pretends that is how people live. Real people in today's South Africa don't lead the life that is seen in cultural villages. Some aspects of that life perhaps are true. But the bulk of what tourists see is the past . . . a lot of it an imaginary past. They must be honest and say that they are attempting to show how people used to live. They must not pretend that's how people live now."

"It seems you intend to oppose everything that I come up with," says Dalton bitterly. "First it was my water project, now you knock down things I have been doing successfully here with NoManage and NoVangeli long before you came to this village."

"I am just saying I have a problem with your plans. It is an attempt to preserve folk ways . . . to reinvent culture. When you excavate a buried precolonial identity of these people . . . a precolonial authenticity that is lost . . . are you suggesting that they currently have no culture . . . that they live in a cultural vacuum?"

"Now you sound like Xoliswa Ximiya!"

"Xoliswa Ximiya is not capable of saying what I have just said. She talks of civilization, by which she means what she imagines to be western civilization. I am interested in the culture of the amaXhosa as they live it today, not yesterday. The amaXhosa people are not a museum piece. Like all cultures, their culture is dynamic."

"I know what you are trying to do, Camagu. You are shooting down my ideas because you want to promote your own cooperative society. You want to benefit alone with your women. I heard that your lackeys, MamCirha and NoGiant, were trying to recruit NoVangeli and NoManage."

"I don't know what you are on about. What would we want with NoManage and NoVangeli? We are in the business of harvesting the sea and manufacturing isiXhosa attire and jewelry, not of milking gullible tourists."

"You want everything for yourself. You don't want me to have a piece of the action. You are greedy! My people will not allow you to get away with this. My people love me."

"Your people love you because you do things for them. I am talking of self-reliance where people do things for themselves. You are thinking like the businessman you are . . . you want a piece of the action. I do not want a piece of any action. This project will be fully owned by the villagers themselves and will be run by a committee elected by them in the true manner of cooperative societies."

◦ ◦ ◦

In no time the village is talking of the fallout between Camagu and Dalton. It is interpreted by the villagers as a power struggle. The Unbelievers are happy that at last they will be able to break the Believers. As long as those who oppose the gambling paradise fight among themselves and are divided into two camps, the plans to develop the village towards the path of civilization will proceed smoothly. Soon the surveyors will be coming.

Tongues wag in all directions. Some say Dalton is jealous of Camagu's success with the women's cooperative society. Dalton is not satisfied with owning Vulindlela Trading Store. He wants to own everything else in the village. Dalton's supporters, on the other hand, claim that Camagu is trying to take over all aspects of the tourist trade, including the cultural tourism of NoManage and NoVangeli. Camagu came all the way from Johannesburg to plant the seed of division in the clan of the amaGcaleka. He is so ungrateful, after Dalton set him up in Qolorha, bought him a cottage, and even got him a bride.

Camagu is despondent. The only bright spot in his life is that soon Qukezwa's people will bring her to his cottage. Qukezwa and Heitsi. He has claimed Heitsi as his child, even though the elders were insisting that since he was born out of wedlock he, according to custom, belongs to Zim and not to Qukezwa's new family. It will be wonderful to have an instant family. He never thought he was cut out to be a father. His ways were wild and carefree. They were ways that were in constant search of the pleasures of the flesh. Any flesh. Until he came to Qolorha-by-Sea. And was tamed by a nondescript daughter of Believers. Heitsi. He will be a good father to him. Heitsi. He who is named after Heitsi Eibib, the earliest prophet of the Khoikhoi. Heitsi. The son of Tsiqwa. Tsiqwa. He who tells his stories in heaven. Heitsi. The one who parted the waters of the Great River so that his people could cross when the enemy was chasing them. When his people had crossed, and the enemy was trying to pass through the opening, the Great River closed upon the enemy. And the enemy all died.

Camagu smiles to himself when he remembers how he learned all this from Qukezwa when she was teaching him about the sacred cairns.

He also learned that the Khoikhoi people were singing the story of Heitsi Eibib long before the white missionaries came to these shores with their similar story of Moses and the crossing of the Red Sea.

A messenger breaks his reverie. Qukezwa will not be coming. At least not for a while. As soon as Camagu and Dalton had left after negotiating the lobola, Zim had declared that he could now go in peace, for his work was done. Then he just sat there staring at nothing. Since then he has not said a word. He does not hear anything. It is as if the world outside does not exist. Qukezwa feels that she cannot leave her father in this state. She will try to nurse him back to good health. Only then will she join her husband.

But Zim remains in this state for many days. And then for many weeks. Nothing seems to help. After a while, Camagu is allowed to visit his wife. He is seen at Zim's homestead at least every other day. He is puzzled by what is happening to Zim.

Qukezwa arranges that they put his father on Gxagxa, his favorite horse, and lead him to Intlambo-ka-Nongqawuse—Nongqawuse's Valley. They place him before Ityholo-lika-Nongqawuse, the bush where Nongqawuse first saw visions of the Strangers who gave her the message of salvation. Qukezwa hopes this will help to jog his spiritual memory back to the world of the living. But it does not help.

An igqirha—a healer and diviner—is called and puts her finger right on the problem. Only after she and her acolytes have eaten the goat that was slaughtered for them, of course.

She says the daughter of the amaGqunukhwebe—by which she means NoEngland—is calling Zim. But Qukezwa is holding him with her heart. She does not want her father to die. She is selfishly holding him very tightly. There is a tussle between the two women who love the elder. He therefore remains in limbo between the world of the living and the world of the ancestors.

"NoEngland will finally win, for she is in cahoots with very powerful ancestors," says the igqirha. "Qukezwa is only a girl, although her heart is powerful enough to hold the elder for so long."

Qukezwa is angry when the elders plead with her to release the poor man so that he may go in peace. Why does everyone want her father to die?

◊ ◊ ◊

While the relatives are waiting for NoEngland's grand victory over Qukezwa, a woman is brought to Zim's homestead on a triangular wooden sleigh pulled by two oxen. She is very sick. But her beauty shines through the illness. She is covered in a gray donkey blanket, and lies calmly on a mattress on the sleigh. Only her head is showing. She wears a bright-colored doek. Her eyes are downcast and speak only of shame.

The sleigh is parked just outside Zim's door, and the man who brought her unyokes the oxen. The Believers who are surrounding Zim hear the commotion outside and are amazed to see the woman on the sleigh and the man driving his oxen out of the homestead.

"She is my daughter," explains the man. "She insists that I leave her here. It is the only thing that will cure her."

And he is gone.

No one knows what to do with the woman until Qukezwa arrives. She takes one look at her and screams.

"What do you want here? Are you not satisfied with what you did to my mother? Have you come to put the final nail in my father's coffin?"

"Please, Qukezwa," the woman whispers wanly, "have a heart. I am dying. This is the last appeal that I can make to NoEngland. I heard that Zim is in the process of dying and that you are holding him. I am glad you held him until I arrived. Perhaps he can take a message to No-England that she remove the curse. I have been to doctors of all sorts. They are unable to stop the flow. Only NoEngland can stop the pain that is racking my body."

The doctors at the hospital in East London gave her disease a name, she tells the men and women who are now surrounding her. Cervical cancer. They told her it was incurable. They gave her tablets to ease the pain. There was nothing new in what they said. She already knew that it was incurable, whatever one chose to call it. The igqirha himself had said so. Only the person who had caused it could reverse it. And that igqirha should know. He was the one who had "worked" her underwear for her to be like this in the first place.

NoEngland cannot be woken from the dead to remove the curse. But at least Zim can ask her to remove the pain when they meet in the Otherworld. The woman says she will not move from where she is until she is given an audience with Zim.

"You set your friends on me . . . to harass me wherever I went!" a callous Qukezwa yells at the hapless woman.

"I will not move until Zim's spirit departs from his body," insists the woman.

Everyone looks at Qukezwa as if the woman's salvation lies with her. As if Qukezwa was responsible for her fate. She runs back to her rondavel, where she breaks down and cries. She is angry that they want to hasten her father's death just so that he can carry their messages to NoEngland. She is determined more than ever to nurse him back to health. But the sick woman is just as determined to keep vigil outside Zim's door. She is grateful for the bread and tea that merciful relatives of Zim serve her. But she will not be moved to any of the houses. She wants to wait outside Zim's door.

Camagu comes the following day to see Qukezwa and Heitsi, and to find out if there is any change in Zim's state. He sees the woman on the sleigh. He takes one look at her and his heart beats faster. His palms sweat. He is out of breath, as if he had been running.

"NomaRussia?" he wonders softly.

She lifts her eyes wearily.

"NomaRussia!" he calls excitedly.

"Who are you?"

"At the wake . . . in Hillbrow . . . you sang so beautifully."

"So I did."

"We spoke. Don't you remember?"

"There were many people there. I do not remember you. All I want is for the pain to go away."

 People were dying. Thousands of them. At first it was mostly old people and children. Then men and women in their prime. Dying everywhere. Corpses and skeletons were a common sight. In the dongas. On the veld. Even around the homesteads. No one had the strength to bury them.

Twin and Qukezwa were determined to keep Heitsi alive at all costs. Twin had extricated himself from his lethargy. While he joined raiding parties that stole food from both Believers and Unbelievers, Qukezwa boiled up old bones that she picked up on the veld and in the dongas. Although the bones had been bleaching in the sun for years, she hoped to get some broth from them. She and Heitsi drank it as soup.

Twin's raiding parties went as far as East London. They broke into the colonists' stables and stole their horses. They slaughtered them and shared the meat. Qukezwa would see her husband approach from afar with a whole leg of a horse on his shoulders. She would rejoice, for there would be plenty of meat that day. The people could no longer afford to be disgusted about eating horsemeat. They forgot that they used to laugh at the Basotho people who regarded horsemeat, especially its biltong, as a delicacy.

Sometimes, even before he reached home, Twin would be attacked by hordes of hungry people who would grab the meat and run away with it. Or, while Qukezwa was cooking it, hungry thieves would steal the whole pot, right from the fire, and run away with it. It was a dog-eat-dog world.

And to their utter shame they did actually eat dogs. They stole the well-fed dogs of the colonists and cooked them for supper.

But death continued unabated. The colonists protected their animals from marauders with barricades and guns. Many Believers just sat in their homes and waited for death. Helpless mothers watched as children fell, never to rise again. Dying wives watched as the family dogs ate the corpses of their husbands. They knew that sooner or later they too would end up in the dogs' stomachs. But then the dogs themselves would end up in some hungry families' stomachs. It was a dog-eat-dog world.

"When things are like this, people will end up eating one another," said Twin as he sat with Heitsi near the fire where Qukezwa was cooking some grass that they were going to eat before they slept.

"Only mad people can do that. Even at the worst of times we would never be reduced to cannibalism as the Basotho were during the Difaqane wars and migrations," replied Qukezwa.

"Some people are mad already," said Twin. "Hunger has made many people raving mad."

"The prophets have failed us," lamented Qukezwa. "We must move. We must seek refuge, or even go to the colony and seek help from our conquerors."

"The prophets have not failed us," declared Twin. "We have failed them. We have failed ourselves. The fault is not with the prophecies, but with the Unbelievers, who failed to obey Nongqawuse! The dead will yet arise!"

"You can sit here, Father of Heitsi, and wait for the dead to rise. I am taking my child away."

"Where will you go?"

"I will go to the land of the amaMfengu. I heard that they have given refuge to quite a few of the starving amaXhosa."

"You can't desert the prophets now!"

"Desert the prophets?" laughs Qukezwa mockingly. "They deserted us. Where are they now? Mhlakaza is dead. The girl-prophets were arrested. Your prophets lied to us. The god of your people is weak. He failed to protect his people. I am going back to the god of my people, the Khoikhoi people."

Indeed Qukezwa went back to the god of her people. She begged his forgiveness for abandoning him. Qukezwa, daughter of the stars, returned to worshipping the seven daughters of Tsiqwa, the one who told his stories in heaven, the one who created the world and all humanity. The prodigal daughter communed once more with the bright stars that were also known as the Seven Sisters.

In the same way that she had led the sons of Xikixa to the land of plenty a few years before, she led Twin and Heitsi to the land of the amaMfengu. But this time there was no Gxagxa to ride. They walked on foot, their hunger belts tightly tied around their stomachs. There was no Twin-Twin and his many women and children. There were no cattle to drive. No pigs. No chickens. Just the three emaciated souls with calloused feet.

On the way they came across many dead bodies lying on the road. Some of the bodies had not finished dying yet. Their sunken eyes showed a little glimmer of life. Their cracked skin looked like land that had been thoroughly punished by drought. Their skin clung desperately to their bones. Twin and Qukezwa knew that they would be very fortunate if they themselves were not eventually counted among the roadside dead.

Although they looked like people risen from the grave, they arrived in the land of the amaMfengu, and found many Believers who had taken refuge with various families. They were provided with shelter in exchange for their labor. They looked after cattle, hoed the rich fields, and did guard duty for their amaMfengu hosts. This was very humiliating to many Believers who came from some of the noblest families of the amaGcaleka clan.

Twin and Qukezwa were quarreling all the time. He was unhappy that she had led them to the land of the amaMfengu, who were known traitors in alliance with the British. They had ignored the prophecies of Nongqawuse and had become rich by buying cattle cheaply from the

Believers. Now they were slaughtering cattle and feeding the *amafaca*, the emaciated ones.

"Would you rather we had died at Qolorha?" asked Qukezwa.

He could not answer that, but continued to moan about the treacherous nature of their saviors. He threatened that as soon as he got strong enough he would leave. He would go back to the land of his forefathers.

"You have nothing. What will you do there?" Qukezwa reasoned.

"I will find Twin-Twin," he said. But there was no conviction in his voice. "Or I will go to Lesotho or to the land of the amaMpondo and the amaMpondomise. Many Believers have taken refuge there. It is not as humiliating as it is here."

Qukezwa just chuckled and said that maybe Twin-Twin would welcome him with open arms after all the mischief that Twin had done against him. Then she went to feed Heitsi with umphokoqo maize porridge and creamy *amasi* sour milk.

Twin-Twin, of course, was in no mood to welcome any of the people who had caused the downfall of his nation. He was still receiving protection from the colonial government through John Gawler and John Dalton. Dalton had been eager to retire from the colonial service to start his own business, but he had been persuaded to remain in the service of the great queen, at least until things settled on the frontier and in British Kaffraria. He was now a magistrate in his own right. He was permanently based at Chief Nxito's chiefdom, and was therefore directly responsible for protecting both Twin-Twin and the aging chief from the marauding Believers.

But Twin-Twin was more disillusioned with the colonial government than ever. The Man Who Named Ten Rivers, who had styled himself The Great Benefactor of the Non-European Peoples of the World, was taking advantage of the defenseless amaXhosa and was grabbing more and more of their land for white settlement. Twin-Twin's scars itched all over when he heard stories of advancing parties of settlers who were demarcating for themselves chunks of farmland on the ruins of the Believers' homesteads. Those amaXhosa who continued to occupy their homesteads suddenly discovered that they were squatters on their own land and now had to work for the new masters.

The Man Who Named Ten Rivers ordered that only those who agreed to work for the colonists would be given famine relief. Many amaXhosa found themselves working as slaves in white settlements, being paid only in food rations.

"We are achieving what we set out to do," he benevolently told his magistrates. "The Xhosa are becoming useful servants, consumers of our goods, contributors to our revenue. Like the Maori of New Zealand, these people are not irreclaimable savages. We should make them a part of ourselves, with a common faith and common interests."

He was happy that all his plans were coming together so nicely. It had always been his intention to break the independence of the ama-Xhosa by destroying the powers of the chiefs, and forcing their subjects from their land to work for white settlers on their farms and in their towns. He was achieving this sooner than he had expected. Thanks to the cattle-killing movement.

The magistrates, however, felt that Sir George was sending mixed messages. He was constantly complaining to them about what he called indiscriminate benevolence. The magistrates were dishing out charity to people who were still able to work. According to Sir George, this was not true charity. Indiscriminate charity would attract hordes of natives to Kingwilliamstown, he said. Some would come from as far as Zulu-land to take advantage of the soup that was being given at the Kaffir Relief House—a charitable institution established by the missionaries.

"I do not understand what Sir George is trying to achieve," said Dalton one day as he rode with Gawler among the skulls and fragments of human bones near the Gxarha River. "He is trying to break the Kaffir Relief Committee because he claims their charity is attracting masses of natives to Kingwilliamstown. Yet at the same time he is sending his officers to recruit more natives to work as laborers in the colony."

"You never know with Sir George," said Gawler. "I think he wants to close the Kaffir Relief House."

"He should just close it and not make excuses. Now he is accusing us of indiscriminate charity."

"He knows what he is doing. He is a brilliant man."

"You like the man, don't you? You are the one who puts his theories into practice."

"On the contrary, I don't like the man. I am faithful to him for the good of the British Empire. He is an excellent governor. And humane too. But I don't like the man."

"You don't like him? I don't believe that."

"Because you do not know what he did to my father, who was the governor of Southern Australia. My dear father lost his job after Sir George's denunciations. They claimed he had mismanaged the finances of the colony. What is more, Sir George denounced my father after my family had given him wonderful hospitality at our home."

The Man Who Named Ten Rivers' opposition to indiscriminate charity extended to the amaMfengu. He could not tolerate their humanity towards the amafaca, the emaciated ones, and instructed their chief to expel those amaXhosa who had found refuge among his people. Twin and Qukezwa were among the thousands of people who were driven out of the land of the amaMfengu. Two thousand of these refugees were handed over to the colonial labor officers. Twin was too weak to attract the interest of anyone at the labor market. He ended up an inmate of the Kaffir Relief House, and there he lived with people who had been made raving mad by starvation, until he went raving mad himself. Meanwhile, Qukezwa wandered from village to village with Heitsi, begging for scraps of food. She hoped that one day she would locate her Khoikhoi people and would be welcomed into their warm bosom.

Twin-Twin heard how thousands of his people had died as a result of the cattle-killing movement. He heard of the activities of The Man Who Named Ten Rivers. He saw with his own eyes white settlements spreading over the lands of his people. He was filled with bitterness and his scars went wild.

He and Chief Nxito shook their heads over the disaster that had befallen their people.

"We have been cheated," he told Nxito. "These people through whose ears the sun shines are spreading like a plague in kwaXhosa."

"What can we do? We are a defeated people," said the old chief.

"It must be true that The Man Who Named Ten Rivers planned all this cattle-killing business," said Twin-Twin. "He is the one who planted these ideas in the mind of Nongqawuse. He wanted the ama-Xhosa people to defeat themselves. Now he is enjoying the spoils of victory without having lifted a finger."

"What can we do?" repeated Nxito tiredly. "We are a conquered people."

"And we helped them to conquer us! Just like that foolish King Ngqika, the very father of General Maqoma, the hero of the War of Mlanjeni. When these white people first came, the alcoholic King Ngqika believed that they were his subjects. He welcomed them and allowed them to preach their gospel among his people. When he woke up the next morning they had taken his entire country and he was their subject."

"Many people are now turning to the god of the white man, for they have seen that he is more powerful than our god," said Nxito.

"He is not powerful at all," said Twin-Twin dismissively. "Is he not the one who sat idle while the white people killed his son? I for one am tired of all these gods."

Twin-Twin went away to brood on the dangers of religion.

Ned, Mjuza, Dalton, and Gawler had all tried, at various times, to convert him to Christianity. But he told them he could not join a religion that allowed its followers to treat people the way the British had treated the amaXhosa. He was indeed disillusioned with all religions. He therefore invented his own Cult of the Unbelievers—elevating unbelieving to the heights of a religion.

Without the dance, the Cult of the Unbelievers is almost dead. Bhonco, son of Ximiya, is at the height of misery. The abaThwa will not lend them the dance even for a single day. The Unbelievers tried to invent their own. But they had no experience in inventing dances that send people into a trance, especially the kinds of trances that send people back in time. Their invention lacked potency.

It really is a pity that the woman-loving ancestor Twin-Twin died before he could perfect the rituals of his cult. Otherwise the present-day Cult of the Unbelievers would not have had to borrow dances from the abaThwa, but they would instead have immersed themselves in the rituals of old, which would automatically have become the cord that connected them to the world of the forebears. A world filled with essential pain and suffering.

When things are like this there is no balm that can soothe Bhonco's scars.

Loneliness devours his insides. NoPetticoat, his once-loving wife, spends a lot of time at the cooperative society. She claims she is still a loving wife, and that her stubborn husband is the one who refuses to understand her needs. But even when she is at home, the once-uxorious Bhonco does not talk with her. He will not talk with her until she stops gallivanting with Believers or their sympathizers. He grudgingly eats the food she cooks, and will not even say when he is not full and he needs some more. When she is not at the coop she sits under the tree that used to be the venue of the harrowing dances of the Unbelievers, and gracefully smokes her long pipe. Since her rebellion she has gone back to smoking her long pipe. And to wearing her traditional isiXhosa costumes of *umbhaco* and beads. At the cooperative society she has gained a reputation as the best sewer of umbhaco, which are decorations of black strips that are made on isikhakha skirts and on modern shirts that are inspired by the isikhakha tradition.

Xoliswa Ximiya finds these habits disgusting. She had successfully weaned her parents from redness, until NoPetticoat's rebellion. She pleaded with her at length, but her mother was adamant that she was no longer going to stifle herself with soulless European clothes. They were an utter punishment for her. She loves the clothes of the ama-homba. She has always loved them. She will always love them. As for puffing on her long pipe, she is no longer prepared to suffer from *ukun-qanqatheka*—the searing desire for tobacco—just to make her daughter happy. She has grabbed for herself the freedom to enjoy her pungent tobacco.

But Xoliswa Ximiya has more to worry about. She knows that she will never get Camagu back. He has decided to forsake all forms of civilized life and to follow heathen ways. He is a lost cause. She wouldn't have been happy with him in any case. She stands for civilization and progress, while he is bent on reinforcing shameful practices and uncultured modes of dress. They deserve each other, he and Qukezwa. They will wallow in redness together. She, daughter of Ximiya, will soon turn her back on this village.

Nevertheless, she is disturbed by the usual wagging tongues of Qolorha-by-Sea. They say she has become a turncoat and now believes in the developments that Camagu and the Believers are advocating. Some say that she has changed sides only because she thinks it is the best way to win Camagu back. Yet others say that Qukezwa stole Camagu to avenge her brother, Twin, whom Xoliswa Ximiya ejected like a jet of spit only because he had no schooling. Gossip has never bothered Xoliswa Ximiya before. But these rumors are getting out of hand, especially this last one. She finds that she has to defend herself constantly, even to people she does not regard as deserving to walk the same earth with her. The sooner she leaves this heart of redness the better.

But this is not the end of Xoliswa Ximiya's troubles. She wakes up one day and finds that the scars of history have erupted on her body. All of a sudden her ancestor's flagellation has become her flagellation. She rebels against these heathen scars. She refuses to believe that they are part of an ancestral vengeance. She curses her father for resuscitating the Cult of the Unbelievers.

"Even if I had not started the cult, the scars would still have come when they wanted to come," says Bhonco. "They have nothing to do with the cult. Even the Middle Generations got the scars though they knew nothing of the cult. It is a burden that a first child of Twin-Twin's line has to carry."

The Unbelievers were shocked to hear of the scars on their daughter's civilized body. They thought that the scars had come to an end, as Bhonco did not have a male heir to inherit them. In all history, they have never been imposed on a woman. Everyone, therefore, believed that the curse of the scars had finally been broken.

When Bhonco was younger, and his wife could not have a son, they had tried to persuade him to take a second wife who could give him an heir. But he was so much in love with NoPetticoat that he refused to marry anyone else. People even said that NoPetticoat had bewitched him with a love potion. She was obviously a witch, like Twin-Twin's senior wife had been. But both Bhonco and NoPetticoat had laughed at this idle talk.

Now here their daughter is getting the scars.

"What else did they expect?" ask the wagging tongues. "She is a man in a woman's body. That is why no man can tame her. That is why even a doctor like Camagu was afraid to marry her. He knew that she was her own boss, and that she would not be controlled by any man. That is why she rules all those men and women at the secondary school with an iron stick."

Xoliswa Ximiya packs up and leaves Qolorha-by-Sea. She has lost the battle for the soul of the village and for the love of Camagu. She has got a new job with the Department of Education in Pretoria. She is going off to more civilized places. Places with streetlights. She will be in a better position to consult specialists—dermatologists and plastic surgeons—to remove the accursed scars.

Once again Bhonco is devastated. Not only has he lost his wife to the Believers, now he has lost his daughter to the city. Worse still, he has lost the prestige of being the father of the principal.

Xoliswa Ximiya is too far away to hear the wagging tongues that insist that she is running away because she is heartbroken. Love has driven her out of the village, they say. And it does serve her right. She is getting a dose of her own medicine. She drove Twin away by being stingy with her love.

Camagu is sorry to hear that Xoliswa Ximiya has left without even a good-bye. But he has no time to worry about this. There are more worries at Zim's place.

There is Zim who is refusing to die. He is hovering between the Otherworld—the world of the ancestors that runs parallel to this world—and the world of today's Qolorha-by-Sea. The Believers appeal to Qukezwa, "It is because you are holding him with your heart. Please release the poor man. He has done his duty on earth. Let the elder go!"

Everyone looks forward to the pleasant life in the Otherworld. It is cruel to hold the elder to this earth.

Qukezwa is angry that everyone wants the old man to die. She is even angrier that she is being blamed for his state.

"How do you people know that this time my father's time has really come?" she demands. "How do you know that he cannot be cured out of this state and enjoy the life of this world again?"

People remember that Zim wanted to die once many years ago. He felt that he had overstayed his welcome on earth. So he slaughtered a goat, by which he was asking the ancestors to give him the road to their eternal place—*ecela indlela*. But the ancestors refused to take him. And now here he is, sitting in the middle of his relatives, and staring at one spot on the wall. How can anyone be sure that this time the ancestors are ready to accept him?

"Oh yes, they are ready," declares an elder of the Believers. "This time for sure he'll succeed to go. NoEngland is very powerful."

There is Gxagxa standing outside Zim's door, neighing endlessly.

Then there is NomaRussia.

While Zim is busy dying, she sits in a vigil on the sleigh outside his hexagon. She pleads with him in a feeble voice through the cracks of his door, "Tell her when you get there . . . tell NoEngland to release me . . . to make me well again . . . to take away the pain . . . to take away all this flow."

"He can't hear you," says a kindly old lady. "He is between the worlds."

From time to time her friends—those who had harassed Qukezwa all over the place—bring her food and water. They sit with her and try to comfort her whenever the pain flares up. They repeat what they have always believed: that whoever caused her this is burning in the fires of hell. Their parents have told them that the igqirha who "worked" their friend to be like this cannot be a genuine igqirha. A genuine igqirha does not harm people. An authentic igqirha has been given only those powers that heal. This one who caused NomaRussia to have this constant flow that is now accompanied by pain is an *igqwirha*—an evil one who only causes harm. He too will burn in the fires of hell.

When the astounded Camagu found NomaRussia outside Zim's door for the first time, he was hurt when she did not remember him. But he was not given the opportunity to talk with her any further. Her friends came and fussed over her and told Camagu to leave her alone. So he went into Qukezwa's hexagon to see her and to play with Heitsi. He was cross with Qukezwa for not revealing the truth about his hopeless quest all those months ago.

"I followed you. All the way from Johannesburg," he tells Noma-Russia one day when he finds her alone on the sleigh. "I came searching for you."

"You are Qukezwa's," she whispers.

"Yes. I am engaged to Qukezwa. But it is you who brought me here. It is about you that I dreamt. She merely invaded those dreams."

"You had no right to dream about me. Do not dream about me. I am like this because my eye roved to a man of this homestead."

"Like this? The curse, you mean?"

"Qukezwa has been talking?"

"Your friends attacked her in my presence. It is because of the curse?"

"Yes. The curse has something to do with it."

Camagu tries to say something that will comfort the dying woman.

"That is the river of life. You are the river. It is from this river that men and women have come. Humanity flows from the same mouth that gushes your curse. It is no curse. I do not mind to swim in that river. I can swim in that river for all my life."

"You do not know what you are saying. Go away. Even if I were not dying you would not swim in any such river. When I heard there was a strange man looking for me, I thought they were talking of a madman. Now I know that you are indeed mad. I do not want any more curses on what is left of my life."

"She is right, Camagu," says Qukezwa, smiling cynically.

Camagu almost faints. He was not aware that Qukezwa had been standing at the door listening all the time.

"At last you will rid yourself of demons that got hold of you in the streets of Johannesburg," she adds, leading him away into the house.

Days pass. Zim refuses to die. Amahobohobo weaverbirds fill the homestead with their rolling, swirling song. They miss the man who spent most of the day sitting under their giant wild fig tree. Gxagxa refuses to move from his vigil outside Zim's door. NomaRussia continues her own vigil.

Qukezwa is amused by Camagu's confusion—his hankering after a phantom he had created in his feeble mind.

"I sought you all over," Camagu tells NomaRussia one afternoon.

"Once I was employed here," she responds. "A man of this homestead sought me and found me. Look what happened to me."

"It has nothing to do with that. You said yourself that the doctors at the hospital in East London say you have cervical cancer. It is a disease that is there and kills many women when it is not found and treated early through radiotherapy or whatever else medical doctors can do. Perhaps if this had been attended to when your bleeding started you would have been cured by now."

"They did say you are a doctor."

"No. Not that kind of doctor. I know nothing about medicine. But cervical cancer is a well-known disease even among laymen like me— that is, people who are not medical doctors. This is not a curse. Please let me take you to hospital. Okay, they have told you there that it has reached an advanced stage and cannot be cured. But you need care and support."

"Do you think just because white doctors have a name for the sickness that it was not caused by NoEngland?"

"No one can cause someone else to have cancer."

"Then how come your white doctors didn't understand how I got this terrible thing at such a young age? How come they said mine was an unusual case?"

"I don't know."

"You have a lot to learn, doctor."

"All I want is to help you. Please let me help you. I am prepared to pay for you at a hospice where they will take good care of you. They will relieve your pain and make your life a bit more comfortable."

"No, I will sit here . . . at this homestead that brought this on me.

I will die here. Let my death hang on their necks for the rest of their days. Now leave me alone and go to your wife," she says, smiling ruefully at him.

She can still smile in the middle of such pain.

Days pass. Zim refuses to die. Once more, relatives come from far and wide to make appeals to Qukezwa. "Please leave the elder alone! Let him go in peace!"

Her anger at being accused like this has dissipated. She assures the relatives that she is not holding Zim. They see her earnestness. Perhaps they should look elsewhere for Zim's stubbornness against the call of the Otherworld. Twin. Zim's son who went to Johannesburg and never came back. Perhaps the elder does not want to leave without saying good-bye to Twin. People must be sent to Johannesburg to track Twin down.

"Where will they find Twin?" asks NomaRussia when her friends tell her about the plan. "He is dead. I sang at his wake in Hillbrow."

Everyone is shocked to hear for the first time of Twin's death. Women wail when they are told that he died in the streets of Hillbrow drunk and frustrated.

Twin had been frustrated for a long time. No one was buying his carvings anymore, for he carved people who looked like real people. No one wanted such carvings. Buyers of art were more interested in twisted people. People without proportion. People who grew heads on their stomachs and eyes at the back of their heads. Grotesque people with many arms and twisted lips on their feet. Twin refused to create things that distorted reality. He could only carve realistic figures the way that Dalton had taught him to. He starved and died a pauper. He was mourned by the aged and forgotten in a tattered tent on top of a multistory building in Hillbrow. He was also mourned by NomaRussia and Camagu.

"You were dressed like a makoti . . . like a newly married woman . . . yet you are not married," wonders Camagu.

"To put men off," explains NomaRussia.

Qukezwa laughs and says, "Obviously it didn't work. Here is a man who came running after you even though he could see you were someone's daughter-in-law."

"What was NomaRussia doing there?" people want to know.

"In my desperation I went to Johannesburg to see Twin," she tells them. "I did not know how he could help. I only remembered that after NoEngland discovered the truth about her husband and myself, Twin was the only one who continued to speak to me. He was the only one who did not harbor any bitterness against me. The igqirha had told me that only NoEngland could reverse my misfortune. NoEngland was dead. Maybe I could reach her through Twin. Maybe Twin would know how to appeal to her sense of mercy."

But she was too late. When she arrived in Johannesburg, Twin had died that very week. The loving farewell that she sang at his wake was a plea to NoEngland to release her from the curse. She was hoping that Twin would take the message to his mother.

People of the village are amazed at the lack of taste of the people of the city, who don't like carvings that look too real. Even so, the Believers blame John Dalton for teaching their son to be true to life in his sculpture.

"It is Dalton's fault," Qukezwa wails. "He is the one who taught my brother to create beautiful people who looked like real people. He pretends to know everything, so he should have known that people of the city who have money to buy carvings don't like beautiful people. Twin could have been successful with his original stumpy bottlelike people."

Camagu agrees that perhaps Twin's original work could have had a market because of its quaintness and folksiness.

That night Zim is told of Twin's demise. For the first time he gives a wan smile. And dies. He dies smiling. NoEngland is victorious. No wonder her call was so strong. Her son had been helping her in the tussle with Qukezwa.

When people wake up the next morning they find that Noma-Russia has also died. This fuels further anger among the Believers. This unscrupulous woman would not leave Zim alone, they fume. Even when he was called by his wife, she forced her way to accompany him. Now Zim has taken his mistress with him to the world of the ancestors. There is going to be a big war between her and NoEngland. They send for her father to fetch the body of his daughter for burial.

Bhonco, son of Ximiya, is enraged when he hears that Zim is dead. Zim was always one up on him. Now he will reach the world of the ancestors before him. He is going to become an ancestor before him. When Bhonco finally dies and goes to the world of the ancestors, Zim will have been there for a long time. When Bhonco is a newcomer, Zim will be familiar with all the corners of the Otherworld. And in the meantime, while Bhonco is still on earth, who knows what lies Zim will tell about him to the other ancestors? Who knows what havoc he will create in the homesteads of the Unbelievers? Zim will be a very unfriendly ancestor. A vengeful one who will not be appeased even by slaughtered goats and oxen. The Believers have won one more time. A final victory that Bhonco will never top as long as he lives. His scars itch woefully.

During Zim's burial, graveside orators say that when a soldier falls, another one rises. Heitsi's generation will carry forward the work left by those who came before. Another orator says Zim's is a family well beloved by the ancestors. A family of death. First it was NoEngland. Then it was Twin. Now it is Zim himself.

A month after Zim's funeral, Qukezwa has not yet joined Camagu at his cottage. She can join him only after the *isizathu*, the ceremony for the dead that happens months after death. At the isizathu women wear the best of their isikhakha skirts and the beads of the amahomba. A beast is slaughtered and beer is brewed. Men and women dance the *umxhentso* dance together, in memory of the dead.

Camagu is at Zim's homestead, where he spends a lot of time playing with Heitsi. He sees a number of villagers going down towards Nongqawuse's Valley. They tell him that the government people are here to survey the place. The construction of the holiday paradise and gambling complex will be going ahead. The war has finally been lost.

At Nongqawuse's Valley he finds a group of men talking with the surveyor, a scrawny white man in a khaki safari suit. Bhonco, son of Ximiya, is at the center of the group, which includes Chief Xikixa. There is another group a short distance away, looking dejected.

Camagu recognizes them immediately as those people who have stood with him in opposing the gambling complex.

The surveyor is excitedly showing Bhonco's enthusiastic crowd his new equipment. It is a tellurometer, he says. And guess what? It was invented here in South Africa. It can pinpoint a location with great accuracy, beyond the capability of any other instrument. So they must not worry. He is going to finish the surveying in a very short time, and soon their wonderful gambling city will rise in all its crystal splendor and glory where wild bushes and trees once grew.

"Well, son of Cesane, you and your Believers have lost in the end," says Bhonco.

"Did you allow this?" Camagu directs this question to Xikixa.

"It is not for me to allow it, son of Cesane," says the chief. "The government wants this development. It may be good for the village after all. The wheels of progress are grinding on, son of Cesane. No one can stop them."

With a flourish the surveyor begins his work. Bhonco and his followers cheer. Camagu and his followers look on hopelessly. They are about to leave when John Dalton arrives in his four-wheel-drive vehicle. He is hooting all the way. He halts abruptly next to the surveyor, and majestically steps out of his bakkie brandishing some papers.

"And what do you think you're doing, my friend?" he asks.

"What am I doing? Surveying, of course. Surveying the site that will have the gambling city and the tarred road that will lead to it," responds the surveyor animatedly. "You see over there? That's where we'll have all the rides. And then the cable car . . ."

"I am afraid there won't be any gambling city, my friend." Dalton hands him a piece of paper. It is a court order forbidding any surveying of the place. It is accompanied by a letter from the government department of arts, culture, and heritage declaring the place a national heritage site.

"No one is allowed to touch this place!" Dalton shouts triumphantly.

People cheer and lift Dalton to their shoulders. He is the savior of their village. They ululate and sing songs of victory. Bhonco, however, is like a raging bull. His followers try to calm him down. He shouts insults at everyone in sight, both friends and foes. Once more he is defeated.

Dalton also gives Camagu a victorious sneer. He has won his people back from the clutches of the overeager stranger from the city of Johannesburg. That is why he had not told anyone that he had applied for a court order to stop the developers, or that he personally drove to Pretoria to get the government letter. That is why he had insisted to the sheriff of the court that he serve the court order himself. That is why he had kept the government letter and the court order until the last minute. To win his people back.

 She sings in soft pastel colors, this Qukezwa. She sings in many voices, as Heitsi plays on the sand. He is six years old, yet he has shown no interest in the sea. From the day he was born to ululations and heckling, his mother dreamt of the day she would take him to the sea and teach him to swim. His upbringing would be different from hers. Her mother had never allowed her near the sea. Heitsi would swim better than any fish. But, to her disappointment, Heitsi has no interest in the sea. He has come because his mother dragged him along. He plays on the sandbank as Qukezwa paddles at the shallow end of the lagoon and sings in split-tones.

She sings in glaring colors. In violent colors. Colors of gore. Colors of today and of yesterday. Dreamy colors. Colors that paint nightmares on barren landscapes. She haunts yesterday's reefs and ridges with redness. And from these a man who is great at naming emerges. He once named ten rivers. Now he rides wildly throughout kwaXhosa, shouting at the top of his voice, declaring to everyone who cares to listen, "Finally I have pacified Xhosaland!"

Pacified homesteads are in ruins. Pacified men register themselves as pacified laborers in the emerging towns. Pacified men in their emaciated thousands. Pacified women remain to tend the soil and build pacified families. When pacified men return, their homesteads have been moved elsewhere, and crammed into tiny pacified villages. Their pacified fields have become rich settler farmlands.

Twin-Twin's sons are back from the Amathole Mountains and have rebuilt their homestead. But it is much smaller than before. He is one of the few people who still have cattle. They are as emaciated as the sunken-eyed ghosts that walk the land. Their milk is thin and watery. It produces amasi sour milk that looks like dirty dishwater. But people eat. Sometimes beggars get the remains.

Qukezwa is a beggar who will get nothing. Even though her eyes are sunken like those of the other ghosts that walk the land, and her high Khoikhoi cheekbones have been rendered sharper by famine, she will not even walk close to Twin-Twin's homestead. She spends all her life at the wild beach. Like those of her people who are called strand-lopers. She goes into the sea and gets some shellfish. She eats it raw and takes some to Heitsi. Heitsi is old enough to catch his own. But he seems to have some aversion to the sea. He would rather watch his mother from the safe distance of the rough beach.

Twin-Twin knows that the woman of the sea that everyone talks about is his brother's wife. He knows that Heitsi is his own nephew who will be the bearer of Twin's progeny. He knows that Twin died a raving lunatic at the Kaffir Relief House. He knows. But he does not care. He wakes up every day with yesterday's anger. His heart is full of bitterness. There are two big regrets that dominate his life: that his brother died before he could gloat over him, and that he never took the chance to strike out at John Dalton, to avenge his father's head. It is too late for that now. He missed many opportunities when Dalton and he were riding together from village to village, when Dalton was still a magistrate. He is a well-placed trader now. Has built a huge general dealer's store at Qolorha, on a hill. From this hill he can see down below, a number of miles away, to a mission station where his son is a missionary. It is too late now. It is left to future generations to avenge the headless ancestor. If they think it is worth it. He himself has a lot to lose.

Bhonco thinks he has nothing to lose. He has already lost everything. The Believers have been victorious at every turn. There is no gambling complex at Qolorha. None of all the wonderful things of civilization that his daughter used to tell him about. Instead there is a tourist place, which started as a backpackers' hostel but has now developed into a holiday camp. Those villagers who decided to join the cooperative society own it. It is managed by Vathiswa, who learned the ropes at the Blue Flamingo Hotel. To make things worse—from Bhonco's perspective, that is—this holiday camp is at Zim's old homestead. When Qukezwa moved to Camagu's cottage she gave the homestead to the coop. More chalets in the form of isiXhosa rondavels and hexagons were built. The place now gives the Blue Flamingo Hotel tough competition. Tourists are attracted by the gigantic wild fig tree and the amahobohobo weaverbirds that have built a hanging city on its branches. And by the isiXhosa traditional costumes and beadwork that are created by the coop women who are led by MamCirha, NoGiant, and NoPetticoat. These are displayed in one of the hexagons.

To Bhonco, all these things represent defeat. The Believers have won. He has nothing more to lose. And it is all John Dalton's fault. He brought that despicable Camagu to this village. They both stood with the Believers against the Unbelievers. As a result he lost the abaThwa dance, he lost his wife, he lost his daughter, and he lost the respect and prestige that he enjoyed in his village. The village itself lost a glittering gambling paradise that would have changed life for everyone. Instead it got a rustic holiday camp that lacks the glamour of the gambling city.

And there is Zim. It is almost six years since he left. A new millennium has dawned. The excitement it caused has died, and people have now become used to the idea. Yet he hasn't forgotten that damned Zim. The Zim who is now venerated as an ancestor. The Zim for whom the living slaughter animals so that he may communicate their messages to Qamata, while Bhonco languishes on earth. The Zim who is capable of telling lies about him to the other ancestors, and of influencing them to distance themselves from him.

Bhonco feels that everything has gone wrong for him. He must avenge Xikixa's head. Somehow it must be restored. Dalton must speak with his ancestors to see to it that Xikixa's head is restored. Only then will things come right for Bhonco and his divided homestead.

He takes his panga and knobkerrie, and casually walks to the cultural village that Dalton established a few years back in direct competition to the holiday camp. It is also a cooperative society, run by Dalton with the assistance of NoVangeli and NoManage. Although it is called a cultural village, it is not really a village. There are four mud rondavels, thatched with grass and fenced in by reeds. The outside walls of the rondavels are decorated with colorful geometric patterns. Inside there are clay pots of different sizes, which are for sale. Grass mats are strewn all over the cow-dung floor. There is nothing else. In a large clearing in front of the rondavels, village actors walk around in various isiXhosa costumes. Some are sitting on tree stumps, drinking sorghum beer. When the tourists come, the amagqiyazana, the young girls who have not yet reached puberty, are invited to dance. They are always happy for the tips they get from the visitors, who are usually guests at the Blue Flamingo.

Bhonco demands to see John Dalton. NoManage tells him that he has left for his store. Bhonco climbs the hill to Vulindlela Trading Store. He finds Dalton arranging the black credit books in readiness for the nkamnkam day tomorrow, when old-age pensioners come to cash their checks. When he sees Bhonco he assumes that the elder has come for more ityala, more credit.

"There cannot be any ityala for you today," says Dalton.

"Who says I want ityala?" replies Bhonco.

But Dalton is not listening. He just prattles on, "I know your daughter sends you money regularly. She has a good job, that Xoliswa Ximiya. A deputy directorship in the national Department of Education is not to be sneezed at. You must be proud of her. But I will only give more credit to people after nkamnkam day."

"I do not want ityala, Dalton," says Bhonco calmly. "I want you to ask your forefather to restore the head of my forefather."

"The head of your forefather? Have you gone crazy?"

"Give me the head of Xikixa, Dalton!"

Before Dalton can answer, Bhonco hits him with his knobkerrie on the head. The trader falls down, unconscious. Bhonco gives him two whacks with his *panga*. Blood spurts out and sprays the walls. Missis runs from her tiny office wailing. Screaming clerks and salespeople join her. Bhonco lashes out at everyone. He is foaming at the mouth as he screeches something about the head that has caused him misery. Customers and passersby finally grab him and disarm him. Dalton is unconscious on the floor. He is bleeding profusely from a gaping wound on the head and another one on the arm.

Gxagxa neighs. Qukezwa does not stop her song of many voices. She only looks up and smiles. Whenever the horse has had its fill of grazing, it comes looking for her everywhere. If she is not at the cottage, it goes to Nongqawuse's Valley. If she is not there still, it goes to the sea, particularly to the lagoon. She is sure to be there. They love each other, Gxagxa and Qukezwa. It was her father's favorite horse. Her father lives in this horse. She wouldn't dare do anything shameful in its presence, nor utter words she would never have uttered in her father's presence. She gives it the same kind of respect she gave her father.

It neighs again. She jumps out of the water, and goes to caress its neck. She tells it to go and graze some more, for she intends spending the whole day playing in the sea. She hopes that Heitsi will finally agree to follow her into the water. She will make a swimmer of Heitsi yet. Heitsi is afraid of the sea.

Qukezwa fills the valley with her many voices. She fills the wild beach with dull colors. Colors that are hazy and misty. Gray mist, not white. She sings of Qukezwa walking in the mist. She is so bony. Her eyes are bulging out of her skull. They are resting on her high cheekbones. Her hide skirt is tattered. She does not sport a single strand of beads. Beads were long since exchanged for food. She is the woman of the sea. She is a strandloper. A beach scavenger. As long as the sea yields, she and her son will not go hungry. It is high time Heitsi learned to harvest the sea. How will he survive if something happens to her? Heitsi is afraid of the sea.

She sings of prophetesses walking in the mist.

A white woman is teaching them ring-a-ring of roses. She is Mrs. Gawler. They live with her and her husband, Major John Gawler. Mrs. Gawler finds them quite amusing, although they can't get the hang of the simplest of games. She teaches them beautiful children's songs that celebrate death: *Ring-a-ring of roses. A pocket full of posies. Atishoo! Atishoo! We all fall down!*

These children. These prophets. They do not know how to fall down. They do it so artlessly. So gracelessly. So crudely. Their heads are so hard they cannot catch the simplest of games. Well, Nonkosi catches on faster. And knows how to have fun. She plays hopscotch too. Nongqawuse and Nombanda are difficult to figure out. Especially Nongqawuse. She seems confused most of the time. And unkempt.

Mrs. Gawler tries to teach them the rudiments of good grooming. They are immersed in a bathtub, and she sees to it that they scrub their sacred bodies with pebbles, and wash themselves thoroughly with soap and water. Until the layers of dirt have peeled off. She dresses them nicely in colorful dresses. Young prophets in summer dresses. She and Dr. Fitzgerald—the miracle doctor that The Man Who Named Ten Rivers brought from New Zealand—take the prophetesses to a photographic studio for their portraits.

"Smile Nonkos!" she says.

Click.

"Come on, Nongause! Don't be so sullen! Smile!"

Click.

These prophets. Not only do they not know how to fall. They do not know how to smile either.

Click! Click!

Then they all sail to Cape Town in the *Alice Smith*. Throughout the voyage the sacred girls are a showpiece. Everyone wants to take a good look at them. In Cape Town the prophetesses are taken to the Paupers' Lodge, where they are incarcerated with a large number of female prisoners and transportees.

"Nongqawuse really sells the holiday camp," Camagu tells John Dalton, who is lying in a hospital bed. "When we advertise in all the important travel magazines we use her name. Qolorha is the place of miracles. It would have been even more profitable if she had been buried there."

Dalton groans and tries to move. The drip shakes. He groans again. He looks like a mummy with bandages all over his body. All sorts of strange contraptions lead to his body. They are taking good care of him at this very expensive private hospital in East London. The doctor has told Camagu that he is lucky to be alive. He will survive. But there is no guarantee that he will have all his faculties functioning as before.

"You will be glad to hear that Bhonco has been arrested," says Camagu, trying to stretch the conversation to fill the time. Dalton lets out a long groan as if to say he wants to near nothing of the madman.

"You must get well soon, John," says Camagu sincerely. "This rivalry of ours is bad. Our feud has lasted for too many years. Five. Almost six. And for what? Nothing! There is room for both the holiday camp and the cultural village at Qolorha. We must all work together. You must come back home quickly, John. We need your business expertise at the holiday camp."

Dalton groans his agreement. He tries to lift his heavily bandaged hand. Camagu shakes it gently.

As he drives back home he sees wattle trees along the road. Qukezwa taught him that these are enemy trees. All along the way he cannot see any of the indigenous trees that grow in abundance at Qolorha. Just the wattle and other imported trees. He feels fortunate that he lives in Qolorha. Those who want to preserve indigenous plants and birds have won the day there. At least for now. But for how long? The whole country is ruled by greed. Everyone wants to have his or her snout in the trough. Sooner or later the powers that be may decide, in the name of the people, that it is good for the people to have a gambling complex at Qolorha-by-Sea. And the gambling complex shall come into being. And of course the powers that be or their proxies—in the form of wives, sons, daughters, and cousins—shall be given equity. And so the people shall be empowered.

Qukezwa sings in soft pastel colors and looks at Heitsi. Qukezwa swallows a mouthful of fresh oysters and looks at Heitsi.

Oh, this Heitsi! He is afraid of the sea. How will he survive without the sea? How will he carry out the business of saving his people? Qukezwa grabs him by his hand and drags him into the water. He is screaming and kicking wildly. Wild waves come and cover them for a while, then rush back again. Qukezwa laughs excitedly. Heitsi screams even louder, pulling away from her grip, "No, mama! No! This boy does not belong in the sea! This boy belongs in the man village!"